E.G. FOLEY

THE GRYPHON CHRONICLES, BOOK THREE:

THE DARK PORTAL

Also By This Author

Don't miss the previous books in The Gryphon Chronicles series:
Book One: THE LOST HEIR
Book Two: JAKE & THE GIANT

Credits & Copyright

T 96314

At the door of life by the gate of breath,
There are worse things waiting for men than death.

~ Algernon Charles Swinburne

TABLE OF CONTENTS

PART V

Coming Soon!
About the Authors
About the Illustrator

PART I

PROLOGUE
The Sorcerer's Tomb

A hundred and fifty feet underground in perfect darkness, a labyrinth of black, twisty tunnels snaked beneath the mountains of Wales. And in one such little-explored passage of the Harris Mine, a simple man called Barney had just discovered a curious phenomenon.

He angled his handheld wedge against a big, tough knuckle of coal and gave it a whack with his hammer to show his fellow miners. "See what I mean? Got a funny sound just there, ain't it?" He tapped again, harder. "Sounds...I dunno, hollow."

"Yer head's hollow," grumbled crew chief Martin. Nevertheless, to Mr. Martin's experienced eye, the problem was plain: They'd hit a stubborn section of the coal seam. He gave his men a nod. "Let's blast it."

Crawling about awkwardly in the narrow, claustrophobic space barely four feet tall, the men fetched the heavy hand-cranked drill and started churning it.

The tip of the drill slowly pierced a thin hole into the rock face, where they would soon pour in the blasting powder. Cranking the drill was backbreaking labor, just like every other job in the coalmine and its sister company, the Harris Ironworks. But coal made the steam that forged the iron that ran the British Empire, which, in turn, ruled the world. And so these rough, rugged miners saw themselves as unsung heroes of a sort. To be sure, not a one of them was ever afraid of the dark.

Even when they should be.

At length, the skinny hole into the bedrock was drilled, the blasting powder carefully poured in.

Daredevil Collins volunteered to light it—always a dangerous job. Cocky as ever, he held the squib carelessly between his teeth and lit it as if it were a cigar instead of a type of firecracker. Swiping it quickly out of his mouth, Collins shoved it into the hole the men had drilled.

As it burned its way toward the little pile of blasting powder, he scrambled after his crew, who had already scuttled out of range to wait for the explosion.

All four men held their ears and opened their mouths slightly, waiting for the shift in air pressure.

BOOM!

"Ha, ha!" The miners cheered out of habit at the blast. "That'll teach her!" said Martin.

With pickaxes and hammers at the ready, the men crawled back to harvest the chunks of coal that had been knocked loose from the mountain's grip by the explosion.

As they approached, the air was so thick with dust and smoke that it blackened their faces until all they could see of their mates was the whites of each other's eyes. As the men pressed on, the tiny oil lanterns on their hats glowed like four lonely lighthouses in that thickest type of fog, known as a London Peculiar.

Martin whistled for Jones to bring the coal cart so they could load up their fresh haul and carry it topside.

The more coal they brought up to the surface each day, the more money they made for their families. Of course, their pay went right back to the Company through the rent on their houses, owned by the Harris Mine, or through the goods they bought at the Harris Company Store.

The Company, in short, was more powerful around here than Queen Victoria.

"Look!" Barney suddenly burst out with a gasp. "I don't believe it! I-I was right! It *was* hollow!" He pointed as the smoke cleared to a *hole* they had blasted in the underground wall.

It should not have been there.

Indeed, it was impossible. There shouldn't be a hollow space left after their controlled blast, just an indentation exposing deeper layers of the earth's solid bedrock holding up the mountain.

"Well, beggar me," he murmured, marveling at it.

Bending forward to shine his headlamp in, Barney peered

through the hole that opened into a darkness ten times blacker than even the rest of the mine. Then he waved his crewmates over. "Fellas, come and see!"

"What is it now?" Martin grumbled, coming up behind him.

"You got to see for yourself. There's some kind of room in there!" Barney said in wonder, pointing.

"Don't be daft. A room? Underground cavern, maybe..."

But as the others crowded round, even stern Mr. Martin had to admit that it was, indeed, an ancient-looking room with smooth, chiseled walls.

Smith squinted into the midnight darkness beyond the hole. "What's a room doing all the way down here?"

"How should I know," Martin said. An uneasy chill ran down his spine, for Wales was not just the land of coal and mist and unexpected spellings. It was also a place of legend. The sacred homeland of countless bards and sorcerers of old; the birthplace of Merlin himself, according to some; a land of ancient magic, mighty castles, and time-forgotten kings.

Collins had that daredevil gleam in his eyes once again as he glanced around at the others. "Fancy a look, boys? C'mon, let's go in!"

"I'm not so sure that's such a good idea," Barney warned him, but coalminers as a rule were not afraid of much.

Even when they *really* should be.

"C'mon, leave it. We've got to cut our support timbers to prop up that hole," Martin said. "It ain't stable."

"Ah, just for a moment." With a laugh, Collins vaulted through the hole, and so was the first to see the ancient, heavy table in the center of the mysterious chamber and the chair...

With a skeleton sitting in it.

A skeleton decked in strange jewelry and wearing the floppy hat and moldy velvet robes of a Renaissance-era scholar.

Collins stopped in his tracks when he saw it and pointed, aghast. "Bones!"

Barney, who was following right behind him, ran into Collins's back on account of not watching where he was going. He was too busy staring all around at the strange subterranean chamber, his eyes wide.

The rest followed, and when they all saw the skeleton, they let out exclamations of wonder and shock; the four big, fearless coalminers unconsciously started huddling together with a creeping, superstitious sense of doom.

For they now realized that they had just disturbed the dead.

"This is no ordinary chamber, my lads," Martin said in a hushed voice, taking control of the situation, as their leader. He looked around at all the odd things inside the chamber, and the bones. "It's a tomb."

"But whose?" Smith murmured, while Barney just gulped.

"His," Collins whispered, staring at the skeleton. "Whoever he is."

The skull's empty eyes stared right back at them from the darkness, giving them no answers.

Sitting upright, as if he had died right where he sat, whatever soul had once owned those bones had left this life surrounded by his books and papers.

This seemed odd to Barney. "But surely not a tomb, Mr. Martin. I mean, folk ain't usually buried at their desks, is they?"

"Well, you do have a point there," the crew chief admitted, growing ever more aware of some unseen evil lurking in this place.

"Maybe he died alone down 'ere and nobody ever noticed," Collins opined.

"Likely so," Martin quickly agreed, but Smith shook his head and whispered, "Maybe he couldn't get out."

Somebody gulped in the inky darkness.

"Maybe we'd better leave," Barney squeaked, but unfortunately, Collins had now recovered his nerve.

"Wonder who he was, poor bleeder." As he ventured closer, his hat-lamp shone on the long-dead occupant of the crypt.

Strange jewelry hung around the scholar-skeleton's neck, an intricate metalwork necklace with all sorts of arcane insignia. They had no idea what all the strange little symbols meant.

A chunky ring hung loosely off the skeleton's bony finger. The thick band was probably made from locally mined gold, but none of the men recognized the unusual black rock in the center, though they unearthed gems and semi-precious stones in the Harris Mine nearly every day.

None of them could explain it, either, when the black stone took on a cloudy green glow.

"Why's it doing that?" Smith asked.

"Probably oxidation," Mr. Martin said sagely. As foreman, he was well aware that lots of the minerals buried in the earth changed color when the air touched them. "Lord, it's dank!" he added with a cough.

Air from the mine's ventilation system had begun seeping into the chamber, which had apparently been sealed off for centuries.

The draft poured in, stirring the ancient cobwebs that hung off everything; a puff of breath in the dust, as if the room itself sucked in a deep, agonizing gasp for air.

Smith nodded at the walls around them. "Look at all the quartz."

Giant crystals of glowing, colored quartz poked out of the natural cave walls everywhere. Milky white, candy pink, glassy cornflower blue.

The weird spiritualist lady in town, Madam Sylvia, who claimed to be a medium, sold crystals, Barney thought. The sign on her shop window advertised such stones as having mystical properties. But she had nothing in her shop like these ones, big as railroad ties.

"You know," Collins said abruptly, "there could be something valuable down here. Maybe treasure." He gave Smith a sudden, jolly punch in the arm. "We could be rich, man! Let's have a look around."

Martin harrumphed. "Anything we find will belong to Mr. Harris and the Company," he sternly reminded his crew.

"Ha! We're the ones who risked our necks for it," Collins muttered. "Finders keepers. What they don't know won't hurt 'em. Everyone, spread out! Let's see what we got down 'ere."

Martin still grumbled, but couldn't resist joining in their perusal of the chamber. The miners' hat-lamps shone in all directions as they moved off to explore the strange, sealed room.

Smith went to examine the giant crystals.

Collins poked around the skeleton's desk with considerable caution, frowning at the grinning stone statue of a little gargoyle crouched atop a pile of old books.

Martin went reluctantly to look on the shelves that edged the chamber. These were piled with parchments, drawings, and designs. Haphazardly strewn along the shelves, also, were odd weapons; ancient instruments of science; vials and bottles of potions that had long since dried up. And a crooked stick that Martin feared looked very much like a wand. He got a chill down his spine and started sweating.

Barney, meanwhile, stared down at the strange shapes carved into the stone floor. Astrological signs, alchemy symbols or something.

Then he gazed apprehensively at the large gargoyle statues that posed in all four corners of the room. Silent stone guardians, they resembled a hideous mix of apes, frogs, lizards, and hideous, giant bulldogs with horns and tails. Their fanged, ugly faces were frozen in mid-snarl. He grimaced and backed away. *Horrible beasties.*

The oxidation Martin had mentioned must be the reason that some of the gray stone the gargoyles were carved from had started flaking off their muscular bodies.

Indeed, when he glanced over at the desk, he saw that the oxidation was making the skeleton's ring glow ever brighter. The strange stone on the ring was turning a ghastly shade of malevolent green.

Hold on. Was it a trick of his imagination or was there some kind of black cloud floating up out of that ring? *Lovely, now I'm seeing things.* With a slight shudder, Barney turned away and headed back toward the center of the chamber, when something growled behind him.

He stopped and turned around slowly, looking back at the nearest gargoyle statue. *What?* Had he inhaled too many fumes, or had that thing just *moved?*

Suddenly, on the far end of the chamber, Collins laughed aloud in the gloom. "Gold! I knew it!" He had opened the small wooden cask on the skeleton's desk. "Look at this, boys! Didn't I tell you there'd be treasure here? Come and see! This box is filled with gold and jewels! We're rich, I tell ye, rich!"

Barney put the gargoyle out of his mind and rushed over to see the gold.

"We're rich, rich, rich!" Collins was laughing like a lunatic. He scooped two handfuls of gold together and buried his nose in them, like he was splashing his face with water. "Ha, ha! Mother always said I was born lucky!"

"Put that down!" Martin scolded. "You know it isn't yours!"

Just then, Smith, who was out of sight, called to them from a lower level of the chamber. He had ventured down some black stairs carved into a distant corner of the tomb, and now yelled up to them: "You have *got* to see this, lads!"

They could barely drag themselves away from the gleaming beauty of the gold horde in the little wooden chest, but Martin called back to him. "What did you find?"

"Some sort o' doorway!"

They ran to see it, but no one was prepared for what they found.

Carved into the rock was a huge skull, and the door Smith had found waited inside its open mouth.

"Crikey," Martin said.

Barney frowned, nervously bringing up the rear. "I-I don't think I want to go in there." But he didn't want to be left behind either, so he followed his companions.

They all went cautiously creeping down the few steps into the lower cave.

It was one strange door. Peering into the stone-carved skull's gaping mouth, they saw that massive slabs of gray rock framed the dark portal, like a subterranean Stonehenge. The thick door itself was made of ancient hawthorn wood and covered in strange locks and bolts of intricate, swirling metalwork, like intertwined serpents.

"What on earth?" Martin murmured, squinting at it in disbelief.

"I knew it. It's a vault," Collins said. "That must be where Boney up there hid the rest of his gold! The full stash!"

"I don't think so." Martin shook his head, staring at it.

"Why else would he have it locked up like a bloody bank vault?"

"What should we do?" Smith asked breathlessly.

Then he and Collins looked at each other and shouted the answer simultaneously: "Blasting powder!"

"Are you mad?" Martin cried. "You can't set off an explosion in here! It could cause a cave-in. Use your heads! We haven't even put up any support beams yet!"

But gold fever had taken hold. Smith and Collins ignored him, racing to set everything up so they could blow the weird, formidable door off its hinges and get to the treasure inside.

They weren't listening to their foreman, nor to Barney, who

tried to help Martin convince them for a moment, before he became transfixed by the eyes of the great skull.

He gazed up into them. There was a layer of transparent quartz fitted into each eye socket, like windows made of thick block glass. But he could swear the eyes glowed a little, as though lit from within by burning torches.

Too weird. Unnerved, he glanced around at the corners of the chamber, tingling with ever-increasing terror. "Fellas, I got a bad feeling about this place. I think we need to get out of here..."

They ignored him, Smith and Collins busily working to set up the blast, Martin scolding them in a halfhearted manner—for, in truth, he was just as curious as they were to see if there was a horde of treasure in there.

"Did you hear that?"

As Barney froze, the others stopped and turned to him.

"Hear what?" Smith grunted.

Grrrrrrr...

The sound came from a foot or two behind Barney.

He saw Smith's jaw drop, but he knew they were really in trouble when even Collins turned white.

"Aw, drat," Barney mumbled in terrified dismay. "There's something horrible behind me, ain't there?"

"Run!" Mr. Martin bellowed, his voice echoing off the chamber's stone walls.

But unfortunately, they were too late.

Awful sounds echoed out of the chamber at the bottom of the mine. Bloodcurdling screams, ferocious snarls.

And a low, sinister laugh that grew and grew, until it reverberated throughout the hollow stone chamber.

"FREE! Free at last! Feed, my children, and I shall do the same."

With that, a mysterious black vapor that seemed no more than a puff of smoke floated up from the skeleton's ring and headed for the hole the men had blasted in the wall. It whooshed out of the chamber into the mining tunnel beyond, then headed for the world above.

The hated world of light, and happy living things.

CHAPTER ONE
Welcome to Wales

Two Days Later

It is a well-known fact that too many hours of travel can make a person silly. Especially if he is twelve and confined in a vehicle with three of his closest friends, one dog, and of course, his pet Gryphon.

Thus, it was not surprising that after the past couple of days—including five carriage changes, a long steam-train ride chugging over the border from England into Wales, and their present slow, plodding slog, rumbling along in the coach sent from Jake's Welsh estate in the mountains of Snowdonia to collect them—the passengers were very silly indeed.

Boisterous laughter and the clamor of four young friends in a state of merriment came from inside the heavy coach winding its way up a hill through the forest.

When the coach abruptly stopped, however, so did all the noise.

"Hoy! Shush, you lot!" ordered Jake, the twelve-year-old in question. "Why are we stopping?"

"Are we there?" a piping voice exclaimed.

"Dunno! Let's see."

Four young faces, still shining with humor, promptly peered through the windows of the sturdy coach to find it had just emerged from the jewel-toned autumn woods.

Now they were surrounded by broad open fields, beyond which lay breathtaking valleys and misty mountain vistas. But when the high-spirited travelers saw what had halted their progress up the road, their eager smiles faded.

"Well, that's grim," declared Archie, Jake's cousin, the boy genius, age eleven.

The two girls, Dani and Isabelle, exchanged a startled glance. Then they, too, stared at the ominous scene ahead.

A long, elaborate funeral procession was crossing the road in front of them, making its way toward the nearby cemetery that covered the bleak brow of a windy hill.

Hundreds of people dressed in black marched slowly on foot all around the coal-black hearse, a solemn, stately carriage drawn by four black horses with ebony plumes on their heads.

Under the cloudy October sky, the slow-moving funeral procession inched by in morbid quiet. Professional hired keeners followed the coffins, moaning and wailing in sorrow. Some slowly beat funeral drums.

Unsmiling men in top hats walked by with clusters of crying women, their faces hidden by long black veils. In this sea of midnight, only the priest had some white on, his long cassock flapping in the breeze like a shroud.

"Gracious, I wonder what's happened," murmured Isabelle, Archie's sister. She was the eldest, at fourteen.

"Derek will find out." Jake nodded through the window at their escort on this journey, Guardian Derek Stone.

Even now, the big, dark-haired warrior rode his powerful black horse ahead, reining in at the edge of the funeral parade. He dismounted and took off his hat in a show of respect for the dead.

Meanwhile, Miss Helena, their half-French governess, looked on from her perch up on the driver's seat of the carriage, where she had fled when the children had grown sillier than she could stand.

To be sure, the grim sight before them quickly put a damper on their fun, especially when still *more* hearses came into view as the procession moved along.

"Sweet Bacon!" Archie murmured. "One, two, three—*four* coffins! What the deuce do you suppose happened here?"

"I hope there isn't a fever in the town." Dani O'Dell hugged her little brown Norwich terrier a bit closer. Teddy went everywhere with her, even on holiday.

As for his own pet, Jake quickly turned to his Gryphon. The lion-sized beast was lying peaceably on his belly in the center of the carriage between the children's seats, his scarlet wings folded against his sides.

"Stay down, Red." Jake threw his discarded greatcoat over the Gryphon's feathered head, hiding at least part of his large, unusual pet from the hundreds of people streaming past. "Sorry, boy," he added when a low, indignant "caw" came from underneath his coat. "You know we can't let you be seen."

With Red safely hidden, Jake rose from his seat and opened the door, leaning out with one foot braced on the metal carriage step. The brisk wind riffled through his dark blond forelock as he scanned their surroundings.

Hmm. On the hill opposite the cemetery stood a decidedly spooky-looking, old institution building. With its redbrick towers, it was designed to look like a castle, but to him, it looked more like a jail. Or maybe a madhouse. A wrought-iron fence wrapped around the property, with tall gates closed across the entrance to the long drive that led up to the place. Then Jake spotted the sign planted outside the gates: *The Harris Mine School.*

Well, that explained the presence of the few dozen children he now noticed milling around up by the building. The students must have been at recess, but most had stopped playing and stood motionless, watching the funeral procession in silence.

It was odd to see so many kids in one place and yet hear so little noise, he mused. Then a robed figure caught his eye, walking back and forth along the school's porch—a teacher or headmaster in long black robes and a tasseled cap. He seemed to be in charge.

But when the teacher suddenly dissolved into thin air, Jake's eyebrows shot up. *Oh, a ghost.*

Right. First one he'd seen today. He had had his abilities for six months now; seeing spirits rarely startled him anymore. Still, he couldn't help but smile wryly to himself. Those kids must love going to a haunted school, he thought. But although the headmaster ghost was his first apparition of the day, it wouldn't be his last.

Across the way, scores of them were floating around the cemetery—transparent, bluish versions of who they had been in life. It was a busy day up there, all right.

At least a dozen spirits wandered among the headstones. Some sat idly on their gravestones, chatting as they leaned against Celtic crosses or sculpted stone angels while they watched the living crowd into the cemetery to bury the new arrivals.

It wasn't as though they had much else to do.

For a moment, Jake watched a couple of child ghosts chasing each other in circles around one of the fancy white marble mausoleums where the richer folk were laid to rest.

As he scanned the row of miniature mansions for the dead, he barely noticed the little gargoyle statue peering down from atop the roof of one, watching the proceedings with a sinister grin.

Or maybe he had just imagined it, because when he looked again, it was gone.

Jake frowned, ducked his head back into the carriage, and sat down in his seat again.

Archie was right. This was an altogether grim way to start a holiday.

They had been so jolly a moment ago, but now a vague, creepy feeling had silenced all four. Of course, the grand funeral was a tad depressing, but it was more than that.

Something just felt...off.

An ominous undercurrent of something very wrong in this place.

He conceded, however, that it could be just his own private dread of their upcoming tour of the goldmine that he (a former pickpocket, of all people!) had inherited from his parents.

He looked askance at Isabelle.

Unusual talents ran in their family, and if the eerie atmosphere around here—the presence of evil he felt—was real, then surely his cousin the empath would sense it, too.

Instead, her delicate face betrayed the fact that all the sadness at the funeral was starting to affect her sensitive soul like a contagion. Her porcelain-doll complexion looked even paler than usual; her golden curls drooped with sorrow that did not quite belong to her.

Jake realized she was picking up on the grief of all those hundreds of mourners. *We need to get her out of here,* he thought, but the road ahead was still clogged.

He gave her a light, fond kick from across the carriage to distract her. "Hey! Come back to us, Izzy. They're them, you're you. Now block out their emotions like Aunt Ramona taught you."

"Easy for you to say," she mumbled.

Dani put her arm around the older girl's shoulders and Archie, sitting beside Jake, pulled faces at his sister until she finally smiled.

When the whole funeral procession had finally crowded into the cemetery for the burial and the road was clear once more, Derek swung back up onto his horse and trotted over, coming alongside the carriage.

"Everyone ready to move on?" he rumbled, skimming the four of them with his usual protective glance.

"More than ready. What happened?" Jake asked, while Archie helpfully pulled the coat off the Gryphon's head. Red snuffled and shook himself, happy to be rid of it.

"Some sort of accident at the Harris Coalmine," the fierce-eyed warrior said.

Isabelle flinched at this news and turned her morose stare out the window.

Archie shook his head sagely. "Dangerous business, mining. Explosive gases, cave-ins, collapses. Long hours, fires, floods in the tunnels. Dangerous machines. Fantastic machines, of course," he added with a grin, "but dangerous."

"Did you say Harris?" Jake asked, trying not to ponder the list of underground dangers Archie had just rattled off, for they only intensified the, er, *slight* phobia he already had about descending into the mine. "That's the same name as that school over there. Which is haunted, by the way."

Derek glanced in the direction Jake had nodded and saw the sign by the wrought-iron fence. "Must be a Company school, for the miners' children."

"How much farther, Derek?" Dani asked wistfully, petting Teddy on her lap. The little brown terrier wagged his tail as if he, too, couldn't wait to get out of the coach.

Derek squinted toward the road. He alone of their party had been to Plas-y-Fforest before, the Everton family's Welsh cottage, having come here on holiday long ago with Jake's father when the two were only boys themselves.

"No more than twenty minutes, I should think. Good thing, too." He glanced at the sun to judge the hour. "We don't want to be late for our tour. The dwarves are a prompt people. They'll be offended if we're late. Best get moving."

So, they did, and as usual, Derek was right.

Only another two more miles up and down the winding country road, the coachman turned in at a narrow dirt driveway that disappeared up into the woods. Beside the drive entrance sat a quaint, old, mossy sign that read: *Plas-y-Fforest.*

Which, in Welsh, meant *Mansion in the Forest*—so Jake had been told.

Up the long, bumpy drive the horses climbed, passing through a deep, mysterious pine wood that Jake was sure was full of magic. He could feel it in the air and could almost swear he saw some tiny people in the trees. Not fairies—about that size, but no wings or sparkly trails, and clad in bits of leather and colorful autumn leaves.

He pointed them out, but the others didn't look fast enough to see.

The tiny people followed, spying on them and running atop the branches to keep up with the carriage.

Hmm! I wonder what they are, Jake thought, but they couldn't be anything dangerous. His ancestors had protected all three thousand acres of their land here centuries ago with countless magical spells.

Plas-y-Fforest was a very special place in Everton family history, which was why they had come. As the long-lost heir of the Griffon earldom and the family fortune, Jake still had much to learn about his heritage.

At last, near the top of the mountain, they reached a clearing where his ancestors' rambling old holiday cottage came into sight.

As the carriage rolled to a halt in front of it, the children stared in delight. The sun had come back out; the sky was blue again; the earlier gloom and the sinister feeling up by the cemetery were forgotten.

For there in the sunny clearing before them, hidden among the woods, sat a large medieval cottage right out of a storybook—a wonderful old hodgepodge of gray stone sections, haphazardly joined, and seemingly held together by nothing but the climbing roses and dark green ivy that grew up its sides.

It had banks of narrow mullioned windows, some with colored glass, and a funny little arched doorway at the entrance. A dozen chimneypots poked up from the steep slate roof; gables peered out in all directions like watchful eyes.

Jake loved the place on sight. Despite having "Mansion" in its name, Plas-y-Fforest was not at all grand and imposing, like Everton House in London, but cozy and quirky, and full of nooks and crannies that the children suddenly couldn't wait to explore.

They burst out of the coach, freed at last from the stifling confinement of their journey. Teddy dove out, barking, and started running around in circles.

Red leaped out of the carriage and soared skyward to stretch his wings with a few minutes of much-needed flying.

Perhaps the Welsh-born beast also wanted a moment alone to reacquaint himself with his homeland.

Meanwhile, Derek dismounted from his horse and went to hand Miss Helena down from the driver's box.

At that moment, the cottage door banged open and out rushed a little human whirlwind.

Well, maybe not *human,* exactly, Jake thought.

"Welcome, oh, welcome, lords and ladies! Guardian Stone, so good to see you again! Welcome, children, oh, do please, all of you, come in, come in! Snowdrop Fingle at your service!"

Snowdrop Fingle was no taller than the children and bore a strong resemblance, Jake thought, to a cheery little hedgehog, with shiny dark eyes, slight sideburns, and pointy ears sticking out from beneath her white house cap.

She wore an apron over her plain cotton work dress; the dress hung to her ankles, revealing her odd bare feet.

The feet seemed just a bit too large for such a diminutive woman: strong, callused feet with slight fuzz growing on them.

Dani elbowed Jake. *"Quit staring,"* she whispered.

Derek did the introductions. "Children, Mr. and Mrs. Fingle have been the faithful caretaker couple here at Plas-y-Fforest for many years."

The coachman tipped his hat as he jumped down from the carriage and started getting their luggage.

"And if I may say so," Derek added, "your family is very lucky to have them, Jake. One house brownie can do the work of twenty servants, but you're blessed with two."

"Oh, Guardian Stone, such flattery!" The small, hairy she-brownie tittered nervously as she stood by, waiting to hold the door for everyone.

Jake was astonished. House brownies?

He had thought the Welsh driver was merely a short man rather in need of a shave. It was only when Mr. Fingle's top hat slipped that his pointy ears popped out from beneath the brim.

"Well, dash my wig," said Jake, but the Fingles were just as mystified by him.

"Sweet bees' wings," Snowdrop fairly whispered, "is this the young master who was missing all those years? Oh, but it must be! He looks just like his father."

"Doesn't he, though?" Derek agreed with a smile.

Jake swelled with pride, though he felt a bit self-conscious. She took a step toward him. "Welcome to your little Welsh cottage in the woods, Lord Griffon. My Nimbus and I, we do our best to keep it perfect for you at all times. If there's anything you want changed now that you're the new owner, you have only to let us know. The same goes for all your guests. House brownies live to make their masters comfortable."

"Thank you, Mrs. Fingle, you're very kind," Jake answered.

"Welcome to you all," she added, beaming at the others. But when Red landed in their midst, the little house brownie gasped.

"Crafanc!" Snowdrop cried.

"Huh?" Jake said.

She forgot all about the rest of them and went running to throw her arms around the Gryphon's neck. "Oh, my most noble Lord Crafanc! How marvelous to see you again after all this time!"

Red hugged her back with his front lion-paw.

Apparently, they were already well acquainted, but Jake was puzzled. "Why'd you call him that?"

Snowdrop released the Gryphon and wiped away a tear of joy. "Because it is his name, of course, my lord! Crafanc-y-Gwrool."

"Really?" Jake exclaimed, astonished. "I always just called him Red. Or Big Red."

"Well, he does seem to like that, too," Snowdrop admitted. "But his real name, his old name, his Welsh name, his royal name, is Crafanc-y-Gwrool. Claw the Courageous," she translated in a reverent tone.

"Claw the Courageous?" Jake echoed, impressed, as were they all. "Well, that certainly suits you, boy."

The Gryphon snuffled through his sharp golden beak as though making light of his own magnificence, then fluffed out the scarlet feathers of his mane in kingly fashion and prowled off to the cottage.

He pushed the front door open with his beak and went strolling in like he owned the place—and for all Jake knew, maybe he did. The Evertons would still be peasant farmers if it weren't for the gratitude of a gryphon long ago.

"Is anyone hungry?" Snowdrop asked brightly. "How about some nice warm bannock cakes with honey?"

That got them moving.

Inside, the pokey old house had low, plaster ceilings crisscrossed with dark, heavy, wooden beams in the old medieval style. Underfoot, the ancient flagstone floors were uneven, tilting this way and that, and the sconces on the walls were for ordinary candles; Plas-y-Fforest had never been updated with gaslamps and probably never would.

While Mr. Nimbus Fingle carried in their traveling trunks far faster than would have been *humanly* possible, Snowdrop showed them around the cottage. She pointed the way to the bedchambers upstairs, where the children chose their rooms for the trip.

But there wasn't time for unpacking quite yet, or they'd be late for their tour of the Everton Goldmine.

On Derek's orders, they changed their shoes and put on wellies or good, sturdy boots for the hike up to the mine entrance and for traipsing around through the underground tunnels that awaited them.

Four sets of clomping footfalls rushed back downstairs to the kitchen, then the kids scarfed down the traditional Welsh bannock cakes that Snowdrop had prepared for them. Cut into wedges, they were very much like scones.

They were wonderful.

"Quickly, now." Miss Helena tapped the dainty watch that hung on a ribbon around her neck. "You mustn't keep the dwarves waiting."

"Aren't you coming?" Isabelle asked.

"No, my dear, I'll stay behind to get your things unpacked," said the governess. "You go on, now, and do as Derek tells you. You're due there in twenty minutes."

"Time is short," Jake agreed, flashing a grin at Archie.

"Ah, yes!" the boy genius drawled. "We don't want the dwarves getting angry. They can be short-tempered."

"We all have our shortcomings," Jake rejoined.

"But I'm sure their anger at us would be short-lived," Dani chimed in.

Isabelle just looked at them. She hadn't found the game very amusing in the carriage, either, during their bout of silliness. But then, empaths were incapable of making fun of people or hurting others' feelings, since they shared them.

Jake snorted. Little Miss Perfect was too bloody nice. No wonder she had been chosen as a Keeper of the Unicorns.

"Enough, you lot," Derek grumbled, rising from the table. "Crack a joke like that in front of one of the dwarves, and you'll see what you get."

"They'll make short work of us," Archie said under his breath.

Jake tried not to laugh.

"You're not exactly tall yourself, Master Archie." Derek scowled at them. "Time to go." He stalked out of the room, leaving them to scramble after him.

"I'll grow!" Archie assured the others as they left the table, thanking Snowdrop for the snack and grabbing a few extra bannocks to bring along on their hike.

Miss Helena accepted temporary charge of Dani's dog. Teddy growled as the governess took him in her arms; he accepted Miss Helena but would never quite trust her, considering she was a shapeshifter whose other form was feline.

Dani waved a finger at him. "Teddy, be nice!" Then the Irish redhead ran outside after the others.

Before the group set out on their hike up to the mine's hidden entrance in the woods, Derek gathered them around to reiterate the warning he had already given them several times along their journey.

"Now, children. About this goldmine. Listen well. I know you're tired of hearing it, but as Jake's bodyguard, it is my duty to remind you one last time. It is of the *utmost importance* that you keep everything you're about to see today in strictest secrecy. Understood?"

"Yes, yes, we understand," they mumbled.

"Even knowing about the Everton Mine's existence, let alone its location, brings a certain risk," he continued. "You may discuss it amongst yourselves or with us, but never speak about it in front of outsiders. Never forget, having great wealth, like magical abilities, can make a person a target for those with bad intents. Of course, you're well protected here, but always be discreet. We don't need the wrong sort of people hearing about the goldmine and deciding to try to kidnap Jake or any of you, as his closest friends, to make a fortune in ransom money."

"I'd like to see 'em try it," Jake drawled.

The battle-hardened warrior eyed him with a cynical frown, then turned away with one of his meaningful low growls.

"What?" Jake asked in an innocent tone.

"We all know you hate caves, Jake," Derek shot back over his shoulder, "and that you're already dreading going underground into the mine. Your showing off, boasting, and making fun of the dwarves isn't fooling anybody."

"Am not! What do you mean?" he protested, his cheeks coloring as Derek stalked off. "I'm not scared!"

But even his friends chuckled at his protests.

Archie slapped him on the back. "It'll be fine, coz. We'll be right there with you."

"We'll protect you, Jake," Dani teased as they walked away to follow Derek.

Jake scowled after them. What did they know? They had never been sent off from an orphanage at age nine to work in a coalmine. Maybe he had a reason for how he felt!

He shuddered at the memory of the older boys' cruel pranks on him—and his own, even worse retaliation on them. The meanest thing he'd ever done in his life. And that was saying something.

The darkness just seemed to bring out the worst in some people, he guessed. Even a future Lightrider.

He thrust the unsettling memories out of his mind and ran to catch up with the others, still irked—which was probably a very strange emotion for someone who had inherited a goldmine.

Let's just get this over with.

CHAPTER TWO
Master of the Mine

Marching up the mountain path toward the mine's secret entrance in the woods, Derek pointed out the distant boundaries of all the lands belonging to Plas-y-Fforest, practically the whole mountaintop. The outer world believed the property to be simply an outdoorsman's retreat for the Earls of Griffon, passed down from father to son.

The woods and streams were rich grounds for hunting and fishing, after all—a fine country getaway from the hustle and bustle of London life and the Parliamentary duties that Jake would have to take up after he turned the ripe old age of twenty-one.

But the truth was, inside this sprawling parkland, the entrance to the Everton Goldmine was hidden, along with the clan of dwarves who worked it—not to mention the herd of unicorns who roamed inside the magically protected bounds of the wilderness preserve.

As a designated Keeper, Isabelle could hardly wait to go and check on them, find out how the unicorns were faring. The Welsh herd at Plas-y-Fforest was supposed to be much wilder than the tamer group she tended back home at her family's country estate in England, Bradford Park.

For his part, Jake saw no sign of the elusive species, though he scanned the green, leafy shadows constantly as they hiked up the sun-dappled path. Of course, according to unicorn lore, the wary creatures would not come near when they smelled male humans in the area.

They had been hunted by men for too many centuries ever to trust one again, according to Isabelle. The creatures barely even trusted grown women, only young girls, and even the most docile unicorn mare could be extremely dangerous if she decided she didn't like you. Though the boys were envious of the girls' good standing with the creatures, they had no desire to be impaled, and thus were content to keep their distance.

Fortunately, other sorts of beasts had no problem with boys.

Gryphons, for example.

A loud caw from the sky signaled the arrival of Red, or rather Crafanc. Jake grinned as the winged beast landed lightly on a mossy outcropping of rock above them.

"There he is!" Archie beckoned to Red with a cheerful grin. "Come on down and join us, boy!"

Red bounded down onto the trail ahead of them and proceeded to lead the way to the goldmine, strutting up the path with a grand, lion-like stride.

"You're feeling very pleased with yourself today, aren't you, boy?" Jake asked in amusement.

"I think he's just happy to be in his homeland again," Isabelle said.

"Wait, is he *purring?*" Archie exclaimed as they followed the Gryphon through the woods.

They paused to hear the sound.

"How cute!" Dani ran after him and rested her hand on Red's withers as she walked along beside him.

Derek shook his head with a rueful smile, but since Red had taken the lead, he waited to bring up the rear, waving all his hikers past him. "Keep going, we're almost there." He gave Jake a friendly clap on the back as he went by him.

Actually, nobody minded the walk after being cooped up in the carriage. It was a perfect autumn day. The path was steep but not difficult, with a little brook trickling alongside it. Overhead, the sun shone through the changing leaves so they glowed like stained-glass, red and gold and orange. The forest floor around them was covered in ferns turning russet, and squirrels frolicked here and there, arguing with each other in funny chirps as they scampered around, rustling the fallen leaves.

The way Red kept watching the squirrels, Jake suspected his large feathered friend was thinking of gulping one down for a snack.

Fortunately, he didn't; Isabelle, who could communicate telepathically with animals, besides sensing other people's emotions, would have been horrified.

At last, the Gryphon stopped where the path ended in front of a small but steep section of the hillside. Red summoned Derek over with a low caw, nodding at the spot.

Derek strode to the front of the group, his long black duster coat trailing out behind him. "I'll get that." He started brushing away the tangled growth of vines, uncovering a small, arched, slightly rusty metal door.

It had a round metal handle, like that on a ship's hatch. He grasped the metal wheel in both hands and began turning it—or trying to.

Rusted into place, the handle squeaked and creaked in protest as he strained to get it working. "Thing seems...stuck." Just as he heaved the handle into motion, a little metal peephole in the door suddenly slid open at about Derek's waist level.

"Hello!"

The greeting startled the mighty warrior so much he nearly fell back onto his rear-end on the path. The kids stifled laughter as he caught himself with a curse.

A pair of blue, twinkly eyes peered out at them through a rectangular peephole opening halfway down the door. "Oh, good, you're all here! Right on time. One moment, please. I'll let you in." The eyes disappeared.

They could hear the small door-guard on sentry duty shuffling about behind the metal barrier, talking to himself. "There's a mechanism here somewhere...too dark, can't see. Where did I put my lantern? Can't believe I dozed off. Oh, here it is. Humph. Be right with you!" he called politely.

"Take your time," Jake answered, glancing wryly at the others.

"Jump!" the little old dwarf said to himself.

They heard an odd thud and a rusty metal squeak, but nothing happened.

"Oh, blast. Did it open?" the dwarf called.

"Not yet," Archie answered.

"Hold on! I'll only be a minute! Drat it," he muttered to himself. "Jump again, Ufudd."

Thud-squeak.

"Must be a weight-triggered mechanism of some kind," Archie murmured sagely.

"Almost got it! It's just that I'm not quite...heavy enough. Must be losing weight. Maybe I'll buy a nice apple tart for dessert tonight. Hm, wait, let me get a rock," the dwarf mumbled to himself. "There. This should do it."

A pause.

Behind the door, the little dwarf jumped with all his might onto the square metal mechanism, and suddenly, the door popped open.

"Ha! There she goes!"

They heard him throw down the large rock he had picked up for extra weight, then he appeared in the doorway, beaming at them—an old fellow, white haired and white bearded, with a pointy brown hat. "Welcome to you all! Sorry about all that. These outer doors get rusty in the rain. And, er, don't tell Emrys I dozed off, would you?"

"We won't say anything," Dani answered, tilting her head as she stared at the little fellow in wonder.

"Well then. Greetings to you all!" he said in a more formal fashion, clapping his little hands to his chest. "I am Ufudd, and you are all most welcome." His wrinkled face wreathed in smiles, Ufudd beckoned them in. "Come, come. Mind your head."

When Red hopped in first, the dwarf was overcome with joy, much as the house brownie had been. "My Lord Crafanc! Such an honor to see you again!"

While Ufudd made much of the Gryphon, the rest of them filed into the small, dark antechamber—first the girls, then Archie, each bending down to be able to fit under the dwarf-sized doorway. The six-foot-plus Derek practically had to crawl through on his hands and knees.

Jake was the last to follow, wiping the cold sweat off his palms onto his tan trousers. *Now or never.* Tilting his head back, he took one last, longing look up at the sunshine and the bits of blue sky showing through the parti-colored trees.

Then he braced himself, ducked his head down low, and stepped through the doorway.

As his eyes adjusted to the darkness, he was surprised to find a towering metal door ahead of them, far grander and more formidable than the small hatch behind them.

It was covered with intricate carvings depicting dwarven warriors clad for battle.

"Now then, are we all in?" Ufudd asked. "Security procedures! We cannot open the Great Door until the outer one is shut and locked again. Would you hold this, dear?"

Ufudd gave Dani his lantern, then he marched back to the small door, dusting off his hands.

They watched curiously as he jumped up (it took a few tries), reaching for a knotted rope that dangled down from beside the outer door. When he finally grabbed hold of it, he hung from it with a grunt for a moment, pulling down on it with all his might, making the door creak shut, until his feet touched the ground again.

Jake exchanged a wry glance with Archie, realizing it was another weight-triggered mechanism, this time to get the door closed.

"Ah! There we are. Mind you don't step on that square there or it'll pop open again." Ufudd waddled back to the Great Door ahead of them, taking his lantern back from Dani on the way.

With the outer door shut, the antechamber was plunged into gloom. One lantern hardly drove off such darkness.

Caught between the two heavy doors, Jake instantly started feeling a tad claustrophobic. Dani must have known—she poked him in the ribs.

"Well, Lord Crafanc, would you like to do the honors?" Ufudd asked the Gryphon as he stood aside and gestured at the mighty magic door with a flourish.

Red walked up to it proudly and lifted his front paw, placing it in a sculpted indentation that turned out to be a metal paw print.

It fit him perfectly, and when he leaned into it, giving it a slight push, he triggered the mechanism that, otherwise, would have taken a bevy of magical incantations to overcome.

The kids stepped back in caution as great gears and interlocking parts rumbled and rolled. Slowly, the Great Door to the Everton Mine slid open.

But if they had been expecting to see shiny mounds of gold ahead, they were disappointed.

There was only a dark tunnel with small train tracks leading off into it; sitting on the tracks before them were four little wooden mining carts hitched together in a row.

Ufudd gestured toward them. "Your transport awaits, my lords and ladies! If you'll kindly take a seat, I will bring you down to the Atrium for the Welcome Ceremony. Better let the boys know you're coming," he mumbled to himself.

While Jake and the others climbed into the carts, Ufudd hurried over to pull several times on another dangling rope behind the Great Door. This one apparently operated signal bells like those in any great house, wired to the servants' quarters.

They could hear the signal echo traveling along the taut wires, ringing bells strung together at intervals, and fading off into the distance.

Having sent Master Emrys the alert that their guests were on their way, Ufudd triggered some other mystical mechanism that sent the Great Door rumbling shut again.

It closed with an ominous slam.

Jake swallowed hard and gripped the metal bar across from his seat in the second cart with the boy genius.

"You're not nervous, are you?" Archie asked.

"Of course not," he lied.

"I can't see," Dani said. The girls were sitting behind him and Archie.

"Everyone hold on tight," Derek warned from the back car, where he barely fit. His shoulders were as wide as the cart itself, and he had to bend his knees out at an awkward angle to wedge his long legs into the vehicle.

Ufudd hurried back and sprang up into the first cart, where the Gryphon waited. "Here we go, then. Have you there in a trice!" He pulled a wooden handle and threw a metal switch that gave off sparks, and the cars started to roll down the tracks.

Jake's hair started blowing around as the carts picked up speed. The tunnel was lit with dim lanterns here and there along the way. They began to blur into a chain of staggered lights, a dizzying effect, as the carts began to whiz faster and faster along the tracks.

Around turns, down drops, over bumps, they flew every which way, the girls shrieking now and then behind them. Jake was trying hard not to yell, too, as he was thrown around inside the crazy cart beside his cousin.

With Red's tall, winged form blocking the view in front of him,

Jake's disorientation grew. He couldn't see where the tracks were taking them next. He hung on to the bar for dear life, trying not to scream.

He lost that battle when they burst out of the tunnel and plunged down a nearly vertical drop into the great, open hollow of the mine beneath the mountain.

"Ahhhhhhh!"

Jake's stomach lifted inside him as they fell through what felt like empty space, though the rails were still before them. Hair standing on end, he pressed with his feet against the wooden floor of the cart, his grip white-knuckled on the bar.

In the cart ahead, little Ufudd was perfectly serene, driving his vehicle, while the Gryphon seemed to be enjoying every minute of the ride, his feathers fluttering with the wind.

If not for his terror, Jake might have taken more notice of the vast working mine all around him.

Everywhere, an intricate web-work of ladders, walkways, scaffolding, buckets on ropes, pulleys and supports, little tracks with more carts full of gold and precious stones, and little wooden footbridges spanned the yawning gulf. It was as busy as an underground city.

As their wee train flattened out again at last after that nauseating drop, they zoomed through the dark underground canyon on a gentler downward spiral, circling down toward some yet-unseen destination.

Far below them, meanwhile, deep in the heart of the mountain, Jake glimpsed the white-hot glow of the forges processing the gold, burning off the dross, shaping and refining it with blasts of pitiless heat.

Sixteen hundred degrees Fahrenheit, to be exact, Archie had informed him earlier.

All the while, the whole mine reverberated with the low, constant echo of a pounding rhythm, like distant giant drums, as rocks were crushed down to gravel size, then pulverized into dust to free the flecks of gold inside.

"Impressive operation," Archie remarked as the carts began to slow.

Ufudd hauled on the brakes as they approached a large stone archway ahead: the entrance to the Atrium. Bright gold light shone from inside it, but they could not see the interior of the Atrium until the tracks had carried them under the archway. Then the kids gasped at what they saw.

"Now that's more like it," Jake breathed as the mining carts glided to a halt in the middle of the Atrium.

All four sat motionless in the carts for a second, staring all around them. It was hard to say which was more of a wonder: the soaring, gold-plated dome above them; its walls, honeycombed with the entrances to countless tunnels, like the center chamber of a beehive, all lit up with pure, carved crystal chandeliers; or the hundreds of dwarves standing on a semi-circle of tiered bleachers, waiting to greet them.

Red pounced out onto the platform, then prowled up the few wide steps to the Atrium. After him, Ufudd jumped out of his cart with a polite "Ahem!" to jar the others out of their daze.

"Let's go, kids," Derek ordered in a low tone, untangling himself from the back cart.

They got out, still wobbly from that wild ride, their hair askew. Jake's legs felt rubbery beneath him as he climbed out onto the platform and followed Red up the broad, rounded steps.

The dwarves on the bleachers craned their necks and peered over each other's hats and shoulders, trying to get a look at them. Ufudd escorted them over to where five chairs waited for them, but Jake could not stop staring at the central feature of the Atrium: a life-sized, solid gold statue of a gryphon rearing up on his hind legs, wings spread, claws bared.

The wings were inlaid with chips of ruby to resemble Red's scarlet feathers. The statue's sharp claws were of platinum, but Jake did not recognize the jewels that had been embedded in the gryphon statue's eyes. Maybe diamonds?

"Sit, please," Ufudd invited them, gesturing toward the chairs. For Red, there was a round, tufted ottoman with purple velvet cushions like a throne.

As soon as they all took their places, someone doused the lights.

"What's going on?" Dani whispered, clutching Jake's arm.

"How should I know?" he mumbled.

"Quiet!" Derek ordered in a low tone.

Then they learned why, as the dwarves welcomed them to their underground stronghold with a song.

Jake listened, enthralled by their deep, sonorous harmonies. He did not understand the words, for the lyrics were in Welsh, but the melody was brave and stirring.

How could a choir of such small fellows produce such a rich, powerful sound? He could feel the vibrations of their song resonating in his chest. The sound swirled and reverberated under the dome, then he suddenly noticed a peculiar thing happening.

Something began to twinkle in the darkness.

It looked a little bit like Gladwin's fairy trails, but more silver than gold. Puffs of it appeared here and there in midair in the center of the dome and drifted down slowly like confetti.

"What's that?" Jake breathed.

"I can't believe it! It's Illuminium!" Archie whispered in excitement. "I've heard about it, never seen it before. It's a very rare phosphorescent mineral that's said to have many magical properties. It lights up when it contacts sound waves of certain frequencies. The dwarves sing to make it glow."

"Shh!" Derek scolded.

Archie lowered his voice further. "I've heard they use it as a backup light source underground. It helps them avoid methane explosions and whatnot. It doesn't burn."

"It twinkles!" Dani whispered in excitement.

"It's beautiful," Isabelle sighed.

Sparkling dust shimmered in the darkness as the dwarves sang one of their ancient songs, bathing the cloud of Illuminium particles in the sound waves that made them shine. Meanwhile, other dwarves posted at various spots high up all around the Atrium used fireplace bellows to puff powdered Illuminium into the air.

The louder those in the bleachers sang, the brighter the darkened Atrium grew. Before long, Jake could see his friends' faces clearly by the mystical, silvery lights twinkling in the darkness, as if the stars had floated down close to hear the song.

Jake was sufficiently impressed to be filled with remorse for having poked fun of these good folk earlier.

Then he noticed that the gryphon statue's eyes must have been made from two rounded chunks of Illuminium, for they, too, glowed as the dwarves sang.

When their medley ended with a final, fading harmony, the lights came back up on all the chandeliers, and instantly, Jake and the others erupted with applause.

The dwarves themselves joined in the cheering, but Jake soon realized that the hero's welcome was for Red.

The Gryphon bounded down off his purple throne and bowed to his short fans, then launched into the air and took a victory fly around the Atrium, letting out a grand, lion roar. The dwarves went mad with celebration at this display, but Red wasn't quite done showing off yet.

To Jake's amusement, his pet landed in the center of the Atrium and reared up on his hind legs, mimicking the gryphon statue.

Fluffing out the scarlet feathers around his mane and looking very grand indeed, Red came prowling over to Jake and took his wrist gently in his beak.

"Huh? What are you doing?" Jake asked.

Red pulled him out of his chair and led him over to stand with him in the center of the stage-like Atrium.

Jake realized Red—or rather, Crafanc—was presenting him to the dwarves as the new, rightful owner of the Everton Mine.

They all stared, waiting to see what he might do.

Jake had no idea what to do. Suddenly remembering all of Miss Helena's work with him on his manners, he offered the watching assembly of dwarves his most gentlemanly bow. "Thank you all so much for that wonderful singing," he said, his voice echoing under the hollow dome of the Atrium. "I, er, we are all very pleased to be here."

A murmur of approval ran quietly through the bleachers. Red seemed pleased as well.

Whew, Jake thought. He must have done all right, because next, a stern-looking, red-bearded dwarf formally dressed in a kilt and tartan marched out carrying a golden key on a satin pillow.

He cleared his throat nervously. "Ahem." Of course, his first words were to Red. "Noble Lord Crafanc-y-Gwrool, we make you welcome. We are most honored by your presence, and we thank you for confirming the bloodline of the rightful heir." The head dwarf seemed uneasy, himself, with all the formality.

He was tall for a dwarf, for when he turned to Jake, Jake

noticed they were about the same height. "My lord, I am the mine manager, Emrys, at your service. It is my great honor to present you, as the seventh Earl of Griffon, with the key to the Everton Mine."

The dwarves all applauded as though Jake were accepting an award.

"Thank you," he answered uncertainly, lifting the large key off the pillow to examine it. He couldn't believe how heavy it was. "Blimey, is this solid gold?"

The words slipped out at once while the dwarves were still applauding.

Emrys's stony face cracked a smile. "Aye, lad," he mumbled in a low tone, "but it's only ceremonial at this point. You'll find our security measures have come a long way since that was forged back in the 1400s."

"I imagine so." Wonderstruck, Jake started to put the key back gingerly on the pillow.

"Er, sir—they usually want you to lift it up and show it around a bit," Emrys coached him in a confidential tone.

"Oh, right," Jake said gratefully. Then he did as Emrys suggested and lifted the key over his head, showing it around so all the dwarves in the bleachers could see how pleased he was to accept it.

Red was practically smiling with pride as he watched him. Having satisfied tradition, Jake laid the heavy golden key back down on the pillow for safekeeping until one day, when he was old, he'd bring his own son or daughter here to pass the mine down to *his* rightful heir.

A lump came into his throat as he thought of his parents' portrait hanging over the fireplace back at Griffon Castle. Wishing his father could have been here to be a part of this, Jake dropped his gaze to the floor.

With the key returned to its pillow, Emrys announced it was time to return it to the Great Vault. At once, nine kilted dwarf guards marched out and gathered to stand in a half circle around the front of the gryphon statue with Emrys. "You might want to step back a bit, laddie."

Jake obeyed.

"We ten were chosen by your father as his most trusted, loyal dwarves. We are the only ones who can open the Great Vault, and only three of us know how to get there."

Jake returned to his seat and watched, intrigued, as the ten most loyal dwarves began to sing a very peculiar, unexpected melody, each one chiming in at various intervals.

Archie drew in his breath. "It's a sound lock!"

Jake furrowed his brow, unsure what that meant, but the Illuminium eyes on the gryphon statue had begun to glow. As the ten most trusted dwarves finished their song, harmonizing the final bar with impressive precision, the gryphon statue began to rotate aside.

The children watched in astonishment as the heavy statue rolled away, revealing a hollow, dark space beneath it. When Emrys beckoned to Jake, Archie and Dani and even Isabelle glanced eagerly at him.

"Can they come, too?" Jake called.

While the dwarves in the bleachers chuckled fondly at his request, Emrys cracked another rueful smile. "It's up to you, my lord. You're the Master of the Mine! If you trust them."

"With my life," Jake declared. "Come on, you lot! Derek, too."

The kids ran over to the opening beneath the gryphon statue, where they were surprised to see a few metal steps leading down to an elevator. Red jumped down and led the way, going into it.

Intrigued, Jake and the others followed. Emrys beckoned to Ufudd, who came hurrying over to join them.

"But he's not one of the most trusted dwarves," Archie pointed out in a delicate tone.

"Oh, but he was for many years. He's mostly retired now," Emrys answered.

"Your grandfather appointed me as one of his ten," Ufudd informed Jake with an affectionate poke in the stomach, as if he were a cute, chubby baby.

"Grandfather?" After so many years as an orphan thinking he had no family at all, Jake was thunderstruck at the notion that he had once had a grandfather.

Blimey, it had seemed such a miracle to discover only recently that he had actually had *parents* at one point—before they were murdered—that he had never contemplated the having of actual grandparents until that very moment, when Ufudd said it.

He was still in shock, and Dani was eyeing him with some concern, as Emrys handed off the pillow and key to Ufudd in order to haul the railed metal elevator door shut. The other nine most trusted dwarves waited above, presumably to guard the opening to the Great Vault while they went to see it and put the ceremonial key away.

"You might want to hold on," the head dwarf advised.

Remembering the cart ride, they did, gripping the wrought-iron rails of the boxy elevator.

Then Emrys threw the switch.

They dropped. They screamed. Except for Derek, who laughed, probably remembering when his old friend, Jake's dad, Jacob, had brought him here for the first time, too.

Archie let out a loud "Woo hoo!" after a moment. As an inventor of flying machines, the boy genius was a bit more used to such wild rides than the rest of them.

They gripped the rails, laughing and terrified, as the elevator careened through a series of underground passages. There were lots of intersections shooting off in all directions, though some were blocked with redoubtable metal doors fortified with rivets.

One such door straight ahead separated into four steel panels that retracted into the walls as they zoomed toward it. Jake realized Emrys was operating the doors as well. This one shut with a puff of steam right behind them, then the elevator immediately jolted to the left, then up, then down.

"We change the pattern through these tunnels every week!" Emrys explained, yelling to be heard over the whooshing noise of wind and motion and the occasional clanks of metal on metal, which produced little showers of sparks in their wake. "Anyone taking the wrong path will be instantly vaporized before they ever reach the Vault."

"Oh, that's comforting," Dani mumbled, holding on for dear life. "I hope he knows the way."

He did.

Through one last separating door beneath them, they dropped down into the center of a tall underground cavern, where the elevator glided to a halt.

The doors opened with a pleasant *bing!*

But amazement was already replacing Jake's dizziness, for

when they had come through the last door, it had automatically switched on the gaslights, illuminating the inside of the Great Vault.

All their jaws dropped.

Emrys stepped out and waited for them to follow, but all four children stayed motionless for a second, agog at the gleaming gold mountains of treasure all around them.

Jake could not believe his eyes.

He staggered out of the elevator in an utter daze. He had had no idea that anyone was this rich.

Especially him.

He barely even heard the others laughing in astonishment as he took a few steps out of the elevator, dazzled and, to his surprise, slightly queasy at the sight of gold ingots piled high on all sides.

He went down the center walkway, numb with shock and not quite sure how to feel. Half of him was elated at the endless possibilities his fortune represented.

But the other half looked back on all the times he had nearly starved to death—one homeless orphan among many on the streets of London—and that half of him was furious.

What was the point of all his suffering? Wasn't this gold half the reason his parents had been murdered?

Compared to that loss, this gain was meaningless.

He shook his head, overwhelmed and confused. Money was supposed to solve all a person's problems—and look at the mounds of it he had!

But his heart sank as he realized it would never be enough. It could never replace what he had lost. In his most secret heart of hearts, he was still painfully poor, and probably always would be.

Meaningless.

"You all right, kid?" Derek asked softly, appearing out of nowhere to lay a steadying hand on his shoulder.

Jake looked up at him, unable to find his voice.

Derek knew what he had been through. The Guardian, after all, was the one who had finally hunted him down in the rookery and saved him from his wicked Uncle Waldrick, who had tried to have him killed.

Rage filled Jake from out of the blue as he felt the wound afresh of all that he had been deprived. His mother's hugs, his dad's advice.

And his grandparents, whoever they were.

It really wasn't fair.

But if this inheritance was all that he had left, well then, so be it, he thought bitterly. Might as well make the most of it. And why not?

It's mine. All mine. As he glanced around at the treasure on every side, he felt his heart grow cold and hard inside of him, just like it used to when he would go into the market to steal in order to survive.

His jaw clenched with anger, he strode over to pick up the nearest golden cup.

He inspected it while Dani came toward him cautiously, noticing the strange mood that had come over him. He held up the gold cup to show her. "Nice, ain't it?" he bit out sharply. "You like it? Here, it's yours." He thrust it into her hands.

She looked at it in astonishment, marveling at the fortune he had just handed over without a second thought.

Sure, it was enough to buy her dirt-poor family's whole house back in London, but what did he care?

It was the least she deserved, after all her loyalty to him ever since their rookery days.

He nodded at her, his eyes narrowing, then he grabbed a golden bowl to go with it. "Here. Send this home to your Da. At least you still have some family left." He turned away with a brooding glower.

"Jake, are you feeling all right?" Dani ventured.

"Never better!" he barked, whirling around angrily to find all of them staring at him. "Why wouldn't I be, when I've got all this? Archie, you need some new funding for your research?"

"Er, not really. But...thanks."

Jake ignored his protest and shoved a gold bar into his hands, then stepped past him. "Isabelle! You always said there should be a proper animal hospital in the village back at Gryphondale? Here, I'll have one built for you." When she didn't take the gold ingot fast enough, he nearly dropped it on her toe.

"Jake?" Derek asked in a worried tone.

"Ah, Derek!" Jake strode toward the tall, muscled warrior. "You saved my life. I'll have the dwarves forge a blade worthy of you! And a solid gold necklace with jewels for Aunt Ramona, and one for Miss Helena, too! What can I give to Henry? Make me a life-sized statue of a wolf for our tutor," he ordered Emrys, who blinked in surprise.

"Jake, I'm sure Henry wouldn't really want that," Isabelle said gingerly, and for some reason, her gentle protest set him off.

What did she understand about being poor?

"*I am the seventh Earl of Griffon!*" he roared, turning on her. "He'll take it from me whether he wants it or not! What, you think I can't afford it?" He threw an angry gesture at the treasure around them. "Look at all this! It's mine. I can do whatever I want! Who's going to stop me? I could buy off half the Parliament if I wanted to—"

"Snap out of it, Jake. That's dangerous talk," Derek growled.

"You can't tell me what to do. You're not my father. What do I care what anyone has to say, when I'm *so* bloody rich!" With an angry laugh, his heart aching, Jake dove right off the walkway into a sea of gold coins.

Clanking sounds filled his ears as he sank beneath the surface, laughing carelessly, rolling around in his money—aye, swimming in it—and trying to tell himself he was the luckiest bloomin' mumper in the world.

It was too late now for whining, anyway; he willed himself to believe that this treasure more than made up for what he'd lost. Who needed stupid parents, anyway?

Whoever once said you couldn't buy happiness was a fool. He'd prove them wrong.

Come to think of it, he thought, drowning in his money, he had the means now to bankrupt every apprentice-master who had ever been cruel to him.

Aye, this gold could be used as a weapon—

All of a sudden, his exultation came to an abrupt halt as a large beak dove into the mound of coins, grabbed the back of his collar, and fished him out by the scruff of his neck. Gold coins rained off him, falling out of his hair and his ears and his pockets and the folds of his clothes as Red pulled him out.

But if Jake assumed his overprotective pet had meant to rescue him, he was sorely mistaken.

Red dropped him on the walkway, tossing him angrily onto his back like a salmon he'd just caught out of the river for a meal.

Jake's eyes widened as the Gryphon reared up over him, tail thrashing, claws bared, his eyes glittering with fury as they did when he was in battle-mode.

Landing on all fours, his lion-paws planted wide before him, Red's scarlet mane-feathers stood on end.

Then the fierce beast roared, full throttle, in his face—and Jake suddenly remembered who all that gold *actually* belonged to.

Claw the Courageous.

Who alone could not be corrupted.

CHAPTER THREE
All That Glitters

Jake had never been scared of Red since the night he had first met him, when they were both Uncle Waldrick's prisoners. But at the moment, he cowered from the beast, terrified that the noble Crafanc might rip his throat out.

Instead, satisfied he had made his point, the offended Gryphon flew away, disappearing far above them through the elevator shaft.

Jake let out a shaky exhalation and sat up slowly, trembling. Oh, he got the message, all right.

He had just humiliated himself with a spectacular show of greed. He felt like an utter fool. At least Archie and Dani didn't seem to mind his complete lack of character, he thought with a wince as they rushed over to help him up.

"Jake! Are you all right?" they asked.

But he wasn't, especially when he saw Derek looking about as disappointed in him as Red was. The warrior lowered his head, pivoted, and walked back to wait in the elevator without a word.

"I'm sorry," he forced out as Dani and Archie managed to pull him to his feet between them.

He still felt so weird and out of sorts. And kind of nauseated by his own demented display.

This was the first time, moreover, that he had ever had a real spat with Red. "I-I don't know what came over me."

"Oh, that would be the gold fever, I should think," Emrys said kindly. "Don't worry, lad. It'll pass. You'll feel better in a moment."

"Gold fever?" Jake echoed, steadying himself. "That's a real thing?"

"Looked to me like a horrid attack of self-pity," Isabelle said with a cool stare.

Jake cringed, knowing she was right. He mumbled another apology for his behavior, and his cousin gazed at him intently for a moment, no doubt sensing all his tangled emotions with her telepathic powers.

"You've had a hard life, Jake, no doubt" she said at length. "But the other orphans, the ones you left behind in your old life? They're still there."

"Right," he whispered, barely able to find his voice at her simple reminder of the kids he used to know back at the orphanage and in his homeless days as a pickpocket.

Still there.

Her frank words were more effective than a much-needed slap across the face and worked at once to clear his head.

Then she, too, walked away, returning to the elevator.

Jake stared at the floor, his blond forelock hanging in his eyes, veiling his embarrassment. *What an idiot I am. What a selfish, greedy fool.* Between Red's rebuke, Derek's disappointment, and Isabelle's soft-toned skewering, he felt lower than a worm.

Dani propped him up by his elbow and searched his face with a frown. "You don't look so good. Maybe we should go back to the cottage."

"No," he managed. As much as he wanted to go and hide under a rock, the dwarves had gone to a lot of trouble to welcome him here today. He couldn't just ruin the day for everyone—that would be selfish all over again. "I'll be fine," he said, and swallowed hard. "I'm...looking forward to our tour."

Emrys exhaled in relief when he said that.

Then they all started back toward the elevator. Jake glanced upward, wondering where Red had gone.

"Don't feel too bad, laddie," little Ufudd offered, noticing his anxious look. "Lord Crafanc is likely just a bit touchy after how things went here at the mine with your Uncle Waldrick."

"What do you mean?" he asked in surprise.

"Well, when your uncle inherited everything, after what he and the sea-witch did to your poor father and mother, and since *you* couldn't be found, the rightful heir—well, as the new Earl of Griffon, your Uncle Waldrick came here to look at all the gold."

"He spent ten hours in the Vault," Emrys said. "We could

barely pry him out of here for breakfast."

No wonder Red had reacted so angrily. Jake did not want to be *anything* like his horrid Uncle Waldrick, who was even now imprisoned in a tower for his crimes, deep in the heart of dragon country, where he would remain.

They stepped back into the elevator, rejoining the pure-and-virtuous Isabelle and the always-honorable Derek.

Jake knew they would never behave like he just had. "I-I wish to apologize for my outburst. I had no cause to be rude to you—Derek, especially. I hope you can forgive me. I guess the past just sort of hit me. Still, that's no excuse." His cheeks flamed and his voice faltered with the awkwardness. "I just wanted to say—I'm sorry."

The Guardian gave him an understanding nod. "It's all right, lad. We'll help to keep you honest."

Isabelle smiled ruefully at him. "It was a nice idea about the animal hospital, anyway," she said.

Then Emrys closed the door, and when they all held on, the elevator went shooting up again.

Generous-hearted as they were, Jake's friends spared him any further mention of his unseemly temper tantrum.

As the elevator ascended, he reflected on how he was fortunate, indeed, that the people he cared about were willing to let his ugly moment pass as water under the bridge.

But when they returned to the Atrium, Jake worried that the Gryphon might be another story. Red was already there, surrounded by dwarf engineers and geologists who were showing him maps of the mine's newest tunnels and trying to get the beast to indicate where they ought to dig next, for gryphons had an instinct for finding gold.

Red sent Jake a chilly glance over his winged shoulder and huffed through his beak, then turned away again.

Jake's heart sank. But there was no time to waste, for the dwarves' workday was waning. They had to get on with their tour of the mine.

Emrys put the gold key away while Ufudd passed out rain slickers and a hard protective hat to each of them. Goggles were optional, but each received a little pouch of powdered Illuminium to light their way back in case they got separated.

If being underground weren't bad enough in itself, Jake blanched at the thought of getting lost by himself in that labyrinth of subterranean tunnels.

Of course, Emrys had no intention of letting that happen, so the Illuminium was really just a keepsake from their visit to the mine. Dani was jumping up and down with excitement over having some Illuminium of her own when Derek announced that he'd be staying behind with Red in the Atrium, where he'd wait for them to return.

He'd been on the tour many times before, he said, and for a fellow of his size, some of those passages, tunnels, and low arches were just a bother.

Jake instantly worried that this was just an excuse, that Derek really just wanted to get away from him after his obnoxious outburst in the Vault.

Not that he could blame him.

Before they set out, Emrys issued a formal invitation to them all to come tomorrow night to Waterfall Village and enjoy the dwarves' hospitality. They eagerly accepted the invitation, then with a final warning from Derek to do as Emrys said, they marched off into the wide main tunnel off the Atrium to begin their tour.

Crews of dwarves with all their tools and gear bustled about in all directions, heading for their assigned work areas. Halfway down the tunnel, Emrys led them past an alcove hollowed out of the bedrock, with a few small tables built into it like a tiny restaurant. Here some of the dwarf miners were taking their breaks until a signal bell rang; then the hardworking miners picked up their tools, put on their hats, and trudged back to work.

Next, their tour proceeded into even darker, narrower underground passages, where they saw many wonders. Great stone arches, dramatically lit with lanterns. Rock formations in an array of colors, like natural sculptures formed by water and erosion. Startlingly bright white calcium formations grew next to sleek, jet-black coal. Reddish clumps of iron mingled with sparkly green galena and silvery lead sulfide. Bright blue copper sulfate striped bold yellow deposits of garish sulfur.

"Whew, that stinks!" Dani declared, holding her nose.

"It wasn't me," Jake said on cue.

The girls rolled their eyes at his joke, but at least Archie laughed. They were just glad he was starting to act like his normal self again.

"Ah, that's sulfur for you! Rotten egg smell. Well, way down here, we're not that far from the underworld, you know," Emrys jested. "We always joke we mustn't dig too deep, or we might accidentally crack open the Pit of Hades and let the devil out. Then we'd have some explainin' to do."

The boys laughed, but Dani's eyes became like saucers. Ufudd stamped his feet. "You hear that, Old Scratch? You stay down there where you belong!"

Dani O'Dell, the good Irish-Catholic girl, was suddenly looking over her shoulder, obviously wishing she had brought her little rosary. She seemed to fear that every shadow thrown out by the lanterns might be a demon lurking in the tunnels.

Jake resisted the urge to sneak up behind her and scare her with a roguish "Boo!" He could hardly blame the carrot-head for believing in the devil, considering that a bona fide angel had once saved her life.

Come to think of it, it had been a while since they had seen Dr. Celestus.

Ufudd also noticed Dani's uneasiness and spoke up to put her at ease, for at age ten, she was the youngest of their party. "Now, now, don't you worry, my pip," said the little old dwarf. "We'll not dig that deep. We're very careful here, as you can see. Master Emrys, tell them about how we make the gold."

"Right." They continued on their tour with the head dwarf narrating as they went. "Gold, you see, is nearly always mixed with other kinds of minerals. That means it has to be separated out from them. Fine gold has to be purified. All the worthless stuff has got to be burned away. Just like with people," Emrys added with a chuckle.

He led them along to watch the dwarves at work at all the various stages of the process, from the initial taking of samples with a diamond-bit drill to the final smelting process that turned out pure, solid-gold bars.

"You may not realize it," he continued, "but it takes one whole ton of rock to get just six and a half grams of gold."

"Really?" Archie exclaimed. "No wonder the alchemists back in the olden days tried so hard to do it the easy way, changing lead into gold."

Emrys snorted. "Legend has it there was a local wizard once in these parts who succeeded. Unfortunately for him, it turns out that gold made from magic only lasts for a couple of hours and crumbles when sunlight touches it. What we bring out of the Everton Mine is the genuine article, 99.9 percent pure. Now, let's head up this way. Watch your step. It can be slippery."

Indeed, they had long since realized why Derek had told them to wear their boots. Water trickled down the walls of the mine here and there and made their footing treacherous in places.

They steadied each other as they went, with Emrys at the head and Ufudd bringing up the rear of their party.

As they trekked on through the twilight, Jake was able to forget about his phobias from working in the coalmine. Bit by bit, he finally relaxed until he noticed he was actually having fun, trekking through tunnels, up ladders and down slides, over wooden footbridges suspended high above the central canyon of the mine.

At one point, they had to stop and wait while a line of carts buzzed by carrying its load. They felt the breeze of it whizzing past, then Emrys showed them one of the many ventilation shafts. "Keeping the oxygen flowing down here through twenty miles of tunnels can be tricky."

"Twenty miles of tunnels!" Dani said.

"Ah, we've had a lot of time to dig them out, considering this mine was started away back when, in medieval days. You *have* heard the story of how the Everton Mine first came to be, haven't you, young lady?"

Before Dani could respond, Emrys launched into the tale, obviously a favorite of his. "Long ago, in medieval times, a humble farm boy called Reginald was sent off by his father to serve as page to a great warrior lord, who had promised to train the lad as a knight.

"Well, it happened that the baron and his men were called up to join the king in some battle. So they came here to Wales from England, and Reginald had no choice but to follow his master to the war.

"But one evening, the baron sent him out to gather kindling for their campfire, and that was when Reginald discovered it—a large, mysterious egg. This big." Emrys held up his hands over a foot apart, then trudged on, leading the way down the dark tunnel. "It was just sitting there, wedged between some rocks in the hillside.

"He'd never seen anything like it. The shell was gold and glittered in the sunset. He knew that if he showed it to his master, the baron would think it was a dragon egg and have it destroyed. But the boy wasn't so sure. So, he picked it up and carried it around the woods, trying to find where it had come from.

"He brought it all the way up to the top of the mountain, where he found the huge nest it had rolled out of." Emrys glanced over his shoulder. "It was a gryphons' nest, and the egg turned out to belong to a mother gryphon, and you know who was inside that, waiting to be born?"

"Red!" Dani cried.

"That's right: Crafanc-y-Gwrool."

"Claw the Courageous," Isabelle said with a smile.

"It seems that while the mother gryphon was off catching food, the egg had rolled right out of the nest and down the mountain," Emrys said. "Our dear Crafanc would have been lost forever if it weren't for Reginald's kindness." He shrugged. "Perhaps, being just a boy, he did not realize the priceless value of the treasure he had found. So he simply gave it back.

"I can assure you, if any of the knights or warriors would have found it, they'd have kept it, or given it as a present to the king in exchange for royal favors. The poor mother gryphon would have never seen her cub once he hatched.

"Well, she was so grateful that Reginald had returned her prize—and so pleased to find a human who had proved he could be trusted—that she led the boy to a cave hidden in the mountain. There he saw the vein of gold sparkling in the rocks.

"Young Reginald gave his master some excuse and rushed right home to the family farm to tell his father what had happened. Fortunately, his father believed him and made the journey back to the mountain with him to see it for himself. Once he had confirmed his son's tale with his own eyes, he sold the family farm and used the proceeds to buy this land instead. I understand he got it cheap.

"No one could fathom why a sane man would trade a nice, fertile farm for a wild mountain, but the Everton family got to work chipping the gold out of the cave walls with their own hands, and that's how it all began." Emrys held up his lantern and beckoned them on. "This way, now. Come along, and watch your step down here by the water."

With his tale completed, he led them down to the tunnel's end at the edge of an underground waterway, where they all got into a boat.

The dwarves and the boys took up the oars. The dwarves steered the way through the maze of flooded caverns and old, quarried tunnels, while the boys added muscle to the rowing.

They passed a number of little waterfalls pouring in from several directions above. At length, they came to an underground chamber where the water was a bright, unearthly blue, very cold and very deep. Emrys directed them to row out into the middle of the vaulted space to show them its interesting acoustics. "We call this the Echo Chamber. Try it. *Halloo!*" he called up into the hollow space above them.

His shout bounced around and came back to him three times over, clear as a bell.

They had a grand time yelling out words and silly phrases just to hear the echo, then they finally rowed on, still laughing. The deep, resonant sound of male voices singing came from ahead, with a steady, clanking rhythm.

They went to see what it was, rowing onward. Gliding past another waterfall that spilled from a hole far above them, they paused at the mouth of another tunnel where the dwarves were hard at work.

The children marveled to see the dwarf miners perched on scaffolding or hanging halfway down the wall with knotted ropes around their waists.

"That looks dangerous," Dani said as they rowed past.

"That reminds me," Archie spoke up. "We heard about an accident at the Harris Coalmine not far from here. Have you heard what happened? A collapse? An explosion?"

"Neither," Emrys answered with a frown.

Archie furrowed his brow. "What then? Problem with machinery?"

Emrys shook his head, knitting his bushy eyebrows together with a skeptical frown. "Believe it or not, the rumor is, it was some sort of animal attack."

"*What?*" Archie and Dani exclaimed in unison.

"An animal attack in the mine?" Isabelle echoed.

"What sort of animals live down here?" Jake asked rather anxiously. *Great.* Yet one more reason not to like dark, deep caves and underground places.

"Don't worry, nothing lives down here except for us and maybe a few bats," Emrys said.

"You're not saying bats attacked them?" Archie asked with a dubious arch of his eyebrow.

"No, no, I'm not saying that. It couldn't have been bats! After all..." Emrys hesitated. "Bats don't usually eat people."

"Eat people!" Dani exclaimed.

Ufudd leaned closer. "Aye, according to the pixies, all they found of those men was a few wee bones!"

Emrys snorted. "As if you can take the word of a pixie. Troublemakers!"

Ufudd ignored him, holding up his pinky finger. "All they found was a finger bone of one. Part of a toe of another..."

The children stared at him in horror.

"What Ufudd is trying to say is that nobody really knows," Emrys said in a longsuffering tone. "The Company is being very hush-hush about it."

"Well, the bones looked like they had been gnawed! According to the pixies," Ufudd said.

Dani finally found her voice. "You...have pixies around here?"

"Oh, Wales is crawling with 'em, poppet," Ufudd assured her.

"Wait," Jake said, striving for clarity. "So, those coffins we saw at the funeral earlier today—they were empty?"

"Except for the few bones they found in the dirt," Emrys answered with a sigh. "Poor fellows. That's no way to go."

"Eaten," Archie echoed, pondering it.

"But by what? It wasn't bats!" Jake exclaimed.

"Wolf, bear," Ufudd suggested.

"Impossible!" Emrys blustered at the senior dwarf, leading the kids to realize that this had been an ongoing topic of debate in recent days. No doubt, as overseer of the mine, Emrys was responsible for his workers' safety. He had to be concerned. "I don't know what happened to those coalmen, but bears and wolves have both been extinct in Wales for centuries."

"Not the tame ones! Years ago when I was a boy," Ufudd told

the children, "a traveling circus came through and one of the trained bears escaped—"

"Oh, don't start with that again, you daft old thing," Emrys muttered.

But the littler dwarf ignored him, earnestly addressing the kids. "Maybe it found its way down into the mine and has been living there ever since."

"That was fifty years ago! Bears don't live that long!"

"Maybe it had cubs!"

"What, by itself?"

Ufudd just ignored him. "Bears *like* mountains. This is the sort of place where bears can thrive." He nodded sincerely at the children.

Emrys dropped his chin nearly to his chest. "Don't listen to him, please. I swear he's going senile." He lifted his head, heaving a sigh. "A pack of feral dogs, maybe. But if you ask me, it was just an explosion blew those poor men to smithereens and the Company doesn't want to admit it. Either that or someone deliberately killed them."

"What, like a murderer?" Jake asked.

"Well, it's a dashed lot more likely than a bear! Look around you. Anything can happen if someone isn't careful. Lots of nooks and crannies where an enemy could strike under cover of darkness. Maybe somebody wanted those men dead."

"But there has to be a bear," Ufudd insisted, "because the pixies were spying on the coalmen, who are all beside themselves with fright at this point—"

"I should think so," said Archie.

"And the pixies said they overheard the humans saying that now a few of the pit ponies have gone missing, too."

"Pit ponies?" Isabelle asked.

"Over in the coalmine, dearie, they use small ponies underground to pull the coal carts. They've got a whole underground stable at the Harris Mine, from what I'm told. And I'm very sure a bear would like to eat a pony if it got the chance."

"Ew," said Dani.

"All I know is that someone ought to get to the bottom of it!" Ufudd declared.

"On that much we agree," Emrys said. "Now can we please

change the subject, Master Ufudd? You're scaring the children."

"Oh! Dear me." Ufudd hesitated, realizing that perhaps Emrys was right. "Well, no worries, children. If there *is* a bear, he won't be getting into our mine! Not with doors like that." The old dwarf pointed to a massive metal door at the top of a stone pathway that sloped up from the other side of the water. "Not even a goblin can slip past our security! Nasty little thieves."

"Goblins, too?" Dani cried.

"Oh, don't worry, my dear, they're just little tree goblins. More of a local pest problem than anything," Emrys hastened to assure her.

"Talk about gold fever! They're obsessed with it," Ufudd chimed in.

Emrys nodded. "They've set up a whole colony in the trees beyond that door just so they can be near the gold."

"What's a goblin going to do with gold coins? Go on a shopping spree?" Archie asked in a quizzical tone.

"They eat it, poor wretches," Emrys said. The children marveled at this information. "They'll swallow a gold coin whole if they get their little green hands on one. Pop it right into their mouths and gulp it down. Half the time they'll choke to death—it gets stuck in their wee throats. If that don't kill 'em, the gold is poison to their system and makes them dreadful ill. But that doesn't stop 'em from wanting it." Emrys shook his head. "You'd be shocked at the lengths they go to." He leaned closer. "Want to see?"

They eagerly agreed to this. None of them had ever seen a goblin, after all, and Emrys seemed to think it was perfectly safe.

So off they went.

CHAPTER FOUR
A Goblin Mystery

They rowed across the water until they reached the stony ledge on the other end of the flooded quarry. There, they climbed out of the boat and walked up the slope toward the mighty metal door.

A few feet in front of the security door, Emrys opened a small hatch and pulled down a periscope, like one might find on a submarine (Archie's newest craze, having completed his flying machine).

Emrys beckoned Jake forward, cordially offering him the first look through the periscope. After all, he was the owner of the mine, not to mention the fact that goblins had established their colony on *his* property without asking anyone's permission.

"You can observe them through the scope without them noticing you. It's camouflaged in the landscape. I like to come up once a week or so to make sure they're behaving," Emrys said. "Haven't checked on 'em in a while. You'll see we put up nets twenty yards outside the door to help keep them off. By this time of day, with the sun going down, the nets are probably covered with goblins. Yes?"

"No," Jake said in surprise, peering through the periscope. "There's a crowd of them gathered around the base of one of the tree trunks. So those are goblins!"

"I want to see!" Dani cried.

Emrys stared at Jake. "They're not on the nets? Are you sure?"

"Are they little green creatures, about knee-high, with big heads and little skinny bodies? Pointy ears, gold eyes?"

"Aye, that's them," Emrys said, sounding confused. "May I?"

Jake stepped back so the head dwarf could confirm it.

Emrys grasped the handles of the periscope and stared through the viewer for a moment. "Hmm…" He turned the periscope this way and that. "The boy's right," he said after a moment, turning to Ufudd. "There's something going on out there. I'd best go see what's got 'em all riled up. This won't take long. You're welcome to come along and see the goblins if you like," he told the children.

Dani gasped.

"You'll be safe behind the nets, dear. Don't worry, we dwarves have been dealing with the greenies for a very long time. Occupational hazard, you might say. Where there's gold, there's goblins."

"So, they're not dangerous?" she asked.

"Aye, unless you're a pixie!" Ufudd said.

Emrys explained this remark: "Tree goblins mainly eat grasshoppers and other insects, but they'll gobble down a pixie without even thinking about it if they happen to catch one."

"So will birds, since they all share the trees," Ufudd said, nodding sagely.

"Yes, but they're still *goblins*," Archie pointed out.

"Well, it's true none of the goblin species are what you might call lovable, but the greenies are relatively harmless, especially to folk of your size. Granted, they can be vicious when they're cornered. They've got the claws and teeth to do some damage if they feel threatened. But in general, they're more scared of you than you are of them."

"Master Emrys knows how charm 'em," Ufudd said.

"Harrumph." The head dwarf glanced at Jake. "I do think that at least Your Lordship ought to come along and see them, since they're on your property, after all."

"I'd be glad to." Jake welcomed the chance to step out onto the surface world again, among the trees and grass and sky. He could barely wait to get a breath of fresh, country air after these few hours underground.

Emrys stepped forward to undo various complicated locks on the huge hydraulic door.

Jake tilted his head in thought. "Do you think I should have the goblin colony removed?"

The head dwarf gave a noncommittal shrug. "Nuisance that they are, I don't really know where else they'd go, poor little wretches. I can't speak for others, but myself, I can't help but feelin' a little sorry for 'em."

"I don't," Ufudd said flatly. "They remind me of this one's Uncle Waldrick, only smaller. And green."

Jake arched a brow at the elderly dwarf in amusement, while Emrys stepped onto another weight-triggered mechanism; the massive door opened slowly with a puff of steam. Then Emrys put on a pair of little, wire-rimmed spectacles with darkened glass lenses to shield his eyes from the sun. "I'll go first. You stay back a bit until I figure out what's got them in a fuss."

Emrys marched out.

Jake and the others followed a few cautious paces behind him, as instructed. The moment they stepped out into the fresh evening breeze, rich with its autumn smell, the pink and orange sunset dazzled their eyes after the twilight underground.

Emrys was wise to carry his dark glasses with him.

Since the kids' vision had not yet adjusted, they could hear the chattering of the frightened little goblins, but missed the startling sight of them rushing back up into the trees by the hundreds.

By the time the world came back into focus for them, they would not have seen the tree goblins anyway, on account of their chameleon-like skin.

When Jake had seen them on the ground, they had been the same pleasant green as the surrounding ferns and mosses. But as they scampered up the tree trunks, holding on and climbing with their large yellowed claws, they began turning brown and grayish; and when they vaulted back up into the branches, some of the goblins turned red, others yellow or orange, depending on the colors of the autumn leaves in the trees where they hid.

Emrys walked about twenty yards ahead and pulled up a section of the sturdy brown netting that protected the door to the goldmine. He ducked under it, then walked over to where Jake had seen the goblins gather.

The kids watched the head dwarf walk around, looking up into the trees, and then searching around on the ground.

Emrys suddenly stopped, staring down at something by his feet.

"Did you find something, Master Emrys?" Archie called.

The head dwarf glanced over grimly and nodded, beckoning to

them.

"No thanks, think I'll stay back here," Dani said with an uneasy glance at the colorful canopy of trees overhead.

Isabelle stayed back with her behind the safety netting, and little Ufudd remained to guard the girls, but Jake and Archie hurried out to see what the head dwarf had found.

Emrys gestured to them to slow their strides as they approached. "Be careful, don't step on them."

"What is it? What have you found?"

He pointed at the ground.

Jake looked down then and saw them: three dead goblins.

Their little greenish bodies were but stiff, dried husks, as if all the life had been sucked clean out of them.

Alarmed and yet fascinated at this morbid sight, the boys bent down slowly, staring. Jake was surprised to find how the other goblins of their colony had apparently laid out their dead, arranging them in a row on a mossy stone veiled by a tuft of tall grass.

The first looked newly deceased, but the other two had obviously been dead longer.

"What do you think happened to them?" Archie murmured, poking at one with a twig.

"Honestly? I have no idea." Emrys shook his shaggy head uneasily. "Pixies didn't do this. They'll set traps for tree goblins to protect their own people among the branches. But pixies can't do this."

"Do you think they might have found some gold somehow and eaten it?" Jake inquired. "You said it made them sick."

Emrys shook his head. "It doesn't look like that when they die of gold poisoning, either."

"Maybe some other disease, then?"

"Not one that I know of," Emrys said.

"Maybe they fell out of the trees and broke their necks," Jake suggested.

"That would be extremely strange. They're born up there, it's their natural habitat." Frowning, Emrys glanced up into the trees again. "Maybe I can lure one down to tell us if any of them saw what happened."

He reached into the pocket of his waistcoat and pulled out a small nugget of gold. Lifting it toward the treetops, he gave a low whistle. "Come on, now, I know you're up there. Look at this here! Nice shiny gold. Come on down and have a word with your old pal, Emrys." The head dwarf let out a few sharp, chattering sounds, at which the boys glanced at him in surprise.

He shrugged. "I've picked up a little of their language over the years." He did it again, clicking his tongue in a way that was difficult to imitate.

It was enough to snare the tree goblins' attention. Of course, the real lure was the little gold nugget in his hand. Jake watched in wonder as a few small silhouettes crept cautiously down the tree trunk, head first. You could just barely make them out, so well their chameleon-like skins matched the mottled tones of the bark.

As they moved closer, it was easier to see them despite their inborn camouflage. Their movement gave them away, along with the gleam of their yellow, catlike eyes.

They wore tattered remnants of brownish rags around their waists for clothing. As three of the creatures crept into position a few feet above Emrys's head, chattering warily, not taking their eyes off the gold nugget, Jake noticed that they had nasty sharp teeth. They looked like some strange blend of minor devils, squirrels, and tree frogs.

Emrys used the gold nugget to persuade the goblins to explain what had happened to their dead companions.

Jake and Archie listened to the exchange, mystified by the quick, staccato sounds the creatures made—even more so by Emrys's attempts to answer them.

"What are they saying?" Jake prompted at last.

Emrys shook his head with a frown. "This one here, with the tip of his ear bitten off—you see him?"

The boys nodded.

"I call him Striper. He's usually one of the friendlier ones. Striper says this is the third day in a row that they've found one of their colony dead."

"Really!" Jake said. "No wonder they're upset. Did he see what happened?"

"Striper says he doesn't know for certain what happened to the first two, but this third one today, he claims he witnessed the whole thing."

"What did he see?"

"Striper says he was just sitting on a branch eating a chestnut when he happened to look over to where this one, called Momp, had wandered off by himself and was sharpening his claws against a stone. Then Striper says a black cloud floated up and suddenly surrounded Momp."

"A black cloud?" Archie echoed.

"Or a bit of fog, or a wisp of smoke, or something like that. That's what he said." Emrys shrugged.

Jake furrowed his brow in confusion. "What happened next?"

"Momp went stock-still, staring straight ahead like he was frozen, while the black cloud swirled around and around him. A moment later, it disappeared, and as soon as it flew away, Momp fell over, stone dead."

The boys were silent, trying to make sense of this mystery.

"A black cloud..." Archie pushed his spectacles higher up onto his nose in thought. "I wonder, could it be some kind of gas escaping from the mine?"

"Gases don't pick specific victims," Emrys said.

Jake nodded with a wary frown. "It does sound like a deliberate attack."

"Besides," Emrys added, "the gases that can hurt you don't have a color or a smell. This was a black cloud of some sort."

Jake scanned the surrounding landscape uneasily, looking for any sign of this mysterious black vapor. "Have you ever heard of anything like this happening before around here, Master Emrys?"

"No! Can't say I have." The head dwarf scratched his shaggy head, obviously confounded.

"What do you think it means?" Jake asked.

"Bless me, I haven't a clue. Come along, lads. Let's get you back inside. We'd better let Guardian Stone know about this."

When they turned away, the goblins protested, complaining in chatters, stretching out their little grasping hands toward Emrys, and whining for the gold nugget. "Oh, stop that!" the dwarf scolded them. "It'll only make you sick! Now, shoo!"

Walking back toward the netting where the girls waited with Ufudd, Jake suddenly stopped, struck by a new thought. "Are we still on my property in this part of the woods?"

Emrys glanced around. "Yes. Why?"

"I thought the whole acreage here at Plas-y-Fforest was

supposed to be protected by ancient magical spells."

"Aye," Emrys said.

"Then how could these creatures have been attacked here? We're still on my property."

"Maybe this has nothing to do with magic, but with science," Archie suggested. "Perhaps it's some sort of virus."

"But you heard about the black cloud!"

"It could have been toxic smoke or fumes coming off the mine, or even a cloud of insects, like gnats or mosquitoes or even wasps with a sting to which the goblins are allergic."

"Archie," Jake muttered.

"What? Some people can die from beestings!"

"I didn't see any sign of bites or stings on those dead goblins."

"I'm just trying to say we shouldn't jump to conclusions before we know the facts," Archie said. "For that matter, how reliable are these creatures as witnesses? Can we be sure that Striper really saw what he thinks he saw? Maybe there was no black cloud."

"Why would he lie?" Jake retorted.

"How should I know?" Archie exclaimed.

"Well, you must admit these goblins do seem genuinely scared of something."

"I won't argue that," Archie agreed.

Emrys nodded. "Master Archie could be right, I suppose. There may be a perfectly logical explanation for all this. It does sound like a deliberate attack, but on the other hand, I never heard of any creature that's like a black fog."

"Well, I never heard of tree goblins till now," Jake mumbled under his breath.

What really bothered him was a sudden, gnawing worry about those magic spells that were supposed to be protecting Plas-y-Fforest.

If this was an attack of some sort, then maybe those protective spells were no longer as strong as everyone assumed. They had been cast hundreds of years ago, after all. Maybe some of their power was starting to wear off.

And if that was the case, then maybe the other creatures who lived on the grounds of Plas-y-Fforest and depended on that magical protection for their safety were also at risk.

The dwarves, the unicorns, the house brownies...

Even Red himself?

Jake couldn't say, but it seemed an excellent time to send a message to Great-Great Aunt Ramona. If those magic spells were indeed getting weak, he was fortunate to have a very powerful old witch in the family.

As an Elder for the Order of the Yew Tree, the Dowager Baroness Bradford would know what to do. No black fog, natural or unnatural, would ever bother her.

Jake decided to send a message to her at once.

"Come along, boys," Emrys mumbled with another uneasy glance around. "We should be getting back."

Jake and Archie ducked back under the netting with the head dwarf. Then they all filed back into the mine and returned to the boat, rowing back to the Atrium to conclude their day's visit.

Bit by bit, drip by drop, life, so long banished, was slowly returning to the sorcerer. But he was still so weak.

He had to feed again—and this time, he wanted something more satisfying than the life-force of a few scrawny tree goblins.

Such fare would never be enough to restore him to his full power, let alone reconstitute his body in due time. Without it, not even *he* could say for certain what manner of creature he was: a wraith, a vapor, a shadow in the moonlight.

A half-forgotten nightmare...

Of course, the goblins were a vast improvement over the vile diet he had started with upon first bursting free of the coalmine.

Too ravenous to care, he had practically inhaled the tiny souls of the first wriggly crawling things he had found. Worms and beetles.

Draining their struggling bodies of life had given him just enough feeble strength to fly on toward the nearest farm. There, he had devoured a baby chick he had found pecking about in a chicken coop. That had helped.

Feeling stronger, he had fed for a while on the farmer's fat old cat that was too lazy to run away. The cat had finally broken free of his hold before he drank the whole thing, but still, its energy helped immensely. Its stolen life-force had given him enough strength to return to the chicken coop and devour a whole hen.

By the time he had finished that feast, he was feeling almost like himself again and found he could even fly properly once more.

With every life he drank, more of him came back from the void into which he had dissolved himself by dark magic centuries ago, storing away his soul in a state that was neither death nor life, until such time as he could return.

Only a madman would attempt it, his best apprentices had warned. The devastating spell with which he had preserved his own consciousness was dangerous and rare. But with the Lightriders closing in, he'd had no other choice.

He had turned his faithful gargoyles to stone to preserve them, too, then had worked the Spell of a Hundred Souls. It had been his final act of defiance as a living man—and, indeed, it seemed he had cheated both death and the devil, and somehow, had got the last laugh.

But he still had to feed. Thanks to the goblins, he was doing much better, but he was still a very long way from being Garnock the Sorcerer again, in the flesh.

Truly, he marveled to find himself in such a weak and wispy state, when he had once been so mighty that the very elements obeyed him: air, fire, water, earth. Lead had turned to gold at his command.

Still, he had to give himself some credit. The fact that he was alive at all—even in this regrettable form—proved how powerful he had been.

And would be once more, he vowed, in due time.

For now, he had many questions. But as weak as he was, the answers were slow in coming. He was not even sure how long he had been entombed in that underground chamber. At least a few decades, judging by the state of his skeleton back in that room—poor bones!

In the hopes of orienting himself to his shadowy new existence, he summoned up the energy from the last goblin he had consumed and flew up high into the night sky to look down upon this strange, modern world and try to get his bearings.

Egads, his old village had quadrupled in size!

A sleek metal bridge with towers had replaced the ancient stone one they'd copied from the Romans.

He marveled at the baffling inventions of the day. Torches lined the streets yet burned without a flame. Magic of some sort?

Wires strung on huge wooden crosses split the skyline and hummed like they had something important to say.

Off in the distance, a huge metal snake with wheels on its belly slithered on tracks through the hills with smoke puffing out of its head. Fearsome beast! Maybe some new breed of dragon? Garnock wondered.

As for the people he saw in the streets, the men were no longer wearing hose and breeches, but odd, long trousers and jacket-y sorts of things—not a link of chain mail to be found on any of them. Such times!

But he only truly grasped how many years had slipped away when he saw the ruined Cistercian abbey.

It had been a working monastery in his day, a center of power and authority, but now the ancient structure was in shambles.

He could barely believe it. It had taken a hundred years for men to build and now it lay in ruins. Where were all those blasted White Monks? Dead, too?

Well, good riddance.

But as it finally hit him that, indeed, *centuries* had gone by since he had last walked the earth, he was stunned.

After shock came depression. Because this meant that everyone he'd ever known was dead, dead, dead. Including his former apprentices.

Not that he would miss them. Nevertheless, it hit him hard, because in his weak and vulnerable state, it meant he had no allies left to help him orient himself in this strange new world.

He was profoundly alone.

Well, except for his familiars, his loyal gargoyles—especially his two favorites, little Mischief and fearless Mayhem.

Still, as companions, they were little more than animals. They knew less about this frightening new age than he did.

Garnock let out a sigh as he wondered what ever happened to his once-young apprentices of centuries ago...

No doubt they were long dead.

The stark reality was he had no one to help him navigate through this alien new era or assist him until he was himself again.

A situation of this magnitude, waking up after centuries of a twilight slumber, could give even the greatest of sorcerers pause.

Garnock found himself drawn to the old cemetery outside of town. At least it was still there, though much larger now than he remembered.

He wasn't sure why he wanted to see it. Maybe just for nostalgia's sake, an urge to read the names of the people he used to know, there on the oldest headstones.

Somehow, it seemed the best place to start. In this place of death, he was *alive*, when he absolutely shouldn't be.

Well then. The Spell of a Hundred Souls had worked. But if *he* was all that he had left, then he had better get on about his own survival. With that thought, the dark fog that he was grew even darker.

He glanced around with an evil gaze and saw some of the local cemetery ghosts staring at him in alarm.

They didn't know what to make of him. He wondered if it was possible for him to feed on ghosts as well.

They fled when he moved toward them, but on his way to chase them, he suddenly caught a whiff of something better on the air. A lovely, enticing aroma of one the most powerful magicks on earth. *I know that smell...*

He forgot all about the ghosts and followed his nose (such as it was in his spirit state), sniffing the air to guide him.

He came to a road and saw a tall wrought-iron fence ahead, guarding a looming sort of castle on the opposite hill. The scent was getting stronger. He flew closer and read the sign: *The Harris Mine School.*

If he had still possessed a proper face, he would have smiled as understanding dawned. And if he'd had a belly, it would have grumbled with hunger.

Dear little children!

He flew across the hills at top speed and floated through the brick wall of the school. Suddenly, he was in the upstairs dormitory, hovering near the ceiling, looking down on the feast before him.

All the sleeping little innocents! That sickening smell was the goodness of children, and though personally, it nauseated him, he was well aware that nothing would restore him to his full power faster than drinking the elixir of their life-force.

Why, he would regenerate to his full wicked glory in mere days if he took his time resting and recuperating from the centuries here.

Here at this school, he could feed on the students as he pleased, stealing their life-force to restore his own. Children usually had too much energy anyway, he thought. No one would even notice, as long as he did not drain them to the point of death.

As for the brats themselves, when they awoke strangely tired in the morning, if they remembered any part of his attacks, they would think him nothing more than a dark dream.

And perhaps for now, that was all he was.

But not for long, Garnock vowed. And with that, he whooshed down from the ceiling to prey upon their bright, sparkly souls.

PART II

CHAPTER FIVE
The Secret Archive

Y ou didn't have to be an empath like Isabelle to sense the grim mood that hung over the cottage that evening.

Dani O'Dell could feel it, too, and no wonder.

Between the dead tree goblins and the men who'd been eaten in the coalmine (by a bear or not-bear), their holiday had turned unexpectedly morbid.

Everyone was worried, moping, cross. Red hadn't even come back to the cottage, but had flown off to Waterfall Village to visit with the dwarves' wives and children.

Clearly, the Gryphon wanted no part of Jake quite yet.

Only Teddy seemed oblivious to the ominous atmosphere that had invaded their fun.

Glad for her dog's cheerful company, Dani took the little Norwich terrier outside to do his business. Wrapping her arms around herself to ward off the chill, she followed the speedy terrier down a garden path, where Teddy insisted on sniffing every blade of grass.

But when she heard low voices in the garden and spotted Derek and Helena flirting in the moonlight beneath the grape arbor, she stifled a grin and tiptoed away. At least those two were getting along.

Of course, they usually did. Too bad Guardians were not allowed to get married, and anyway, Miss Helena refused to accept any suitors after her twin brother, Henry, the boys' tutor, had given up on winning the heart of the lady he liked. Poor, bookish Henry seemed to think the scientific Miss Astrid would never be able to accept him if she knew he could turn into a wolf at will.

That was the reason Jake's aunt, Lady Bradford, had hired the twins to mind the Bradford children. They were not just fine educators, but vicious protectors when their charges were in danger.

At any rate, the dejected shapeshifting tutor had gone off to some mathematics seminar at a university in Germany somewhere. He had to study hard to stay ahead of the boy genius.

Such troubles all these magic folk had, Dani mused as she waited for her dog. Sometimes she was oh-so-truly glad just to be a normal person. Somebody around here had to bring the common sense.

Retreating to a respectful distance—though she was highly tempted to eavesdrop—she left Derek and Helena alone and minded her own business. It was a beautiful autumn night. She gazed up at the black sky full of twinkling silver stars and smiled at the memory of the dwarves' Illuminium.

A few minutes later, the jaunty little terrier came racing back to her, tail wagging, his bright eyes shining merrily, as if to say, *"What's next?"*

She bent down to pet him—then suddenly had an idea of how to change the grim mood and cheer everyone up. "Come with me, Teddy!" She scooped him up into her arms. "I'm going to need your help."

"Mr. Fingle, I was wondering if you'd drive me into town—oh! Sorry to intrude." Jake paused in the doorway of the kitchen, where the two house brownies, having served them dinner, were now having their own meal.

"No, no, it's all right!" Snowdrop waved him in, dabbing at her mouth with her napkin. "Please, come in, Lord Griffon."

Nimbus did the same and rose from his chair. "Right away, sir. Just let me hitch up the horses."

"No, please, there's no hurry," Jake insisted. "I just need to send a telegram to my Aunt Ramona. Do you know her? The Dowager Baroness Bradford."

"She visited here once," Snowdrop said.

"Er, I'm afraid the telegraph office is closed at this hour, my lord," Nimbus said. "But I could go to the clerk's house and ask him to return to his office if it's urgent?"

"Oh, no need. It's not an emergency like that," Jake said, waving off this suggestion. "I've just been wondering if the old spells protecting Plas-y-Fforest may need refreshing after all these years. I have no idea how to do that myself. She'll know. She can send me back the instructions."

"Not sure you ought to send that sort of magic-related communiqué by telegram," Archie said. Jake hadn't heard his cousin wander up behind him, hands in pockets. He glanced over his shoulder as Archie shrugged. "Too bad you don't have an Inkbug."

"Oh, but we do!" Snowdrop exclaimed. "Does Her Ladyship have one to receive the message?"

"Yes."

"Perfect!" she said. "Then you can send it right away."

Jake glanced back at Nimbus with a smile. "Never mind about the carriage."

Snowdrop was already in motion, sailing down the hallway out of the kitchen. "Come with me, gentlemen!"

"You can finish your supper!" Jake told her, hurrying after her.

"No, no, business before pleasure!" she replied. "This way!" Snowdrop led them into the cozy, oak-paneled sitting room and marched straight over to the fireplace. She climbed up onto a stool, then reached up to grasp a candle-sconce embedded in the wall above the thick timber mantel.

Jake furrowed his brow, wondering if she meant to light the candles. Instead, she pulled the metal arm of the wall-mounted candelabra forward until they heard a click.

"Whoa," Archie murmured as a bookcase beside the fireplace swung open, revealing a hidden room beyond.

"We call it the Archive," she said as Nimbus handed her down from the stool. "Thank you, dear."

"A mechanical trigger to open it?" Archie mused aloud as they walked over to the opening. "I'm surprised they didn't use magic of some sort."

"Not all the Evertons in His Lordship's family line had magical powers," Snowdrop said. "They had to be able to get in here, too."

Jake stepped through the opening into the secret room behind the bookcase. Archie followed a step behind.

Isabelle joined the boys a moment later, having come down from her bedchamber. "What are you two getting up to?" She looked around in surprise. "What is all this stuff?"

"The Archive," Jake said absently, staring all around him at the fascinating array of magical objects that cluttered the small room.

Wands, weapons, shelves full of grimoires and spell-books. Great leather-bound tomes on all sorts of paranormal subjects. Isabelle rushed over to one whose spine was engraved with gold letters: *Veterinary Care for Unicorns.*

"I can't believe you have a copy of this! It's a classic," she said.

"Then you'll like this even better, Miss Bradford." Snowdrop pointed out the pearl-white staff, like a tall, heavy walking stick, leaning against the wall. "I imagine you already have a Keeper's Staff at home."

She nodded with a smile.

"You're welcome to use this one while you're here, if you should need it."

"Thank you." Then she happened to notice the odd brass or bronze gun-like thing her little brother was playing with. "Archie, what is that?"

"No idea." He squinted through his spectacles and fiddled with the round crank handle on the side.

Isabelle shook her head. "I don't think you should be touching that. Especially if you don't know what it does."

"Don't worry, sis, I'm a scientist," he said, flashing a breezy grin.

"Actually, that's the Phantom Fetcher. For arresting poltergeists." Snowdrop hurried over to him.

"You're joking."

"No, you hold it like this. May I?"

Archie handed it over, mystified.

Jake arched an eyebrow as the diminutive house brownie took the weapon in her hands sort of like a rifle—or more like one of those antique blunderbuss guns with the muzzle that flared out at the end like a bell.

Steadying the butt of the weapon under one arm, she cranked the brass handle on the side round and round. "Once you get this handle thing going, it builds up the electrical energy or what's-it-called, and once you hear—"

Bing!

"Ah! That means it's ready to shoot," she said.

"Shoot what?" Archie asked, folding his arms across his chest as he studied the Phantom Fetcher.

"It throws out some sort of energy field like a net made of, of ecto-what's it called? Ecto-something."

"Ectoplasm?"

"That's it! Once you've got your problem spirit in the force field, you can put him in one of your Spirit Boxes. There's a stack of them in the closet."

"Brilliant," Archie said.

"Mind you don't open any of them that's already occupied!" Snowdrop warned as she handed the Phantom Fetcher back to him. "Lord only knows what might be in there."

"Yes, ma'am," Jake and Archie said.

Meanwhile, Isabelle was twirling the staff like she actually knew how to use it. Jake turned and stared at her. The 'delicate young lady' looked like she could take someone's head off with that thing.

She smiled mysteriously at him and stopped swinging it, the demure soon-to-be debutante once more.

"Hm," Jake murmured.

"Look at this. And this. And this!" Archie had moved on from the Phantom Fetcher and was examining still more strange devices that cluttered the shelves.

There were ancient articles of magic clothing. He held up a white vest that looked like it had been woven from spider webs. "Giant silkworm body armor! Practically impenetrable."

"This is like your ancestors' old attic," Isabelle remarked, looking around at everything. "All their old, magical junk."

"Junk?" Archie echoed indignantly. "Look at this." He unfurled a scrolled parchment map and pointed to the title at the top.

"Atlantis?" Jake cried.

"Junk," Archie said with a snort, then he rolled it up again. "Mind if I borrow this?"

"Be my guest."

There were colored candles with unknown mystical properties, and a mortar and pestle for crushing up magical cures.

The Inkbug, however, lived in a wooden box on a table in the center of the room. Snowdrop leaned down and tapped gently on the lid.

A few seconds later, the caterpillar-like insect trundled out and scurried to the center of the desk, where it waited at attention.

Snowdrop glanced at Jake. "Have you ever sent a message by Inkbug before, Lord Griffon?"

Jake shook his head.

"It's quite simple. All you have to do is tell him what you want to say and he'll transmit the message for you through his antennae. Then, on your aunt's end, Her Ladyship's Inkbug will receive the message through *his* antenna and write it out for her in the usual way." Snowdrop pointed at the flat, open inkpad on the table.

That part Jake had seen before.

When an Inkbug received an incoming message, it would run across the inkpad to get ink on all its many tiny feet. It would run back and forth across a sheet of paper to spell out the message for the recipient.

Snowdrop gestured toward the door. "We can step out if you want to send your message privately—"

"No, no, that's all right."

"Try to keep it short or you'll confuse the little fellow," Isabelle advised.

Jake nodded, then turned to the Inkbug. "Er, are you ready?"

The little furry caterpillar rose up onto its many back legs; the front half nodded.

"Right. Ahem, well then," he said uncertainly, "here's my message. Dear Aunt Ramona: How do I refresh the old protection spells around the estate? Please send instructions as soon as you receive this message. Thanks, Jake."

For the next minute, the Inkbug twitched its antennae around with a great air of concentration, sending out the message through the ethers to Aunt Ramona's Inkbug all the way back in England. Jake hoped the grand old baroness was at home, and not in London or off at Windsor Castle visiting her friend of many years, Queen Victoria.

"That should do it," Snowdrop said when the Inkbug stopped flicking its antennae around and collapsed on its fuzzy little belly after its efforts.

"Thank you," Jake told the creature, then turned to the others. "Do you think we'll hear back from her soon?"

"Sure, though she may have to do some research on whichever spells were used," Archie said.

When Jake glanced over at him, the boy genius now had an odd-looking black cylinder thing like a camera lens over one eye, with a leather strap around his head holding it in place. "What are you wearing on your eye?"

"I don't know, but I like it."

"That would be the Vampire Monocle, my lord," Snowdrop told him. "It lets you see in the dark. One of your ancestors had to clear out a coven of vampires once in London. Horrid people, vampires. Can't turn your back on them."

"Blimey," Jake said.

Just then, Dani O'Dell peered through the secret bookcase doorway, which was still open behind them. "Hey, you lot! Come out front, I have to show you something. And hurry!"

"You come and see some stuff!" Archie called back, but she had already dashed away again, giggling.

Jake cast his cousins a rueful smile. "Carrot-head's got something up her sleeve."

"Indeed," Archie said.

"Let's go see what she's up to," Isabelle said.

"You're all through here?" Snowdrop asked.

Jake nodded. "Will you let me know as soon as my aunt sends back a reply?"

Snowdrop assured him she would, then they all left the mysterious Archive room to see what Dani wanted. They found her out front, waiting for them with Teddy.

"Well?" Jake asked as they filed out into the darkness.

"Ladies and gentlemen, presenting...the world's first glow-in-the-dark dog!" She started singing some jaunty old Irish song, and Teddy began to sparkle.

They burst out laughing in amazement.

"You dusted him with Illuminium?" Archie asked.

Dani nodded but kept singing.

The twinkling terrier wagged his tail eagerly, glancing around at them. He clearly thought he looked very handsome doused in sparkles, and loved being the center of attention. Dani got him to dance, balancing on his hind legs, which made them laugh harder, but nobody was prepared for it when Teddy began lifting off the ground.

He started floating as he glowed and Dani stopped singing with a gasp. Her dog landed back on the ground and she quickly picked him up. "I don't want him to float away!"

The others were applauding the show.

"Well done! Bravo!"

The girl and her dog took a bow. "But I don't understand why Teddy started floating. The dwarves didn't say anything about that."

"Illuminium is a magical element with unknown properties, Miss O'Dell," Archie said. "It may react differently on animals or even vary among individuals. In short, you probably shouldn't be fooling around with it."

"Like you weren't fooling around with the Phantom Fetcher and the Vampire Monocle?" Jake drawled.

"I am a scientist," Archie informed him.

"You're a quiz," Jake replied.

But since Archie usually knew what he was talking about, Dani quickly dusted the Illuminium off Teddy's coat. She did not want to take any chances of her beloved dog floating away. "Well, as long as we cheered everyone up."

"You did. Thanks." Jake glanced at the starry sky, but his heart sank a bit. Still no sign of Red.

Isabelle glanced around at them. "I have another idea of something we could do." She bit her lip against a shy smile, then said, "How about I take you all to see the unicorns?"

"Really?" Jake exclaimed.

"It's a little late, isn't it?" Archie asked.

"It's not yet eight o'clock. We could go out for an hour and still be back well before bedtime. You won't regret it," she added. "They're even more beautiful in the moonlight."

"Do you think you can find them out there within an hour, Izzy? The woods are huge," Dani said.

"I can always find them. Being near them fills a person with the most peaceful feeling. I just thought we could all use some of that after today."

"True. But what about the boys?"

"They'll just have to stay back a little and keep a safe distance."

"Er, and the tree goblins?" Dani ventured with a nervous glance over her shoulder. "If we go out into the woods at night, what if the greenies crawl down from the trees and try to get us?"

"Nah, Emrys said they're more scared of us than we are of them," Jake reminded her. "Besides, they're even more rattled after the black-cloud incident. They'll probably just cower and hide from us. I doubt we'll even see them."

"Vampire Monocle!" Archie shouted, then dashed back inside.

Of course, they were used to such oddness from him.

"Anyway, don't worry," Jake said. "If the greenies try to come close, I'll zap 'em." He wiggled his fingers at her with a grin.

There was a time when Dani had objected to him using his strange, inborn ability to move solid objects with his mind. She had feared with a superstitious dread that such a talent could only signify something evil.

But after Jake had used his telekinesis on several occasions to save their necks during past adventures, she no longer scolded him about it. He had got very good with his aim, too.

"We'd better get our coats," Isabelle said. "It's chilly out here. Oh—and we'd better ask permission."

"Um, I don't think Miss Helena and Guardian Stone want to be interrupted right now, if you know what I mean," Dani said, and started giggling again. "I'm not *sure* if they were kissing, but..."

Jake feigned gagging at this information, and Isabelle blushed a bit, but they all agreed to leave the pair alone.

As Isabelle had pointed out, it wasn't that late yet. It was merely the time of year that made it so dark out.

The older two ran to get their coats, but Dani stayed behind for a moment to pat Teddy on the head. "Good job, boy. You did great!"

"Arf!" Teddy answered, tail wagging.

She grinned and tossed him a wee biscuit, then ran to get her coat.

A few minutes later, the rapid clomping of footsteps filled the old medieval hallway once again as Jake and the others stampeded toward the door.

Jake was especially thrilled that Isabelle was letting him and Archie come along. For boys, it was a very rare treat. Unicorns didn't generally like male humans. At all.

As they crowded around the door, Jake grasped the handle to lead the way, as usual, but when he tried to push it open, it was stuck. "What the...?"

"What's wrong?" Archie asked.

"The door's jammed. It's like something's blocking it from the outside."

"But we were just out there."

"Oh, that would be the climbing roses, children!" Snowdrop suddenly reappeared, wiping her hairy little hands on her apron as she hurried over to help them.

"The roses?" Dani echoed as the kids stepped aside to let her go to the door.

"The rose vines round the house. Enchanted flowers," she explained. "Every night at precisely eight o'clock, they wrap around the cottage to keep us snug and safe, thorns at the ready, so no intruder can possibly get in."

"Can we get out?" Jake asked.

"There's a password, but you mustn't share it with outsiders." When they agreed to keep it a secret, Snowdrop revealed it. "All you have to do is say, 'Roses, retreat!' Then they'll pull back. You have thirty seconds to get through the door before they close again. Be careful of the thorns."

"Mrs. Fingle," Isabelle spoke up, "if Miss Helena asks where we are, would you please tell her we went out for a walk?"

"I hope she won't mind?" Snowdrop asked with a frown.

"We won't leave the property. We'll be back within the hour."

"Besides, we *are* on holiday," Jake pointed out.

"Very well." Snowdrop knocked twice on the front door to alert the enchanted flowers that someone wanted out. "Roses, retreat!"

As soon as she spoke the password, they heard a rustling sound outside and a bit of scraping as the retreating thorns scratched across the door.

"Look!" Dani pointed at the window.

The thick, tangled vines with gnarled, woody branches were slithering back away from the doors and windows.

"Thirty seconds, don't dally!" Snowdrop called after them as they raced through the doorway. "Just say it again when you need to come back in!"

"Thank you!"

"Oh, and will you children want a bedtime snack when you return?" Snowdrop asked hopefully as the flowers started sliding back into place. "Something sweet, perhaps?"

"Mrs. Fingle," Jake declared, "I like the way you think. Yes, please!"

Then the door slammed shut in her smiling face.

"She's really going to spoil us," Archie remarked when they had all made it safely outside.

"Everyone should have a house brownie," Isabelle agreed.

"Look at that." Jake nodded at the cottage as the enchanted rose vines rustled and scraped and creaked back into position, like fragrant, flowery chains spiked with giant thorns.

The four glanced at each other in amazement, but could only shake their heads over this latest wonder.

Then they set off through the moonlit garden on their night's adventure of the unicorn hunt.

CHAPTER SIX
The Headless Monk

A s Isabelle led them through the forest, Archie scanned the branches above them through the Vampire Monocle, watching out for any sign of tree goblins.

"Nothing yet," he reported.

"Good!" Dani said.

Above them, dark clouds floated across the bright October moon. The crisp night air turned each breath into visible puffs of vapor, reminding Jake of the tree goblin's account about the black fog. So weird...

He pondered the mystery as he trudged along the path after the others, dead leaves crunching underfoot.

Near the top of the hill, Isabelle stopped and turned slowly, scanning the landscape and trying to home in on the herd's whereabouts. They all listened for hoof beats but only heard the warbling of a night bird.

"I think...that way." She pointed, and they followed her down another trail that slanted off to the left.

After a few more minutes of walking, the path left the woods and opened out into one of the fields.

"This looks right. Come on," she murmured.

They strode out into the sloping meadow and got halfway across it when Archie pointed toward the top of the cleared hill. "Whoa, what's that?"

They followed his gaze and discovered the outline of a lonely old building standing on the crest of the hill.

"It's a house," Dani said.

"No." Archie had the advantage of the Vampire Monocle, so he could see it clearly in the dark. "It's just ruins. Looks like an old medieval church or something. It's missing a couple of walls. Jake, did your ancestors build a family chapel on the grounds?"

He shrugged. "Maybe."

"Looks like it might've burned down a long time ago."

"Let's go see it!" Dani said.

"What about the unicorns?" Jake protested as the carrot-head started running up the hill through the tall grass.

He didn't care about some rotting old ruins now that he was finally getting his chance to see some unicorns.

Isabelle had never given him this privilege before because of the animals' general dislike of male humans. He wanted to see them before he got any older. After all, unicorns feared and loathed grown men because of all the knights and princes who had hunted them nearly to extinction in the Middle Ages, which they had done on account of the magical properties in the unicorn's horn. It could practically bring someone back to life.

"Aw, Dani!" Irked at taking time away from their main adventure just to see some moldy old ruins, Jake was about to demand she come back when he suddenly spotted the eerie blue glow of a ghost wandering around up there.

Gliding through the ruins, it moved too fast for him to see it clearly before it disappeared again behind one of the crumbling stone walls.

"We might as well join them," Isabelle said to him, since her brother was already following Dani up the hill.

"Something wrong?" Isabelle asked, noticing his frown.

"Ghost," he said in a rueful tone, nodding toward the ruins. But then he brightened. "Maybe it'll be able to tell me something about that black fog thing that killed the tree goblins."

"Good idea."

Then he and Isabelle followed the younger two, arriving a few minutes later at the ruins of the old church or abbey or whatever it once had been.

It must have been an impressive structure in its heyday, Jake thought. What was left of the walls had pointed gothic arches and pillars with ornately carved stone tops. Pieces of the ancient slate roof had long since caved in and crushed some of the rotting pews.

"There's rubble everywhere, so be careful where you step,"

Archie warned, inspecting the ruins through the Vampire Monocle. "Don't touch the walls, either. This place is falling down."

"I wonder what happened here," Isabelle murmured.

"Look! Some of the stained-glass windows survived. Over there." Dani pointed to the east wall. "Let's go see!"

"You're not going to see anything through them," Jake said. "It's too dark."

"There's moonlight," she replied.

As the others began picking their way through the ruined nave to go and see the ancient stained-glass, Jake went off alone to have a chat with the resident ghost.

It did not take long to find the spirit out on the old church grounds, but Jake stopped cold when he saw it.

Blimey. A chill ran down his spine. He had never seen a ghost in this condition before.

Namely, without a head.

Even the headless traitor ghost he'd seen when he'd been sent to Newgate Prison had had his head with him, and could put it on or take it off at will. But this poor soul...

He winced, watching in confusion as the ghost bumped around into the ruins of the open cloister, zooming this way and that like it was lost. It wore the long, simple tunic of a monk or friar with a cord tied around its waist. Jake suspected it had been here for an awfully long time.

Oh, blazes. The pitiful thing lowered itself onto its hands and knees and began feeling around in the grass, trying to find its missing head.

"Uh, hullo?" he called. "Are you all right?"

It did not respond.

He moved a few steps closer. "Do you need any help?"

But still, nothing.

Then he realized why. It didn't have any ears. It couldn't hear him. Couldn't see him, couldn't talk to him, either, without its mouth.

It probably wasn't even aware that he was there.

Oh, this is terrible, Jake thought, wishing there was something he could do. *Nobody should have to go through eternity without their bloomin' head.*

Before long, the ghost gave up its search for its missing

cranium, as it had surely done too many times to count over the passing centuries.

Jake looked on, the hairs on his nape standing on end as the spirit's bluish-gray shoulders slumped with disappointment. Climbing unsteadily to its feet, it went sailing back toward the church, bumping into things now and then along the way.

The poor thing. Jake followed as it floated back into the stone shell of the ruined church.

The others turned when he stepped into the wide opening that had once been the doorway.

Dani beckoned to him with an air of excitement. "Jake, come and see! You're not going to believe this!"

"Bit busy," he replied, hurrying after the ghost as it crossed the church.

The headless apparition made its way across the rock-strewn nave to a small side alcove that was somehow still standing. It glided away, disappearing through the ornate stone archway that served as entrance to the alcove.

Still following, Jake scrambled over fallen chunks of roof and stone pillars in his effort to keep up with the headless monk ghost.

"Where are you going?" Dani persisted.

Jake didn't know where the ghost was leading him, so he gave no answer. The others grew curious and followed.

With his head start, Jake was the first to arrive under the ancient archway into the side alcove.

To his dismay, the ghost had already disappeared.

But what he did find astounded him.

Inside the alcove were three large marble tombs, bathed in the beams of pearly moonlight slanting in through the gothic window.

Each pale stone sarcophagus was elevated on its own rectangular dais. Each also had a white marble statue carved on top of it, depicting a sleeping person—a knight, a lady, and a priest—their stone-carved hands folded in prayer.

Jake stared in wonder. *Eerie.* He knew that back in London, lots of dead folk were buried in the great cathedrals like St. Paul's or Westminster Abbey, with its Poet's Corner, where many of England's greatest writers were laid to rest. But he had hardly expected to find ancient tombs in this small, time-forgotten chapel—probably the tombs of his own ancestors who had built the place, he realized, moving closer.

It seemed logical to assume that the lifelike statue on top of each grand coffin was a three-dimensional portrait of the dead person buried inside.

Which meant he was looking at likenesses of his own long-dead ancestors.

Jake quickly circled the coffins, searching until he found engravings on the sides of the platforms to tell him who they were. Unfortunately, he could not decipher them.

"Hey, Archie!" he called over his shoulder. "You read Latin, don't you?"

"Sure do!" the boy genius answered as the others joined him in the alcove.

"Criminy," Dani muttered when she saw what Jake had found.

Archie came over to stand beside him at the sarcophagus of the knight. The knight statue wore a funny pointed helmet, his shield and broadsword resting on his chest.

"What does it say?" Jake asked, pointing to the Latin words engraved along the side of the dais.

Archie leaned closer, reading the Latin inscription in the dark with the help of the Vampire Monocle. "Great Euclid, Jake! This is Sir Reginald himself—the page boy who found the gryphon egg!"

They all stared in amazement at the tomb.

"Was Sir Reginald the first Earl of Griffon?" Dani asked after a moment.

Archie shook his head. "No, if he's a 'Sir,' that means he only got to the rank of knight or maybe baronet during his lifetime. After that, his descendents would've had to be promoted to Barons, and then Viscounts before they worked their way up to Earls through their service to the Crown. That's generally how it works."

"I see." Dani grinned and elbowed Jake. "So, if you play your cards right, maybe you could get promoted to Duke when you grow up."

Jake snorted, then he wandered over to the lady's coffin. "So, would this be Sir Reginald's wife, then?"

Archie followed and read the inscription. "Must be. Her name is Lady Agatha Everton."

"Agatha?" Jake murmured.

"Good medieval name." Archie nodded. "I'm glad we came up

here and got a chance to pay our respects."

"Me, too."

"So, what about the priest?" Dani asked, nodding toward the third sarcophagus.

"Monk, actually," Archie replied.

That was probably the headless ghost, Jake thought, but he remained behind for a moment, lingering by the knight and his lady.

Now that he knew who they were, the pair of sleeping marble statues of his long-dead ancestors brought back an uneasy memory of something he had seen on his last adventure. Something that still didn't make any sense.

When he had sneaked into Valhalla to help his friend, Snorri the Norse Giant, Jake had glimpsed into Odin's crystal pool, which showed the king god images of what was going on in all the Nine Worlds.

What Jake had seen in the pool's reflection had unnerved him. A vision of his parents—who had supposedly been murdered when he was a baby. He was sure he recognized them from their portrait hanging over the fireplace mantel back at Griffon Castle.

The image in the pool had shown them, not dead and buried, but sleeping, rather like the knight and his lady, inside two glass coffins side by side in some dark place.

Jake didn't know what to make of it.

Thinking of that memory sent a chill down his spine. He could not be sure if Odin's crystal pool showed true things or the things you only wished were true.

He was afraid to hope there might still be some faint chance that his parents were alive somewhere, somehow.

After all, the only person who had ever claimed they were not quite as dead as everybody thought was the sea-witch, Fionnula Coralbroom.

But Uncle Waldrick's treacherous ally would have said anything to save herself. Only a fool would trust her.

"Hoy, Jakey, come and look at this one!" Dani beckoned him over to the monk's tomb. "Archie says he's from a later century than those two."

He went over.

"Sir Reginald and Lady Agatha were from the twelfth century, but this one died in the early 1400s," Archie told them.

Jake nodded. "Am I related to him, too?"

"I don't think so. His name is Brother Colwyn, and er, the inscription says he was murdered right here on the premises of the church and its community of Cistercians. I believe they used to call them White Monks. Anyway, if he wasn't a relative, I'd assume the murder was why they had him buried here."

"Brother Colwyn," Jake murmured. "I'm betting that's our ghost."

Dani and Archie looked at him in surprise; he told them what he had seen.

"Did you speak to him about the black fog?" Isabelle asked, hands in her coat pockets.

"Er, no. He was in no condition to answer me." And when he told them why, all three reacted with gasps and low shrieks of horror—which, naturally, Jake rather enjoyed.

"That's awful!" Dani exclaimed. "Maybe we should try to find his head for him."

"It's only been missing for, what, five hundred years?" Jake said skeptically.

"How do you take off a ghost's head, anyway?" Archie wondered aloud.

"No idea."

"Sounds like there must have been dark magic involved," Isabelle murmured, which immediately brought back the ominous pall of fear they had only just started to forget.

Jake frowned. At least her answer made sense. Bad business, black magic. The white kind was dangerous enough. Great-Great Aunt Ramona always told them magic was only to be used as a last resort, and even then, you could never be entirely sure there would not be unintended consequences.

Jake shook off the gloomy mood. There were unicorns waiting out there somewhere for them. "Right," he said. "So, what did you want to show me before?"

"Oh, you've got to come and see!" Dani gripped his arm and started dragging him out of the alcove. "You're not going to believe what we found. Don't tell him!" she chided the others. "I want to see if he has the same reaction we did."

She led him back out into the rock-strewn nave, where they

picked through the rubble to stand before one of the two remaining walls.

Dani pointed up at the last stained-glass window that was somehow still intact. "Look like anybody you know?"

Jake gazed at it.

Only a little moonlight shone through the window, just enough to reveal the figure it portrayed: a white-robed male angel with nearly white-blond yellow hair, gold-tipped wings, and a knotted cord around his waist. He had sandals on his feet and a silver sword in his hand. Jake took a step closer, staring in fascination. Why, if you put that fellow in a black suit, top hat, and opera cloak...

He turned to them, squinting in confusion. "Dr. Celestus?"

"It is! It's got to be him. I'd know him anywhere!" Dani declared, and well she should, since this was the very angel who had saved her life.

"But that was just back in May," Jake said. "This window must have been made over five centuries ago."

Isabelle shrugged. "I guess he's older than he looks."

Puzzled by the thought that he might personally know an actual immortal being, Jake stared up at the stained-glass window a moment longer.

The air of mystery around this night had definitely thickened.

Still, they didn't want to risk being gone too long and get in trouble with Derek and Helena. So they left the old church ruins and continued on with their nighttime trek across the countryside.

It was time to find the unicorns.

CHAPTER SEVEN
The Unicorn Hunt

"**L**et's try over there," Isabelle suggested, pointing across the moonlit meadow.

They agreed to this and marched on in their search, crossing to the far side of the field, where the path led into the woods again.

"How long do you think this is going to take?" Dani asked.

"More importantly, what snack will Snowdrop have made for us when we return?" Archie jested.

The words had no sooner left his mouth, however, than the dark forest around them began to shake. The thunder of hoof beats filled the air.

Dani gasped. "The unicorns! They're coming!"

"Where are they?" Jake cried. "I don't see them!"

"Me neither," Archie said, glancing around anxiously through the Vampire Monocle.

"Quick, you need to hide!" Isabelle ordered.

"Where?" Jake asked.

The sound seemed to be coming from all directions, making it impossible to guess which might be the safest way to run.

"Isabelle, which way?" her brother demanded with dread in his voice. "I don't fancy getting impaled tonight!"

That quickly, it was too late.

The unicorns burst into view at the top of the ridge just a few yards above them and came galloping out of the darkness straight at them through the trees, horns gleaming like a charge of cavalry sabers.

Jake gasped at their overwhelming beauty, frozen in dread mingled with awe.

"Dani! Put the boys between us. Hurry!" Isabelle ordered. "Take my hands to put them in a circle."

The girls quickly turned their backs to Jake and Archie, their hands joined. Isabelle, as Keeper faced the approaching herd, shouting at the animals as the four of them braced for impact.

Jake was too scared to scream. The boys had never meant to meet the unicorns on the ground. Archie and he had expected to climb a tree nearby and look down on them from a safe vantage point while the girls went to pet them.

His heart in his throat, Jake stayed close to Archie within the circle of the girls' arms.

Isabelle was speaking words Jake did not understand, holding her ground without showing fear as the whole mass of towering, horned horses came bearing down on her.

It was like standing in the middle of a horseracing track. In the next second, the unicorns were practically on top of them.

But somehow the herd split, swerving clear of them on either side with naught but a sure-footed change of lead. A few of the creatures snorted in annoyance, but they went streaming past the terrified cluster of kids as if they were no more than a large boulder in their path.

Jake's heart hammered as he saw the moonlight glimmer on those sleek, deadly horns, any one of which could have run him through like a sword.

Indeed, with the four kids huddled in a ring, one unicorn taking a stab at them would have likely skewered at least a few of them at one go, like a shish kebab.

"I can't believe I'm seeing this," Archie squeaked in terror, his voice barely audible over the thundering hoof beats and the agitated whinnies.

"Don't move," Isabelle warned. "Dani, hold your ground."

The ten-year-old let out a frightened whimper, but she did not budge from protecting the boys. "Isabelle, get us out of here!"

"Just...wait," the Keeper answered. "Steady..."

Jake stared in wonder as the unicorns barreled past, kicking up clods of dirt.

Even though he was petrified, he had never seen anything so beautiful in his life. They galloped by so close that he could feel the breeze of their passing.

Their manes danced as they ran, their tails streaming out behind them. The mares had a hint of pastel colors in their mane and tails; otherwise, they were every shade of white and ivory and silver. There were some smaller unicorns, colts and fillies, which must have been born this past spring. They were growing fast, though their little horns looked relatively harmless.

As the herd swept by, barely seconds passing, it seemed like they might just be all right—until the stallion arrived. He was pure white and larger than the rest, and he clearly did not appreciate this intrusion on his turf. Unlike the mares, he stopped to confront them.

Jake swallowed hard as the kingly beast skidded to a halt in front of Isabelle, then reared up, tossing his head angrily, as if to say, *"Keeper, how dare you bring them here?"*

The mighty pearl-white stallion looked like he wanted to kill the boys to protect his mares and foals, but one look at the kingly creature and Jake almost didn't care.

The unicorns' nearness was having a profound effect on him, putting him in a kind of serene, soothing trance, even though he knew he was in danger.

Meanwhile, Isabelle spoke soothingly to the stallion, keeping her own body between the angry beast and the boys. "They mean you no harm," she was saying. "They're only children, they are not a threat..."

Jake was barely listening. Unicorn magic was taking hold of him, quite the opposite of the gold fever he had experienced earlier in the Great Vault.

He could feel the breeze from the herd still rushing past them on both sides in all their overwhelming beauty.

The way the moonlight glistened on each pearly horn, the charm in each big, brown eye, and the velvet texture of their hides as they ran past entranced him.

Even if one of them chose to kill him, he couldn't help but think it might not be a bad way to go.

All of his own badness from this day seemed washed away from him. All the hurt about disappointing Red and Derek and himself with his display of selfishness, it all felt forgiven, washed away by their presence.

Even the fear he had experienced today—his phobia about

being underground and the even more unsettling news about the animal attack on the miners, then finding the dead goblins...all that darkness dissolved like a night fog burned away by the morning sun.

He had never felt such peace, never mind the fact that the unicorn stallion half wanted to kill him. Jake wanted to stay with them forever.

Finally, Isabelle's words placated the stallion, who left with a last, angry kick of his hind legs into the air. With the boys present, the unicorns did not linger as they normally would to visit with the girls.

Instead, the herd moved on.

Jake stared after them with an inexplicable lump of emotion in his throat. How could men ever have killed these creatures?

But perhaps there was no bottom to the depths that human beings could sink to, once they decided to turn bad.

In any case, their encounter with the unicorns ended nearly as quickly as it had begun.

The herd left the woods and cantered out into the meadow the kids had just crossed.

At last, the girls released each other's hands, lowered their arms to their sides, and stepped away from the boys. All of them were shaking.

Without a word, they watched in wonder and relief as the unicorns cantered off to the far end of the meadow and stopped to graze, though they still seemed restless.

The big white stallion pranced along the outer edge of his family herd, making sure all his mares and babies were accounted for. He nudged a wayward colt back to the group from where the little one had stopped to stare at the kids.

It skipped back to its mother in the herd.

Dani looked at Isabelle. "You think we're safe now?"

She nodded in relief. "You did well."

"They are beautiful. Still, they could've killed us!" Archie exclaimed, finally recovering his voice.

Isabelle just looked at her brother.

"What did you think, Jake?" Dani asked.

Jake just shook his head, tongue-tied. "Quite an experience," was all he could manage.

"We'd better be getting back," Isabelle said.

"My legs feel like rubber," Dani mumbled.

Archie took a deep breath and let it out again, composing himself once more. "I don't think we'd better mention this to Miss Helena or Guardian Stone."

They all agreed. Then they walked back down the path through the woods to the edge of the meadow. It was the only way back to the cottage.

"Keep to the edge of the woods as we go around them, everyone. I don't want to scare them any more than we already did." Isabelle scanned the herd out in the pasture.

Jake noticed that she looked worried. "What is it?"

"I don't know. Something, more than just us has got them spooked tonight."

"Like what?" Dani asked.

She shook her head. "I don't know. I'll have to come back later by myself and try to find out what's got them so skittish."

Following Isabelle, they gave the herd a wide berth as they passed, hugging the edge of where the meadow met the woods.

Soon, they had put a safe distance between themselves and the amazing animals, leaving the unicorns behind.

Jake remained silent, all of his emotions churning after the two extremes of this day. His own ugliness in the Great Vault, and the beauty of those innocent creatures. It made his heart ache for reasons that he could not explain.

All of a sudden, he was filled with inspiration, and words came out of his mouth that not even he quite expected. "We should do something for those orphans," he blurted out. "The coalminers' kids. The men who got buried at that funeral, I mean. I'll bet their kids go to that school that we passed across from the cemetery."

Everyone stopped and looked at him in varying degrees of astonishment.

You would have thought Teddy the dog had just uttered a sentence in perfect English.

"What?" he mumbled, a trifle defensively. "We should! I mean, blimey, their dads got eaten by a bear or whatever. They've got to feel just terrible. Maybe there's something we can do to cheer them up or something."

Isabelle smiled as though she knew perfectly well that this un-

Jake-like suggestion could only be the result of his encounter with the unicorns. "What did you have in mind, coz?"

Dani's Irish eyes beamed at him in approval, while Archie grinned. "Capital notion! We could go into town tomorrow and buy some toys and such to cheer them up. And you can pay, old boy!" he added, giving Jake a jovial slap on the back.

"I think that's a beautiful idea, Jake," Isabelle declared. "Perhaps when we drop the gifts off at the school, you could say a few words to comfort those children, since you've already been through it, losing your parents. You know how it feels. I'll bet they'd really appreciate that."

He nodded uncertainly, then they all walked on toward the cottage.

Jake still felt strange after his encounter with the unicorns, but deep in his heart, he felt oddly better about this place, the world, and everything.

Even his own, woefully flawed self.

But despite his earlier behavior in the Great Vault, maybe he wasn't a totally lost cause, Jake mused as they walked on. Maybe this was just...burning away the impurities.

Like with the gold.

Although the night was black, the stars shone out and dazzled with their light.

CHAPTER EIGHT
A Visit to Town

The next day, they set out on their mission to buy presents for the miners' orphans and the other poor children of the Harris School. After what had happened in the mine, no doubt all the kids were afraid for their fathers and elder brothers who worked down there.

It would be fun cheering them up.

By midmorning, the four of them were racing through the cobbled streets of the nearby town of Llanberis, going from shop to shop on the hunt for gifts.

Tucked between a lake and a dramatic mountain pass, Llanberis nestled in the shadow of Mount Snowden, the tallest peak in either Wales or England.

The mighty mountain's old Welsh name was Yr Wyddfa, which meant, *'The Tomb.'* There was nothing *grave* about the busy town, however.

Llanberis was bustling with life. The quaint row of shops along the High Street were brightly painted: yellow, blue, orange, green, pink. It made for a very cheerful effect, especially with the train chugging past along the lake, toy-like, behind its shiny red engine.

Puffing a trail of smoke behind it, the locomotive blew its steam-whistle as it passed the town.

The kids waved to the conductor before the train went winding off through the colorful autumn trees. Then they bounded on into the next shop to find out what trinkets and treasures it held that the students might enjoy.

They bought them toys, books, games, edible treats like gingerbread and Welsh cakes, a few inexpensive musical instruments, and an assortment of knitted hats, gloves, and scarves, since winter was just around the corner.

Townsfolk smiled as they passed by, but the shopkeepers were especially happy to see them coming with money to spend. For Jake, it was a new experience *not* having shop clerks and managers follow him around their establishments and watching his every move in suspicion.

Of course, here in Wales, nobody had any idea that he used to be one of London's most notorious boy-thieves.

After all, people could change.

Jake was finding this whole experiment in generosity most interesting. The only item he bought for himself was a Welsh cake when he (naturally) got hungry.

It was only this sweet snack that gave him the strength to keep up with Dani O'Dell, who proved to have the most stamina for shopping.

Jake would have thought it was a talent that all girls possessed, but no, Isabelle was halfhearted about it. Of course, she was having enough of a time managing her telepathic awareness of all the passing townsfolk's emotions. Llanberis was not overly crowded, otherwise she probably would have opted to stay back at the cottage.

Dani, however, marched along like a little redheaded general, on the watch for bargains.

Archie pronounced her 'indefatigable,' whatever that meant. The carrot-head, in turn, almost didn't let the boy genius buy the children anything educational.

"An abacus? You can't be serious!" she exclaimed as they loitered in one aisle of a splendid toy shop. "We're supposed to be bringing them fun things. How's that going to cheer them up?"

"An abacus is great fun!"

"You're loony," she said.

"No, I'm a good eccentric Englishman. We are a lovable and well-established breed. We dig up ancient cities, we discover island chains, we invent things nobody has ever seen before—"

"Loony, like I said. Pencils, notepads, I could see. Even watercolor paints—"

"But they could use an abacus for math lessons!"

"Just buy the thing, I don't care," Jake mumbled. "This is

exhausting."

"See?" Archie gave up arguing with her and rushed on to the next item. "Oh, look at this astrolabe! They could use this for their science lessons."

"That's kind of neat." Jake stepped over to examine the little model of the solar system, but Dani shook her head, at her wits' end with them.

Instead, she went and picked out some marionettes so the kids could make a puppet show.

When they crossed the street a few minutes later, heading for the dry goods store, a flicker of motion on the roof caught Jake's eye.

But when he looked up, homing in on it, all he saw was a little gargoyle statue sitting on the edge of the roof, much like the one he had seen in the cemetery.

A fanciful decoration for such a mundane type of shop, he thought, but he paid it no further mind and followed the others inside.

Up by the counter, he heard the shopkeeper gossiping with some customers about the Harris Mine reopening this morning for the first time since the accident.

Eavesdropping while he pretended to look at the merchandise, Jake gathered that the townsfolk did not quite believe the Company's story about the mysterious accident.

An aproned woman suddenly poked her head out of the shop's backroom and called to the clerk: "Has anyone seen Whiskers?"

"No, ma'am," he answered, chuckling when the woman disappeared again. "How she spoils that cat."

"Jake! Come 'ere, I need your help."

"Coming." Soon Dani O'Dell was stacking more and more items for the schoolchildren into his arms. "Hold this, hold this. This, too..."

When she was finally satisfied that she had bought up half the store, he carried their things up to the counter and handed over the last of the gold he had permission to spend on this project.

Derek announced he would go fetch the carriage and come right back to pick them up with all their packages.

Miss Helena clapped her white-gloved hands in her prim way and ordered them to start carrying all their shopping bags outside.

They piled all their many, many gifts for the schoolchildren into a mountain on the curb, then waited for Derek and Nimbus Fingle to arrive in the coach.

Dani finally ran out of energy, her shopping crusade complete. She leaned against the quaint front window of the nearest shop and groaned, resting her head against the glass. Isabelle stood guard over the pile of presents while Miss Helena watched down the street.

Archie turned to Jake. "So, what are you going to say to these children when you make your speech?"

He glanced at him in surprise, his mind a blank, because the little gargoyle statue was gone.

"Hello?" Archie snapped his fingers in front of Jake's nose.

"Oh, right. Um, actually...I have no idea. Say, Archie, maybe you should do it—"

"Ah, no, no, no."

"But you give speeches all the time!"

"I am not an orphan."

Might as well be, as little as you see your parents, Jake thought, shooting him a frown. Lord and Lady Bradford were always off traveling for the Order of the Yew Tree, which was why Archie and Isabelle were usually left under the care of Henry and Helena and Great-Great Aunt Ramona.

"No, this is on your shoulders, my friend."

Jake harrumphed. "Well, any advice?"

Hands in pockets, the boys wandered a few yards down the sidewalk while Archie gave him a few pointers on public speaking. "The main thing is to speak from the heart. Don't worry if you get lost for a moment. Just forge on. Probably best to keep it short—"

All of a sudden, the shop door right in front of them blasted open, bells jangling, and the most beautiful girl Jake had ever seen slammed out, bellowing over her shoulder. "I said I don't *like* it, Mother! It's *my* birthday party and I am *not* wearing that horrible rag! I want one from London! As if you have any fashion sense! Just leave me alone!"

The boys stopped in their tracks at the sight of this obviously furious young beauty.

She was about Jake's age, maybe a bit older, with milky-white skin and flashing coal-black eyes, but both boys might as well have been invisible.

She shoved her way between them with a look that invited them both to drop dead for staring at her, then marched off down the sidewalk toward the pile of presents with her cute little nose in the air.

"Blimey," Jake whispered at the same time Archie said, "Great Euclid!"

The boys exchanged a wide-eyed glance.

"Excuse me!" the girl snapped at Isabelle, going around the pile of presents as if it was the most tremendous burden in the world. "You shouldn't crowd the walk."

"Oh, she's a mean one," Archie breathed.

Jake grinned. "Doesn't bother me a'tall." He clapped his cousin on the shoulder, then dashed off and started walking after the mysterious mean girl for a better look.

Suddenly, behind him, the shop door opened again. This time, the ding of the bell had a frantic sound.

"Oh, Petunia! Petunia, Pettie, darling, please come back!" A large, lumpy woman in a brown fur-trimmed coat and an astonishing feathered hat ran past both boys like a mother elephant chasing after her young. "But the satin gown looked so pretty on you!"

The dark-haired beauty tossed her curls in disgust and did not even bother looking back, just as Jake's fine coach-and-four rolled to a halt beside the pile of presents.

That was the moment that Petunia's mother noticed the Earl of Griffon's family crest emblazoned on the door.

The large woman halted as abruptly as the boys had at the sight of her daughter. Petunia's mother turned to stare, her eyes wide, the ridiculous peacock feathers on her hat blowing in the breeze. "Good heavens! It's—you're—him, aren't you, young man? You're the new Earl!"

"I am," Jake said coolly, folding his hands behind his back like the worldly London gentlemen whose pockets he used to pick. All his thoughts, of course, were on the daughter. Aha, now he could get an introduction. "Madam?"

"Goodness me! Why, you're just as handsome as they wrote in the Society pages!"

"Nonsense." Jake laughed uncomfortably.

"No, but how marvelous to meet you. Why, it's a miracle you were ever found, Lord Griffon—after all those years! Please—you must meet my daughter. *Petuniaaaaa!*" she bellowed in a whole new tone.

Rather like an order from a drill sergeant.

At that moment, Archie caught up. His smaller cousin skidded to a cheerful halt and slammed into him in his eagerness, knocking Jake off his balance and rather killing his suave effect.

Jake scowled at him, but Archie didn't notice.

"Hullo!" he said to the big lady, who was clutching at her heart, as if the opportunity to introduce her very own daughter to a young earl was more than she could bear.

"Petunia Harris! Over here—*NOW!*" the matriarch elephant roared.

Jake arched a brow. If this was what it was like having a mother, perhaps he was better off.

"We've met some charming new guests to add to your birthday party...*darling,*" she added through gritted teeth. "It's the new Earl!"

At that, Petunia finally stopped.

Ha, thought Jake with another roguish grin.

Now she was interested. She slowly pivoted and narrowed her eyes at the boys before warily returning.

Thankfully, Miss Helena appeared beside them to smooth the way for proper introductions. Meanwhile, Derek had jumped down from his seat beside Nimbus Fingle and started loading their packages into the boot of the coach.

"I am Mrs. Harris," the woman was telling Miss Helena, "and this is my daughter, Petunia."

"Harris?" Archie echoed. "As in the Harris Mine?"

"Yes, dear," she answered, though she had no interest whatsoever in Archie.

Apparently, she was unaware that he would be a lord, too, one day, when he grew up. Maybe a baron wasn't high-ranking enough for her precious Petunia.

Then Jake studied them discreetly; after all, these were the people who owned half the town.

With Miss Helena's assistance, all the expected pleasantries were exchanged. All the while, Dani O'Dell eyed Mrs. Harris's hat like she worried that some small animal might be lost up there, living among the feathers.

As for Petunia, her midnight eyes narrowed with calculation, she scanned each member of their party one by one, taking their measure. She seemed mildly impressed by Miss Helena for her slight French accent, but only Isabelle apparently lived up to her standards.

Here, at least, was a highborn young lady on her own level of wealth and beauty, she seemed to conclude. She gave her a queenly nod. "Miss Bradford."

"Miss Harris."

Poor Archie and Dani might as well have been clods of horse dung in the street, in Petunia's eyes. Scruffy Derek Stone only warranted a slight, sneering curl of her rosy lips.

As for Jake, Miss Petunia Harris stared straight at him in cold, skeptical suspicion.

Jake was bemused. Usually girls like the aristocratic misses Uncle Waldrick had introduced him to in London fell all over themselves trying to get on his good side. This reaction generally annoyed Jake until he was ready to scream. But no girl had ever dared to look at him like he was a rotten fish-head that some alley cat had dragged out of a trash bin.

He was fascinated.

"I *so* hope you children will be able to come to Petunia's birthday party on Saturday," Mrs. Harris gushed. "It will be held at our estate at two o'clock. It'll be great fun! Good food, games indoors and out, fireworks after dark. I can't believe my little girl is turning thirteen!"

Jake was already nodding eagerly. "We'd love to come," he blurted out, unaware of Miss Helena's faint wince.

"Excellent! Oh, we're so truly honored! This will be a fine chance for you to meet the *better* sort of neighbors. I will send an invitation up to the cottage at once," the grateful matron gushed. "Now I'm even more excited! Aren't you, Petunia?"

Petunia rolled her eyes.

Mrs. Harris cupped her mouth with one hand to offer a loud stage whisper: "She doesn't know the theme of her party yet. It's going to be a surprise!"

"Thank you for inviting us," Miss Helena said with a gracious nod as the female Harrises went on their way.

"Little monster, that one," Derek muttered as he put the last of the bags into the carriage.

"Hey, that's my future wife you're talking about," Jake taunted.

Derek snorted. "You do know you're twelve?"

Jake laughed. "Well! Our social calendar is filling up nicely," he drawled, feeling terribly popular as they all gathered around to file back into the carriage. "Now we've got *two* parties to go to on this trip. Waterfall Village with the dwarves tonight, and Miss Harris's party this weekend."

Archie shook his head with a troubled look. "I'm not sure we should've agreed to go."

"Why not?" Jake asked in surprise.

"It's ghastly bad manners."

"Huh?"

"They shouldn't be having a party just days after four men got killed in their mine! It's not decent," he huffed.

"Aw, come on, that wasn't Petunia's fault," Jake said. "Besides, I'm sure her parents were planning the party for months before the mine thing happened. Were they supposed to call it off and disappoint their daughter?"

"As if she'd let them," Dani said under her breath, but Archie just shrugged.

"He's right about one thing," said Isabelle. "This is going to look terrible in the eyes of the townspeople."

Jake furrowed his brow, then glanced at the governess. "Should we cancel?"

"You can't now," Miss Helena said with a shrug. "You've already accepted. They'd take it as a snub, and we can't have you offending the great merchant family who owns half the town."

"Good point," Derek said. "You don't need to be making enemies of the neighbors around Plas-y-Fforest before you've even met them."

Miss Helena nodded. "We'll have to attend now."

Jake smiled wryly. "If we must." Then he cast Derek a roguish glance. "You see that? It would be rude not to go."

Derek arched a knowing eyebrow. "And that's the only reason you want to be there?"

"Hardly," Jake shot back with a grin. "I'm in love."

"If I thought you really meant that, I would kick you in the shins," Dani said.

Jake laughed. "Just get in the carriage, you lot. Let's go deliver these gifts and get back to the cottage for supper. I'm already half starved."

They all agreed it was time to go.

Derek handed Miss Helena back up onto the driver's seat to ride beside Nimbus Fingle, then swung up onto his horse, while the kids filed back into the carriage.

As Jake took his seat, he leaned his head on the window, rather worn out from shopping.

It was then that a peculiar shop captured his attention—one they had missed before.

On the pavement in front of it sat a wooden folding sign, painted dark blue with small stars. In dramatic gold letters, it advertised:

MESSAGES FROM BEYOND!
ATTEND A SÉANCE WITH MADAM SYLVIA
PSYCHIC MEDIUM AND SPIRITUALIST

He squinted and read it again, drawing in his breath. Suddenly, he shot up out of his seat. "Don't go yet! I have to see something." He stepped over the others' feet and, without warning, leaped out of the carriage.

His greatcoat flapping behind him in the wind, Jake ran across the street to find out if there really was somebody else in this town besides him who could talk to the dead.

The possibility of meeting a fellow psychic took his breath away far more than Petunia Harris's midnight eyes. Having only received his magical abilities about six months ago on his twelfth birthday, Jake had not yet met a single soul who could also see ghosts.

Not even Great-Great Aunt Ramona could do that.

Oh, it would be wonderful to have the chance to talk to a seasoned psychic! Somebody who knew what he went through and how it was, feeling like a supernatural freak all the time.

Maybe this Madam Sylvia lady could even tell him something about the black fog that had killed the goblins, or what sort of creature had eaten the men in the mine.

Unless, of course, she was a fraud.

Unfortunately, he'd have to find out later. The shop was closed.

"What are you doing?" Dani hollered out the open carriage door while Jake stepped up to Madam Sylvia's shop window and cupped his hands around his eyes, staring inside.

The shelves were stocked with crystals and candles, charms, tarot cards, and herbal potions, and the doorway to the backroom of the shop was veiled with red curtains and long strings of beads. *I'll bet that's where she holds the séance.*

Abandoning the window, he strode back over to the sign for more details and learned that the weekly séance would be held tomorrow night at nine o'clock.

Perfect. He was definitely going to this.

It could be a first-rate opportunity to get some guidance from somebody who, unlike him, actually knew what they were doing when it came to ghosts. Usually, he just made it up as he went along.

Meanwhile, everyone was calling him.

"Jake! Let's go!"

"Coming!" He jogged back to the carriage, then they went on their way.

"There you are! Late as usual," Garnock said as Mischief came bounding out of the woods.

The little imp-gargoyle scampered over to the narrow, cave-like opening in the rocky hillside where he and Mayhem had been waiting. "Where have you been?"

Mischief chirped out some typical excuse; the larger, muscled Mayhem snarled in disapproval, baring his fangs.

"Ah, scrounging up some food in town, eh? Find anything good there?" Garnock asked indulgently.

"Meow!" Mischief imitated.

"You ate somebody's cat? Well, I see at least *you* haven't changed after all this time."

Mischief snickered and rubbed his belly as his way of saying it had been a good meal.

Mayhem—a more serious sort of gargoyle—let out a snuffle and hung his horned head in exasperation.

Garnock leaned closer to Mischief. "You had better not have let any of the townsfolk see you."

Mischief shook his head and turned himself to stone for a second to demonstrate how he had blended in. Then he came back to normal.

"Just be careful with that trick. We don't want any undue attention, at least until I've got my body back. Now then." Garnock began floating back and forth as he prepared to address his two troops.

In truth, he was doing much better now that he'd fed on dozens of the Harris School's students. Rather than simply a black fog, he had more of a shape developing.

He was very excited about his progress. Of course, he did not look quite human yet, more Grim Reaper-ish, which rather amused him. But at least it was a start.

He now had wraith-like black robes that billowed in wispy tatters; he had a ghostly skull for a head and skeletal hands, though only in spirit form.

He could not pick anything up, but that would come. And besides, there were certain advantages to being a dark spirit. He could, for example, go through walls.

His gargoyles waited expectantly, hanging on his every word, and thankfully, he could at least communicate with them. "My friends," he began, "we have been through so much together. You have endured a terrible imprisonment with me, and for this, you will be justly rewarded in due time.

"I know how upsetting it must be for you to see your master in such a state. But don't worry. Soon I'll be back to my old self. Until then, the reason I called you here is that I would feel much better about all that lies before me if I had my ring of power back.

"So!" Garnock declared. "Both of you, go back down to my workshop at once and fetch it for me. I'll wait here."

The two gargoyles stared at him and then looked at each other. Apparently, they did not like the prospect of going back into their underground prison any more than he did.

Garnock did not care. He ignored their reluctance. "Mayhem, you handle any miners that might cross your path, and remember, no mercy. Mischief, you'll have to pry the ring off my skeleton's hand with your little fingers. Mayhem's claws are too large for such dexterous work. Be careful handling it," he added. "A sorcerer's ring is no ordinary trinket. Very well, that is all. Off you go."

Mischief chattered in a questioning tone.

"No, I am not coming with you! You can do this yourselves."

The little imp whined.

"Nonsense, you're not going to get trapped in there again. Yes, I know the Lightriders sealed the door once, but that was centuries ago. They are long gone. No, no, stop that crying! I don't care if you're frightened!"

Mischief whimpered, doing his best to play for pity in the hope of getting out of his assignment, until Mayhem couldn't take it anymore. The larger gargoyle grabbed him by the scruff of the neck and gave him a hard shake, then tossed him several yards.

Mischief sailed through the air, landed with a thud, then jumped up, furious. All tears vanished, he leaped on Mayhem's back in a counterattack and grabbed the larger gargoyle by his horns, wrenching his head this way and that.

Mayhem yowled in protest.

"Stop fooling around, you two! I want my ring!" Garnock bellowed.

They stopped.

He glided over to them with a dire stare. "I may seem less to you than I once was, but when I give you an order, I still expect to be obeyed! Now, *go!*" he thundered.

The imp-gargoyle slunk toward the opening, his black, bat-like wings drooping. He cast Garnock a sulky glance over his shoulder before diving into the crack between the boulders.

The fissure in the hillside went just deep enough to give access to an upper tunnel of the mine. Mayhem had a harder time squeezing through, large as he was.

"Don't come back without it, Mayhem," Garnock said sternly. "At least I know I can rely on you."

"Rrrrurrr!" Mayhem answered in an obedient growl. Then the big, fierce gargoyle rammed himself through the opening and disappeared into the hole.

Garnock glimpsed the shine of their eyes in the darkness before his familiars hurried off on their mission.

Daft little monsters! He could not believe they had actually expected him to join them down there.

Go back into that tomb? Garnock gave a ghostly shudder at the thought. *No, thank you.*

He had spent five hundred years locked up in the chamber that had once been his secret lair. He had no desire to face it ever again.

Not that he could avoid the place forever. Certain debts would have to be paid eventually. Sooner or later, he would have to go back down there—not just into the underground chamber, but even through the mighty Portal.

Even in spirit form, the thought of that skull-shaped doorway—and what waited for him beyond it—was enough to give him the cold sweats.

No. Not yet. Must wait until I'm stronger. He resolved to put it off for as long as possible. At least until he had his body back.

Then perhaps it would not seem so final to step through the Portal—and face the terrifying ally he had once betrayed.

CHAPTER NINE
The Haunted School

Beyond the tall wrought-iron gates of the Harris Mine School, the windswept hilltop with a view of the cemetery across from it was every bit as bleak as Jake remembered.

Dead leaves blew across their path as the carriage rolled up the long drive. Ahead, the large redbrick building loomed, jail-like, its shadowed front porch deserted, its pointed turrets scraping the undersides of the gray marble clouds.

At last, they stopped before the entrance.

Derek got out and went to let the school staff know they had arrived for their scheduled appointment; Miss Helena had set it up this morning.

Restless over his upcoming speech, Jake couldn't sit still any longer and jumped out of the carriage, following Derek up to the door. He hoped some inspiration came soon, otherwise, he was going to stand there stammering like an idiot in front of the whole school.

At the same time, he had not forgotten about the ghost he had spotted floating around here dressed in a black scholar's cap and gown.

Wondering if he'd have another sighting, he jogged up the few steps onto the porch, while Derek knocked on the double front doors.

The warrior looked askance at Jake. "Cheerful place, eh?" he muttered while they waited for someone to answer.

Jake snorted. "Haunted, too. They've got a ghost," he added. "Dead teacher or something, I think."

"Nice," Derek breathed. A pause, still waiting. "Think it's a threat to the students?"

"Doubt it. He probably thinks he still works here."

At that moment, the door opened and a thin, pinched-lipped schoolmarm with her hair in a tight bun appeared. "May I help you?"

Derek explained who they were, and the woman admitted them into a gloomy foyer with dark oak paneling.

"I am Miss Tutbury," the teacher said with a harried glance over her shoulder at the classroom she had left. "If you'll wait here for a moment, I'll go fetch Dr. Winston, our headmaster."

"No, need, Tutbury! I saw their coach arriving." A tall, gray-haired man came marching down the staircase, his long black scholar's robes and the tassel on his cap swinging in time with his jaunty strides. "Hullo, hullo! Welcome to our school! I am Dr. Winston. It is so good to meet you. Jolly good, please come in!"

"I-I should get back to my classroom, sir—"

"Yes, yes, run along before a riot breaks out in there, Miss Tutbury. I can manage splendidly from here, I assure you."

"Thank you, sir!" Miss Tutbury raced back to her waiting students, but when the door opened, Jake caught a glimpse of the class and immediately saw that these kids hadn't the slightest interest in rioting.

Even with their teacher absent from the room, there was not so much as a wad of paper thrown.

The children slumped in their chairs, listless and drained, dressed in drab-colored clothes as weary and gray as the autumn colors of the overcast afternoon.

They perked up a little with curiosity when they saw the visitors waiting in the foyer. Still, as their faces turned to him, Jake was taken aback by how tired and pensive they all looked. Pale and thin, dark circles under their eyes.

Blimey, aren't they feeding them? he wondered.

Miss Tutbury closed her classroom door.

"Well then!" Dr. Winston turned to them, clapping his hands together with a jovial air. "Where do we begin?"

Derek introduced them, then Jake told Dr. Winston about the presents.

"Exceedingly thoughtful of you, m'boy!" he fairly shouted with a toothy grin.

Indeed, he was a loud and happy-seeming man, but judging by his glazy eyes, Jake suspected the headmaster had been having a nip of the bottle up in his office.

At least he was a happy drunk. But somehow his false cheer made the school seem all the more depressing.

"Well, er, we can start bringing in the presents," Jake suggested. "Where would you like us to put them?"

"Hmm, yes, dining hall, I should think. That is where we'll have the assembly. It is our largest room. Right through there." Dr. Winston pointed to the central hallway that opened off the foyer and led farther back into the building. "Shall I summon a few of the older boys to help you carry your packages?"

Jake agreed that would be helpful. While Dr. Winston popped his head into another classroom to recruit a few helpers, Jake went outside and beckoned the others in.

They came, each bringing an armload of presents.

"Here are your helpers," Dr. Winston announced as four large boys rushed out of their classroom. A voice droned on about the rules of grammar. They looked relieved to have escaped it.

Miss Helena showed them outside and pointed toward the carriage, where more bags waited. The three older schoolboys hurried out to help bring in more bags and boxes, and Jake went after them.

He soon returned with his arms full and traipsed into the corridor Dr. Winston had pointed to. It led to the students' dining hall at the back of the building.

As he passed the school's sprawling kitchen, he heard two people arguing in hushed tones. Their voices echoed off the metal work counters more than they probably realized.

What he heard made him pause.

"Are you sure you have been giving the students their full rations?"

"Of course I have!"

"Then, honestly, are you using tainted ingredients?"

"Never! Are you trying to insult me, Nurse DeWitt?"

"Of course not, Cook. I'm only trying to figure out what's wrong with all the children."

Jake couldn't resist. He leaned discreetly in the doorway and saw—judging by their uniforms—the school nurse questioning the large, sweaty cook, who was stirring a huge pot atop the enormous black stove.

The nurse rubbed her forehead, looking distressed and confused. "Has anything new been added to the menu? Maybe they're allergic—"

"No, and no," the cook said indignantly. "There's been no change in their food. Three squares a day, snack at tea, same as always. It isn't my fault they're so tired! You ask me, they're not getting enough sleep. The little stinkers are probably staying up past lights out, playing games and misbehaving with their friends up in the dormitory."

The nurse shook her head. "If that were the case, we would surely hear them. But there's never any noise."

"Why don't you ask the teachers?" the cook grumbled, moving to the worktable to chop carrots. "Maybe it's their fault, giving 'em too much homework. Maybe their brains are worn out."

"I've already spoken to the teachers and they've promised to cut down on assignments for a while." The nurse frowned, unaware of Jake eavesdropping in the hallway...

To say nothing of the other listener who had just arrived.

Jake stared at the transparent, bluish figure of the old professor he had seen on the school's porch yesterday, when they had been halted by the funeral procession.

He was floating in the middle of the kitchen, looking very annoyed at both the school employees.

"I suppose it could be all the chores Dr. Winston gives the poorer boarders and the orphans," the nurse admitted.

The cook snorted. "May well be. Cleaning house, washing dishes, doing laundry, pulling weeds. They're just children, after all. He's probably overworking them."

"Yes, but these are coalmine children. Hardy stock. They can take a little labor. Heavens, I hope we don't have a gas leak!" she said all of a sudden. "That could explain why they're all so tired."

"But none of us are affected," the cook pointed out.

The ghost threw up his hands. "It's not a gas leak, you idiots! It's not the food, nor the chores! There's something here, I tell you, feeding on the children! Why won't anyone listen to me?"

Jake sucked in his breath at the ghost's words.

Unfortunately, his gasp attracted the attention of all three.

"Can I help you?" the nurse demanded, her expression darkening as she realized he had overheard them discussing private problems at the school.

"Er, no, sorry." Jake backed away. "I just—I'm a visitor—where's the dining hall?"

"That way." She pointed to the hall behind him.

"Thanks," he mumbled, hurrying away, while the schoolboys brought in the final packages.

Drat it, Jake thought. That meant it was almost time to give his speech.

But before they left today, he needed to talk to that ghost and find out what he knew.

CHAPTER TEN
The Souling Song

S oon all the students were assembled in the dining hall, and Jake stood up at the front of the room to offer a few words of consolation.

He felt butterflies in his stomach, and his hands were shaking as he stood before the sea of faces. Archie gave him an encouraging nod, while Dani sat there with her fingers crossed.

"Ahem." Jake cleared his throat. "So, my friends and I heard about what happened at the mine when we arrived here on holiday. And we really just wanted to say how terrible we feel about your loss. It's awful, what you must be going through, feeling so alone, and wondering who'll take care of you. I should know. My parents died when I was a baby, so I do understand."

The kids stared at him.

"And the rest of you who've got family working in the mine, I imagine you all must be pretty scared right now. But the best thing, I think, is just to take it day by day, and have a little faith. And rely on your friends. You've still got each other, right?"

He floundered on a little longer and wasn't even sure what all he said, but he paused when a ghostly face peered out from one of the oval decorative medallions that adorned the four corners of the ceiling.

It was the headmaster ghost again, studying him with a critical eye; Jake got the feeling the old professor was evaluating him on his rhetoric.

He doubted he got a passing grade.

"Ahem. Anyway, we brought you these things to try to cheer you up a bit." Jake gestured toward the mound of presents on the front table so the other three would begin handing them out. "Thank you for listening. That is all."

To his embarrassment, Dr. Winston started clapping for him. "Marvelous, Lord Griffon! Very fine indeed! Wasn't it, children?"

Jake turned red as the schoolchildren politely followed suit, applauding him.

He knew full well that his speech had sounded kind of idiotic, but they seemed to appreciate it nonetheless. He nodded in thanks and hurried out of the limelight.

Still red-cheeked, he busied himself helping Archie and the girls pass out the gifts. He shook the kids' hands as he met them one by one, pretending all the while that he knew what he was doing. Being an aristocrat could be so embarrassing sometimes, he thought, but what could you do.

Heading back to the pile of presents to get more to hand out, he noticed Isabelle marching stiffly toward the exit. She looked pale and queasy, barely glancing at him as she hurried past. "Izzy, are you all right?"

She shook her head but didn't answer, rushing out of the dining hall like she had to puke. Dani wasn't far behind her. As paid companion, it was her duty to look after the delicate young lady.

"What's wrong with her?" Jake asked the carrot-head.

"Something in the atmosphere here is making her sick," Dani whispered. "Too much sadness, too many people, who knows? She said she needs some fresh air. I'll go see if there's anything I can get for her."

"Well, don't take too long. We need you in here."

"Jake!"

"Aw, c'mon, you can't abandon Archie and me. Girls are better at this sort of thing. She gets queasy all the time."

Dani gave him a look, then hurried out after the highly sensitive empath.

"She probably wants to be alone, anyway!" he added, but she was already gone.

He scooped up another armload of presents, then smiled ruefully at the schoolchildren's happy chatter resounding through the dining hall. They seemed delighted, showing each other what they had got. Some were still waiting patiently, however. Jake made his way toward them.

Approaching the tables of kids who were still empty-handed, he noticed Derek and Miss Helena standing together, chatting with Dr. Winston by the wall.

"Very well done, young man," the headmaster congratulated him.

"Thank you, sir," he answered.

But when Dr. Winston moved to clap him on the back, Jake noticed the portrait hanging on the wall behind him.

He recognized that face.

"Dr. Winston, who is that?" he asked casually, nodding at the painting.

"Why, that's Dr. Ephraim Sackville. Died some twenty years ago. Old Sack, we used to call him," Dr. Winston drawled, hands in pockets like one of the schoolboys.

The tall, slightly tipsy man rocked back and forth on his feet, the tassel on his cap swinging. "Old Sack was headmaster here for forty years. Made the Harris school what it is today. And trust me, he did not take any nonsense. I was in his first class of students when he was a new teacher here. Fierce old buzzard. He could hit a misbehaving boy in the back row square on the forehead with an eraser standing all the way up at the chalkboard. I believe he played cricket in his youth. Quite an arm on him."

"How dare you? Buzzard, am I?"

Jake blinked as the ghostly face of Old Sack peered out from the portrait and scowled at the living headmaster.

"You, sir, are a disgrace to this school and all it stands for. Drunkard! I can't believe they ever gave you my position."

Dr. Winston sighed, unaware of the ghost glaring over his shoulder. "Sometimes I could swear he still hangs around this place. I can almost feel him...watching me."

"Sir, I need to talk to you," Jake blurted out.

The living and the dead headmasters, side by side, both looked at him in question.

"About what, my boy?" Dr. Winston asked, but the strict, dead headmaster snorted.

"I daresay. That speech was a maudlin disaster. Your rhetoric needs serious work. You have obviously put no effort at all into your studies. In my office now, you young dunce."

"Hm?" Dr. Winston prompted.

Jake stared, his mind a blank from that unexpected scolding. Then he realized the living headmaster was still waiting for his question. "Uh, you know, sir, I just entirely forgot what I was going to say."

"Ha! Happens to me all the time," Dr. Winston confessed with a chuckle. "If you'll excuse me." He nodded, taking leave of them to mingle among the students and admire their little gifts in his jovial, tipsy way.

"Something wrong?" Miss Helena asked, smiling at him.

"No." Jake shook his head, but as soon as Dani returned, he took her and Archie aside.

He implored them to cover for him and distract everyone while he slipped out for a few minutes to speak to the grumpy ghost.

They agreed to this readily enough, after he assured them he would explain later. With that, Jake made a stealthy exit from the dining hall and went looking for Old Sack.

Jake hurried down the dark hallway, past the kitchen, then sneaked out into the gloomy foyer at the foot of the staircase. "Dr. Sackville? Headmaster, sir, are you here?" he whispered as loudly as he dared, looking all around him.

"You're really not a very intelligent boy at all, are you?" The ghost of Dr. Sackville materialized, floating, arms crossed, a few feet off the floor. "Does this look like my office?"

"Sorry, sir, there isn't much time," Jake whispered. "I have a few questions—"

"I daresay." Old Sack shook his head in disapproval, and the tassel on his cap swung like the pendulum on a grandfather clock. "But never fear. Rhetoricians are not born, they are made, by study, effort, practice. Now then. We will cover topics such as posture, diction, and the appropriate use of Classical references." He floated grandly toward the ceiling, hands clasped behind his back, peering down at Jake all the while through the small spectacles perched on his nose. "The best way to start a speech is with a Latin phrase to edify one's listeners—"

"Dr. Sackville, that's not what I wanted to talk to you about!"

"Ending a sentence with a preposition? Ugh, my ears may bleed."

"You said something's feeding on the children."

The ghost paused. "You heard that?"

"I did."

Old Sack hesitated over how to respond, then chose to bluster. "Young persons should never eavesdrop on their elders! It is too shocking! No privileges for a fortnight."

"I don't go to school here. If you'd just tell me what you saw, maybe I can help."

"I have no idea what nonsense you are spewing. We here at the Harris School place the highest possible priority on the welfare of our students and maintain the strictest standards of excellence. Now go back to class," he warned, narrowing his eyes, "or I shall have you caned."

A large paddle appeared in the ghost's hand; he tapped it meaningfully against his other palm.

"Good grief," Jake muttered. "Sir, if what you saw is a black fog, your students could be in more danger than you realize."

The ghost leaned down to glower in his face. "You think I don't know that?" he snapped in an angry whisper. "You are asking the wrong question once again, young dunce! Why am I not surprised?"

"Then what's the right question?"

"Oh, you want the answers given to you? I see."

"I'm only trying to help!"

The headmaster ghost glanced around fearfully. "Then ask not *what* the black fog is, but whom!" With that, Old Sack disappeared.

"Come back!" Jake whispered into the empty air.

He rushed across the foyer and threw open the front door of the Harris School to see if the headmaster spirit was floating back to the cemetery across the road, where his body was probably buried.

Jake did not see him, but he did spy Isabelle leaning against their carriage. The brisk autumn air had brought the pink back into her cheeks.

With her psychic sort of allergy to evil, the fact that the atmosphere inside the school had made her sick raised the obvious question: What if the black fog thing was in there even now?

The thought sent a chill down his spine.

He thought of how this mysterious black fog had sucked the life out of the tree goblins, leaving them like little, dead, dried-out mummies. There were no reports of any children dying here, but they certainly looked weary and anemic—enough to alarm even the school nurse.

I have got to get to the bottom of this.

All the more reason to attend the séance tomorrow night, he thought. Maybe one of the ghosts around here would be more willing to talk to him than Dr. Sackville.

The late headmaster seemed more concerned about protecting his school's reputation than the actual safety of the children. It was rather maddening.

Jake marched over to Isabelle. "What did you sense?"

She sent him a dark, troubled glance, then looked at the school again. "There's something evil in this place."

"Do you think it's in there now?"

"Hard to say. It might be. Did *you* see anything?"

She still looked green around the gills, so he chose not to burden her with the news about Old Sack, and shook his head.

"Well, then," she said slowly, "maybe all I'm sensing is the residue it left behind." A shudder gripped her, and she glanced over her shoulder at the opposite hill. "Who knows what might wander over here from that cemetery?"

Jake's jaw tightened at the thought. "Feel better, Izzy."

"Thanks. I'll wait out here till everyone's ready to go."

He nodded, then went back inside, on the watch for any sign of a black fog.

On his way back to the dining hall, he passed a classroom where Archie was talking to the teachers and older students about his latest scientific obsession. He had sketched a picture on the blackboard of the submersible he was building back at home. Jake sent him a grateful nod from the doorway.

This was obviously Archie's way of helping to distract the teachers and older students, as they had discussed. Dani must have agreed to entertain the youngers. As Jake approached the dining hall, he felt a tug on his heartstrings as he realized the carrot-head had got the children singing. *Leave it to the Irish.*

It was a song Jake knew all too well, but it pained him to hear it coming, muffled, through the door. He had sung that song many times. Indeed, the melancholy tune brought back some of the bleakest moments of his former mode of life.

The age-old 'Souling Song' was typically sung by homeless

children going door-to-door to beg for food:

Hey-ho, nobody home,
No food, no drink, no money have I none.
Yet will I be merry!
Hey-ho, nobody home.

They sang it in a round split between two groups. That was how it sounded prettiest.

Jake ignored the slight lump in his throat and pushed open the door.

But the moment he stepped into the dining hall, he stopped in shock. *"What are you doing?"*

Illuminium glittered in a cloud over Dani's head and sparkled over the heads of the smaller children crowded around her, all singing.

Jake took an angry step forward. *Little fool!*

When Dani saw him standing in the doorway with a horrified glare, she abruptly stopped singing.

The schoolchildren followed suit and when the song stopped, the Illuminium went dark in the silence; it fell out of the air, whispering to the floor like ordinary dust.

The kids' eyes shone with wonder, but Dani's green ones filled with confusion when she saw the fury on Jake's face.

"Can I please speak to you for a moment, Miss O'Dell?" he said through gritted teeth.

Usually she would have sassed him for being bossy, but she must have heard the serious wrath in his voice. She furrowed her brow, got up, and hurried over, then stepped out into the hallway with him.

"What do you think you're doing?" he whispered angrily at her before she could speak. "You can't show them that!"

She seemed startled. "What's the harm? You saw how sad they all were. I had to do something to cheer them up. It made them happy."

"It was supposed to be a secret!"

"Well...I forgot!"

"You forgot? Don't lie to me! You know you broke the rules."

"Like you never do that!" she retorted.

"Dani, this is serious," he warned her when she rolled her eyes and folded her arms across her chest. "Anything having to do with the magical world can't be shown to outsiders! You know that perfectly well. Why did you do this?"

"I felt sorry for them!" she exclaimed. "Kids like that, they never get anything."

"What if Aunt Ramona found out? You could be fired."

She drew in her breath, paling at the prospect of being sent back to the rookery. "Are you going to tell on me?"

"Of course not," he snapped. Then he shook his head. "But I have no idea what sort of problems you might have just caused by showing them that. What else did you tell them?"

"Nothing!"

"Did you tell them about the goldmine? The dwarves? The unicorns?"

"Of course not! I'm not stupid!"

"Are you sure about that?"

Hurt flashed across her freckled face. "I was only doing what you asked me to. Distract 'em, you said!"

"Right, so your mistake is my fault?"

"I said I was sorry!" she cried, then she rushed off with tears in her eyes, pounded through the foyer, and slammed out the front door, rejoining Isabelle by the coach.

Great. Jake scowled after her. *Now I have to clean up her mess. Stupid carrot-head.* How could she do such a thing? She knew better than this.

If these school kids started asking questions about the Illuminium, like where it came from, that would lead to questions about the mine, and *him,* as the person who owned it.

Soon Plas-y-Fforest could be plagued with a wave of snooping youngsters trying to sneak onto the property to explore—and then how long before they discovered dwarves and unicorns, and tree goblins, and house brownies, and roses that moved on command?

He'd better come up with something good.

Because if Aunt Ramona found out about this, the old bird would have a fit, and as usual, he would somehow end up getting blamed.

With a harrumph under his breath, Jake stalked back into the dining hall, upset that now he'd also have to put the Oubliette spell on these kids.

Perfect. After all that they had been through, now he'd have to do the mind-wipe spell on them.

That was the usual protocol that Aunt Ramona had taught him when regular folk saw something that they shouldn't. It would make them forget.

But when Jake went in and bent down amid the circle of younger children sitting around on the floor, he looked at their pinched, drawn, pale, hungry faces, and realized he didn't have the heart to take it away from them—that little taste of wonder that Dani O'Dell had just shared with them.

Instead, he hid his frustration, put on a fake, enthusiastic smile and gathered them around closer, then made a game of swearing them all to secrecy.

Fortunately, he was still an accomplished liar.

He told them the Illuminium was one of Archie's scientific projects, a boring old chemical compound of aluminum and phosphorus or something. But he warned that this invention was still waiting on its official government patent, so they mustn't tell anyone, or some other scientist might try to steal Archie's idea.

Once they understood this, the children eagerly agreed, much to Jake's relief. They seemed thrilled to share in the duty of keeping Archie's secret.

Finally satisfied they'd keep their little mouths shut, Jake nodded and left them.

"At last. What took you so long?" Garnock huffed when Mischief and Mayhem finally returned. They did not look too much the worse for wear. "Did you get it?"

Mischief jumped up onto Mayhem's head and perched there, proudly holding out the ring of power on his dusty gray palm.

"Ah, ha, ha, good boy!" Garnock swirled closer with a gloating laugh, but Mayhem let out a low, indignant yowl, as if to say, *What about me?* "Yes, yes, of course, I meant both of you."

Mayhem snuffled at this blatant show of favoritism.

Garnock tried to lift the ring off the little gargoyle's cupped gray palm, but alas, as a spirit, he could not pick it up.

He uttered a low-toned spell to levitate it; Mischief's eyes widened as the ring floated up and spun slowly in midair while

Garnock admired it.

"I will wear this again," he vowed. "As soon as I have my body back. And believe you me, I will use it well." When his concentration broke, the ring plopped out of the air back into the imp's hand. "Keep it safe for me until it's time."

Mischief bobbed his head and clutched it.

"I'm going back to the school. I'm starting to feel peckish. I need to feed again. You two stay out of sight. You've done well for today, but I'm afraid you're going to have to go back down there— no whining!" he scolded Mischief when he complained.

"Tomorrow, I want you to go back to my workshop and then slip through the Portal and start bringing more of your brethren through to our side, in case I need them.

"Have them hide in the mine until I'm ready to mobilize my army," he said in a sinister tone. Then he frowned. "Mischief, be careful with that thing! How many times have I told you a ring of power isn't a toy? Stop fooling around!"

His warning came a bit too late, for Mischief had just given the ring some sort of order: In turn, it sent him shooting backwards twenty yards across the grove.

He landed with a yelp.

Mayhem laughed heartily.

Garnock sighed and shook his ghostly skull of a head at their antics, then made his way back to the Harris Mine School.

It was time to feed again on more of the students' life-force.

Once he had preyed on a total of one hundred souls, the spell to bring him fully back to life would almost be complete. And then...his first order of business?

Revenge on whatever remained of the Lightriders.

Naturally.

PART III

CHAPTER ELEVEN
Waterfall Village

J ake couldn't believe he had such an impressive piece of Nature on his property.

White Lace Falls plunged a hundred feet over the cliff's edge, breaking into five whitewater plumes that pounded the boulders.

Where the last glow of sunset filtered through the spray, the light shattered into a rainbow that hovered in the mist between the thundering cascades.

It was breathtaking, tucked away within the sprawling wooded acreage of Plas-y-Fforest. Because the river with the waterfall cut through his lands, Jake's ancestors had been able to let the dwarves live here in privacy for an age.

Well, there's the waterfall, Jake thought, but peering eagerly out the carriage window, he did not see signs yet of any dwarf village.

"Are we here?" Archie asked when Nimbus brought the coach to a halt beside a grassy clearing on the banks of the river's lower run.

"We must be," Isabelle said.

This was confirmed when the house-brownie coachman came and got the door for them. Everyone climbed out dressed in their best finery for the occasion of the dwarves' celebration.

The girls shone like jewels in satin gowns with puffy skirts that nearly reached the ground. Thankfully, the dwarves' reception was not quite formal enough for the boys to wear tuxedoes. Instead, they had donned the nicest trousers, waistcoats, and jackets they had brought.

Still, without Henry to tie his complicated red cravat, Jake had

had to resort to having Miss Helena do it. Once the knot of his neckcloth was properly sorted out and smoothed down, he thought he looked pretty dashed smart, if he said so himself.

Too bad Petunia Harris couldn't see him, he had thought, mugging in the mirror before they had left the cottage. Ha! Well, she'd get her chance soon.

Derek marched ahead of them to the edge of the river, having somehow found the strength to stop staring at Miss Helena. The half-French governess admittedly looked fetching in her dark purple bustle-gown and elbow gloves, with her black hair all pinned up and a dark ribbon elegantly fitted around her neck.

Truthfully, out here in Nature, though, it seemed like a better place for them to be wearing the hiking boots Derek had insisted on when they had had their tour of the goldmine, Jake thought.

He wasn't quite sure what was going on when Derek nodded, standing at the river's edge, and gestured to Nimbus.

Nimbus took his tin traffic horn out of its holder on top of the carriage and blew it.

Jake surmised that this was some sort of signal.

Derek beckoned to them. "Everyone, follow me. Mind your step." He proceeded to walk out onto the stepping stones that led into the middle of the river.

Jake and Archie exchanged a startled glance.

"Come along, it's quite safe," Derek said.

The boys rushed forward, though, even to Jake, it seemed dicey to undertake this little obstacle course when they were all dressed up.

The girls looked appalled at the prospect of getting their fancy gowns splashed—or worse, falling into the muddy river.

Which Jake thought might be kind of amusing. Especially since he and Dani O'Dell still weren't speaking.

Fortunately, however, Miss Helena was right behind them, moving with her particular cat-like grace, just in case either of the young ladies should wobble.

As it turned out, the stepping stones were very easy to walk on—close enough together for even a dwarf's short strides.

The constant rumble of the falls grew louder as the group picked their way out toward the middle of the river.

All around them, the water pooled and swirled in eddies here and there. Old fallen logs trapped it in spots, creating tranquil little shallows, where fish drifted.

"So, why are we doing this?" Jake called to Derek when he could no longer contain his curiosity.

The Guardian merely smiled over his shoulder, stopping when he reached the center of the river, but it was Archie who first grasped the answer.

"Look! The waterfall's slowing," he said.

Jake blinked. "It looks like the water's shutting off."

"No, the flows are merely being redirected. See? Sluice gates on the upper river temporarily channel the water into the four side flows. That'll leave the middle one dry in a moment. Then we can go in," Archie said brightly.

"The dwarf village is *underneath* the waterfall?" Dani exclaimed.

"Behind it," Derek said with a grin. "Surprise."

Sure enough, as they watched, the middle cascade trickled off, while the four remaining falls—two on each side—poured down all the stronger as the water was redirected.

"The dwarves are really excellent engineers," Archie murmured.

Derek nodded in agreement, but Jake just stared in astonishment as the waterfall parted like theatre curtains, revealing the grand arched doorway to the dwarves' secret realm.

"How do we get up there?" Isabelle asked, cupping her hands around her hair in an effort to protect her golden curls from the mist and spray around the falls.

It was a good question.

The arched entrance to Waterfall Village was set about thirty feet up on the sheer rock face of the cliff, obviously for purposes of defense.

Jake didn't see any way to scale it. No steps, no bridge, no ladder, nothing.

"Surely they're not going to make us climb?" Isabelle asked in dismay.

The Guardian was apparently enjoying keeping them all in suspense. "Let's hope not, hmm?" he teased.

Suddenly, a metallic cranking sound filled the air, and a mechanical platform rolled out from underneath the archway, right out of the cliff face.

When it reached its full length—about the size of a mattress—another layer of metal dropped out neatly from under it and likewise trundled forward. Again and again, this repeated with a series of loud metallic thuds. Clank, clank, clank, the long, broad platforms came clattering down and toward them, creating a dark metal staircase with a red carpet down the middle.

By this means, guests could simply walk up to the entrance of Waterfall Village.

"Voila," Derek said.

"How do you like that!" Archie laughed as the bottom step locked into place with a bang right at their feet.

"After you." Derek gestured politely to the boys to go ahead of him. They did.

Then he waited for the young ladies, who all looked exceedingly relieved. Miss Helena's eyes twinkled as she placed her gloved fingers on Derek's offered hand, lifted the hem of her long skirts, and stepped gracefully onto the bottom stair.

When they had all moved safely off the stepping stones onto the strange mechanical stairway, they walked up in a group. Each metal stair retracted behind them, though not as quickly as they had rolled out.

Jake looked over the edge at the frothing river as they went closer to the falls. The breeze from the rumbling cascades blew his forelock around. "Brilliant."

When they reached the top and stepped through the archway, the stairs disappeared behind them, and somewhere on the upper river, the sluice gates must have been cranked open again, for the main waterfall resumed flowing, arcing over them, and tumbling ceaselessly behind their backs. It was marvelous. Jake stared in wonder at the back of the waterfall.

They were behind it now, invisible to the outer world.

Even more unusual was the sight before them: hundreds of dwarves waiting to greet them. Emrys trudged out with a broad grin, opening his arms wide in a gesture of welcome. Old Ufudd came hurrying along a step behind him.

Miss Helena turned quickly to the four of them. "Children, get into position as we discussed. We are going to meet the dignitaries on the receiving line."

Jake turned to the nearest girl, who happened to be Dani, and offered her his arm to escort her in, as the governess had instructed would be expected of them.

He lifted an eyebrow, however, when the carrot-head turned up her freckled nose and walked away, going over to take Archie's arm, instead.

"Fine," Jake muttered with a scowl. Thankfully, Isabelle did not shun him.

At the head of the row, Miss Helena took Derek's arm; the Guardian stood ramrod straight.

The dwarves were waiting for them. It was time to parade down the receiving line, nodding cordially to the dwarf bigwigs and shaking their little strong hands here and there as they went.

Isabelle was much better at all this than he was, smiling and waving to the crowd like a blasted royal princess. Behind them, Dani and Archie were both waving madly everywhere—pair of cheerful little widgeons, Jake thought. It was all *he* could do not to scowl after Dani's snub, but that would look haughty and rude. So he put a smile on his face.

Honestly, though, it was bad enough still having Red peeved at him without Dani also joining the ranks of those against him.

Just then, the Gryphon bounded over to join their party, landing a few feet away from Jake.

Jake looked over hopefully. The noble beast folded his magnificent scarlet wings against his tawny lion-back and walked along proudly beside them in their formal parade.

Jake noticed that the dwarves had honored Red with a gold medal of some kind.

It hung from a blue ribbon around the Gryphon's neck.

They sure love their mighty Crafanc, he thought in amusement, and the feeling was obviously mutual.

Red seemed very happy here in Waterfall Village. That realization actually came as a relief, for it dawned on Jake that maybe he had misunderstood.

Maybe Red was not so much avoiding *him* as choosing to spend as much time as possible with his dwarf friends before it was time to go back to England.

I hope so, Jake thought. He could certainly see why Red liked it here.

Waterfall Village was snug and dry and extremely cozy. It was underground, true, and a little dim for Jake's tastes, lit only by streetlamps and hanging lanterns everywhere, but it seemed to suit the mining folk who dwelled there, and it was they who made it warm.

The dwarves thronged the village center, crowding around to see their guests, waving and yelling friendly hellos.

Jake marveled at everything, craning his neck to look around in all directions.

The village center sat under a tall, domed ceiling of hollowed-out rock, just like the Atrium back at the goldmine. Under this soaring space, it had all the amenities of an ordinary village, except everything seemed child-sized.

A quaint fountain splashed in the middle of the village square; market stalls sold food around the edges. A clock-tower overlooked the scene, and little railroad tracks ran past for the crazy mining carts that pulled in each morning to take the men to work.

Above all this, which sat on the ground level, the upper walls of the surrounding dome were honeycombed with the dwarves' countless shops and their homes—charming cubbyholes with rounded doors and little flowerboxes on some of the windows. (Shade plants, Jake presumed.)

Everywhere, little ladders and stairways carved into the rock wound their way up the walls; the open space above was crisscrossed with catwalks and wooden footbridges, just like at the mine.

Straight ahead, the back wall of the dome apparently served as the dwarves' shopping arcade. Jake read the quaint wooden signs for each shop in fascination: *Apothecary, Barber, Baker, Butcher, Cobbler – Shoes and Boots, Tinker – Mining Tools and Axes Sharpened Here! Chandler – Candles and Lanterns, Rag & Bone Man,* and up at the top, a *Smokehouse* with a chimney to the surface.

He raised his eyebrows at the sign for the *Bat Catcher. Prompt and Affordable Pest Removal.*

Then Jake grinned as he realized that while most villages aboveground had rat catchers, people who lived in underground caves were more likely to need a bat catcher.

Well, that makes sense, he thought.

Then they arrived by the fountain, where chairs had been set up for them and a raised platform awaited the official welcome speeches.

As soon as the large visitors sat down, the little mayor climbed up onto the platform and spoke with the long-winded pomp of a politician twice his size.

The speech was rather boring, but Jake was just glad he wasn't the one who had to give it.

After the speech came the songs, of course. First, choirs sang rapturous, mesmerizing tunes that fairly put Jake and the others in a trance.

Then came the bagpipers and drummers in their kilts.

Their rousing battle music reverberated so loudly under the dome that they drowned out the constant rumble of the waterfall in the background.

Thunderous applause resounded when their concert was done. With the show over, refreshments were served and it was finally time to socialize. They were charmed to meet Master Emrys's wife and two kids—a boy and girl, ages six and four—and their family dog, a miniature Dachshund.

"His breed doesn't mind being underground, do you, boy?" Emrys said fondly.

The funny little wiener dog wagged his tail with a big canine smile, and Jake hid his amusement to see how the gruff mine boss melted over his dog, possibly more than he did over his children.

"Oh, you want to meet everybody, eh?" Emrys picked up the Dachshund, then they all crowded around to pet the dog while the junior Emryses went tearing off to get some of the honey cakes and sweet biscuits that were presently being served on scaled-down plates and dwarf-sized cups.

His wife couldn't stay long, either. She hurried off to get in line for the Ladies' Axe-Throwing Contest.

"She can use an axe?" Archie exclaimed.

"Of course she can, she's a good dwarf woman! Quite deadly, actually."

"Blimey," said Jake.

"Ah, our people have always had to be ready to fight," Emrys told them. "Why, look at us! Larger folk always start trouble with us, thinking we might be an easy target—especially since everybody knows we've always had a way with gold and precious stones. We've had to teach bigger folk a lesson many times over."

"And don't even get him started on cave trolls!" Ufudd chimed in as he came over and joined them.

They greeted the wee village elder with warm smiles; in truth, Ufudd had become the children's favorite.

"Nuisance species, cave trolls!" Ufudd told them, grimacing.

Emrys shook his head. "Just a part of life underground. Always got to clear 'em out when you start a new dig."

"But never mind us," Ufudd said. "How is your visit going? How are you Bigs settling in up at Plas-y-Fforest?"

They all sat down together and told Ufudd and Emrys eagerly about what they had been up to, and how the climbing roses around the cottage moved on command, and how they had seen the unicorns.

"We also found an old, ruined church where his ancestors are buried," Dani said, nodding at Jake even as she managed to ignore him.

Isabelle nodded. "The tombs of Sir Reginald himself and his wife, Lady Agatha."

"Oh, and Jake saw a headless ghost!" Archie added.

"Ahh, yes, the Headless Monk. Now there's a tale," said Emrys, and giving a thoughtful puff of his pipe, he settled in to tell it...

CHAPTER TWELVE
Just a Legend

"The Griffon lords had sponsored a community of White Monks on their lands from ages back. The monks lived simply with their vow of poverty, farming and brewing ales, and looking after the poor folk in these parts.

"But poor Brother Colwyn," Emrys said with a shake of his head. "He made an enemy of the wrong chap. Remember that alchemist I told you about who lived around here long ago?"

"The chap who figured out how to turn lead into gold?" Archie asked.

"Until sunlight touched it," Dani reminded him.

"That's the one," Emrys said with a mild nod. "Garnock the Sorcerer. If only he had kept to reading the stars and tinkering with gold. But no, the dark arts were too much temptation for him. Ach, he was a menace. Changing folk into unnatural creatures. Calling up storms and floods and pestilence, ruining crops. He was particularly fond of lightning, they say, and he'd zap you if you got too far onto his bad side. He became a mighty wizard. I've heard that the Dark Druids honor his memory to this day. Legend has it the first ones were some of his own apprentices."

"Really!" Jake whispered with a chill down his spine.

Derek had once warned him that, because of his abilities, the Dark Druids would probably come seeking to recruit him one day when he was older.

Nearly everything that Red and Derek and Aunt Ramona and Henry and Helena did was to try to make him as ready as possible for that day.

Personally, Jake hoped he was at least forty or fifty or so before those shadowy villains attempted any such thing.

"Oh, he was a bad one," Emrys was saying. "Then Brother Colwyn found out Garnock had even summoned a demon from the underworld to do his will."

All four drew in their breath.

"That was the fashionable thing all the wizards liked to have back in those days—your own demon to follow your commands and do your bidding. Of course," he added, "there's always a price to be paid for such bargains."

"Like your soul!" Dani said.

Emrys took another philosophical puff from his pipe. "When Brother Colwyn found out about Garnock's meetings with the demon, he sent word immediately to the Lightriders about it. Unfortunately, one of Garnock's ravens warned him what Brother Colwyn had done.

"Well, the wizard readied himself for the battle that was about to descend on him, but before the Lightriders arrived, he paid Brother Colwyn a visit. He swore to punish the friar for his meddling." Emrys shook his head. "Garnock tried again and again to cast terrible spells on the monk, but he was too well protected by the sacred ground of the chapel and his own holy prayers.

"Finding that his magic had no effect, Garnock became so enraged that he conjured an axe and chopped off the poor fellow's head. 'Twas never found," Emrys finished in a spooky tone.

The kids stared, wide-eyed.

"Did the Lightriders kill him?" Jake blurted out.

"Alas, they arrived in Wales too late to save their friend, the monk, but they did overcome the sorcerer. They trapped Garnock in his workshop with some of the most powerful white-magic spells ever cast. He was imprisoned for all time with the gargoyles who were his familiars.

"But," Emrys added, "the other monks at the church who witnessed the murder said that Garnock made a promise. He vowed that, whatever happened, the Lightriders would never destroy him, and he swore that one day, he would come back for revenge."

A hush of doom had fallen over the children.

Having finished his tale, Emrys took a thoughtful puff on his pipe and eyed the four of them in amusement.

"Egads," Archie said at last in a strangled tone.

Emrys and Ufudd both started laughing.

"Ah, laddie, it's just an old legend," the head dwarf chided, his eyes twinkling.

Then Emrys was called away to go and cheer his wife on in the Axe-Throwing Contest, and Ufudd scurried off to fetch another half-pint of mead, still chuckling at their gullibility.

Jake was silent, the daftest notion taking shape in his mind. Could it be possible that this black fog plaguing the area might actually be Garnock, carrying out his promise?

The idea seemed absurd, yet everything going on around here had to be connected. He just wasn't sure how, yet.

It dawned on him who might know more. "Isabelle, could I ask your help for a minute? I need to talk to Red."

"Of course."

"We'll come with you." Archie rose from his chair.

"Um, I think Jake needs to speak to the Gryphon privately." The empath sent the other two a meaningful look to remind them of the recent spat between Jake and his large, feathered pet.

"Oh, right. Of course," Archie answered with a nod. "Good luck, Jake."

Then they left.

"Jake?" Isabelle asked over her shoulder as they wove through the crowd, heading for the spot where the magnificent Crafanc was holding court, surrounded by his admirers.

"Aye?" Jake barely glanced at her, trying not to step on any of the mischievous dwarf children scampering by.

"You know, you really should be nicer to Dani."

"What?"

"Every time you quarrel with her, she thinks she is going to be sent back to the rookery."

"Of course she's not going to be sent back to the rookery," he said impatiently.

"One mistake isn't the end of the world. Besides, in your old life, she was there for you when nobody else was."

"Fine! I'll apologize," he huffed. "I'll just add her to my list."

"See that you do, or I may start to think that you and Petunia Harris might actually be a good match."

Jake scoffed. Being matched with the beautiful, mean Miss Harris did not sound so bad to him, but Izzy had not meant it as a compliment.

"Red's waiting, if you're quite through lecturing me," he grumbled.

"On that subject, yes. But actually, there's something else I wanted to tell you."

Jake welcomed any change of subject. "Aye?"

She glanced at him uneasily. "This afternoon, before we all started getting ready for the party, I had a chance to go out into the forest alone to see the unicorns. I found out why they acted so skittish last night. They've been sensing an evil presence in the area for about a week now. Something new and strange. They don't know what it was. But I'm sure it's the same thing I felt at the school."

"Agreed," Jake said grimly.

"My brother said you came across a ghost?"

He nodded. "The old headmaster, Dr. Sackville. But that dark atmosphere wasn't coming from him."

"Are you sure?"

"Definitely. He's a strict old windbag, but I could tell he really cares about those kids." Jake stopped short of telling Isabelle that Old Sack had actually seen something feeding on the children.

The poor girl had already been through enough for one day. Besides, this was supposed to be a holiday. In any case, as a future Lightrider, Jake felt that dealing with all this was up to him.

"Tomorrow night I'm going to that séance," he reminded her. "The headmaster ghost wouldn't really tell me much, but maybe some other ghost there will."

"Good idea. Are you ready for this?" she asked as they approached the crowd around Red.

Jake nodded, then the crowd of dwarves dispersed when they realized the two cousins were waiting for an audience with the kingly beast.

"Jake wanted to talk to you, Red. Do you mind?" Isabelle asked him.

The careless flick of his red wings was like a shrug, then his golden eyes studied Jake intently.

"I was wondering if you were there long ago, when the Lightriders defeated Garnock the Sorcerer," he said.

All Jake heard in answer was Red's usual "Becaw," but Isabelle could read animals' thoughts.

She turned to him to translate. "He says that was before his time. He was just a hatchling."

"Oh. Too bad. All right, then." Jake hesitated. "Is there, er, anything else he wants to say to me?" He waited on tenterhooks to hear what Isabelle might translate next.

She glanced at Red and then at him. "Actually," she said with exquisite tact, "he's waiting to hear what *you* have to say first."

"Oh." Jake dropped his gaze.

"Think I'll leave you two alone to sort things out." His empath cousin obviously sensed him floundering. "Just tell him what's in your heart, Jake."

"Right. Thanks," he mumbled as she walked away. He looked at Red uncertainly. "Um, could I please speak to you privately?"

Red pounced down off his perch and nodded at Jake to follow him.

He did.

The beast padded back up the red carpet toward the waterfall.

Near the grand archway to Waterfall Village, the cascade thundered past them, but Red's ears were more than sharp enough to hear Jake's heartfelt apology.

"I'm sorry for how I acted in the Great Vault. I-I know I let you down. I want to do better. I know I'm selfish and sometimes rude. I always seem to have the wrong reaction," he said in dismay. "But I'll keep trying, if you don't mind putting up with me."

"Becaw." Red pushed his head fondly against Jake's chest like an oversized housecat showing its owner affection.

Jake was so relieved that he threw his arms around the Gryphon's neck and hugged him. Red curled one large lion-paw around his shoulder in return.

"Thanks, boy," he mumbled.

Moving back again, Red snuffled with nonchalance, as though everything was already forgotten. Then he spotted a trout going over the waterfall and caught it in his beak, gulping it down whole. Jake laughed.

"Caw!" With a cheerful flick of his wings, Red flew back to the party, his tufted tail trailing down gracefully behind him.

Jake gazed after this marvelous, impossible beast that had come into his life with unabated wonder and realized anew how lucky he really was. In future, he'd have to do a better job of remembering that.

Right, he concluded after a moment. *One down, one to go.* Having made peace with Red, he felt like he had the weight of an anvil off his chest.

Now he just had to find the right moment to tell a certain carrot-head that he was sorry, too.

CHAPTER THIRTEEN
The Séance

The next night, Jake rode alone in the carriage as Nimbus drove him into town for the séance. He had been lucky to snag the last available ticket for the night's event, but was glad the others had stayed at home. A séance was not to be undertaken lightly.

He stared out the window at the cold, craggy woods, feeling tense and chilly as he mulled the task ahead.

He had spent the day checking every hour or so on the Inkbug, waiting for word from Aunt Ramona. But the fuzzy little caterpillar had not so much as twitched an antenna. Jake wondered what was taking her so long. Maybe the Elder witch had to do some research on the old protection spells that had been used all those centuries ago.

Well, he hoped she got back to him soon, because he had no idea what he was going to do if one of the ghosts tonight confirmed the black fog was really Garnock the Sorcerer.

There was no point scaring himself silly about it. *Just cross that bridge when you come to it.*

Upon arriving in Llanberis, he found the streets deserted, though it was not yet nine o'clock. The only sounds of life at this hour came from the pub they passed, then Nimbus turned down another murky, shadowed lane.

A few moments later, he parked the coach outside the crystal shop. Jake got out, his hands in the pockets of his greatcoat, his collar turned up against the chill.

He nodded when Nimbus said he'd wait there. Then Jake glanced around at the eerily abandoned streets and crossed to the front door of Madam Sylvia's shop.

A "Closed" sign hung on it.

When he rapped his knuckles on the window, however, and showed his ticket through the glass, the shop clerk let him in.

The medium herself was meditating to clear her mind before the séance, the woman said, but he was welcome to browse the shop while he waited.

Jake greeted the other six guests with a nod, promptly noting that he was the youngest person in attendance. As the adults chatted, trying to hide their nervousness about the imminent arrival of the spirits, he gave no sign of the fact that he, too, was psychic.

He did not want to steal the show from Madam Sylvia, but more importantly, he first wanted to make sure that her abilities were real. There were a lot of frauds out there, and if she was one of them, tricking people who were grieving over loved ones, he had every intention of exposing her.

But, of course, his main goal tonight was to get answers about the black fog from any ghosts who might appear. It would be tricky speaking to the dead without revealing himself to the living as a psychic.

He paced restlessly up and down the shop aisles, inspecting herbal candles, stones with claimed vibrational powers, and an assortment of odd charms.

Then Madam Sylvia made her entrance, appearing with a flourish in the red-curtained doorway at the back of the shop. "Welcome, ladies and gentlemen! Come this way, if you please."

Jake raised an eyebrow and joined the others.

Madam Sylvia waited in the doorway, greeting her guests as they filed into the dimly lit backroom of her shop. She was a short, plump, grandmotherly lady with wiry gray hair and a round face with rosy apple cheeks—but fierce, dark eyes. Her piercing stare seemed at odds with her sweet, Mrs. Claus-like face.

Her clothing was also a study in contrasts, part somber widow in a black mourning gown with a high lace collar, part Gypsy fortune teller, with many rings on her fingers and a wildly colored shawl draped around her shoulders. The countless necklaces hanging from her neck made her jangle when she walked.

In the backroom, all seven guests sat down at a round table with a dark, fringed tablecloth. The lighted candelabra in the middle of the table cast but a feeble glow.

Of course, Jake thought cynically, low lighting could help conceal any trickery the alleged medium had planned.

Meanwhile, anticipation hung in the air, adding a zing of nervous energy to the darkened room as they all waited to see what would happen next.

Obviously, the other guests were not used to dealing with ghosts like he was.

Glancing around the table at the candlelit faces of the strangers in attendance, Jake wondered what their stories were, who among the dead they were hoping to contact. They could be any sort of people, for these days, everybody loved a good séance— men and women, young and old, rich and poor.

Queen Victoria herself was fond of them, and Jake had even heard that Mrs. Lincoln out in America used to host séances right there in the White House, trying to reach the soul of her dead son.

The other guests were looking around, waiting for anything supernatural to happen, though the séance hadn't even started yet.

"Welcome, ladies and gentlemen," their hostess began in a spooky tone. "I am Madam Sylvia. In a moment, I will invite the spirits from beyond to join us, and you will each get your turn to ask three questions. I'll relay their answers to you, but you must keep quiet so I can hear their responses. I am a clairaudient, which means that I can only *hear* the voices of the spirit world. I cannot see them.

"Now then. Before we begin, I would ask you all to rest your hands palms down on the table, fingers splayed, like so. Make sure the tip of your pinky finger is touching that of the people on both sides of you. Take care not to break the circle once we begin, or the connection could be broken."

Now that sounds like a load of rubbish, Jake thought, but he went along with it anyway.

Madam Sylvia closed her eyes and began invoking the phantom folk. "Oh, spirits of the afterworld! We respectfully invite you to join our company."

As she spoke, Jake scanned the dark walls of the small room. They were covered with strange photographs purporting to have captured ghosts on film.

Spirit photography, they were calling it. Quite the new craze.

Living people were usually the main subjects of the portraits, with ghosts of family members showing up in the background.

Some of the pictures portrayed smoky wisps or mere orbs of light, while whitish faces without bodies stared out from others.

"Oh, benevolent phantoms of the deceased! I call on you to come to us and share your secrets from beyond! Speak! Speak!"

Jake felt an extrasensory tingle on the back of his neck; gooseflesh prickled down his arms; and as usual, these were the first warning signs that the spirit world was pressing through to the ordinary dimension of reality.

Suddenly, a glowing circle of swirling milky light opened on the ceiling, right above the séance table.

Well, that's new, he thought, looking up. *Maybe she is real.*

Pale currents of ectoplasm rotated slowly like a whirlpool or some kind of vortex. He was not sure what it was until ghostly heads started peering through it from above, looking down into the room.

Then he realized it was some sort of doorway. Madam Sylvia had opened up some kind of a portal into the afterlife, and once the spirits saw it, they started coming through.

One by one, ghosts floated down through the hole between their two dimensions. Jake watched in wonder as more of them arrived—male and female, old and young. Ordinary people who just happened to be dead.

Soon, the darkened room was crowded with wispy apparitions eager to chat with the living.

"That's right. Come in, come in," Madam Sylvia encouraged them. "You are welcome in this place."

"Please, I'd like to talk to my daughter!" an old lady ghost said, bustling forward with a whoosh.

"Everyone will get their turn," Madam Sylvia replied. "Thank you all for joining us. Now if we could proceed in an orderly fashion, please state your name when you step forward and tell me with whom you wish to speak."

It began.

Within moments, Jake realized he had no desire whatsoever to become a medium like Madam Sylvia.

It was clearly an exasperating job. He watched and listened, marveling at the old woman's patience as she relayed messages from the dead.

Neither side was ever fully satisfied. The living pestered her with many more than three questions each, the guests taking turns around the table. The dead, meanwhile, were all crowding around and talking at once.

"Please!" Madam Sylvia exclaimed after a bit. "I can't understand you when you all keep yammering! One spirit person at a time!"

"Right!" A soldier ghost swept forward and took control of the proceedings on his side of the great veil between life and death. "Order now, ladies and gentlemen! Queue up, you lot!" he ordered the other ghosts, waving them back. "Form a line, now! Take your turn and move on! Don't take advantage of this woman."

"Thank you very much, whoever you are."

He tipped his semi-transparent hat. "Welcome, ma'am."

Jake hid a grin.

Duly chastened for their rudeness, the ghosts obeyed—well, except for the ghost dog, who bounded through the swirling vortex above and ran over to the man sitting next to Jake.

Barking with happy adoration, the ghost dog jumped up on his former master, tail wagging. The man frowned, as though almost sensing something; then Jake saw him smile when his invisible dog licked his cheek.

Touched to witness this reunion of master and pet, Jake made a mental note to tell Dani about it. She'd be happy to hear that people's pets really did go to heaven to wait for their owners there.

Aye, maybe that cheerful news would help her stop hating him.

Of course, he had not yet managed to find the right moment to apologize to her. He felt stupid about it and did not know what to say. In truth, he'd been more or less avoiding her, half hoping she would just forget about their quarrel.

No such luck.

"Back of the line, sir," the soldier ghost commanded when another ghost arrived, not through the vortex, but whooshing through a side wall of the shop.

Jake perked up. It was the headmaster ghost, his black scholar's robes floating out behind him.

Old Sack gave the officer a bow. "Of course, Captain."

As he glided past, the headmaster ghost peered through the

spectacles perched on the bridge of his nose to send Jake a knowing stare full of disapproval.

Jake scowled back at him, instantly wondering what the strict old don was doing here.

He watched him float to the back of the line, where various ghosts had turned themselves into small, shining orbs while they waited, or idled away their time in the form of slowly spinning spirals.

From what Jake had read in one of the books in Aunt Ramona's library, these forms took less energy for spirits to maintain. The ghosts, however, turned themselves back into full-bodied apparitions when it was their turn to speak to Madam Sylvia.

Most of the messages exchanged were sappy, sentimental things like "I love you" or "Tell him I'm proud of him," which Jake cynically thought the spirits ought to have said while they were alive.

Since the information *he* was after was of a more practical nature, he was starting to grow impatient, waiting for his turn. All the while, more ghosts kept coming. It was getting crowded in the little room.

He noticed in suspicion that Old Sack at the back of the line kept letting the new arrivals go before him.

Oh, I see. He remembered very well how concerned the headmaster ghost had been about protecting the school's reputation above all.

Old Sack wanted to go last so that the other ghosts wouldn't hear whatever it was he wanted to say to the medium. Jake couldn't help smirking at the irony, though.

Surely Madam Sylvia was the very embodiment of all the superstitious, hocus-pocus, unexplainable stuff the headmaster would have disdained during his rigidly logical life as an academic.

Just then, a noisy party of four more ghosts arrived, tools clanking from the belts around their waists, lanterns shining on their hats. They were arguing constantly and bantering among themselves, but Jake sat up straight as he realized who they were.

The four dead coalminers!

His heart started pounding. He forgot all about Dr. Sackville as his turn finally came around.

Madam Silvia glanced at him. "What is your question for the spirits, young man?"

"I want to know what happened to the four men who died in the Harris Coalmine recently," Jake said boldly.

In the blink of an eye, the miner ghosts swept over and surrounded him, all talking at once.

"Oh, I'll tell you what happened—"

"It was 'orrible!"

"It was all those two's fault. I told 'em to stay away from that door!"

"Don't blame us, Barney, you're the one who started all this."

"Was not!" a chubby, hapless-looking fellow in coveralls cried.

"Were, too!" said another with a mustache. "You're the one who said it sounded hollow."

"Well, you're the ones who wanted to get the dead bloke's gold."

"Shut it!" bellowed the older fellow, silencing his men. "So help me, if I have to hear this bickering for the rest of all eternity..."

Madam Sylvia touched her temples with a wince. "The spirits are angry—"

"You're bloody right I'm angry!" The big, brawny one with a cigar turned to her. "Wouldn't you be?"

"Please, speak only one at a time. I can hardly hear you across the void."

The four ghosts scowled.

"Right," said the leader. "Martin here. I've got the others with me: Smith, Collins, Barney. We're the ones the kid was askin' about. May we speak now, ma'am?"

"Thank you, Mr. Martin, yes, please do. Do you have any messages for the living?"

"Aye. You need to warn the Company there's something creeping around down there in the mine."

"What's down there?" Jake blurted out. "I mean—was it an explosion or an animal attack, like some of the rumors claim?"

"No explosion."

"Wild dogs—" the mustache fellow started.

"That was no dog!" Barney interrupted.

Once again, the miners all started talking at once, unable to agree on what sort of creature had attacked them.

"I tell you, it was gargoyles, ma'am!"

"Gargoyles?" Madam Sylvia echoed, puzzling all of her guests.

"Gargoyles?" the living echoed.

"They can deny it all they like. They refuse to believe their own eyes. But I'm not so stubborn. Enchanted gargoyle statues came to life, ma'am, and ate us. I swear it on my grave," Barney said with the utmost sincerity.

Jake gulped, wide-eyed.

"You mustn't listen to him, ma'am," Martin grumbled. "He's gonna start a panic with his daft talk. The truth is, we can't be too sure what sort of animal attacked us. It all happened so fast and then, poof! We was dead and sucked up into heaven."

"Much to my surprise," the brawny one drawled.

"It's just that we did find something down there, you see," said Martin. "Some sort of room."

Jake was dying to ask questions, but he only had one question left—plus, he had to go through Madam Sylvia in order to hide his skills. "What was that about the gargoyles?"

The brawny miner ghost was staring at Jake with his eyes narrowed. "Mr. Martin, I think this boy can hear us."

"Really?" Madam Sylvia looked at Jake in surprise, but he made his face an innocent blank, just like he used to do in his thieving days.

Barney intended to make the most of anyone who could hear him. He leaned closer, right near Jake's ear, babbling at top speed while the others argued. "There was a ring, too, it glowed, and there was bones, a skeleton, and this big, daft door carved in the shape of a—"

"*Silence!*" the soldier ghost thundered. "I demand order!"

Strict Old Sack had also had enough. "Stop pestering that boy, you fool-headed peasants. You heard Madam Sylvia. Only one ghost at a time."

"Who you callin' a ghost?" the brawny miner retorted, taking his cigar out of his mouth.

"Easy, Collins, just ignore that old crow," his mustachioed friend said.

Old Sack glanced around and visibly abandoned his decision to keep his secrets. "I do not know what these buffoons thought they saw, but whatever killed them, it isn't half as alarming as what's been lurking in the basement of the Harris Mine School!"

This got all the other ghosts' attention, as well as Jake's and Madam Sylvia's.

"What are you talking about?" the cigar ghost asked.

"The black fog." The headmaster floated into the center of the table, his spectral body superimposed over the candelabra. He glanced around in distress. "I'm afraid there's not much time. It may have followed me here."

Murmurs of fear ran among the ghosts.

Old Sack glanced around imploringly. "It's been feeding on the children. The poor things are having nightmares in droves. It's as if somebody's filling their heads with their worst fears at night, so in the daytime, they can't concentrate on their studies. They've got no appetite. They no longer even want to play outside. The children cannot see this thing, this wraith, that's attacking them. But I've seen it. Feeding on their souls."

Jake gave up trying to hide his abilities. "What does it look like? When does it come? Only at night?"

"Any time," Old Sack answered. "I've even seen it drawing out their energy in the middle of class, while they're sitting, yawning, at their desks! They have no idea anything's happening to them. I've tried to warn the staff, but no one can hear me."

"What do you mean, feeding on them?" Madam Sylvia demanded.

"It hovers over them like a dark cloud, I don't know, sucking out their life-force. One sees a stream of energy being pulled out of them. Oh, I don't know how else to describe it! I didn't even believe in any of this sort of mumbo-jumbo when I was alive. It's all come as rather a shock, I don't mind saying."

"Have you tried communicating with it?" Jake asked urgently.

"Heavens, no! I keep my distance. But...I've been hearing rumors from some of the other ghosts in the cemetery across the road from the school."

"What's the gossip?" Madam Sylvia pursued.

Old Sack hesitated. "Ghosts are disappearing. I fear this dark spirit may be responsible."

"It even attacks the dead?" the medium asked in surprise.

"I can't be certain. All I know is that he's evil and he grows stronger every day."

Jake's heart thudded in his chest. "Is it Garnock?"

"Ask him yourself—he's here!" Old Sack fled with a shriek as all the ghosts started screaming.

Jake stared in horror at the sinister, skull-headed spirit that had just arrived, laughing, through the wall.

It was the black fog.

CHAPTER FOURTEEN
Visions of Darkness

"What's happening?" Madam Sylvia cried, hearing the chaos of ghosts shrieking in panic, though she could not see them running for their afterlives.

Having exploded into their midst, the black fog began chasing after the ghosts with diabolical laughter.

Madam Sylvia paled at the sound, clutched her heart in dread and thereby broke the séance circle. The living guests, oblivious to the attack in progress, were demanding to know what was happening.

All the while, Jake stared at the dark spirit, riveted with fear. The black fog had a ghostly skull for a head and arm-like streams of ectoplasm, with a wispy, tail-like structure trailing out behind it like a loose black robe.

"Who's there? What's happening?" Madam Sylvia demanded, pressing her fingers to her temples.

"Madam Sylvia, what do you hear?" one of the lady guests asked nervously.

She shook her head, waving off the woman's questions impatiently. "Something's wrong. Another presence has arrived."

Some of the guests smirked like they thought this was just part of the act.

The black fog was streaming after several of the ghosts, who whooshed away shrieking with terror. But the soldier ghost and the brawny coalminer and the big ghost dog, as well, were not about to put up with it.

With the dog between them, barking its head off in an effort to scare the black fog thing away, the two brave, manly ghosts rushed up to protect the others from the wraith.

It paused.

"Well, well," it mocked, pausing at the barrier they presented.

"Hoy!" The coalminer spat out his cigar. "What do you think you're doing?"

"In the name of Her Majesty, you'd better stop right there, friend," the soldier warned the thing.

It laughed.

Infuriated by such insolence, the ghost dog grew itself in size, all teeth, every bark a thunderclap.

Madam Sylvia held her ears; Jake could not believe the others couldn't hear it.

Seeing their braver friend make a stand, the other three coalminers floated up nervously behind the big fellow to back him up.

"You're the one who's been feeding on the children at the school, like the old man said," their boss, Mr. Martin, accused him.

The skeleton head of the thing almost seemed to smile. "Guilty as charged. And now, guess what, my good fellow? Now I'm here to feed on you."

"Get 'im!" yelled the soldier.

But as all the angry ghosts working together rushed at the wraith, it ground out an evil incantation in some strange tongue, then opened its jaws impossibly wide.

In the blink of an eye, it chomped its teeth down on the cigar ghost and swallowed him whole.

"Collins!" his three companions screamed in horror.

Having already been eaten once, they did not intend to let it happen again. The miner ghosts scattered and fled in all directions, abandoning the soldier to make his stand alone.

The wraith ate him in a similar fashion. It even bit the dog, who tried to intervene, but escaped and zoomed away with a yelp.

"All of you, run!" Madam Sylvia cried to warn away whatever ghosts still lingered.

While the living guests looked at each other in confusion, Jake gasped to see the black fog take notice of the headmaster, who was peeking out from behind a photograph on the wall.

The wraith sneered at him. "You...annoying little man."

"Stay away from my students!" he yelled bravely.

But when the skeleton-head unhinged its jaws in response, Old Sack rocketed straight upward through the ceiling, his robe and tassel flying. He just narrowly missed being chomped by the horrible floating skull.

"Madam Sylvia, please, what are the ghosts saying?" a gentleman attendee asked the psychic in a nervous voice.

"They've all fled. Something's scared them off. A dark presence. Who are you?" she demanded of the wraith.

"Wouldn't you like to know, old witch!" it taunted her in a low, garbled voice. "I've heard about you from my ravens. Clairaudient, no?"

She did not engage the dark spirit. Jake could hear the terror in her voice as she commanded the thing: "Leave this place! You are not welcome here!"

"Of course, as you wish, my dear," it simpered.

But since she could not see the wraith, she did not know it was obviously lying.

Jake saw the black fog purposely keeping quiet as it turned its attention to the living, now that the ghosts had fled. His eyes widened as it began to feed off the lady sitting across the table from him.

Dr. Sackville had described the awful process perfectly. The wraith opened its mouth and inhaled a stream of life-force energy from its victim's very soul.

Jake watched in dread as a smoky stream of pale life energy flowed out of the lady into the mouth of the evil skull-head. She seemed to have no idea that she was under attack.

He wanted to warn her, but he was terrified of what that sinister thing might do to him if he let on that he could see. After watching it destroy the two manly ghosts who had tried to stand against it, he dared not draw attention to himself.

Having fed off the woman, the wraith began going around the table from guest to guest, preying for several seconds on them all. Each time it fed, its shadowy outline got brighter, stronger. It seemed to grow in size.

As for its victims, nobody dropped dead like the tree goblins had, but they all started looking very tired.

Jake saw that in a few seconds, the wraith would come around to him. *What am I going to do?* It was horrible to see the attack coming and do nothing. He felt paralyzed.

He couldn't bring himself to flee the table, mumble some excuse, and run away. Leaving these people to their fate was hardly conduct worthy of a future Lightrider.

His heart beating like a drum, he was not sure if he could make himself sit there passively for those few seconds while it fed on him and pretend not to notice, though that was probably his safest bet.

As he wrestled with himself, the dark spirit reached the man sitting next to him—the ghost dog's master.

Everyone else around the table suddenly seemed exhausted and rather depressed, except for Madam Sylvia and the last woman, to Jake's right. It hadn't got to them yet.

Jake felt trapped. Then suddenly, his time was up.

The black fog came around to him.

He found himself face to face with its horrible floating skull. Its breath stank of the grave. Its soulless eyes were as black as the pit, with sparks aflame in their depths, proving that somehow, it was indeed, hideously, alive.

Jake was trembling, but strove not to flinch or pull back or give himself away in any fashion.

The foul creature hovered before him, its wispy, smoke-like body snaking back and forth a little behind it.

Jake sat frozen like a mouse mesmerized by the stare of a serpent. He heard a voice in his head, the black-magic spell the wraith was using. The words seemed to wrap around him like the coils of a python, conjuring a darkness in his mind of his own worst fears to paralyze him.

In his mind's eye, he saw that shameful event from all those years ago, when he'd been sent to work in the coalmine. Though he was only nine, his job had been an important one. As door boy, he had to open the door in one of the tunnels for the coal carts whizzing through and for the work crews coming and going.

After the bullies on one crew had made sport of him one time too many, he had locked the door and abandoned his post, leaving them trapped underground.

He had run away and never dared go back, because he knew those boys would have killed him after that. He later heard how they had run out of light down there and might have run out of air before anyone finally wondered where they were.

The worst part was, Jake had not been the least bit sorry. He was glad he had made them suffer.

But the wraith was not done consuming his life-force. To keep its victim still so it could feed, it projected an even worse vision into his mind—horrifying him into a state of helplessness.

Then Jake was swallowed up in dark fascination at what he saw: Himself. Grown up. A man.

Rich, handsome, powerful, the seventh Earl of Griffon at the height of his abilities. He was surrounded by a circle of dark-cloaked witches and warlocks hailing him as...

The new leader of the Dark Druids.

The breath felt squeezed from his lungs at what he saw, but he could not look away from the terrible vision of himself using his supernatural abilities for evil.

He knew somehow, deep in his bones, that in that possible alternate future, he had done terrible things. He had caged Red in the cellar. He had killed Derek Stone. He had cut Dani O'Dell out of his life long ago, and his cousins shunned him.

There he was, using his rank and fortune for evil. He had become everything his Lightrider parents had hated.

Because they deserved it.

Because they had left him.

That was his rationale, and to *that* Jake—that hard, bitter, angry man—the excuse seemed perfectly logical.

Only seconds had passed when the wraith abruptly quit feeding on him and backed away, coughing and gagging.

Released from the dark vision, Jake blinked, still dazed but struggling to come back to himself. Back to the here and now.

As soon as the Garnock-wraith stopped retching, it turned to him with a shocked, angry stare and hissed a single word of accusation: *"Lightrider!"*

Jake thought he heard fear in its spectral voice, but suddenly, it fled. Zooming off through the wall, it disappeared, still choking.

Jake slumped into his chair, staring into space. He felt drained and shaken to the core by that ghastly vision of himself. Surely that was just a possible future, not the definite one. He barely paid attention, sitting there in his own world while Madam Sylvia shushed the guests again, listening to the air for all she was worth.

At last, she gave them all a grim nod. "It's gone."

Thank God. Jake closed his eyes in exhaustion.

Garnock sped across the starlit landscape, back to his lair in the cold, clammy basement of the school, where he would be safe.

What the devil had just happened? He had eaten the souls of beetles he had found among the dead leaves that had tasted better than that! Who was that boy? How was this even possible? But he already knew the answer, even though he didn't want to face it.

As much as he had hoped the centuries might have killed off his enemies, it seemed the Lightriders were alive and well even to this day.

He did not know who that lad was, but he certainly had Lightrider blood in his veins. Garnock couldn't get the vile taste of his soul out of his mouth.

How disgusting!

Even more disgusting to him was how he had no choice but to cower in the basement. Killing ghosts was one thing, but he knew he was not strong enough to face even a baby Lightrider yet.

If his enemies were indeed still out there, then he had better get his full strength and his body back soon.

Unfortunately, he had a long way to go to fulfill the Spell of a Hundred Souls and rid himself of this ghastly spectral form.

At the moment, he was too sickened by the terrible taste of the Lightrider's son even to think about feeding on the schoolchildren right now. Perhaps he'd lie low for a while, just to be safe.

The worst thing that could happen would be for the Lightriders to come looking for him before he was ready.

He vowed to himself that they would not destroy him twice. If they managed to kill him—for real this time—then there'd be no escaping his bargain with the demon, and Garnock had no intention of spending the rest of eternity in the underworld.

He'd seen the place. It was bad enough to visit. He had no desire to live there.

No, best to hide for now. He could be patient. Once the Spell of a Hundred Souls was complete, he'd be practically invincible.

Then he could take his time enjoying his revenge.

Indeed, once he was back to his old self, he knew just where to begin: with that boy, the Lightrider's spawn.

A sudden inspiration put a malignant smile on his face. Why, he would deal with the lad the same way he had dealt with that meddling monk.

Yes, when the time came, he'd take the brat's head.

And keep it for all eternity.

CHAPTER FIFTEEN
Sweet Petunia

D ani O'Dell could not help grinning.

Petunia Harris was so colossally mortified when she learned the surprise theme of her birthday party that she wouldn't come out of her bedchamber.

Indeed, she threw such a monstrous tantrum that all the guests could clearly hear her screaming in rage at her parents in some distant quarter of the Harris family mansion. "How could you do this to me? Oh, God, a Pirate Party? I am thirteen years old, Mother! No, I don't want to hear your excuses, you pair of dolts! Unacceptable! How could you humiliate me like this in front of everyone? You've ruined my life!"

The Harris family servants—who had been forced to dress up as pirates for the occasion in fluffy white shirts and scarves tied around their heads—glanced at each other uncomfortably.

Gloating slightly, Dani took a pirate-themed snack off the Butler-First-Mate's tray (a black olive meant to represent a cannonball) and glanced at Jake. *Let's see how Romeo feels about his Juliet now.*

He was a full-blown idiot if he was still in love with that harpy after all her caterwauling, Dani thought. But when she spotted him on the other end of the great hall, he was standing alone, staring out the window.

Hm, still acting weird. He was not himself at all today. Maybe he was just gazing at the colors of this gorgeous autumn afternoon, but she suspected he had learned something upsetting at the séance last night.

Something he had shared with no one.

Curiosity was killing her, but she refused to ask him any questions. She was not speaking to that rudesby. He owed her an apology, and if he didn't think so, then he and the spoiled Miss Harris deserved each other.

For her part, Dani intended to enjoy herself. A Pirate Party might spell social doom to a thirteen-year-old, but was perfectly acceptable for someone aged ten.

Even Archie liked it, and he was eleven.

Dani skipped over to join the boy genius by the fireplace, where he was listening to the hired storyteller, who was dressed up as the pirate captain, and telling the kids swashbuckling tales about his fictional adventures. "Then the sea monster rose up from the waves, covered in barnacles. Aye, it was nearly as high as me mainmast..."

"I wonder if its name was Fionnula," Dani whispered to her friend.

Archie grinned.

Meanwhile, Isabelle was trying to get away from an older boy who was determined to befriend her. Her cheeks were strawberry red from all his attention, but she was far too polite ever to tell someone to get lost.

She kept trying to walk away from him, pretending to admire all the pirate-themed decorations, for truly, Mr. and Mrs. Harris had spared no expense.

There were tiny Jolly Roger flags popping out of every cupcake. Fishing nets hung here and there from the walls and the vaulted ceiling; one even had a life-sized mermaid captured in it.

The giant birthday cake crowning a table in the corner was made in the shape of an elaborate pirate ship with candy sails. Dani liked the decorations on the dining tables best of all. A little trough of water ran down the center of each long, narrow table like a miniature canal, with live goldfish swimming in it and toy ships floating on the waves.

Even the guests' parents standing around the edges of the party declared it the most charming birthday party for a child that they had ever seen.

Petunia might even have agreed—if it had been a party for a six-year-old.

At last, red-eyed from crying over the unfairness of the world, the guest of honor joined them—probably because she had heard that her future husband had arrived.

Dani quite remembered how Miss Harris's attitude toward Jake had changed when she had heard he was the Earl of Griffon.

Dressed in her dark blue satin gown from London, Petunia lifted her chin as she stood in the doorway, letting the Footman-Ship's-Cook announce her arrival.

Then the haughty guest of honor walked stiffly into their midst, her head held high.

Dani raised an eyebrow as Miss Harris went straight over to Jake. She did not leave his side for the next hour.

Perhaps it was wicked of her to laugh, but Dani found it ever so amusing seeing how annoyed he looked at his ladylove.

She wasn't sure what had changed—maybe it was merely the fickle nature of boys—nice one day, nasty the next.

But when Jake finally cast a desperate look at Archie and her after a good long while of having Miss Harris glued to his elbow, Dani just smiled back sweetly at him and turned away.

The ever-dutiful Archie went to his cousin's aid, but Dani sauntered off to rescue Isabelle, instead.

The overly friendly boy was still pestering her, but Dani got rid of him quickly upon their introduction.

It was easy.

She simply scrunched up her nose when the pest said hello to her, then blurted out: "Ew, your breath stinks!"

Isabelle's jaw dropped, but the boy blanched, mumbled some excuse, and fled in shame.

Dani had a jolly laugh as the irksome toad ran off in search of a mint candy.

"You are terrible!" Isabelle gripped her hand, giggling with her.

"You're welcome," Dani said with a small curtsy.

"I thought he'd never go away."

Dani patted her hand. "Any time, my dear." Then she pointed out Jake suffering with Petunia at the other end of the room and both girls giggled merrily again.

"I think she thinks she owns him," Isabelle remarked.

Dani snorted. "Maybe her papa bought him for her."

"Who, Jake? No, he's too expensive. What with the goldmine and all."

"Your brother's too good to him." Dani shook her head, watching Archie doing his best to save Jake from Petunia.

"Should we help him?"

Dani shrugged. "I suppose."

The girls crossed the great hall to go to Jake's aid.

As they approached, Archie was trying to tell Petunia how he had invented a flying machine that had actually stunned the scientific world at the recent Invention Convention in Norway, but she wasn't the slightest bit impressed.

Only Jake mattered.

"Is it true Queen Victoria is your godmother?" Miss Harris asked him, practically turning her back on Archie, who frowned as the girls joined them.

"Uh, it's just a formality, really," Jake was saying.

"But you've met Her Majesty in person? You've talked with her?"

Dani knew he had. Her Majesty was, in fact, the formal godmother of all the magical children born in her Realm so that she could keep an eye on them and make sure they didn't go over to the dark side. For if they did, they then became enemies of the most powerful government on earth.

No wonder the baddies banded together as the Dark Druids, Dani thought while Petunia was still marveling over Jake's royal connections.

"You've had a personal, private audience with the Queen?"

"Aye."

"La, how funny you are, Lord Griffon!"

"Huh?"

"Nobody says 'aye.' Unless you're trying to sound like one of these stupid pirates," Petunia said gaily.

Jake's scowl darkened. "I say 'aye' all the time, Miss Harris."

If that girl wasn't careful, Dani mused, she was going to get a zap of Jake's telekinesis.

He cast a "Help me!" sort of look over Petunia's head at them and cleared his throat. "Well! Here come the girls. Miss Harris, you remember my cousin, Miss Bradford, and her companion, Miss O'Dell."

Petunia turned. "Miss Bradford." She beamed at Isabelle, as though she fully expected them to be relatives by marriage one day.

Of course, Dani only got a passing glance, not that she cared.

Isabelle began to draw Petunia into conversation in the hope of saving Jake, but one of the hired pirate musicians blew a bugle, calling all the kids' attention toward the fireplace.

"Look sharp now, me hearties! Listen up, all ye Jack Tars and pretty Mermaids! Cap'n has got an announcement for the whole crew!"

"Oh, God," Petunia whispered, hiding her face in her dainty, white-gloved hands.

The pirate "Captain" (the hired storyteller) stepped forward with an artificial parrot clipped to his shoulder.

"Ladies and gentlemen! I seem to have misplaced me pirate treasure out in yonder woods." He pointed at the window toward the sculpted gardens and grounds of the Harris estate. "I need your help! It's a treasure hunt, y'see. So, grab a partner and get out there in those woods on this fine day and find me missing gold— and here's the best part. As yer reward, whatever ye find, ye can keep!"

The dozens of young guests let out a roar of enthusiasm at the announcement of the treasure hunt.

At once, the children began racing outside into the glorious autumn sunshine, choosing partners for the adventure as they went.

"Lord Griffon?" Petunia turned prettily to Jake.

He grabbed Dani by the arm and yanked her over to him so suddenly that she nearly went flying off her feet.

"So sorry," he said smoothly to Petunia while Dani scowled. She did not appreciate being manhandled. "Already promised the little one she could tag along with me."

Petunia looked utterly shocked at the denial, but Isabelle hastened to smooth things over, gently clasping the girl's hands. "My dear Miss Harris! Why don't you and I go together?"

The dark-haired beauty somehow found the strength to smile in answer, though she still looked astounded that Jake had told her no. "Very well. Yes. All right. It should be...fun."

"Hey, what about me?" Archie asked, pushing his spectacles up his nose, but Jake was already dragging Dani out the door in a bid for freedom.

Isabelle, for her part, had only just narrowly escaped being captured once more by Stink-Breath Boy.

Dani looked over her shoulder and saw a very tall girl with braids claim Archie.

The short boy genius looked up at her as if she were a giraffe, but then he beamed with a smile from ear to ear.

Dani lost sight of the mismatched pair in the next moment as Jake marched toward the woods, still clutching her arm as if he feared he might still have to use her as a shield to ward off Petunia.

"Why didn't you take Miss Harris up on her offer? I thought you loved her. She's *so beautiful*," she taunted, mimicking his earlier praises of the birthday girl.

"She makes my teeth hurt," Jake muttered. He let go of her arm once they were safely into the green and gold and crimson woods. Then he shook himself like someone waking up from a bad dream. "What are we supposed to do, then?"

"You heard the Captain. Hunt for gold."

"Oh. Right." He ran his fingers through his hair. "How stupid."

"Easy for you to say. You already own a goldmine. I'm going to find some treasure." Dani strode ahead of him and started hunting for gold coins hidden on every mossy log, behind every rock, in the branches of shrubberies, and under every fern, until she finally found one. "Look!" She picked it up and held it high in victory, then frowned. "Aw, dash. It's only candy!"

"Candy? I'll take it if you don't want it." Jake snatched the gold-wrapped chocolate roguishly out of her hands, but suddenly paused, seemed to think better of it, and gave the candy back to her. "Sorry. There I go again. You can have it."

Dani narrowed her eyes at him in suspicion. This was very un-Jake-like behavior. But she ate the candy and savored it.

She moved on, going up the forest path ahead of him, hunting idly for candy coins again, really just because it was fun to find things. Poor Mrs. Harris had obviously gone to a lot of trouble to make a party her daughter would love, only to be rejected.

Sad, Dani thought. That harpy should be glad she even had a mother. After all, not everybody did.

She eyed Jake over her shoulder. He was frowning at the ground, hands in pockets, brooding again.

"What the heck is wrong with you today?"

"Huh? Oh, nothing."

"Pfft," Dani said.

"Well." He let out a huge sigh. "A lot of stuff." He hesitated. "Actually...I've been meaning to say I'm sorry for barking at you at the school the other day."

She turned to him in shock.

"And also to tell you it was actually kind of a lovely thing you did, cheering up those kids by showing them the Illuminium."

Dani was astonished. "I thought you were mad at me for that."

"I was." He shrugged. "But then I realized it's really no big thing."

"It's not?"

"No. I overreacted. I should've trusted your judgment. It was nice, like I said."

"But I broke the rules—about keeping magic secret."

"Eh, rules. I was never really big on those. Don't worry. I took care of it."

Dani frowned. "The forgetfulness spell?"

"Nah, I didn't have the heart. Lied to 'em."

"Well, sorry you had to lie," she said awkwardly, quite astonished at how civilized he was acting.

Maybe Archie had been a good influence on him these past few months.

Jake kicked a clod of dirt in the path. "I'm sorry I was mean."

"It's all right." Dani gazed up in thought at the scarlet lattice of leaves above her. "I give you a lot of leeway, Jake, because I know you've had a hard time."

"Yes, but how much longer can I really use that as an excuse?" He stared at her. "I'm luckier than most, when you come down to it." He dropped his gaze again, looking a little embarrassed by this heartfelt conversation. "Mainly I just wanted you to know that nobody's ever sending you back to the rookery. Not me, not ever. I give you my word."

She absorbed this news like a thirsty houseplant soaking up some water. "You mean it?"

"Aye, no matter what," he said.

She believed him.

She hadn't realized until that very moment that, deep down, she had still feared being sent back to the harsh, dirty, dangerous neighborhood that she came from. "Thanks, Jake."

He nodded.

Feeling awkward, she turned around and continued her treasure hunt for the pretend pirate's candy gold, but her search was halfhearted now with the weight of all the things Jake had not yet told her.

She could feel them pressing down on him like a dark, invisible weight.

"So, the wedding's off between you and Petunia, eh?" she teased.

"Ugh, that girl's worse than me." He plucked a long piece of grass beside the path and stuck it in his teeth like a farmer as he sauntered along after her. "I wish she'd leave me alone. I don't have time for her nonsense. There's work to be done."

"What kind of work?" she asked in surprise, for Jake had never been fond of chores.

"Lightrider stuff."

"Ohhh." Dani spotted a glint of gold tucked in a woodpecker hole on the trunk of a dead tree nearby. She walked up the angle of a fallen log to reach it.

Jake frowned and took his hands out of his pockets, as though ready to catch her by telekinesis if she fell.

"Don't tell Miss Helena I'm climbing trees. It isn't ladylike."

"Just don't break your neck."

"Got it!" She seized her prize and held it up with a grin. "You can have this one." She tossed the coin down to Jake.

He caught it out of the air. "Are you sure you can get down from there?"

"Of course. I'm not some dimwit debutante." She jumped down, dusting off her hands as she landed back on the path. "So, are you going to tell me what happened at the séance last night? You haven't uttered one word about it to anyone."

He paused in unwrapping the candy and sent her a wary glance. "I met Garnock. At least, I'm pretty sure it was him."

"*What?* Garnock the Sorcerer? From the story Emrys told us?"

Jake nodded grimly. "If I'm right, then he's the black fog. And he's horrible. Way worse than I thought."

Dani sat down on the log she had just climbed while Jake propped his foot up on it and told her the whole, harrowing story of what had happened at the séance.

She could not fathom how the dark spirit could "kill" ghosts, who were already dead to begin with.

But she soon learned that what really had Jake so shaken up was the vision Garnock had implanted in his mind, of himself as the future leader of the Dark Druids.

It took her a long moment to find her voice again after he described it.

She swallowed hard. "Anything else that happened?" she asked, trying to sound calm.

He shook his head, staring at her with dread in his blue eyes. "Afterwards, I got out of there as fast as possible. Madam Sylvia wanted to talk to me, but I couldn't. I just left."

Dani clenched her fists by her sides. "One of us should have gone with you. Derek or Miss Helena or me—"

"He would have only fed on you, too, if you had. Besides, it wouldn't have made a difference. There was nothing anyone else could've done." He paused. "I just wish I knew if that vision was a picture of my fate, or if it was just him trying to torment me."

"Obviously the latter."

"How can you be so sure?"

"Jake, you'd never join the Dark Druids."

"What if they trick me somehow? Maybe by using dark magic?"

"Hold on, now. Slow down. What makes you think this was Garnock in the first place?"

"Who else would know how to use magic to paralyze people, using nothing but raw fear, mere pictures in their minds? This is the master of the original Dark Druids we're dealing with. I wouldn't put anything past him."

"But how could he bring himself back to life?"

Jake shrugged. "I wouldn't call him entirely 'alive' quite yet. I think that's why he's going around sucking the life out of people. It seems to be what makes him stronger."

"Well, what are we going to do?"

"I'll have to ask Aunt Ramona. She hasn't even answered my first message yet. But to be honest, my bigger worry at the moment is myself. I mean, after a vision like that, how can I even trust myself to stand against him? Maybe I'm the wrong person to try to deal with this. You saw how rotten I was in the vault. Selfish, spoiled. Even worse than Petunia."

"Oh, Jake."

"Honestly, Dani. I'm worse than you know." He looked lost as he gazed at her in dismay. "What if the evil thing the unicorns were sensing out in the woods that night...was me?"

"Now you're talking crazy."

"Am I?"

"Yes, and that's enough of that," she said firmly.

He fell silent for a moment. "Dani, I want you to make me a promise."

He knew she'd do just about anything for him, but she didn't like the sound of this at all. "What sort of promise?"

"Like I said, I trust your judgment. You know me better than anyone. So, I want you to promise me that if you ever see me turning evil, you'll buy some rat poison from an apothecary and slip it in my tea."

"What?"

He stared at her, somber and unblinking as an owl.

"You want me to kill you? Murder you?" She jumped to her feet in exasperation. "I'm not doing that, you bloomin' lunatic."

"You have to! Dani, I don't know if what I saw was my own worst fears or a vision of my future! I'd rather be dead than turned into a supernatural monster of a man."

"You're out of your head! What a horrible, horrible thing to ask of a friend."

"Dani, you know what I can do. You know how much damage I could do to the world and other people. If the Dark Druids ever manage to turn me somehow, you know very well I'll have to be stopped."

"Then ask Isabelle to do it, not me. She's your kin. If it's a matter of good and evil, she's the one who'll be able to sense it—"

"She's too tender-hearted. She always believes the best of people. She'd make excuses, probably cover up for me. She'd never be able to do it."

"And you think I could? Jake, the answer's no. I am not going to kill you."

"Well then, promise me you'll tell Derek Stone, if it ever comes down to it. He'll know what to do."

"You're daft if you think Derek would ever agree to hurt you, either. He's sworn to protect you, and he loves you like you're his own little brother or something."

"He's also a warrior and a true knight of the Order. My parents were his best friends. He'd never let me betray their memory. If I ever need to be killed, he's the one to do it. But you're the one who's got to make that call, Dani. Will you at least agree to that much?"

"Not me, ask Isabelle!" she pleaded. "She can sense what's in a person's heart, and she's as close to pure good as anyone I've ever seen. I'm just a regular person."

"You're the one the angel came to rescue, remember?" Jake pointed out. "Please? I'm counting on you, Dani. Promise me!"

"Fine. I'll say it if it makes you feel better, but I don't mean it." She held up her crossed fingers to show him she was lying. "I *promise* I'll tell Derek to kill you if you ever turn evil. Happy now?"

"Yes. Thank you. It helps more than you know," he muttered.

She shook her head at him. "You really are an absolute loonbat."

At that moment, a chestnut fell out of the tree above them and bounced off Jake's head, hitting Dani in the nose before falling to the leafy ground.

"Hey!" they cried in unison.

With Jake holding his head, and Dani cupping her nose, they both looked up indignantly at the oak tree, only to gasp in astonishment.

The slender branch above them was covered with a row of tiny people—*spying* on them!

They could not be fairies. They had no wings, nor sparkle-trails, but carried tiny spears or bows and arrows. They wore bits of brown leather sewn with twine and colored autumn leaves for their finery.

They shrieked as soon as they were spotted and immediately scattered, fleeing higher up the trunk, somersaulting into the canopy of the leaves, or pole-vaulting on their twig-spears onto other branches to escape.

"Come back here!" Jake ordered, only to be ignored.

"What are they?" Dani cried.

"Not sure yet, but they certainly seem to fit what Emrys said about the pixies. Believe me, I intend to find out when I catch one, little spies!"

"How are you going to do that?" She chased after him.

Jake was already following the tiny woodland folk from along the ground, his angry strides crunching over the fallen leaves as he abandoned the forest path. "Good question," he conceded. Then he pulled off his jacket as he walked and tossed it to her. "I'll knock 'em down with my telekinesis. Use this for a net to catch whoever falls."

"Don't hurt them, Jake!"

"I won't. But just because they're small, that doesn't mean they're harmless. They seemed awfully curious about my Garnock story. They could be working with him, for all we know."

"They could?" she asked, scrambling after him.

"Why else would they be spying on us? Keep up, Dani. Come back here, you lot!" he yelled up into the trees. "Why are you eavesdropping on us? I want answers! You're only making it worse for yourself!"

Spotting one of the wee folk running away among the leaves, Jake brought up his hands and shot an invisible lightning-bolt of energy from his fingertips at the slender branch that was their getaway route.

Dani heard a small shriek from above and brought Jake's coat up like a net, racing to catch the mouse-sized fellow as he plummeted past the branches toward the ground.

Miniature, high-pitched voices screamed from the branches above: *"Whorty!"*

Dani dove for him. "Got you!"

CHAPTER SIXTEEN
Pixie Mischief

J ake spun around and saw Dani swiftly close his coat up like a sack.

Then he laughed aloud at the sudden panic on her face as their tiny captive started thrashing around inside the makeshift bag.

She glanced at him in desperation. "Jake!"

"Coming! Don't drop him! He'll get away."

As he ran toward her, Dani grimaced and held the makeshift bag out at arm's length, waiting for him to take it.

All the while, the mouse-sized man inside it was moving around furiously. They could hear his muffled protests. "Let me out!"

"Hang on, Whorty! We'll save you!" With a voice only as loud as a cricket's chirp—but much angrier—one of the tiny men in the tree shouted at his fleeing brethren. "Come back here, you cowards! We need to rescue Whortleberry! Quickly, get into formation!"

A tiny horn blew from somewhere up in the tree, then came a tapping of little running footsteps along the branch. Before Jake could take the sack out of Dani's hands to deal with their prisoner, the wee forest folk rallied and charged.

"Attack!"

Suddenly, Jake and Dani were under siege as the pixies rained down acorns like cannonballs and started shooting their bows at them with splinter-sized arrows.

"Ow! Ow!" Jake and Dani said.

"Release Whortleberry! Put him down, you oversized oafs!"

More pixies were joining the fray with every second that

passed. At their size, they must have known full well that their only hope was overwhelming their enemies with sheer numbers.

It was like walking into a cloud of mosquitoes. The pixie archers and acorn artillery on the branches above them continued to fire, but now the tiny shock troops swung down off bits of twine and landed on their heads and shoulders, where they proceeded to beat them and pull their hair.

"Get off o' me!" Jake yelled to no avail as now the infantry rushed over the leafy ground and stormed the beaches of their feet, and immediately set about climbing up the bluffs of their knees.

Dani shrieked as the pixies swarmed up them, clutching miniscule handfuls of fabric to pull themselves up; they scaled Jake's tan trousers and the puffy skirts of Dani's party dress as easily as squirrels running up a tree.

She kept trying to brush them off, but they'd merely catch themselves on the green satin ribbons of her sash, swing from it, and scamper up once more.

Tenacious as she was, however, the carrot-head held onto the sack containing their prisoner.

Jake was losing patience with the pixies' battle. Their punches felt like harmless finger taps, but the pinpricks from their spears kind of stung. "Stop that!"

"Let Whortleberry go, you ugly giant!" their leader shouted in his ear from his perch on Jake's shoulder.

"Why were you spying on us?" he demanded.

They wouldn't answer, too intent on beating Jake and Dani into submission.

Plagued from all directions by angry pixies, neither of them realized that all the poking and prodding from the tiny fighters' spears was herding them deliberately toward a particular spot on the forest floor.

They were so distracted by the attack, they had not noticed the fat little pony grazing contentedly among the tall shrubberies several yards away; nor did they see a distant team of pixies slide the halter over the pony's head and slap it on the rump.

But the pony suddenly vaulted to attention and broke into a spooked gallop, and until that very moment, Jake and Dani had no idea that they were standing on a trap concealed beneath the autumn leaves.

"Retreat!" the tiny leader hollered to his troops.

Instantly, the pixies dove off them all at once, leaving them standing there, still dazed by the attack and baffled as to why it had suddenly stopped.

But even at that moment, the pony yards away leaped into motion; the ropes went taut, racing through pulleys far above in the tree, and suddenly, the two of them were scooped off their feet, clunking their heads together as they fell into the pixies' snare.

The rope netting instantly lifted them high, higher, into the tree as the spooked pony ran.

Smushed together in the trap, they gripped the ropes of the net that now held them, and neither stopped screaming until they reached the top of the giant oak tree.

Dangling many, many feet above the ground, at least they had an admirable view of the lovely Welsh landscape.

They were terrified but could see for miles around: the town, the coalmine, even the distant school and cemetery.

Jake's heart was pounding and he could hear Dani practically hyperventilating beside him.

"Jake?" she squeaked. "What just happened?"

"You're good and caught, that's what," a small but authoritative voice said. "They don't look like tree goblins to me. Captain Coltsfoot? Explain."

"They kidnapped Whortleberry, sire."

"Is that so?"

As the trap spun slowly on its main rope, rotating to face the tree trunk, Jake and Dani gasped in amazement to find the pixies' base camp right before their eyes.

At an intersection of two main branches, a horde of pixies stood on a ledge-shaped tree fungus, inspecting them with obvious hostility. They were about five inches tall, with pointy ears and pointy noses, rosy cheeks, and outdoorsy complexions. More of them kept hopping out of their papery, round shelter—an abandoned hornets' nest—to see what was going on.

The tiny, robed king with an intricately carved walnut shell for a crown turned to his Captain of the Guard, awaiting an explanation.

"Your Majesty," Coltsfoot started, stepping forward.

Jake furrowed his brow when he saw him. Coltsfoot turned out to be the same tiny fellow who had stood on his shoulder seconds ago. *How did he get up here so fast?*

Dani couldn't contain herself. "Who are you?" she burst out.

Captain Coltsfoot started to protest, but the king looked pleased by the question. "I am King Furze—oh, and here is my wife, Queen Meadowfoil. Hullo, my little sweet sedge." King Furze took his wife's hand and kissed her knuckles as the tiny queen stepped out of the hornets' nest and joined them.

"What's afoot, my dear?" she inquired, staring at their captives in the net.

"Our brave head of security has informed me these hideous giants have kidnapped one of our people."

"Oh, no!" said the queen.

Jake strove to take control of the situation. "First, we aren't giants—"

"Well, you're certainly not tree goblins," the king replied. "That is what my soldiers usually catch when they venture into our territory."

"We are humans," Dani said.

"And your men were spying on us," Jake said.

"Well, you're the one who's trespassing. These are our woods. We have every right to eavesdrop on intruders if we wish, and besides, without humans, who would we make fun of?"

The pixies laughed at the king's jest.

Jake and Dani exchanged a scowl. Coltsfoot stepped over to King Furze. Hiding his mouth behind his hand, he whispered something in His Majesty's ear.

"Really?" King Furze murmured. "Indeed...hmm." The tiny chieftain then passed along the secret message to his wife.

Queen Meadowfoil's dainty face turned grim. She turned to Jake and Dani. "Humans, we have just been informed that the reason our soldiers were spying on you is because you were discussing a matter of some interest to our tribe. The so-called black fog. You have information on who or what this thing may be?"

"It's just a theory—" Dani started, but Jake interrupted.

"Careful, Dani. This could be another trick. Emrys said that pixies are crafty. He also said they're thieves. They can't be trusted."

"I beg your pardon!" King Furze looked outraged.

Coltsfoot aimed his spear at Jake in warning. "You'll show Their Majesties respect!"

"Nice pony. Where did you get him, eh?" Jake retorted. "See, Dani? I'm sure they stole him."

"We liberated him!" King Furze exclaimed. "Poor Tim. He used to be a pit pony down in the coalmine before we freed him. Trust me, he's much happier with us."

"Underground is no place for a pony," Queen Meadowfoil agreed, then she hesitated, with a slightly nervous look. "Especially with the strange beasts lurking down there lately."

"Now answer the King's question!" Coltsfoot ordered Jake. "Tell Their Majesties what you told the orangey girl about the black fog and who it really is."

"Orangey girl?" Dani muttered.

Jake narrowed his eyes at the tiny soldier. "Make me."

"I could always cut you down. Long fall for your kind," Coltsfoot warned.

"But first, free Whortleberry—or else!" said the king.

Dani gripped the rope netting with a frightened look at the distant ground. "Jake, I think we should do as he says. This is no time for your stubbornness. I'm going to let Whortleberry go."

"Fine," he muttered.

Smushed as she was by the trap, Dani gingerly opened the makeshift sack of his coat and freed their pixie captive. She let him climb onto her palm and then stretched out her hand so he could hop off onto the ledge-fungus.

"Starchwort, Featherfew, quickly, go and help him," the queen said.

"Whorty!" The other two pixies steadied Whortleberry, slapping him on the back with smiles all around. "We thought we'd lost you!'

"I'm all right, I'm all right," he assured everyone, though he still looked rather shaken.

After Featherfew had walked Whortleberry in toward the safety of the hornets' nest to recover from his ordeal, King Furze eyed Jake closely. "Starchwort?" he said all of a sudden. "Bring out Wake-robin. I think these two need to hear his story."

"Yes, Your Majesty." Starchwort dashed into the hornets' nest.

"Who's Wake-robin?" Jake asked.

"One of our finest pranksters." The king paused. "At least, he was, until he saw something dreadful several days ago. Something so terrifying that it turned his hair white, though he's only twenty-seven. I think it's a story you'll want to hear, if you are interested in the black fog."

Starchwort soon returned with another pixie leaning on him like a frail old man.

Sure enough, his hair was snow-white, though his face still looked young.

Coltsfoot brought over a chair for the weakened pixie, and the king gave him leave to sit in his presence with a wave of his hand.

"Wake-robin, tell these human younglings what you saw the other day in the mine," King Furze ordered.

Still swinging in the net, Jake and Dani waited while Wake-robin sat down and slowly collected his thoughts. He still looked dazed by whatever it was that he had experienced.

Jake knew the feeling.

"Where do I start?" Wake-robin asked.

"Begin at the beginning," the queen said kindly.

He nodded and gathered his strength. "Very well, Your Majesty. It all started when Starchie and me—that's Starchwort." Wake-robin nodded at his friend. "We were bored, so we thought we would lasso a mole. Always fun to lasso a rabbit and then you can ride it, flippity-fast they are, great fun. But we never heard of anybody trying to ride a mole. So we decided that we should be the first. Well, we did." He shook his head, lost in his thoughts. "But it didn't go as planned."

"Poor planning all around," Starchwort admitted with a pensive nod.

"Moles live underground, y'see," Wake-robin pointed out.

"Everybody knows that," Jake said impatiently.

"The mole was stronger than we thought. We got the rope around its neck, didn't we, Starchie? But then it ran. Dove into its hole, it did, and pulled us underground. It was dark down there.

"Starchie had the good sense to let go of the rope, but I hung on. That's me. I never know when to quit." He shuddered at the memory. "The mole ran so far underground into its dark, moley tunnels that it came down to the ceiling of the Harris Coalmine.

"When it turned a corner at top speed, I fell through a crack in the rock and we got stuck. There I was, dangling into one of the coalmine tunnels, hanging onto the lasso by my fingertips." He gulped. "That's when I saw them."

"What? What did you see?" Dani asked.

"The eyes," he whispered, fixing his haunted stare on a memory that only he could see. "Glowing eyes in the blackness. Two of them."

"Two eyes?" Jake asked.

"No. Two creatures in the mine. Maybe more. Beasts."

Dani blanched. "What were they?"

"Big. Horrible."

"Yes, but what sort of beasts?" Jake persisted. "Wolves, bears?"

He wished for a moment with all his might that the pixie would say *anything* but gargoyles. He still hoped his theory about Garnock might be wrong.

Wake-robin shook his head, looking lost. "I don't know."

"Well, what did they look like?" Dani asked. "What color were they?"

"Hard to tell, it was so dark. Maybe gray. Black? They had horns. Tails." He gulped at the memory and held up his hand, curving his fingers into hooks to show them. "Claws. They were..." He couldn't bring himself to say it.

Starchwort put his hand on the traumatized pixie's shoulder. "We believe poor Wake-robin stumbled onto a nest of dragon hatchlings."

"Baby dragons?" Dani whispered.

Starchwort shrugged. "Wales used to be infested with dragons, long ago. The glowing eyes. Horns and so forth. It adds up!"

"Did any of them breathe fire?" Jake asked.

"The young ones don't, until they reach a certain age," King Furze pointed out.

"Well, what about wings?" Jake asked.

Wake-robin shook his head, looking desperate. "Can't be sure. I think they might have had them. Please, no more! I can't bear it."

Just then, a clamor in the distance drew everyone's attention.

"Look! The pit ponies are escaping!" Dani cried, pointing toward the entrance of the Harris Coalmine.

She was right. Jake turned and scanned the landscape, then squinted at the strange sight.

A large herd of ponies was fleeing out of the mine. They had broken free and were stampeding right down the main street of the town.

Jake stared with a chill of realization down his spine. "Something must have spooked them."

Dani turned to him, wide-eyed. "Maybe there's been another attack in the mine!"

He believed she was right. Indeed, maybe this time, the gray beasts had tried to eat one of the pit ponies.

Then Jake gripped the ropes of the snare. "Please, you have to let us go."

"Oh? Why is that?" King Furze replied.

"So we can get down there and do something about this!"

"Er, we?" Dani looked askance at him.

He glared at the king. "Haven't you realized who I am yet, Your Majesties? I am Lord Griffon of Plas-y-Fforest, the Lightriders' son, and this is my friend, Dani O'Dell. Now put us down! Unless you want those dragon hatchlings growing to full size in your back garden?"

King Furze considered this, then finally relented. "Very well—since this has all been a misunderstanding, I will let you and the orangey girl go. But take care to pay the forest folk the proper respect when you venture into our territory again, or next time, you might not be so lucky. Goodbye—and good riddance," he added under his breath.

Then he nodded at his head of security. Coltsfoot lifted a tiny flint hatchet with a gleam in his eyes and chopped away a few fibers of the main rope holding up their net.

Loosened, the rope slipped through the pulley, running them down the length of the tree at top speed. They held on for dear life.

A moment later, Jake and Dani tumbled out onto the ground in a heap atop the soft leaves.

"Blimey!" she exclaimed, looking up at the height from which they had plummeted by a few strands. "We're lucky we didn't break our necks."

Jake grabbed his jacket and jumped to his feet, giving her a quick hand up. "Come on, no time to lose!" With that, he was up and running back to the path, then racing down it toward the Harris family mansion.

Dani was right behind him. They pounded over the packed dirt trail, leaped the fallen logs, and carefully dodged over the rocks that littered the path here and there.

A few minutes later, they burst out of the woods just in time to see a lanky uniformed messenger from the telegraph office arriving. It was not difficult to guess the contents of the telegram he was bringing Mr. Harris—news concerning whatever had just happened at the mine.

Pink-cheeked with exertion, Jake and Dani exchanged a worried glance as they jogged toward the stately manor house. The messenger was already knocking on the door.

"Sorry to interrupt, ma'am. Message for Mr. Harris. It's an emergency," he told the unsmiling housekeeper, who had apparently refused to be forced to dress up like a pirate crewmate.

The stern, black-clad woman instantly opened the door wider and showed the messenger into the house.

Jake and Dani followed, unnoticed.

But as they hurried to the door, a honeyed voice called his name with cloying sweetness. "Oh, Lord Griffon! Would you like to help me look for treasure?"

Jake scowled straight ahead, refusing even to look over at Petunia, who was waving at him from across the lawn and starting to hurry toward him.

"Act like you don't see her," he said to Dani through gritted teeth. Then they slipped into the house.

They saw the housekeeper showing the messenger down the hallway to the oak-paneled library, where Mr. Harris had sought refuge from the party with the other children's fathers.

A mirror in the hallway offered a perfect angle, allowing Jake and Dani to see into Mr. Harris's stately library, even as they kept a safe distance back, remaining unnoticed.

The wealthy gentlemen were lounging around on brown leather club chairs, smoking cigars and drinking port, when the housekeeper knocked thrice on the open door.

Mr. Harris glanced over, a portly, red-faced man with impressive muttonchop sideburns. "Yes?"

"Telegram for you, sir. Sorry to disturb, but the lad says it's an emergency."

"Very well." Mr. Harris waved his chubby fingers, summoning in the messenger to bring it to him.

The lanky lad with a silly pillbox hat crossed the room and handed the message to the coal-factor.

"Egads!" Mr. Harris shot to his feet and turned pale, then looked away and let out a harsh curse under his breath.

"I say, what is it, Harris?" one of his gentleman friends inquired as their host crumpled the note in his hand.

"No use hiding it. There's been another attack in the mine." Mr. Harris glanced grimly at the gentlemen, who let out varied exclamations of shock.

"Did anyone see what it was this time?" one of them asked.

Mr. Harris shook his head. "Blast it, I thought it had surely moved on by now. But whatever's down there, it just attacked one of the pit ponies, and now the whole herd has escaped."

"Now, see here, Harris." An aristocratic fellow in a red coat stood up, ready to take matters in hand. "I am the president of the local foxhunting club, I host shooting parties throughout the autumn at my country estate, and I daresay some of the chaps here are jolly good shots, as well. Why, Carrington is our most avid sportsman. He just returned from a lion hunt in Africa, didn't you, old man?"

Carrington nodded, then pointed at the man by the window. "Thurlowe over there has shot bears in the Alps."

"You see? You must let us help you eradicate this creature," the foxhunt president informed Mr. Harris. "So here's what we shall do. First, you must evacuate your workers, and then, we shall form a hunting party amongst ourselves. We will hunt this beast and destroy it."

"Capital sport, old boy!" Thurlowe exclaimed, jumping to his feet. "My new rifle just arrived, imported from one of the top gunsmiths of Switzerland. I can hardly wait to try it out in the field against worthy game."

"Jolly good!" Carrington replied. "Whoever fells the beast gets to keep the brush!"

"What does that mean?" Dani whispered.

"I think they cut the tail off and keep it as a hunting trophy."

Dani wrinkled up her nose. "That's disgusting."

But the great British hunters were growing more enthusiastic by the minute for their quest.

"Better still, why not have the beast stuffed and mounted once

we've felled it for you, Harris? You could hang the head up there."
The foxhunt president pointed to an empty spot on the oak-paneled
wall.

"I don't think I'd, er, quite like to see it every day."

"Not a sporting fellow, eh?" one teased with a condescending
smile.

"But if you think you're able to track the creature down..." Mr.
Harris said hopefully.

"Of course we can, old man!"

Mr. Harris already seemed half persuaded by these worldly
fellows. After all, they outranked him by a mile.

The word "Lord" in front of their names seemed to guarantee
that they must know what they were talking about on any subject.

Mr. Harris had lots of money, but they had all the class. Filthy
rich as he was, a coal-factor was merely a great merchant. With no
title of any kind, he might as well have been (horrors!) middle class.

No wonder Petunia was already hard at work trying to land a
young lord like Jake for her future husband. Her papa's money
wasn't much good without "class"; but then again, class was
hopeless without money. Lots of the aristocrats' lives revolved
around hiding the fact that they were nearly bankrupt.

"There, Harris," Lord Carrington decreed. "You see? Leave it to
the aristocracy to look after the safety of the lower orders." The
foxhunter-in-chief raised his glass to his fellow noblemen with a
smug smile. "Tally-ho, gentlemen."

They clinked their glasses and drank.

"Ha! Now, let's go hunting!"

"They're going to get themselves killed," Jake muttered.

"Where are you going?" Dani called after him as loudly as she
dared when Jake got up from his crouched position by the wall and
headed for the library.

"I need to talk to Mr. Harris privately," he answered over his
shoulder, keeping his voice low. "He can't let those idiots go down
there. They have no idea what they're getting into. They'll get torn
apart. Get the others together, will you? We need to leave soon."

We've got gargoyles to catch, he thought grimly. Or dragons,
which could be even worse.

"Good luck!" she said.

Jake nodded in thanks, though he had no idea how to make

the coal-factor listen to him, a mere kid, offering suggestions. Mr. Harris was never going to listen to him.

Guess I'm just going to have to prove it to him, then.

Jake braced himself before stepping into the open doorway. "Ahem, Mr. Harris, might I have a moment of your time, sir?"

The foxhunting gents started laughing. "I say, lad, aren't you a bit young to be coming to beg for his daughter's hand in marriage?"

Jake turned scarlet as they laughed. "It's not that."

"This really isn't a good time, Lord Griffon," Mr. Harris started, but Jake was prepared to insist, especially once the great hunters had marched out of the library to go prepare for their adventure.

Jake turned to him imploringly when they were alone. "Mr. Harris, if you let those men go down there, they're going to get eaten alive. They have no idea what's waiting for them down there."

The coal-factor looked at him in surprise. "And you do?"

"I have a notion," Jake said shrewdly. "For one thing, there's more than one of those beasts down there."

He leaned forward. "You've seen it?"

"No, but I've just talked to an eyewitness."

"Really? What sort of creature is it, then? No one seems able to give me a straight answer!"

"That's because…" Jake trailed off as he debated with himself over how much to say without sounding insane. He opted to be vague. "Sir, I have reason to believe these beasts are…well, supernatural in origin."

The muttonchopped man squinted in confusion. *"Wot?"*

"They're not…of this world."

Jake could read the jumble of emotions on Mr. Harris's face. He was a brass-tacks, down-to-earth businessman.

On the other hand, he had just enough Welsh blood in his veins to stop for a moment and consider that there might just be a magical explanation for all of this.

Then he shook off that fleeting moment of open-mindedness. "This is no time for boyish pranks, my lord."

"It's not a prank! Sir, you've got gargoyles in your mine." There. He had said it.

"Gargoyles," Mr. Harris repeated slowly.

Jake nodded. "That's right. The ugly blokes you've seen carved on old stone churches. Sinister-looking faces. Claws, horns. Some with wings. You'd better let me and my team handle this, or once again, there won't be anything left of those men but a few bones. Only, with Their Lordships, I doubt you'll be able to cover it up the way you did with your lowly mine workers."

This pointed comment obviously angered Mr. Harris, for his red face grew even redder. "You actually claim that you, a mere boy, are better suited than grown men to deal with some sort of rampaging creature?"

"Mr. Harris." Jake strove for patience. "This is not an ordinary situation, and these are not animals like anything your friends have ever hunted before. Surely you have heard the stories around here about my parents and strange doings on my lands."

"Aye," he admitted, "everyone's heard the old peasant tales about faeries or some such enchantment on the grounds at Plas-y-Fforest. I've heard those local legends since I was a boy. How, if anyone steps over the boundary of your property, they can't quite remember what happened to them when they come back."

"Yes, well, that's because my lands are protected by ancient magical spells—which were put there for a reason, I assure you."

"I don't have time for this nonsense." Mr. Harris headed for the door, but Jake used his telekinesis to slam it shut from across the room, preventing him from leaving.

The coal-factor turned to him in confusion.

"I wouldn't lie to you, sir. You've got gargoyles in your mine. I've spoken to the spirits of the men who were killed. They experienced it firsthand and told me what they saw."

"Oh, they told you personally, did they? I suppose you are referring to the séances held by that madwoman in town, Madam Sylvia or whatever her name is."

"She can only hear the spirits, Mr. Harris. I can see them, plain as I see you. Trust me, sir, there's more to this world than what you can see and touch and taste." With that, Jake made his point by slowly levitating a picture frame off the knickknack table by the door and making it float in the air before the coal-factor's eyes.

Mr. Harris looked entranced as he watched it, speechless.

Just in case he still doubted, Jake waved his hands and sent various objects floating hither and thither across the room. Mr. Harris watched them all in shock.

Jake figured he could always use the Oubliette spell on the

man later if it came down to it, but Mr. Harris did not seem the sort to blab about such things. He was the sort of person who really didn't want to know.

"Gargoyles?" he forced out at length, finally ready to listen.

Jake nodded firmly. "Gargoyles," he said. "But don't worry, we'll take care of them."

"How?"

"I'm not exactly sure yet, but this is what we do—Derek Stone and I, and several other of my companions. But I need you to close down the mine, just for a day or two. Evacuate the workers. Then we'll clear the mine of whatever's lurking down there. Trust me, we've dealt with worse," Jake assured him. "After that, feel free to take Their Lordships on a nice hunting party down into the mine. I'm sure they'll have great fun, but they're not going to find anything. Better yet, nothing's going to eat them or anyone else down there again. On that, you have my word."

Won over by his show of confidence, Mr. Harris dazedly agreed and went to give the necessary orders.

On the bright side, however, Jake doubted he'd have to worry about Petunia hanging on him anymore. There was no *way* the coal-factor would ever let his daughter marry a supernatural freak after that demonstration, earl or not.

What a relief!

PART IV

CHAPTER SEVENTEEN
Into the Dark

They left the Harris mansion a short while later, and when they returned to Plas-y-Fforest, Jake went immediately into the secret Archive room. The others followed, but to Jake's dismay, there was still no answer from Aunt Ramona.

He sent another message by the Inkbug, requesting even more urgent help. Then, for the next three hours, they pored over the Lightriders' old grimoires. At last, Archie (who was very good at research) discovered a spell they could use for dealing with gargoyles.

It was called the Petrificus spell, from the Greek root word 'petra,' meaning stone. It would turn the gargoyles back into the stone statues they were supposed to be—but only for thirty seconds. In that short window of time, the stony gargoyles had to be smashed, or they would come back to life and attack again.

You could repeat the spell as many times as needed until the creatures were destroyed, and indeed, between the wand and chant and his telekinesis, Jake realized that, technically, he should be able to destroy one by himself.

Still, he was very glad that he didn't have to.

Derek had put together a formidable team, and by that evening, they all were ready for battle.

With the Guardian himself as their fearless leader on the mission, there was also the Gryphon, who already had that familiar, warlike gleam in his eyes. Red liked a good fight as well as any mythical beast. Miss Helena shapeshifted into her other form for the occasion, ready to pounce, as a lethal black leopard.

Derek had also called in Emrys with his hand-picked crew of

warrior dwarves, their axes sharp and shining. They feared nothing, cracking jokes the whole time.

Archie and the girls, however, stayed back at the cottage, along with Snowdrop and Nimbus and little Ufudd to look after them. Jake felt better knowing his friends would be safe here behind the thorny barrier of enchanted climbing roses and all the old protective spells that girded his property.

At least he wouldn't have to worry about them during this ordeal. For his part, he had no choice but to go along for the adventure. Out of everyone on the team, he alone had the magical bloodlines that could make the Petrificus spell work.

Well, if he wanted to be a Lightrider one day, he was going to have to get used to facing these sorts of dangers, he told himself as their unlikely band of heroes rode along in the carriage, the dwarf warriors laughing at each other's ribald comments the whole way up the road to the Harris Coalmine's entrance.

They didn't seem afraid of the gargoyles in the slightest.

Maybe ignorance was bliss. But, of course, they were used to fighting cave trolls.

Emrys noticed Jake watching the short but hearty crew in awe, and sent him a manly wink to shore up his courage.

Jake managed a smile in answer, then tried harder not to look scared. He just couldn't help wondering what would happen if the Petrificus spell didn't work.

He really didn't want to end up getting eaten today—neither himself nor any of his companions. It seemed a particularly bad way to die. From what he'd heard, there had been little left of the pit pony, sadly enough.

In fact, he was half hoping the pixies were right and it *was* baby dragons, because they were not as smart as gargoyles, and as mere hatchlings, nowhere near as vicious.

Derek had a talent for dealing with dragons, anyway. Aye, Jake thought, gripping the wand in his pocket. Maybe they'd get lucky and go home without a scratch.

Either way, the team was prepared.

Jake just worried if they'd be fast enough to smash the gargoyles within thirty seconds, once he did the spell. If the gargoyles came back to life that quickly, there wouldn't be time to escape. Plus, it was going to be pitch-dark down there, and he was guessing the creatures moved very fast.

What unnerved him the most—and made him all the more sure, deep down, that these were, indeed, Garnock's familiars—was something else the old spell-book had said.

It had warned that gargoyles came from another dimension, another world.

The underworld, to be exact.

An unnerving fact to ponder. But it made sense, considering Garnock's dabbling in deals with the devil, according to local legend.

Whatever was down there, all Jake knew was that somebody had to deal with the beasts before hunger drove them aboveground to hunt for more prey. They had already eaten four miners and a pit pony.

Next they'd be picking off people in the town. That would never do. He took a deep, shaky breath and let it out, feeling his fear climb higher. *One step at a time.*

Still, he couldn't help wondering what ever happened to that boy who had been so bold and confident in Mr. Harris's library just a few hours ago? He smirked at the memory of how he had boasted to the coal-factor: *Don't worry, this is what we do.*

Now he sat here trembling with dread—and if tonight weren't bad enough, as soon as they had dealt with Garnock's pets, they'd have to figure out how to defeat the sorcerer himself.

Jake had no idea how to fight a dark spirit, but it seemed easier to destroy Garnock in his black fog form, rather than waiting for him to get any stronger.

Hopefully, they'd hear from Aunt Ramona before then.

Disgusted with his own pre-battle jitters, Jake thought back to his Viking ghost friend, Ragnor the Punisher, whom he had met on his last adventure. Now there was someone who had courage!

The long-dead Viking chief had believed in two notions: glory and fate. The Norns wove the Tapestry of Fate, and therefore, destiny was set, according to Norse legend. Thus, Ragnor had explained, he was never frightened when he had rowed off in his Viking ship on one of his mighty adventures.

After all, if he was meant to die at that time, then he could not possibly survive, and if he was meant to live, then he could not possibly die until it was time.

Either way, he said, was fine with him. If he lived, he'd have victory and the riches he had taken on his raid, but if he died, he'd enter Valhalla and bask in the glory of a hero's reputation.

Perhaps the Norseman had been a little nickey in the head, Jake mused, but that way of looking at things had allowed the Viking adventurer to charge headlong into life with nearly superhuman bravery.

Right. Jake decided to think more like a Viking to get himself through the ordeal ahead. He wasn't sure it was working, but at last, they reached their destination.

Sunset painted the sky with dazzling colors as they arrived before the black, yawning mouth of the coalmine.

The place looked deserted except for the herd of ponies, who had been gathered back into a corral after their earlier escape.

Mercifully, the ponies had not been forced back into their underground stables in the mine. They would stay aboveground until the problem had been handled.

More importantly, Mr. Harris proved true to his word. The workers had been sent home for the day, as promised, and tomorrow, the mine would stay closed so they could finish this.

It was a good thing there were no people about, Jake mused as he watched their odd company of fighters jumping out of the carriage. Such a crew would have been difficult to explain.

Derek had been driving, which might have appeared normal enough to outsiders, except for all the weapons strapped to his muscle-bound body, to say nothing of the black leopard riding along on the seat beside him.

The erstwhile governess leaped down gracefully onto her four paws, her black tail snaking back and forth in anticipation of the battle. Meanwhile, the Gryphon and all six dwarves jumped out of the back.

Derek gave everyone a couple minutes to clear their heads and make their final preparations. The dwarves lit a few torches and checked the weapons one last time. Red and Leopard-Helena walked up to the opening of the mine, sniffing the air for any trace of gargoyles' scent, while Emrys and Derek consulted the schematics of the coalmine one last time, planning their route.

"The pony was attacked here, which means they could have come at it from any of these three directions..."

Meanwhile, a few of the warrior dwarves went to the back of the carriage and dragged out the large slabs of raw beef they would use to lure the gargoyles close, so they could kill them.

Well, so I can kill them, Jake corrected himself with a gulp. He wiped the sweat off his palms while butterflies danced in his stomach. *I hate caves.*

Going underground was bad enough, but knowing that man-eating monsters from the underworld were lurking somewhere down there was going to make things even more...interesting.

Tucking the yew wand into the waistband of his trousers, he paced back and forth, nervously waiting for their ordeal to begin.

He had armed himself as well as he knew how, with his magical runic dagger, Risker, sheathed at his side, a gift from Odin himself. He had his pouch of Illuminium in case he got stranded in the darkness, though he was not too sure about having to sing to light it up. Wouldn't the singing only lead the gargoyles straight to him?

Anyway, lastly, he had also put on his lucky seashell necklace that his parents had left him—not because it was useful in this situation. Its only real purpose was for summoning the freshwater mermaids known as naiads. He had put it on because wearing it made him feel closer to them somehow, even though he could barely remember either one of them. They had been Lightriders, and someday, so would he.

Derek finished consulting with Emrys, who folded up the map of the mine and nodded. Red and Helena finished sharpening their claws on the stone entrance to the mine, then Derek walked over to Jake.

He had never seen the warrior entirely geared up for battle before. The Guardian was armed to the teeth, a bayoneted rifle slung across his back, a revolver tucked into a shoulder holster next to his ribcage, his favorite pair of Bowie knives strapped to his sides.

He had tied back his long, dark mane and abandoned his long duster coat, wearing only a black vest with no shirt or jacket, along with his usual black trousers and boots.

Aunt Ramona would have been scandalized by his ungentlemanly apparel, but then, this wasn't gentlemanly work.

Not quite the elegant hunting party that Their Lordships had bragged about earlier, in Mr. Harris's library. It was going to be dark and scary—and probably bloody, too.

Jake swallowed hard and looked up at his idol.

"How are you feeling?" Derek asked.

"F-fine." Jake cleared his throat to try to force the fearful quaver out of his voice. "I'm fine," he repeated in a firmer tone.

"Good. You've got the wand, memorized that spell?"

Jake nodded anxiously.

The Guardian gave him a fond clap on the back, then scanned his face in concern. "Are you sure you're ready for this?"

"I don't like caves, that's all."

"Well, I don't like gargoyles," Derek said with a smile.

"You're probably wishing that they *were* baby dragons," Jake joked, trying to dissipate his tension.

Derek flashed a grin. "They're cute when they're small." Narrowing his eyes in thought, he gazed toward the mine entrance. "Your aunt's going to kill me. I really wish you didn't have to come along for this, but since you're the only one who can—"

"I'll be fine." Jake squared his shoulders. *Think Viking.* He lifted his chin a notch. "It'll be fun."

"That's the spirit, kid." Pride flashed in Derek's eyes. He tousled Jake's hair. "Just stick close to Red and me. We'll keep you safe. Stay between us. Whatever happens, don't get separated from the group. And, ah, don't drop that wand."

"Believe me, I won't."

It was the only real defense they had against the gargoyles.

"Good. Let's go." Derek strode ahead of him, waving toward the others while Jake followed, clutching the magical twig from a yew tree.

The Guardian turned to his troops. "All right, you lot. If anyone gets hurt down there, yell for Red. His feathers have magical healing powers; he'll give you one, and you should be all right. Of course, not even gryphon feathers are going to help if you let yourself get eaten, so stay sharp. Everyone ready?"

Jake looked around at their team: one towering Order knight; six grim-faced dwarves with axes gleaming (except for Emrys, who was carrying a sledgehammer instead, on account of the smashing part); a black leopard with greenish-yellow eyes agleam; a lion-sized Gryphon with claws bared, ready for battle; and one twelve-year-old boy trying to act like he wasn't scared.

Jake hid a private gulp. Everyone said they were ready to go. Even Leopard-Helena let out a low feline snarl.

Derek sent his ladylove a pointed look. "Don't do anything foolish down there," he warned her.

She growled at him in answer.

No doubt they were both wishing her twin brother Henry were with them, too; the boys' mild-mannered tutor was terrifying in his other form as a mighty wolf.

They would just have to do without him. And without Aunt Ramona and her formidable magical powers...

Then Derek lowered the Vampire Monocle onto his eye. "All right, then. Let's do this."

He signaled for them to follow, and with that, the whole team ventured into the Harris Mine.

CHAPTER EIGHTEEN
Monsters in the Mine

As they walked deeper into the coalmine, everyone continually scanned the inky blackness all around them.

Jake gripped the wand like a weapon while his pulse pounded in his ears. At any minute, he half expected some unholy beast to come charging out of the shadows.

So far, nothing.

Still, the place was impossibly eerie with all the workers gone, the machinery quiet, the coal carts parked on the tracks, and the drip-drip-dripping of unseen rivulets of water trickling down the walls.

Heart-stopping echoes of faint noises whispered to them from the distant ends of every tunnel.

Following the coal cart tracks on a steep downward slant, they pressed on. The mine grew darker with each step. Just beyond the feeble glow of the dwarves' few torches, it was as black as the coal the crews pulled out of here each day.

Jake wished he could see better in the dark. Everyone else had excellent night vision. The dwarves were used to working underground. Helena was in her feline form and everyone knew cats could see perfectly at night. Likewise, Red was half-lion, with sharp eagle-eyes, and Derek was wearing the Vampire Monocle.

He must have sensed Jake's uneasiness, for he took it off and handed it over. "Here."

"No, that's all right—"

"Take it. I've got my Guardian instincts. Supernatural senses, remember? I should have thought of it before."

"Are you sure?"

"You need to be able to see what you're doing when it comes time to use the spell."

"Good point." Jake accepted it gratefully and strapped the Vampire Monocle around his head, then fixed the camera-type lens over his eye. *That's better.*

At once, his surroundings appeared greenish-charcoal-gray instead of pitch-black.

He could finally see his companions, too. He saw the feathers on the back of Red's neck standing up, like they always did when he was in battle-mode, then he noticed Emrys somehow reading the map.

"This way," the head dwarf told them.

They turned to the right, continuing on a smooth downward angle deeper into the mine.

There was some sort of square wooden structure ahead. Leopard-Helena meowed in warning.

A moment later, Jake, too, could smell the blood.

He squinted toward the structure. "It's the pit ponies' stables."

And that splash of darker color on one of the stall doors was apparently blood.

"That must have been where the pony was attacked," one of the dwarf warriors said, pointing.

Derek shook his head. "Daft keeping horses down here."

"We're getting closer. Let's find a good place to set the bait," Emrys said in a grim tone.

Red trotted ahead of them and quickly located a good spot for their ambush: a junction where two coal cart tunnels met, with a tall, round ventilation shaft high above it.

Jake frowned at the four-way intersection. "Won't this give them an easy escape? They've got four tunnels to choose from as their getaway path."

"Yes, but what interests us more for the moment is to see which direction the gargoyles will arrive from when they come to take the bait," Derek said. "That should tell us where they've been hiding—which direction to look. Then we'll know where to hunt them. Otherwise, this mine is vast. They could be anywhere."

"Oh." Jake nodded. "That makes sense." Also, the intersection was relatively close to the pit pony stables, where the creatures had already proven their willingness to attack.

Derek gestured to the dwarf warriors to drag the slab of beef to the middle of the tunnels' intersection, then they all climbed up the service ladders and clambered onto the metal catwalks halfway up the ventilation shaft. This gave them a good vantage point of the dark junction below.

The dwarves and Red and Helena spread out around the metal walkway, but Derek stayed next to Jake.

"Have that wand ready," the Guardian advised. "And do me a favor, Jake."

"What's that?"

"Don't miss."

Jake gripped the wand harder. Then they all conformed to a rule of silence, watching and waiting for their quarry to appear.

Jake was surprised that no one else could hear his heart pounding like a kettle drum in the quiet. He fought the shivers that ran down his spine in an effort to stay motionless.

Soon, time seemed to creep to a standstill. He could not tell how many minutes had passed. Half an hour?

Waiting for the monster to appear was agonizing when nobody was quite sure what to expect. Little was known about gargoyles' daily habits. The grimoire in the archives had simply said that they came in a wide variety of sizes and shapes, with varying degrees of intelligence and aggression.

Some were meaner than others. Some displayed the reasoning power of the average human child, while others functioned as mere brute beasts.

Jake was pondering the question of what kind lived in the Harris Mine and how they might have got here, when suddenly, a sinister, low sound came from the tunnel.

The blood froze in his veins.

The voice he heard next was not of this world. A chatter and a chirp with an occasional wary hiss, rather like some sort of a demonic squirrel.

This was accompanied by the low, rasping rhythm of claws scraping stone as it approached, drawn by the bloody, raw bait.

Jake held perfectly still as the creature stepped into view in the dark opening of the northern tunnel.

He stared through the Vampire Monocle in disbelief.

He had seen gargoyles carved on old churches, but to see one standing there, alive...

All he knew was that that thing did not belong to this world. It came from somewhere below, and it was hideous.

Ape-sized and dark gray in color, the gargoyle had a grotesque face, a pug nose, and drool dripping off its up-fangs as it crept toward the bait. It had little blunt nubs of horns on its head and leering, wide-set eyes.

It hopped closer, investigating the slab of beef.

Jake flinched when it opened its mouth wide and ripped off a chunk of the raw meat.

Derek nudged him with his elbow. Jake's heart was racing. The Guardian gave him a nod as if to say, *Go on. What are you waiting for?*

Jake tried to settle his frayed nerves. His hands were shaking so badly he feared he'd miss the nasty creature.

Concentrate, he told himself. Though a little unnerved by the sight of the devil's imp gnawing on the beef ribs, he shoved his revulsion away, bringing up the wand.

Just as he was about to do the spell, a second gargoyle appeared, drawn to the bait; Jake floundered, unsure what to do. He glanced at Derek in question.

The Guardian gave him a firm nod, silently indicating that he should get them both.

Jake gulped. But as he aimed the wand at the gargoyles, the first gargoyle chased away the new arrival with a vicious snarl. It seemed the ugly beastie had no intention of sharing the banquet with his comrade.

As the second one shrank back into the shadows, Jake pointed the wand, focused his mind on his target, and summoned up all the magical power in his blood.

A bead of sweat ran down his face. Then he suddenly shouted: *"Petrificus!"*

Energy crackled out of the wand's tip like a miniature lightning bolt and hit the feasting gargoyle square in the belly.

A direct hit!

At once, the gargoyle started changing into stone. First its stomach turned to solid gray rock, spreading outward from there, traveling down the creature's limbs and up to its ugly face.

"Go!" Derek waved the dwarves into motion.

Quick as a wink, they were racing down the ladders.

"Hurry! You've only got thirty seconds!"

"Oh, I need less than that." With these bold words, a scruffy, dark-haired dwarf brought up his axe and struck the gargoyle statue in the middle.

It cracked in half at the waist and fell in two pieces.

"Ha, ha! Thank you very much." Wallace took a bow while his hearty mates crowded round to cheer him and to get a closer look at the beast.

"Lord, that thing's uglier than my mother-in-law."

"Pshaw, it's even uglier than yer wife."

"Hey!" The two dwarves pushed each other back and forth in harmless horseplay, while Wallace turned to grin and wave at Jake.

"Well done, lad! That wasn't so bad, was it? And you were so nervous!"

"I think you really have to smash it!" Jake called down, but his warning came too late.

Wallace suddenly yelped in pain and fell to the ground, bleeding profusely from the back of his leg.

His friends rushed over to pull him clear of the two halves of the gargoyle, which had just come—separately—back to life.

Helena roared, Derek vaulted off the catwalk, and Jake leaped to his feet for a better view.

Meanwhile, the two halves of the gargoyle were flopping around, trying to cause trouble. The lower half was trying to escape, bumping into everything.

But the upper half with the claws and the big, nasty fangs was furious, lashing out at anyone in arm's reach.

Wallace groaned as his friends dragged him farther back to safety. "I can't believe it bit me."

"Jake, the spell! Again!" Derek bellowed from below, clearing everyone else back. "Out of his way, you lot! You'll be turned to stone if it hits you!"

"*Petrificus!*" Jake shouted, waving the wand again, and again, the lightning flew.

He repeated the spell for both the upper and lower halves of the gargoyle. In seconds, the halves turned back into stone, then Derek took the sledgehammer from Emrys, and pounded them both into dust.

Then the ugly gargoyle was no more.

"Lord Crafanc! Will you help him?" Emrys called from beside his wounded man.

Red glided down at once to give Wallace one of his healing feathers, using his beak to pluck it off his wing. The Gryphon offered it to Emrys.

The head dwarf took it gratefully. Unlocking the healing powers in Red's feathers was a simple process. Emrys was obviously familiar with gryphon magic, for he took the feather at once between his hands and started rolling it back and forth quickly between his palms, like someone trying to start a fire with sticks.

White smoke started coming up from the feather. A burst of bright sparkles rose in the darkness as the red feather disintegrated into magical golden dust.

Emrys sprinkled the powdered feather all over the torn flesh on the back of Wallace's leg. The golden dust sank in, easing the pain from his face.

"Uhhh," said Wallace.

Jake and everyone else waited anxiously to see what would happen.

Several seconds later, Wallace started laughing. "Woo-hoo! Well, you don't see that every day, now, do you?"

Emrys flashed around a rueful smile. "He's all right! Thank you, Lord Crafanc."

"Becaw," Red replied, giving the head dwarf an extra feather in case somebody else got hurt.

One of the other warriors gave Wallace a hand up. "Atta boy! On your feet, you lazy lie-about."

"Always have to learn the hard way, don't you, Wally?" Another dwarf warrior clapped Wallace on the back.

He grinned, the blood still wet on his clothes. "You know me. I just do it for attention." He winked at Jake. "At least we know what to do now. When the lad says smash 'em, he means smash 'em. Into itty-bitty bits."

"Sure, I think we're getting the hang of it!" his friend teased. "Better late than never. Before *somebody* gets his butt bitten off."

They laughed heartily.

Jake could not believe the dwarves were back to joking around after what had just happened, but they clapped each other on the back, took a few discreet swigs from their flasks, and seemed ready to fight again.

He shook his head, dazed. Mad, they were. Like wild, miniature Vikings.

"All right, everybody, listen up," Emrys ordered. "Now that we know what we're dealing with, we'll go deeper into the mine and set another trap—" His words broke off abruptly as he was interrupted by the sound of a long, rumbling growl.

"Ahh, we've got company, boys," one of the dwarves said under his breath.

Indeed.

Whether it had been the smell of the bait or the scent of Wallace's blood, they had lured more gargoyles than anyone expected.

Certainly more than they were quite ready for.

The beasts began appearing in the shadows of all four tunnels around them.

Now it was they who were trapped in the center of the junction—in about the same spot where the bait had lain before the first gargoyle had devoured it.

Jake felt dizzy with fear as he glanced around, finding all four tunnels blocked by large gargoyles.

"Don't move," Derek ordered softly. "We're surrounded."

"How did that happen?" one of the dwarves asked angrily through gritted teeth.

"Stealthy little buggers," said another.

"Hungry, too," Wallace added.

"Jake, to me," Derek murmured.

Everyone backed toward the center of the intersection, facing outward in all directions, the dwarves with the spears, Derek with his Bowie knives, Red hissing, Helena baring her fangs.

Jake held the wand out before him as he moved to Derek's side. Red crept into position on his right.

"Fire at will, Jake. I suggest you clear the tunnel we arrived by first, or they'll have us trapped down here," Derek said softly.

He gulped and nodded. "Petrificus!"

The battle exploded.

With his heart pounding in his ears and terror narrowing his senses down to tunnel vision, it was impossible to follow everything that was going on around him all at once. The gargoyles attacked; the dwarves swung their axes, chopping at the beasts to ward them off. Jake turned one monster after the other to stone; Derek smashed them into bits; it seemed to last for hours.

When one tall, horned gargoyle with crazed, glowing eyes put its head down and charged at Jake like a possessed bull, he froze for a fraction of a second that he could ill afford; then he fumbled with sweaty, shaking hands and only managed to drop the wand.

He cursed and bent to pick it up, and would have had his head bitten off if Red had not pushed in front of him and roared in the charging beast's face.

It skidded to a halt.

The ugly bull gargoyle stood as tall as Red; the two creatures had a staring contest. It only lasted about three seconds, but to Jake, it felt much longer. Then, to his astonishment, the bull gargoyle turned tail and ran from the Gryphon.

"Petrificus!" Jake got it in the back while it fled, having recovered his wand.

The nearest dwarf used the blunt end of his axe blade to knock the statue down and pound the parts to gravel.

Someone screamed.

"He got me!"

"Hang on, Joffrey! We'll get you a gryphon feather!"

"Petrificus!"

"This one's mine!"

Smash!

Another gargoyle statue crumbled under a blow from Emrys's sledgehammer.

Jake looked around, chest heaving. "Is that it? Is that all of them?"

He could hear the hurt man whimpering in the dark. Red hurried to give him a feather, then suddenly, a feline roar from above made Jake look up.

He was just in time to see a gargoyle with ugly, stunted wings dropping down toward him from the ceiling.

But Helena leaped off the metal catwalk and slammed the creature aside, driving it against the opposite wall with the force of her jump.

They both tumbled to the ground. The stunned gargoyle got up and ran, galloping away on all fours.

The leopard-governess ran after it in blind fury, chasing it down the tunnel with the single-minded purpose of a cat who had already got a taste of its mouse.

"Helena, come back here!" Derek ordered. "Everyone needs to stick together! Blast that woman. Shapeshifters!"

"She can't help her instincts," Jake blurted out, feeling like his life had just flashed before his eyes.

"Come on," Derek ordered everyone.

They all ran down the tunnel after Helena, already hearing the snarls and growls of a ferocious fight echoing from the darkness ahead.

Strangely, they also heard the unmistakable sound of running water.

"Oh, perfect," Derek muttered.

At the end of the tunnel, they arrived in a large, hollowed-out cavern with an underground river cutting through it.

The high, sloped walls of the craggy cavern had rough-cut rock ledges here and there, and a rock dome ceiling some forty feet high.

There were all sorts of ladders leading to higher tunnels above, with barrels and mining equipment clustered around the walls of the ground level. The rushing water was noisy, reverberating through the cave.

Through the Vampire Monocle, Jake scanned the cavern until he spotted the governess-leopard on a rock ledge twenty feet above them. She had caught her gargoyle in her jaws and was shaking it violently by the back of its neck, just like a cat with its prey.

"Helena, really!" Derek scolded her.

She flung the gargoyle from her jaws, tossing it against the rock ledge.

Jake lifted the wand to turn it to stone, but the gargoyle recovered with surprising speed; it jumped up, shook itself, then launched at Helena in a counterattack.

Derek grabbed his arm and stopped him. "Wait for a clear shot. You might hit her."

Jake obeyed, but he glanced around the cavern and saw fit to warn the others of what the monocle showed him. "Stay on your toes. I'm counting six more of them in the shadows."

"I see seven," Emrys countered in a low tone.

It was true. They were everywhere. This was starting to look more like an infestation than a mere pest problem.

But after the group had successfully fought off the first wave back at the intersection of the tunnels, these ones did not seem too keen to attack, other than the one Helena was battling.

"If she gets hurt, they're goin' to be all over her," Emrys said grimly.

"I know. Helena, that's enough!" Derek yelled. "Get out of there!"

He had no sooner shouted the warning than the gargoyle swiped at her ribcage with its claws. The cavern echoed with the shrill, sudden scream of an animal in pain.

Derek was instantly in motion, both Bowie knives in hand. He dashed across the wooden footbridge over the river, scaled the ladder with effortless speed, and leaped up onto the rock ledge, turning to put the wounded shapeshifter behind him.

Helena tried to get up, but Jake could see she was hurt badly. Derek kicked the bloodied gargoyle off the ledge, but another one came at him.

"Red, get Emrys and me up there!" Jake cried. "Emrys, you get the gryphon feather to Helena; I'll turn the gargoyles to stone. Hurry up! Derek can't kill them, he can only hold them off, but not forever. We have to help him!" Jake rushed Emrys onto the Gryphon's back, then jumped on behind him. "You'd better hold on. Hurry, Red, they need us!"

The Gryphon lifted off and headed for the rock ledge, avoiding gargoyles who leaped at them from all directions.

"*Petrificus!*" Jake yelled again and again, zapping each attacking beast.

When they fell out of the air as stone statues, the dwarves below smashed them—though the drops from various heights did much of that work for them.

Emrys held on tight as they neared the rock ledge where Derek and Helena were still under siege; the head dwarf grimaced at the strangeness of riding on a gryphon, muttering dwarven curses to himself.

Red managed to land, though there wasn't much room on the ledge, with nasty, snarling gargoyles on all sides.

Jake swung off the Gryphon's back, then steadied Emrys, but

he couldn't help thinking they were in as much danger from Derek's whirling blades as from the beasts' big, curved claws.

Wand in hand, Jake went to the edge to stand beside the Guardian, casting the Petrificus spell on one gargoyle after another, while Emrys got another scarlet feather from Red and hurried to turn it into powder, as before.

Poor Helena. They could hear her meowing pitifully behind him. Jake had never seen Derek so furious. Guardians were dangerous under normal circumstances, but never more so than when someone they cared about was hurt.

"Petrificus!" Jake sent another bolt of lightning flying from the wand, then made a halfhearted attempt to cheer Derek up. "I'm getting pretty good at this if I do say so myself."

Another gargoyle turned to stone on the other end of the wand's lightning bolt and dropped, instantly rolling back down the cavern's sloping wall.

"There you are. Steady, girl," Emrys encouraged his black, furry patient.

"How is she?" Derek demanded as he parried a slashing blow from a drooling gargoyle's sickle-shaped ivory claws. "Jake," he urged in an aside.

"No problem. Petrificus!"

Zap!

"Nasty little blackguard got her pretty good," Emrys reported from behind them. "But she'll be feeling better in a moment."

"Next time maybe she'll listen to me," Derek muttered.

"Next time?" Jake retorted. "Petrificus! Look out below!"

Smash.

"Kind of fun."

Derek shook his head and kept on fighting. "You are your father's son."

Within another moment, the attack trickled off.

"Did we get them all?" Jake asked eagerly.

"I think...maybe," Derek murmured.

But no.

Jake scanned the cavern through the Vampire Monocle. There were still some gargoyles left, but they had retreated to the distant edges of the cavern, worn out and perhaps realizing it was a losing battle.

Then Helena sprang to her feet, or rather, her paws behind them. "There she is!" Emrys said with a broad grin as the leopard shook herself. "Right as rain. She's all right!" the head dwarf yelled down to his followers.

The warriors cheered.

"Nice work, Master Emrys," Jake said.

"You, too, laddie."

But Derek turned to stare at Helena and slowly shook his head, his rugged face etched with a smitten look of relief. Helena reared up onto her hind legs and gave Derek's cheek a tickle with her dainty whiskers.

The Guardian scowled at her. "No, don't try to be all sweet. You were bad."

"She did save my life," Jake pointed out.

"Then she got carried away. Typical! Shapeshifters," Derek grumbled.

Helena nipped his arm for that remark.

"At least she's got nine lives," Jake said. "Can we get down from here, please?"

Emrys nodded. "Aye, we need to regroup and figure out where we go from here."

They all headed off the rock ledge. Jake took the easy way down, riding on Red's back, but Emrys preferred to climb down the ladder with Derek. Helena simply pounced off the rocky outcropping down the sloping cavern wall.

Not even she could cross the river in one jump, however. The three of them went in single file toward the footbridge, Emrys leading the way, and Derek bringing up the rear. Even in her leopard form, Derek let the lady go ahead of him. "After you."

Jake had already made it to the other side of the river and was sliding off Red's back over in the center of the cavern.

The dwarves were counting up their kills and congratulating each other, and when Jake joined them, they congratulated him, too.

"I think we're getting good at this, I really do. How many more do you reckon are creeping around down here?"

"No idea."

Emrys crossed the spindly wooden footbridge and stepped off onto solid ground on their side of the river.

"All right, you lot, settle down. Somebody give me the map..."

Derek and Helena hung farther back on the bridge, having a private word before rejoining the others.

All of a sudden, Jake saw a hideous, one-horned gargoyle leap off the very rock ledge they had vacated, launching one last sneak attack.

They didn't even see it coming—but Jake did.

"*Petrificus!*" he shouted, bringing up the wand with a flourish.

Instantly, the beast turned to stone, thank goodness, but then he gasped in horror as, too late, he realized his miscalculation.

The gargoyle turned into a statue and dropped out of midair like a boulder, landing on the footbridge and smashing it to splinters.

Derek and Helena were instantly thrown into the rushing water, and before Jake's eyes, were washed away.

"*No!*"

Horror-stricken, he took a few running steps to the water's edge, trying to use his telekinesis to pull them back, but it all happened too fast.

Before he could even summon up his powers, they were swept away under the low stone arch where the underground river descended deeper into the mountain.

Jake pushed the Vampire Monocle up above his eye and stared at the churning, dark water in disbelief.

Just like that, they were gone.

CHAPTER NINETEEN
The Black Wand

J ake felt as though the room was spinning.

Red swooped through the cavern with a furious roar, but not even he could do anything to help Derek and Helena.

The current had swept them away.

Shocked to the marrow, he didn't realize he was teetering on the edge of the river himself and might have fallen in and joined them if two of the dwarves had not rushed over and grabbed his arms.

Steadying him, they pulled him back. One of them caught the Vampire Monocle when he nearly dropped it into the river in his state of shock.

"Easy, lad."

"They're going to drown!" Jake shouted.

"Now, now, you mustn't say that—"

"It's all my fault," he choked out.

"Calm yourself, Lord Griffon!" Emrys barked.

The sharp-toned order brought Jake back to his senses like a much-needed slap across the face.

"We don't have time for panic. Pull yourself together. This gargoyle hunt is over for now," the head dwarf announced. "We need to get after them at once if we're going to save 'em. Now, let's go, people, hurry!"

That was when Jake turned and dazedly realized the dwarves were already making preparations to rescue the pair. They scurried about with orderly speed, lighting the rest of the torches; somebody thrust one into his hand.

While Jake just stood there, at a loss, the dwarves went about efficiently tethering themselves together, each tying a knot around his waist with the same long rope.

He lost track of which one of them had caught the Vampire Monocle when he dropped it, and was so out of sorts that he forgot to ask for it back.

He turned his bewildered gaze to Emrys as the head dwarf came over to him.

"Don't worry, lad, we're miners. We deal with these kinds of accidents all the time. We'll get 'em back safe." He snapped the map open, poring over it by torchlight. "I just need to figure out where this river leads..."

"Can she change herself back whenever she wants?" one of the warriors muttered to his friend. "Last I heard, cats can't swim."

Jake glanced at him, aghast at this point, then he looked at the river again. The water never stopped for a second.

It just kept flowing full force constantly through the cavern, frothy, rough, and rapid, like it had not just swallowed up the closest thing he had to a father.

Life had robbed him of his parents. Was it about to take Derek away from him, too?

Suddenly, Wallace pointed at the water. "Look!"

Bubbles were rising from the middle of the spot where the footbridge had broken in half.

For a heartbeat, Jake thought it might be Helena or Derek. But no, he had seen the water carry them away.

Then he realized.

Thirty seconds had passed since he had turned the gargoyle attacking them to stone, but he had not destroyed it.

After falling onto the bridge, the gargoyle statue must have sunk to the bottom, too heavy to be washed away.

Still intact, now it was coming back to life.

Jake narrowed his eyes. This time, he wanted revenge. He took out his wand and readied himself to use his telekinesis, waiting the final few seconds for the gargoyle to appear.

"Stand back," he told the dwarves through gritted teeth. Red pounced over to stand by his side.

"Here it comes!" Wallace yelled as a dark shape glided into view just under the water's surface.

Suddenly, the big, fanged gargoyle shot up from the river. It had no sooner cleared the surface than Jake aimed the wand at it. *"Petrificus!"* he shouted for all he was worth.

Instantly, it started turning back into stone, but it fought against the spell, struggling to keep flying.

Jake let out a yell of effort as he cast a bolt of his telekinesis at it. The gargoyle exploded spectacularly in midair. The other gargoyles screamed from all the high, rocky places around the cavern upon seeing this.

"That's what you're all going to get!" he roared at them, turning in fury to pick his next target. He cast the spell at another big one of them from across the cavern, then shattered it, too. "You want to hurt my friends?"

The gargoyles fled from him into any tunnel they could find. He could hear them chattering in fear as they raced into the shadows.

Wallace looked askance at him. "Remind me not to get on your bad side."

Jake paid the dwarf no mind, fixated on the fleeing monsters.

His furious vow echoed after them. "Run if you like, but the darkness won't save you! I'm going to hunt down every one of you and turn you all to dust!"

"No, you're not, my lord. At least, not yet." Emrys pressed Jake's arm down before he tried again. "First we've got to get moving. Tether yourself to the safety line! No time to lose." Emrys marched off and tied himself to the front end of the rope, obviously assuming that Jake would obey.

But Jake clenched his jaw and debated what to do. Killing gargoyles was vastly preferable to watching Emrys pull Derek, dead, out of the river.

He could not bear to see it, and after losing his parents, he felt certain that would be the outcome. Life always pulled the rug out from under you just when everything started going well.

Red nudged him. "Becaw?"

"I can't, Red." Jake shook his head and gave the Gryphon an imploring glance. "You know what Derek would do if he were here— he'd go after those monsters. So I say, let's go and finish them off, for him. C'mon, boy."

"Becaw?"

"Yes, I'm sure. Mine rescues are the dwarves' expertise, but I'm the only one that can kill those beasts with the Petrificus spell, so I might as well do the part I'm good at. How many people are they going to eat? So you coming with me or not?"

"Caw!"

As the dwarves jogged off, all tethered to their safety line, then filed under the low, narrow ledge alongside the river one by one, Jake and Red exchanged a grim glance, but made no move to follow.

When they were gone, probably assuming that he and Red were right behind them, Jake climbed onto the Gryphon's back. "Let's go kill some gargoyles," he said in a hard tone that would have made Derek proud.

Red lifted off the ground and flew up into one of the tunnels that had served as the gargoyles' escape route.

Then they pressed on into the dark.

For an hour, Jake and Red stalked the gargoyles through the maze of coalmine tunnels, pressing ever deeper into the mine. With the wand in one hand and the torch in the other, he destroyed many more along the way.

Meanwhile, to avoid getting lost in the black labyrinth of the mine, he left a trail of Illuminium powder behind them like breadcrumbs, pouring out small dribs of it every twenty paces, so that Red and he could find their way out again when their work was done.

As for his horror over what had happened to Derek and Helena, he had almost managed to convince himself that Emrys and his crew had rescued them by now.

Hopefully, the dwarves had also figured out what he was up to and would not panic, realizing he had Claw the Courageous with him.

The gargoyles seemed to be figuring it out, too. They cowered in the shadows after seeing him turn a dozen of their kind into statues and then smash them to smithereens.

The beasts were doing all they could to elude Red's keen eyesight, hearing, and sense of smell, and Jake's wand.

Well, except for one.

Jake had noticed some time ago that one of the gargoyles was actually following them. Both Red and he had whipped around a few times trying to catch a glimpse of the bold creature, to no avail.

The hair on Jake's nape prickled as he sensed this unseen enemy watching their every move, as if it was sizing them up. He turned around and held up the torch once more, searching the shadows, but still he could not see it.

"Becaw," Red urged him.

"All right, I'm coming," he answered uneasily.

They moved on but both stayed vigilant, determined to track the gargoyles back to their point of origin and finish the rest off there. The hunt led them farther away from the coal cart tracks and all the more frequently used passages of the mine, to a distant tunnel, low and narrow and very dark indeed.

Jake had to hunch over to walk down the angled slope of the passage and bumped his head on the ceiling more than once. "Ow," he muttered.

"Caw?"

"I'm fine," he grumbled, but what happened next took him completely by surprise.

Out of nowhere, the little, demented, monkey-looking gargoyle that he had seen—and mistaken for a statue—in town and in the cemetery, leaped out of the darkness into the torch's ring of light, and snatched the wand right out of his hand.

Before Jake could even react, the creature took off running.

"Hey! Come back here!" he shouted. "Red, he took the wand!"

Which meant they were suddenly defenseless.

At once, Jake hurried after the thief, trying not to bump his head again, and crouching awkwardly in the low tunnel as he ran. Red was right behind him.

He couldn't believe that little gargoyle 'statue' had been one of Garnock's minions all along.

"Have you been spying on me?" he hollered.

Even more surprising was that the imp was clever enough to have realized that he should steal the wand.

Without it, Jake could not destroy the gargoyles, and it was only a matter of time before the larger, nastier beasts figured out that they were now free to turn the tables on them.

Jake did not intend to give them enough time to put it together. Nor did he intend to get eaten alive. "Get back here, you!"

Just ahead, the little imp-gargoyle vaulted through a hole in the rock face into some hollow space beyond—probably some sort of underground cavern.

Jake rushed up to the hole, but it was too dark to see inside. "I've got to go in after him."

"Caw!"

"I've got no choice! If I don't get that wand back, we're dead." Jake shoved the Gryphon away from the hole. "Move aside, boy! You're too big, you can't fit."

Red let out a sound of frustration, straining to jam himself through the hole, but he was lion-sized with huge wings and the hole was narrow like a fox's den.

"Don't worry, Red. He's just a little one. I can handle him. Maybe I can't turn him to stone without the wand, but I can certainly keep him at arm's length with my telekinesis. Besides, I've got Risker to defend myself if it comes down to a fight. I'll be right back. Hope you don't mind, I'm taking the torch." With that, Jake thrust the torch through the hole first, and then climbed through, tumbling into the hollow space.

Blimey. He stared all around him, wide-eyed. "It isn't a cave, it's some sort of room!" he called back to Red in astonishment.

Climbing to his feet, Jake dusted off his trousers with one hand, then drew Risker from its scabbard and gripped it tightly. In his other hand, he lifted the torch, while butterflies of fear danced in his belly.

He ventured another few steps into the stone chamber, marveling at great, pointy-tipped beams of colored quartz that grew right out of the living rock.

Then he stopped with a low gasp. The moment he saw the robed, jeweled skeleton sitting at the ancient, cobwebbed desk, he had a feeling he knew who that was. A certain black fog of his acquaintance—a dark spirit with no body.

Well, he thought with a gulp, *there's the body.* Garnock the Sorcerer in the flesh. Actually, no flesh, just the bones. But first things first.

He needed that wand back *now.*

Red fussed outside the chamber, peering in as best he could. "Caw!"

"All right, all right, I'm hurrying. But I think we can conclude that this is definitely where the gargoyles came from. That hole I climbed through has got to be where they got out. Oh, crikey!" He stopped cold at the sight of a miner's boot sitting by itself in the middle of the floor right in front of him.

It had a moldering, ripped-off part of a dead foot still in it.

He winced and stepped around it, scanning the whole place for the devilish little monkey thing that had run off with his wand.

"Those four miners must have broken through the rock into this chamber by accident. One of them tried to tell me they had found a room... I had no idea what he meant. Poor beggars, probably never knew what hit them. The rest of Garnock is in here," he informed the Gryphon as he searched the chamber for the imp. "What's left of him, anyway."

Jake noted the desk with the skeleton's hollow eyes staring over an ancient grimoire. The shelves built into the walls were laden with magical accoutrements, while the stone floor was carved with an intricate spread of strange symbols.

"This place looks like it must have been his workshop centuries ago. But it seems the Lightriders made it his tomb. Must have sealed him in down here somehow. Whatever spell they used, it must've been broken when the miners blew that hole in the wall." Even as he spoke those words, Jake remembered a worrisome detail about mining procedures from their goldmine tour with Emrys.

Whenever the miners (dwarves or men) used explosives to break open a vein of gold or coal in the earth, they quickly had to put a support beam into the hole they had created. Otherwise, it could cave in under the weight of the rock layers above it.

But there had been no timber beam jammed into the opening of Garnock's tomb. The coalminers mustn't have had the chance to complete that step of the job before they had been attacked and eaten by the gargoyles, Jake mused. *Better be careful.* Without the proper supports in place, this whole chamber was probably unstable.

Then there were the huge quartz crystals all around him, complicating matters.

Before the séance, wandering around Madam Sylvia's shop, he had read something about how quartz crystals could amplify psychic energy. No doubt that was the very reason Garnock had chosen this place for his lair.

Jake realized that if he used his powers in here, with all these massive quartz crystals pumping up magical energies, there was no telling how strong his telekinesis might come out. He did not want to bring the whole cave down around his ears.

Best to recover the wand and get out of here, he thought, scanning the darkness for that wicked little imp.

"Here, little evil monkey-squirrel-demon," he called softly, searching the chamber for the annoying creature. "Come out, come out, wherever you are. You know, you shouldn't take things that don't belong to you. Believe me, I would know. Now, give it back and maybe I won't hurt you."

He heard a mocking cackle from above, looked up, and saw the little maniac scampering up the angle of one of the tall quartz beams. The imp was hugging Jake's wand tightly in both of his wee gray monkey-paws.

"Come back here!" Jake sheathed Risker and brought up his hand to freeze the little menace by telekinesis.

But the pint-sized gargoyle must have been observing him long enough back in the tunnels to see more or less how the wand worked.

It let out a wild screech and waved the wand at him; Jake dove for cover with a startled yelp.

"Don't you point that thing at me!" He lifted his head up from behind the ancient desk, only to duck down again with a cry of alarm as the gargoyle shot another bolt of magic at him.

The creature laughed in delight as the jagged stream of blue light from the wand hit the wizard's astrolabe and sent it shooting off the desk.

"*Right.* That's quite enough, you little runt," he muttered. Setting the torch down, he left it burning where it lay on the stone floor in order to have both hands free.

Then he listened carefully, lost patience, and peeked over the skeleton's desk. *Now!*

He shot to his feet and ran out from behind the desk, tearing after the little imp before the wand-thief could take another shot at him.

His goal was to float the gargoyle into midair by telekinesis and refuse to let him down until he dropped the wand.

But the imp moved too fast. The thing was scampering all over the tomb, laughing as Jake tried to catch him and mimicking human speech as if he was saying the words to various magic spells.

Miniature explosions of poorly aimed magical power were going off all over the tomb as a result.

"Stop that! You're going to kill us both! Oh, when I get hold of you, I'm going to wring your neck," Jake vowed under his breath.

If he could just get close enough to work with some finesse, he could use his telekinesis to yank the wand out of the imp's hand and pull it through the air, drawing it back to himself.

Several times he had to dive out of the way to avoid getting hit by crazy gargoyle magic, but he finally saw his chance.

Using the utmost balance, Jake ran through the gloom right up onto one of the wide crystal beams near the shelves filled with some of Garnock's magical equipment.

But just when he nearly had the imp in reach, something growled behind him.

Jake froze.

A sickening premonition dropped like a stone in the pit of his stomach. A tingle of pure fear traveled up his spine. Terrified that he already knew what he would find, he looked back slowly over his shoulder.

Sure enough, three large gargoyles with fangs, horns, and gleaming eyes surrounded him below. Cutting off his exit, they were already licking their chops over the anticipated meal.

Jake blanched, but managed not to scream. For now, only his elevation, standing on the quartz crystal beam, put him slightly out of their reach. Unfortunately, he had seen how high these beasts could jump during their battle back at the cavern.

Pressing his back against the stone wall behind him, he forgot all about the imp and the wand, caught up in morbid fascination with his more immediate problem: this ugly trio, who clearly wanted to eat him.

They inched closer, giving him a fine view of their astonishing ugliness, not to mention their deadly claws.

The first had stunted black batwings; the second had a spiked tail that it thrashed back and forth; the third sported a row of pointy little knobs down its spine.

But they all had weirdly glowing eyes and squat, sinewy bodies, muscle-packed, like guard dogs made of stone. Aye, they were pets fit for a devil, Jake thought.

When the little imp snickered at him from above, Jake glanced up and suddenly wondered if this had been a trap all along.

Were the gargoyles clever enough to have planned this?

The way the little one preened, looking so proud of himself, Jake thought he must be the brains, while these massive dog-lion types were the brawn.

With a bead of sweat running down his face, Jake shook his head, but had to give them credit. By stealing his wand, they had not only left him defenseless, but separated him from his protector Red, luring him in here alone, apparently so they could kill him.

Not good.

He pulled his dagger out of its sheath. Meanwhile, Red was roaring in wild, useless fury outside the chamber.

Jake ignored him. The Gryphon simply couldn't fit through the hole to help him. He was on his own in this.

When the gargoyles snarled again, Jake brandished his knife to ward them off, even as he began inching higher up the smooth quartz beam.

Not that he was optimistic in the least about escaping them. Earlier tonight, he had seen how the fiends could practically run across the ceiling.

"Get back!" he yelled when the knobby one reared up suddenly onto its hind legs and slashed at him.

Jake struck back with Risker and warded off the beast, but the tip of the gargoyle's talon nicked his cheek.

The creature retreated to its prior position between its companions, still snarling at him; Jake lifted his hand to his cheek where the beast's razor-like claw had slashed him.

He glanced at his fingers and found them smeared with crimson, then he looked at the gargoyles again, taken aback.

Out of all his previous adventures, this was the first time any foe had actually drawn blood.

Likewise, the gargoyle who had cut him licked the drop of Jake's blood off his claw, then hissed at the taste of it. *"Lightrider!"* it rasped in a barely intelligible voice.

Its two companions reacted with wild hatred.

They all started hissing, bristling, slashing at the air with their claws as the glow in their eyes intensified.

If I don't get my hands on a wand, I'm dead.

Jake suddenly realized that the shelves at his back were covered with the tools of the sorcerer's trade.

Not taking his eyes off the gargoyles, he reached for the nearest wand resting upright in a golden goblet on the shelf, where it had lain untouched for ages.

Garnock's wand, he thought with a shudder. But he was past caring.

From the corner of his eyes, he measured the distance to the cup, knowing full well that the second the beasts saw him reach for the wand, they would attack. They seemed to have figured out that a wand meant bad things for them.

He licked his dry lips, readying himself to make his move. He would have only about one second to cast the Petrificus spell, and it had to count for every gargoyle in the chamber. Who could say how many might still be lurking in the shadows? He would have to freeze them all at once, and then shatter them in rapid succession. Thirty seconds, or they'd come back to life.

Then have him for supper.

All right. Might as well try it. He didn't have much choice. Still, even as he braced himself to do it, he could hear Aunt Ramona's direst warnings ringing in his ears. *"Never use the weapons of the enemy, Jacob. It is the most dangerous risk you can take. It always ends up bringing terrible consequences."*

Oh, yes, he believed her, every word.

But he did not intend to end up as some half-gnawed foot in this godforsaken coalmine. Caves alone were bad enough, but he simply refused to get eaten.

Concentrate. Heart pounding, he suddenly shot out his hand and grabbed the ancient wand.

The gargoyles leaped, all flying at him at once; in a heartbeat, Jake circled the wand over his head and screamed, *"Petrificus!"*

His voice echoed in the hollow chamber as he flung out the spell in all directions, and the quartz crystals amplified its magic.

The big gargoyles turned to stone just inches away from him and plummeted to the floor. The little imp, too, became a statue and tumbled off the quartz beam where he'd been sitting, smashing into bits when he hit the chamber floor.

The big ones merely chipped in places, and Jake, in a frenzy of survival, summoned up his telekinesis to finish the job. One after another, he lifted them off the ground using his powers and hurled the heavy stone statues into the distant wall of the chamber.

Boom!

Boom!

Boom!

They all smashed. He did not give them anywhere close to thirty seconds to come back to life.

But Aunt Ramona was proved right once again. He had used the tools of the enemy and at once, bad consequences followed. For the impact of the massive stone statues slamming against the cavern walls rattled the unstable layers of hollowed-out rock.

Jake heard a terrible crack from the direction of the ceiling, followed by a mighty rumble. The last thing he heard was Red's muffled roar from outside the chamber as the cavern collapsed all around him.

CHAPTER TWENTY
Trapped

When the rumbling stopped, the air was choked with dust and Jake lay coughing on the ground, knocked off his feet by the reverberations. He slowly sat up, waving the dust away from his nose and mouth, and squinting to see anything in the darkness.

Oh, no. The cave wall where he had climbed through the opening had collapsed. Now it was a giant pile of rubble. He was cut off from Red and the outer world.

Trapped in Garnock's tomb.

Well, maybe he should've expected something like this after using the evil sorcerer's wand. He threw it down in revulsion. Worse, he noticed that the rush of air from the collapse had left his distant torch barely flickering.

If that flame went out, he'd be swallowed up in pitch-black darkness and never find a way out of here. Too bad he had used up most of his Illuminium leaving the trail behind them.

Since he had no intention of sharing Garnock's tomb with the sorcerer's skeleton and the dead gargoyles for the rest of eternity, Jake climbed unsteadily to his feet, and, still coughing, made his way over to the torch.

Garnock's bones and his spell-book and all the other things on his desk were still intact, though now coated in a layer of dust.

Jake bent down and picked up his torch, then blew on it gently, making the slow-burning tar that coated it glow a little stronger. "Come on, perk up. Don't you dare go out on me." The light it gave was still feeble.

He realized the air was so thick with crushed rock and dust particles that the flame couldn't get enough oxygen to burn very brightly. *Aw, crud.* The last he checked, people needed oxygen, too. In short, he had no time to waste.

He held up the light once more and made sure the gargoyles were no longer a threat.

Indeed, the ugly beasts were beyond dead. They had been pulverized. Unfortunately, the yew wand from Plas-y-Fforest was lost, buried under the pile of rock where half the chamber had caved in.

Compared to the prospect of eventually running out of air, though, losing the wand seemed the least of his worries. Trying to shrug off a frisson of dread, he joked to himself about what a remarkably bad day he was having. First Petunia Harris practically trying to kiss him. Abduction by pixies. Hungry gargoyles, and then seeing poor Derek and Helena swept away.

Now this. If he lived to see the morning, he would count himself most fortunate.

Beyond his own fears, however, there was a Gryphon outside the caved-in chamber who sounded beside himself with panic, poor thing.

He could hear Red roaring, apparently running back and forth along the other side of the rockfall, calling for him, and stopping every now and then to dig through the rocks as best he could, obviously desperate to rescue his young master.

Jake leaned closer to his side of the mound of tumbled rocks and boulders and yelled, "Red, I'm all right! Can you hear me, boy? Over here! I'm alive and the gargoyles are dead!"

"Caw?" The Gryphon's muffled query now came directly from the opposite side of the rock-pile.

"I'm not hurt. Try not to worry, big fellow. I'm fine. I just need to find another way out of here."

"Caw!" Red eagerly replied. Then Jake heard the dear beast starting again to try to scratch away the stones, as if he'd dig him out with his bare paws.

"Red, stop! I don't know if that's the best idea, boy. The whole thing is unstable. If we're not careful, we'll shift the weight wrong and the rest of the chamber will come down and crush me. We don't want to start another rockfall. Just hang on and let me take a look around. There's got to be another way out of here."

Red gave an unhappy yowl in answer, as if to say, *"If there were, Garnock would have used it."*

Jake suddenly remembered he had Risker. "If all else fails, I still have my magic dagger. Remember how Odin said the blade can cut through solid rock? I'll saw my way out of here if I have to, don't you worry. I hate caves. I am not going to die down here."

Well, as long as I don't run out of air.

"Becaw," Red answered uncertainly, and Jake could almost picture him nodding his feathered head and gathering himself after that scare.

"Right, so give me a few minutes to take a look around. Maybe I'll find something useful." Knife in one hand, torch in the other, Jake returned warily to the skeleton's desk.

Though finding an exit was paramount, this chamber certainly seemed like it must have been Garnock's secret wizarding headquarters in life.

Jake figured if he had to be trapped in here, he might as well seize the chance to try to learn more about the sorcerer. Maybe he could even dig up a clue about how to defeat him.

He bent down and blew the thick layer of dust off the page of the skeleton-sorcerer's grimoire, which had been left open all these centuries.

"Blimey," Jake murmured as he held the torch up and saw what Garnock had been working on just before he died. The ancient grimoire was open to a page titled *'The Spell of a Hundred Souls.'*

Unfortunately, the instructions, the ingredients list for whatever potion was involved, and the details of the spell were written in Latin, so Jake had no idea what it said. It would have to wait for Archie to translate, but it might well yield the secret of what devilry the black fog fellow was up to right before he ran out of air.

Jake ripped *'The Spell of a Hundred Souls'* page out of the spell-book. Folding it up, he put it into his pocket, then scanned the dark lair one last time before he tackled the task of trying to find an exit. *Anything else important?*

Just then, a ghostly glimmer caught his eye, a bluish-white spirit orb in the black shadows.

Jake's eyebrows shot up. *Crikey! There's a ghost down here?*

He took a few steps toward the faintly glowing ball of spectral energy. "Hullo? Excuse me?"

Maybe it couldn't hear him. It just kept floating on its way. It never held still, continually skimming back and forth along the chamber walls, up and down, to and fro in all directions, as though it were searching for something.

Probably a way out, Jake thought with a chill down his spine. He wondered if the ghost had been trapped down here the whole time with Garnock.

"Er, pardon me, spirit, could I speak to you, please?"

Finally noticing him, it stopped abruptly on the far end of the chamber and spun in midair to face him, no doubt surprised.

Since the first question every ghost asked was always a shocked *"You can see me?"* he volunteered the answer.

"Yes, I can see you," he informed it. "I'm Jake."

He expected the orb to turn into a full-bodied apparition so that he could see who he was dealing with, like the other ghosts at the séance.

He would have guessed it was one of the miners coming back to brood over the place of his death.

But the orb did not reveal itself as an apparition. Instead, it zoomed straight over to him, and when he saw it up close, his eyes widened as he realized his mistake. The ball of light was not a spirit orb, technically speaking.

It was a head.

A ghost-head. A skull, actually, its jawbone working up and down like it was trying to talk, but couldn't.

Jake gulped. *Well, you don't see that every day,* he thought. Although the ghost-head was certainly startling, he wasn't exactly scared of it. He found it rather comical, actually, in a pitiful way, which was probably bad of him.

But at once, he had a strong suspicion of who this head belonged to.

He winced at the memory of the poor Headless Monk stumbling around the chapel ruins, searching all this time for his...

"You wouldn't happen to belong to Brother Colwyn, would you?"

Floating right before his eyes, the ghost-head nodded in excitement, bobbing in midair while its jaw worked as if to say, *I am! Have you seen my body?*

Or perhaps: *Help!*

Poor man. Isabelle must've been right, Jake thought. Only dark magic could have done this to the friar. Maybe Garnock had used an enchanted blade or something.

Whatever the case, Jake resolved to help him.

"Really sorry about what Garnock did to you," he mumbled. How awful for Brother Colwyn to have been stuck in the same tomb with his murderer all these years.

Jake shuddered on the Headless Monk's behalf, but he was puzzled. "Why didn't you leave when the others broke out of here? When the miners blew up the wall, I mean?"

The ghost-head nodded toward the wall of shelves, then swept toward it.

Jake followed, torch in hand, as he picked his way among the rubble of broken stone gargoyles.

Arriving at the shelves, he saw what Brother Colwyn wanted to show him—his actual skull. After murdering the monk, Garnock must have set his grisly trophy on display here all those centuries ago.

Now it was nothing but pearly white bone.

He stared at it for a long moment. "I see. Something about the spell he used to do this to you keeps you from straying too far from your actual skull."

The ghost-head nodded.

"So, er, we've got to bring your skull back to where the rest of your bones are buried? Does that sound about right?"

The head cocked sideways as if to say, *I think so.*

"All right, then." Jake grimaced in disgust, not at all eager to touch a real human skull, but he knew that, whatever happened, he was getting out of here.

If he left the gross thing behind, Brother Colwyn would never rest in peace as he deserved.

When Jake considered how the monk had helped the Lightriders—and paid such a terrible price for it—returning the head to the body was the least that he could do.

So Jake took off his scarf and draped it over the ancient skull, using the cloth to pick it up. He swaddled it in the fabric, then tied the ends into a sort of satchel so he could easily carry it over his shoulder.

"We'll have you back in one piece in no time," he assured the ghost-head. "Say, you wouldn't happen to know another way out of here, would you?"

The ghost-head went very still, staring at him for a moment. Jake wasn't sure if it was thinking or just hesitating. At last, it nodded slowly.

Jake immediately brightened. "Really? Excellent! Let's go, then! Oh, but hold on—I've got to tell my Gryphon first." He dashed off to give Red the good news. His loyal pet hadn't budged from the other side of the rock pile. "Hey, Red! Guess what?" he called. "Brother Colwyn's ghost-head is in here—"

"Becaw?"

"You know, the monk who helped the Lightriders? Never mind, long story. The important part is, he knows a way out of here. I'm not sure how long it'll take or where I might come out, but I'm going to follow him. So go back to Plas-y-Fforest and tell the others not to worry, I'm all right. I'll see 'em when I see 'em."

"Becaw!" Red said eagerly. "Caw!"

"Yes, I'll be careful," Jake assured him. "Thanks for staying with me, boy. We're leaving now. See you soon—hopefully." Then he turned to the ghost-head, which was hovering a short distance behind him. "Lead on, Brother Colwyn."

The ghost-head glided through the air to the far end of the chamber, where Jake only now noticed the opening into another room.

He lifted the torch and followed, carefully descending a few stone steps carved into the cave floor.

These led down into a smaller, darker chamber, which had been left in more of its natural cave condition. More giant quartz crystals grew out of the living rock in a range of unearthly hues.

But when the room's main feature came into view, Jake stopped in his tracks.

Straight ahead loomed a huge, ghastly skull statue carved into the cave wall. Its open mouth offered a treacherous-looking doorway.

Where it led to, he barely dared guess.

"What...is that?" he whispered under his breath, staring at the ominous portal.

The ghost-head floated toward it warily.

Again, Jake followed, but only so far, stopping in front of the open mouth. "Through there? Please, tell me you are joking."

The ghost-head swung back and forth. *No.*

Jake looked again at the yawning maw of the skull door, waiting to swallow him. "At least tell me what's in there." The ghost-head's jaw worked, but of course it couldn't speak. "Oh, right. You can't." Jake's heart sank. "At least tell me there won't be any more gargoyles?"

The ghost-head tilted to the side, apparently unable to promise this, either.

Jake closed his eyes. Unfortunately, he knew his options were few. Zero, to be exact.

Brother Colwyn had been stuck here because dark magic had tethered him to his physical skull, but if someone as intelligent as Garnock had not found a way out, then there mustn't be any other way.

Jake wondered vaguely why Garnock hadn't used this doorway to leave. Was something even worse waiting on the other side?

Brother Colwyn waited while Jake struggled to resign himself to what had to be done.

"I wish you could tell me what's in there."

The ghost-head motioned to him to hurry. No doubt the monk was eager to be back in one piece after all this time.

Jake stepped cautiously into the mouth of the huge, carved skull and studied the massive door before him. "Any idea how to open it?"

The ghost-head descended toward a smaller, pyramid-shaped crystal outside the carving's mouth. It was only about knee-high. Jake bent to examine it, cautiously touching the crystal.

After much trial and error, he eventually discovered that it actually worked as a lever. When he tilted it back, the door rose up into the skull carving, like a castle's portcullis being raised.

At once, a wave of heat and a foul sulfur stench blew out of the opening. Jake stood up slowly, staring without a single blink—and disbelieving his own eyes.

A fiery vista had opened up before him.

Emrys's tale of Garnock summoning demons to serve him rang like doom in Jake's ears.

Well. At least this solved the mystery of how—or rather, *where*—the alchemist would meet with his demon allies. Because through the portal, Jake found himself staring into the netherworld.

Hell was huge.

A black city with sinister towers clawed the red, smoky sky in the distance.

Farther off, countless volcanoes spewed flame and ash. Rivers of lava oozed across the landscape, glowing red.

Deep black canyons of despair cut through this unholy ground, crisscrossed here and there by treacherous, craggy footbridges.

Blasts of flame rose at odd intervals from the unseen depths of those gorges. It was an obstacle course fit for a condemned soul.

He blinked a few times, but the nightmarish realm did not disappear. Finally, Jake uttered a low, shocked curse, backing away from it and shaking his head dazedly. "I am not going in there. No, sir!" He followed Dani O'Dell's habit of making the sign of the cross as he backed away.

The ghost-head nodded eagerly and tried to coax him down the steps that led to an open space atop a cliff.

Jake narrowed his eyes when he saw the stone table near the cliff's edge. Table?

No, he realized with a chill in spite of the heat that had rushed out. It was an altar.

He swallowed hard, but he still couldn't understand why Garnock had not escaped through this doorway when the Lightriders sealed him in.

Then the answer came to him as he stared into the distance. Horrible demons as tall as giants were herding chain-gangs of the wicked dead to their eternal punishment. Didn't Emrys say that Garnock had promised his soul to a demon? Maybe he had regretted the deal once he was finally staring death in the face.

If the wizard had found some magical way to bring himself back eventually in some form—say, maybe as a black fog—then surely he would've done all in his power to avoid going down there and handing himself over to pay his debt, as promised.

Had Garnock cheated death and the devil? Was that how he had ended up as a black fog, suspended between life and death? *Hmm.* Archie's translation of the Spell of a Hundred Souls was sure to reveal more.

You're stalling, Jake told himself.

Meanwhile, the ghost-head was floating in the air a few yards ahead of him, staring out at the underworld, as though eager to get their trek over with.

"You're sure about this? There's no other way? You want me to sneak through—Hades?"

It bobbed emphatically.

"What if we get caught by one of those demons?"

It swung right to left in a negative fashion.

"What, you think they won't bother you just because you were a holy man? What about me? I was a thief!"

The ghost-head stared at him as if to say, *Trust me.*

Jake conceded that maybe after being dead for several centuries, Brother Colwyn probably knew a thing or two about the afterlife.

Still, his stomach flip-flopped with nauseated fear, though the sulfur stink might have had something to do with that.

Perhaps Brother Colwyn's being a man of the cloth *would* afford them some sort of divine protection down here, Jake thought. As for him, he *was* descended from Lightriders. That had to count for something.

He shifted his weight from foot to foot, torn with indecision. "Is it very far?"

The ghost-head tilted side to side. *Not really sure.*

This is madness, Jake thought, but at the end of the day, he didn't have much choice. "Fine! Let's go, then. Before I change my mind." Bracing himself, and already quite sure that he would regret this, he stepped over the threshold into the underworld and started marching down the hot stone stairs.

He cast a glance full of dread over his shoulder when he heard the portal bang shut behind him.

No turning back now.

The only way out...was *through.*

CHAPTER TWENTY-ONE

Through

And so, they set out.

Jake followed the floating ghost-head, hoping against hope that it knew where it was going. He could not tell how long anything took. There was no time in such a place. A minute, an hour, a thousand years—it was all the same.

He scrambled over wobbly, gnarled bridges that seemed too small and flimsy for the endless black canyons they spanned. They might as well have been made of rotting toothpicks.

Each spindly bridge rocked precariously in the hot, smoky, sulfur winds of the netherworld that blew so strong over those yawning gulfs. Jake looked over the bridge's side in wide-eyed terror. What lurked at the bottom of these pits, he did not want to know.

Every now and then he could just make out the hideous shapes of huge chained things in the darkness that had been there, groaning in pain—but still hardened by the same hatred and rebellion—that had landed them there after the original war in heaven.

When Jake cleared the other side of the canyon, he looked around and could have sworn that he had just ended up somehow, diabolically, back in the exact same spot from which he had started out.

He nearly panicked, but thankfully soon realized this was just one of the underworld's illusions, and somehow, Brother Colwyn was able to steer him through.

The floating ghost-head bobbed along before him like a beacon; Jake focused on it against swirling confusion that was increasingly building in his mind, along with a sense of lost desperation.

The very air down here was like a poison gas that messed with his mind. By turns, he wanted to scream in rage or sit down and bawl his eyes out for no apparent reason.

It was a terrible place that played terrible tricks on a person. But that was the whole point, he supposed.

Yet every time he heard one of those distant devils let out a sinister belly-laugh at the horrified screams and suffering of all his new arrivals, he nearly jumped out of his skin.

Jake shuddered. Any thought of ever stealing anything from anyone again melted in the river of lava he had to cross next.

He hopped from shifting stone to stone, sweating profusely in the impossible heat. It rose in shimmering waves from the fiery flows, making him feel as if he were one of the dwarves' gold bars, thrust into the furnace to have the impurities burned out of him.

How he ever made it to the other side, he'd never know.

Brother Colwyn's head waited patiently, letting him catch his breath when he reached the jagged black cinder beach of the far shore.

"What's next?" he panted, his lips parched and cracking.

His heart sank as the ghost-head indicated the mountain before him.

The way up was liberally sprinkled with broken glass.

The master of this place had really thought of everything.

Jake sighed, then wiped the sweat off his brow with a pass of his forearm. "How much farther?"

He wasn't sure how much more of this he could take.

The ghost-head glided ahead and back several times, urging him to look upward. He did. Way, way up at the top of the mountain, Jake saw a small door plunked up against the red sky.

He furrowed his brow. *That's odd.* On second thought, why expect anything logical, under the circumstances?

And for that matter, maybe Garnock wasn't so smart, after all. What sort of nitwit made bargains with the lord of the underworld? No wonder he had preferred to put that Spell of a Hundred Souls on himself to try to cheat death.

Better to be trapped for centuries in an underground chamber and end up as a black fog—anything to avoid being sent down here.

Not that Jake felt sorry for Garnock after what he had done to

Brother Colwyn. The wizard had made his choice long ago and would not be able to escape his just desserts forever.

Bracing himself for the last leg of his journey, straight up a barren mountain without a tree or shrub in sight, Jake nodded to Brother Colwyn's head. "Ready."

The climb was steep and tedious and awful. Any stumble meant a shard of glass in the knee or the hand, and the scent of blood lured nasty half-crab, half-spider creatures that lived among the rocks.

Again and again, Jake had to kick them away or use his telekinesis to zap them off. Meanwhile, the dizzying illusions of this place made him swear that either the path stretched ever longer as he climbed it or the mountain itself grew.

Every time he thought he was halfway up, he found he had the same distance still to go. The frustration almost made him give up. He would never get there.

Somehow he found the strength to press on, and then the mountain got even weirder.

The path looped so that at one point, he was actually crawling upside down on his hands and knees. Apparently gravity had no more sway down here than linear time.

When he slipped and fell back down the trail about ten feet, cutting his hands again and slicing open his shin, he came to the point where he simply couldn't do it anymore. He put his head down on his arm and gave way to tears of futile fury and absolute despair. *I'm going to be stuck down here forever. What's the point?*

The ghost-head floated back to him and worked its jaws, as though to give him a bracing pep talk. "Go away! It's no use! I can't do it!"

The head zoomed around him, backing off the spider-crabs.

It dawned on Jake that they were probably scavengers that would pick his bones clean the moment they determined that he had given up, or was either dead or too weak to fight.

Ugh! Well, they weren't gargoyles, but the renewed threat of being eaten was enough, finally, to make Jake get a hold of himself and shake off his despair.

He gritted his teeth, narrowed his eyes, and ignored the cuts and bruises and burns all over his body, and vowed that he was getting out of here. With a rush of determination, he got up one last time and kept climbing. *You're not keeping me here, devil.*

All of a sudden, the sound of vicious barking filled the air. The ghost-head spun toward it in alarm.

Clinging to the side of the mountain, Jake looked over his shoulder and promptly had to stifle a scream.

Whatever demon was on security duty must have realized someone was trespassing and had loosed a pack of huge, monstrous dogs to hunt them down.

Hellhounds? Whatever they were, they made the gargoyles look like sweet little kittens, and with the way they came racing over the landscape toward him, they'd be upon him soon.

Instantly, Jake redoubled his efforts, rattling off a few silent prayers as he scrambled up the rest of the path as fast as humanly possible.

Somehow he made it to the top.

But now he had to jump up and catch hold of the bottom of the doorway so he could pull himself up and go through it. He tried a few times with no success as the barking grew louder. The hellhounds were at the bottom of the mountain. Jake swallowed hard and tried again.

His legs were so wobbly and weak after that climbing that he stumbled and nearly fell back down the path. He caught himself mid-tumble, but his hands were bleeding from the sharp rocks and broken glass.

As he lifted his gaze, half ready to give up, he wondered if putting an exit door right here—almost in reach, but not quite—was just another torture.

Please help me.

With every last ounce of his strength, Jake found the will to get up one more time. He rose to his feet, walked up the slope to the top again, and jumped with everything he had left, catching hold of the bottom of the doorway.

His heart pounding, he climbed up precariously, bracing one foot on the threshold while his free hand flailed for the doorknob.

With a sense of victory, he grasped hold of it and turned it.

Miraculously, the door opened; the ghost-head zoomed through while Jake threw himself over the threshold.

Behind him, the devil-dogs were racing easily up the mountain path. Jake glanced back at them in terror, then slammed the door on that terrible realm.

In the place they had come to, it was pitch-dark.

He could still hear the monster-dogs howling on the other side of the door. They rather reminded him of the Fire Wolf from his last adventure.

His heart still pounded with lingering terror. *Where am I?* "Brother Colwyn?" he whispered. "Are you here?"

The ghost-head gave off just enough of an astral glow to let Jake see the small, cramped proportions of the room he was standing in.

It was only the size of a shed, but, oh, the smell was horrible. As his eyes began adjusting to the darkness, he sensed hollow alcoves or shelves or something on the sides of the walls.

Gooseflesh rose on his arms. *The smell of death.*

"How do we get out of here?" Jake's anxious question came out muffled as he used his sleeve to shield his nose and mouth from the tainted air.

Brother Colwyn showed him. The pale glow of the ghost-head led him a few steps forward to a thick door. Out of patience and fighting panic, Jake blasted it open with his telekinesis and pushed his way out blindly, gagging from the rotting-body smell and gasping for air.

He came stumbling out of an elegant white marble mausoleum in the cemetery across from the Harris Mine School.

The ghosts socializing in the graveyard before dawn screamed and fled from him, flying off in all directions.

"Who is that?"

"No idea!"

"Is he dead or alive?"

"I-I can't tell!"

After his trek through the underworld, Jake wasn't sure himself.

He rushed down the few front steps of the small, stately white building and halted; pulling for air, he leaned forward, resting his hands on his knees.

The ghosts warily ventured closer.

"Isn't that the boy from the séance?"

"Lord Griffon? Yes! He's the one everyone's talking about!"

"Sorry, everyone," Jake said in a shaky tone. "Didn't mean to scare you."

"Young man, what were you doing in there?" a matronly ghost demanded.

"Uh, just passing through, ma'am."

The ghosts stared at him in bewilderment.

When he had finally caught his breath, Jake straightened up and turned, looking around to try to get his bearings.

Sunrise was only just beginning to glimmer in the east.

To the south was the very intersection where he and his friends had waited for the funeral procession to pass, just a few days ago.

It felt like a lifetime since then.

Then he stared across the road at the prison-like school on the opposite hilltop, behind its bristling wall of wrought-iron fences.

As the first pinkish-gold rays of sunrise reached over the horizon and fingered the turrets of the ominous brick building, Jake knew his enemy was in there, lurking in the shadows. Feeding on the children.

But not for long, he vowed.

One way or the other, he would make sure that Garnock got exactly what he deserved.

And soon.

PART V

CHAPTER TWENTY-TWO
A Hero's Welcome

J ake, exhausted, shuffled out of the cemetery like the walking dead, while the ghost-head zoomed off alone.

Freed at last from the cursed tomb, it hurried off to tell its ghost-body the good news that they'd soon be reunited.

Jake still had Brother Colwyn's lost skull safely wrapped in the makeshift knapsack of his scarf, slung across his shoulder.

As the ghost-head disappeared down the road, Jake didn't really mind being left alone for the last leg of his journey. After all, Brother Colwyn had seen him through the hard part—that horrible shortcut through the devil's kingdom. Of course, bad as it was, Jake was still glad he had seen the place firsthand and now knew that all that scary stuff was real. One wanted to know such things.

It made a difference in how one lived. Indeed, logic would suggest that those who snapped their fingers at Hades and called it stuff and nonsense did nothing but increase their own odds of ending up there.

Anyway, crossing Hades was still better than being trapped in the mine. Jake was sure he'd have either run out of air or light by now. Not a happy prospect. The thought of losing either of these essentials made him enjoy the beauty of the morning, with its fresh air and birdsong, all the more, even though more walking was the last thing he wanted to do right now.

As he dragged himself down the dusty road with slow, shuffling steps, he would've given a large portion of his gold for a horse or carriage or even a friendly gryphon to give him a ride.

Ah, well.

At last, the entrance to his property came into view. *Wonder if*

Aunt Ramona has written back yet, he thought as he stepped over the invisible magic threshold that bounded Plas-y-Fforest. Maybe he should try contacting her again or even asking her to come, since a battle with Garnock now seemed imminent.

But she's just so very old, he thought with a frown. He couldn't help wanting to protect her.

Powerful as she supposedly was, Jake hated to drag a three-hundred-year-old witch into danger. Surely her battling days were done. She didn't even like using magic anymore for the most part. Too many unpredictable side effects.

As he was mulling the question, a flicker of movement in the branches above drew his eye. *Pixies.* The wee forest folk were watching him again. They looked quite fascinated. He had no idea why. But he certainly remembered King Furze's warning that the next time he crossed a pixie's path, he had better show respect.

Though he was the lord of Plas-y-Fforest, Jake gave them a cordial nod and went on his weary way up the steep, wooded drive. He had no sooner reached the top, where the cottage came into view, when he heard a familiar voice yelling: "Everyone, I see him! He's coming up the drive! Hurry, everybody! Jake! You're alive!"

Jake spotted Archie on the roof watching for him through his telescope. He waved back, smiling; his cousin was practically jumping up and down with excitement.

The next thing he knew, everyone came flooding out of the house and rushed over, surrounding him with quite the hero's welcome.

"We thought you were dead!" Dani cried.

"I knew you weren't," Archie said.

Jake drew in his breath to see Derek and Miss Helena safe and sound. He was so overjoyed that he actually ran and hugged them. Then everyone hugged him. The girls were crying with relief to have him back. Archie was glued to his side. Amid the hugs and tears and handshakes, licks (from Teddy) and nuzzles (from a purring Red), however, the Guardian was none too happy with him for going off with Red to clear the gargoyles from the mine.

"I couldn't help it after I saw them nearly kill you, Derek," he said. "How could I let them go, right when we finally had them on the run?"

The warrior frowned, but mostly he was pleased that Jake had come back in one piece. "Well," he said in a brusque tone, "you'll have to apologize to Emrys. He thought you were following the group the whole time. Poor fellow nearly had an apoplectic fit when he realized you weren't there. He thought one of the gargoyles ate you. He was ready to tear the whole mine apart."

"I'm just glad the dwarves were able to rescue you like they promised. I take it you two were all right?"

"We got washed out into a lower cavern about a hundred yards downstream."

"Poor Miss Helena got dashed against the rocks and broke her leg in the fall," Dani reported. "Thankfully Master Emrys had an extra one of Red's magic feathers. After Red came back to us, he told Isabelle how you killed the gargoyles but were stuck inside the sorcerer's tomb. Then Isabelle told us."

"Red said you were confident you could find another way out," Archie chimed in.

"And he did," Isabelle finished with a sniffle.

"How? A tunnel or something?" Dani asked.

"Something like that." Jake wasn't ready to talk about his stroll through the underworld quite yet. First things first. He was a little choked up by their outpouring of concern for him. He cleared his throat, trying to stick to business. "I found some things of interest in the tomb. Here." He pulled the folded page from Garnock's grimoire out of his pocket. "Archie, can you translate this? I think it's Latin. Be careful, though, it's a magic spell. Don't speak the words aloud. No telling what could happen if you do. I'm fairly sure this was what Garnock was working on right before he died. It may give us a clue about his next move."

Archie took the paper from him, glancing over it with a nod. "Shouldn't take long."

"What's in there?" Dani pointed at his makeshift satchel.

"Oh," Jake said, "I found the Headless Monk's head."

She jumped back, aghast. "You've got a *head* in there?"

He laughed. "Don't worry, it's just an old skull. High time poor Brother Colwyn got his noggin back. Then he can finally rest in peace. I'm going up to the chapel ruins as soon as we're done here."

"Well, I'm going with you!" Dani declared.

"Me, too!" said Archie.

"Me, three," Isabelle added.

Derek gave Jake's shoulder a brotherly squeeze. "As you can see, this lot won't be letting you out of their sight any time soon."

"I only have one question," Dani said in a thoughtful tone, staring at the top of Jake's head. "What happened to your hair?"

"Huh?" He touched his hair self-consciously. Had he singed it off crossing the river of lava?

"You look like that pixie, little what's-his-name. Wake-robin."

"What?" Jake cried in alarm. "Oh, no!" He ran inside to find the nearest mirror, with Teddy chasing at his heels.

A moment later in the parlor, he leaned closer to the looking glass, studying his reflection in dismay. Thankfully, not all of his hair had turned white like the pixie's—just a streak of it at his left temple, curling back around his ear.

"Great, now I even look like a freak," he mumbled.

"I think you look very distinguished," Archie declared, folding his arms over his chest.

This from a lad who insisted on wearing a bowtie most days. Jake just looked at him.

"I don't suppose anyone's hungry?" Snowdrop Fingle asked from the doorway to the kitchen.

Jake shot his hand up. "Me!"

The house brownie beamed. "Oh, goody! I thought you might be after all that, my lord." She whirled off, mumbling to herself about preparing "a wee snack" for them, which to Snowdrop usually meant a celebratory feast.

"Go on now, wash up," Miss Helena urged, rumpling his white-streaked hair. Jake dashed off to do as she said.

It was awfully good to be back.

Mrs. Fingle did not disappoint. The celebratory meal was grandly begun with partridge stew flavored with bits of bacon and lots of button mushrooms, as well as a Toad in the Hole of juicy mutton chunks baked in batter.

Everyone had a merry time at table, passing around the bread and then the butter, talking nonstop, on through to the final course, a baked apple pudding.

Jake described the gargoyles and told how the dwarves had

joked the whole way through the mine.

At length, Derek and Miss Helena stepped out for a walk in the garden, after which came a great deal of giggling from Dani O'Dell.

She reported in hushed tones that she had personally seen the governess give Derek a kiss on the cheek for saving her life down in the mine.

"Ew," Jake said. "As a lady or a leopard?"

"A lady, you nit!"

Took her long enough, Jake thought in satisfaction, pleased for his warrior friend. Derek had liked the shapeshifting lady for a very long time.

Dani prattled on in her lively, nonsensical way while Jake munched happily on everything in sight, only half listening. He took a second helping of the pudding, just happy to be back.

The festive mood darkened, however, when Archie returned with the full translation of the Spell of a Hundred Souls.

"All right," he said. "Let me put it this way. This spell lets you put yourself into a state where you're not technically dead, but you're not fully alive, either. It's a way of cheating death...sort of like a legal loophole."

"How's that?" Dani asked.

"It allows you to magically separate your spirit from your body. You can then store your soul in some inanimate object for an indeterminate length of time, to be brought back later."

"What sort of object?" Jake recalled something the miner ghost, Barney, had said at the séance about a glowing ring. "Would a sorcerer's ring work?"

Archie nodded. "I should think so, but it doesn't really matter now. Garnock has obviously left whatever object he had stored himself in for those five hundred years that he was stuck down there. His main challenge now, according to this, is to reconstitute his body. In order to do that, he's got to drink from the life-force of a hundred different beings. That's why it's called the Spell of a Hundred Souls."

"So, that's why he's going around sucking the life out of everybody," Jake murmured.

Archie nodded. "I have no idea *how* he does it, of course. You'd know better than I, since you actually experienced it. Once he's reached his quota, he'll be back to his full strength. Except for, ah, one final step in the spell that's, um, well, a bit worrisome."

Jake paused with his fork halfway to his mouth. "What's the final step?"

"After he feeds on ninety-nine people's souls, he has to seal the deal, as it were, by feeding on the soul of, um..." Archie hesitated, glancing at his sister. "A unicorn."

"*What?*" Isabelle swept to her feet, the color draining from her face. "Over my dead body," she declared, then ran out of the room.

"Isabelle?" Dani jumped up and ran after her. "Isabelle, where are you going?"

Jake and Archie exchanged a grim glance.

"How can Garnock get anywhere near a unicorn?" Jake asked in the ponderous silence. "You and I can't even go near them, and this sorcerer's pure evil."

Archie shrugged. "If Garnock's not in corporeal form when he approaches them...how will they even know he's there? I mean, unicorns are like any herd animal. They rely on sharp senses and their instincts to flee from danger. But if he's just a dark spirit, a black fog, they won't be able to hear him coming, or smell him, or see him..."

"They won't know to run away," Jake murmured, a cold shadow of premonition passing over his heart.

Just then, Isabelle ran past the doorway with the ivory Keeper's Staff in her hands. She must have gone to the Archive, Jake thought. She disappeared just as quickly, going past the doorway and pounding up the stairs, a girl on a mission.

"Where's she going?" Jake called to Dani, who followed the older girl just a few steps behind.

Dani came back and leaned in the doorway. "We're going to stand watch over the herd."

"No, you're not, don't be daft," Jake replied. "It's too dangerous."

To which Dani gave him a withering look.

She dashed upstairs without waiting around to argue, apparently off to change into her boots and warmer clothes for traipsing around in the woods.

Her silence spoke volumes. It told Jake she would not be dissuaded. When she argued over something, at least she would listen to his opinion. Unfortunately, he knew her well enough to understand that in some situations, Dani would do what Dani wanted to do.

Archie sent him a worried look. "Jake, this sounds really dangerous. If Garnock means to go after the unicorns, I don't want my sister caught in the middle of this."

"I don't think the girls are asking our opinion, coz. Isabelle's a Keeper. It's her calling. And the carrot-head is obviously determined to assist her."

"Well, I don't like it one bit," Archie said, ever the chivalrous English gentleman.

"Neither do I. But you know those two. I doubt they're going to let anyone stand in their way. The most we can do is try to keep them safe. If they mean to go out into the forest, maybe we can talk them into walking up to the chapel ruins with us first. I have a little something to return to Brother Colwyn."

"At least that would get us out there with them," Archie mumbled with a worried frown. "I'd better go tell Guardian Stone and Miss Helena about this."

Jake nodded and wiped his mouth with his napkin, then he rose from the table and gave the house brownie a grateful smile. "Everything was delicious as usual, Mrs. Fingle. Now then! Where the deuce did I leave that head?"

CHAPTER TWENTY-THREE
Reunited

S ome time later that afternoon, they gathered around Brother Colwyn's tomb inside the ruined chapel.

Everyone was there. The girls had agreed to walk up with them before leaving to go and watch over the unicorn herd. Red had come along, as had Derek and Miss Helena, since those two had not yet seen the chapel ruins with the tomb of Sir Reginald.

The girls stood back while Derek and Archie used crowbars to loosen the seal around the heavy marble lid carved with the statue of the dead man inside.

Then Jake lifted it off the ancient stone sarcophagus using his telekinesis. With keen concentration, he levitated it to the side, then floated it down gently to the ground.

Letting out a low "whew" that he had not dropped it, he stepped closer and braced himself to have a look inside.

The others did the same; Dani grimaced.

Inside the coffin lay a headless skeleton draped in the tattered remnants of a simple ancient tunic, its bony arms wrapped around an illuminated manuscript.

Everyone was silent as Jake took the poor, murdered friar's skull out of his makeshift satchel.

"This feels a little sacrilegious," Archie remarked.

"We're only doing it to help him," Jake said. Flicking a spot of dirt off the surface of the skull, he reached down into the sarcophagus and put it back reverently where it belonged.

He had no sooner set the skull back in its rightful place when a dazzling beam of light suddenly blasted straight up from the coffin and filled the space.

Everyone stepped back, gasping and shading their eyes. The brilliance grew until all of them were squinting and trying to shield their eyes with their hands.

Suddenly, a disembodied voice came out of the air. "All of you, join hands. *Join hands!*" it repeated when they just stood there in astonishment.

They looked around at each other in confusion, then obeyed. Even the Gryphon joined the circle, with Miss Helena and Archie on either side of him, each resting a hand on his tawny withers.

"Now, *look*," said the disembodied voice.

The dazzling light beaming up out of the coffin expanded in a circular wave all around them; as it spread out, fading to a more tolerable level of brightness, it surrounded them with a breathtaking vision of the church and monastery as they had been in their heyday, when Brother Colwyn would have lived and worked here.

They stared in wonder, craning their necks to look this way and that at the towering sanctuary in all its glory, with the sunlight streaming through the stained-glass windows, plainchant hymns wafting out from the choir loft.

"It's beautiful!" Dani exclaimed.

"How are we seeing this?" Archie cried.

"He must be channeling the vision to the rest of us through Jake and Isabelle's psychic abilities!" Miss Helena replied.

"Who?" Dani asked.

"Brother Colwyn," Isabelle said, smiling at a spot behind Jake's shoulder, where the glowing spirit of the now re-headed friar stood, beaming.

"Welcome, friends," said Brother Colwyn, a humble, rather chubby man in a long white tunic with the oddly shaved tonsure haircut particular to monks.

They gazed at the smiling apparition in amazement.

"It's so good to be able to see you all—and oh, thank you, Lord Griffon! It's been centuries since I could talk! I owe you more than you can possibly know. Thank you for restoring what was stolen from me."

"Well, thank you for getting me out of that horrible tomb," Jake answered with a modest blush.

The smiling friar-ghost nodded. "Likewise! Now then, I don't know how long I will be able to sustain this vision before Celestus comes for me—"

"Dr. Celestus?" Dani cried, glancing up at the last remaining stained-glass window depicting the angel.

Nodding, Brother Colwyn hastily continued: "So, please, listen well. There's something very important I have to show you. Take that book out of my coffin. Open it, please. And hurry."

Derek left the circle to fetch it; the others quickly joined hands again. The ghost hovered nearby as Derek pried the massive leather-bound tome out of the skeleton's bony arms, then lifted it out of the coffin.

Brother Colwyn floated over to it. "Ah, my dear old book! It was practically my life's work."

When Derek opened the book, the spirit made the pages flutter rapidly, finally arriving at one particular passage near the back.

There were still more blank pages after that, but this was as far as the friar had got during his lifetime.

Brother Colwyn sighed, gazing sadly at the final page of his manuscript. "This was the last thing I was able to jot down before Garnock came for his revenge. I was lucky I managed to hide it from him in time." He paused and glanced at Jake. "You do know by now you are dealing with Garnock the Sorcerer?"

Jake nodded.

"This is the spell the Lightriders used to bind him inside his workshop so long ago. Use it well. If he completes the Spell of a Hundred Souls and then takes his place as the head of the Dark Druids, he'll free the demons under his command—and this time, there'll be no stopping him."

Jake nodded in grim resolve. "We had better go after him as soon as possible. The way he's been feeding on those children at the school, he must be close to meeting his quota of a hundred souls by now. At least now we know where to find him. But I'm going to need some reinforcements."

"You know you've got me," Derek said at once.

"And me," Archie chimed in.

"Becaw!" Red agreed.

Miss Helena glanced at the girls. "We'll watch over the unicorns. Last line of defense. If Garnock gets past you somehow and makes it to the final step of his dreadful spell, we won't let him anywhere near the herd."

"It's dangerous," Archie protested.

"Brother, this is bigger than all of us," Isabelle said softly.

Jake nodded, encouraged by all their offers of help, even though, deep down, he already suspected that it was going to come down to that hideous wraith and him. "Thanks, everybody. But there's just one problem. He's a spirit—at least for now—and none of you is a psychic. So, anyone fancy a trip into town? There's somebody there I need to go and see."

"I knew you had the gift." Madam Sylvia fixed Jake with a piercing stare as they stood in her charm-and-crystal shop. "Why did you try to hide it when you were here last?"

"I had to make sure you weren't a fraud," he admitted.

She humphed. "A skeptic. Well, I suppose that is understandable. But tell me." Her dark eyes narrowed. "What happened that night? What was all the screaming?"

Jake shuddered at the memory. "That's actually what I'm here to see you about." Then he told her everything about Garnock the Sorcerer.

She clearly didn't like what she heard. She pondered the information—and his perilous request—in silence for a long moment.

"Let me see if I've got this right. You sat here and watched this wraith, this Garnock fellow, tearing through my spirit guests, and you never said a word?"

"Madam Sylvia, please," Derek said, "he's only twelve."

"People like us have a responsibility!" She gestured at Jake in annoyance. "If we don't help the spirits, who else can? Oh, I knew something had shaken you up, the way you ran right out of here that night with your tail between your legs. Apparently you were more worried about saving your own skin than trying to help those ghosts. So why should I trust you now?"

"Because now I know what I'm dealing with!" Jake cried, red-cheeked with embarrassment at her blunt words. "It was extremely upsetting, ma'am. If you could have seen him! Besides, what point was there in telling you what had happened to those ghosts when there was nothing you could have done about it?

"Honestly, be glad you couldn't see it," he continued. "It was horrible to watch. If you must know, I was terrified. But I kept my mouth shut because I didn't know what the wraith could do to me if he realized I could see him. Bad enough he tried to feed on me! And right now, at this very moment, he's up there at the Harris Mine School, feeding on the poor children. Please, won't you help?

"We have to stop him before he completes the Spell of a Hundred Souls and comes back properly to life. I can't do it alone. I've got my team assembled and they're armed as best they can be for this, but Garnock is still in spirit form. I need another psychic on hand in case he tries anything."

Madam Sylvia frowned.

"I realize what I'm asking of you must sound mad," Jake said. "I wouldn't bother you if I could get a hold of my aunt. She's a very powerful witch, but she isn't answering my messages—which worries me enough in itself, considering her age."

"Better not let Her Ladyship hear you say that," Derek muttered under his breath.

"She'll turn you into a frog," Archie jested, trying to ward off the tension. "Temporarily, of course."

"I just hope she's all right," Jake said.

He had given up on the Inkbug and ordered Nimbus off to the telegraph office in town to send a regular sort of telegram to the baroness. *Somebody* had to be at home at Bradford Park, if only the butler.

Jake couldn't imagine what was keeping the Elder witch from writing back, and he really didn't need anything extra to worry about right now, like her health.

Provided she was all right, he just hoped she wasn't angry about his mentioning magical matters in the dispatch. He'd really had no choice.

He turned his attention back to Madam Sylvia. "Obviously, what I'm asking of you is dangerous. I know that, and I'm sorry. I also realize you'll be at a distinct disadvantage, since you can only hear the spirits, not see them.

"If Garnock keeps quiet, you won't be able to tell where he is; but I'll warn you if he comes anywhere near you." He glanced at Derek and Archie. "That goes for you two, as well. You've all got to trust me." He turned back to the local medium. "I know we can do this. Brother Colwyn gave us the spell the Lightriders used before to bind Garnock's power. It worked once. If we all say it together, we should be able to do it again."

"Hmm," she said, narrowing her eyes.

"So what do you think, ma'am? Are you willing to help us?"

"I'll have to check my schedule. When did you want to do it?"

"Er, now?" Jake answered, startled.

"The sooner the better, I'm afraid," Derek said.

"Like before we lose our nerve," Archie mumbled.

Jake cast the boy genius a rueful half-smile.

Archie already had the Phantom Fetcher slung across his back like a hunting rifle, and a Spirit Box to go with it, though Jake doubted the container was strong enough to hold the likes of Garnock the Sorcerer.

Derek was armed as usual—not that his Bowie knives and pistols were going to be much use against a wraith. No doubt, carrying them at least made him feel better about the battle ahead.

The girls had stayed back at Plas-y-Fforest to keep watch over the unicorns with Miss Helena, but Jake did not intend to let Garnock get that far in the Spell of a Hundred Souls.

Much better to stop him well before he got to number ninety-eight or ninety-nine; for once he had fed on the life-force of a unicorn, there was no telling what sort of effect that might have upon his abilities.

Unicorns had many potent and mysterious magical properties. Garnock was evil, but if he could somehow assimilate some of their spirit into his being, it might make him all the stronger.

But as for Jake, privately, even more than he wanted to keep Garnock away from the unicorns, he wanted him nowhere near the girls.

"Humph." Madam Sylvia let out a snort, still regarding him with a cynical stare. "Very well. Let me get my things. I have a few items here that should prove useful."

Jake and Archie exchanged a discreet look of relief while the plump little psychic bustled off and started sorting through the shelves of her shop. She tossed crystals and herb-laced candles of various sorts into a parti-colored cloth bag. "Out of sage," she mumbled to herself, then glanced at them. "I have more in the back. Wait here. Sage is highly effective in helping to clear any building of evil spirits—"

Her words broke off abruptly as a spectral scream echoed from somewhere outside.

"*HELLLLP!* Help, please!"

Jake looked out the window and glimpsed an orb speeding over the roofs of the shops across the streets, leaving a faint trail of ectoplasm streaming out behind it.

Madam Sylvia rushed back and glanced around, able to hear the voice, but unable to see the screamer. "What—who—was that?"

"I don't know, an orb—"

Suddenly—*whoosh!*—down it came through the ceiling.

"Madam Sylvia! Oh, Lord Griffon! Thank goodness you are both here!"

Jake's eyes widened as the orb turned itself into Professor Sackville. The headmaster ghost materialized suddenly, right there in the shop's middle aisle.

"Please, you must come quickly!"

"What's the matter?" Jake asked in alarm.

"Who's there?" the medium called.

"It's Dr. Sackville," Jake told her. "The old headmaster from the Harris Mine School."

"He's here?" Archie asked in wonder. "Why?"

"I think he needs help. Sir, what's wrong?"

"It's not me, it's the children! Hurry, please!" the old ghost said frantically. "You must come! It's Garnock. He's attacking all the children! It's like a feeding frenzy!" Old Sack cried. "He's draining the students to within inches of their lives! Please, you must hurry!"

"We'll be right there," Jake assured him.

"What's happening?" Derek asked quickly, since neither he nor Archie had the psychic gift.

"We need to go," Jake answered.

"Let me get my sage." Madam Sylvia ran into the back, while Derek turned to him for an explanation.

"Garnock must have heard about our foray into the mine. I think he figured out we killed his gargoyles. He must know we're coming for him next. Sounds like he's scrambling to reach his full strength before he has to face us."

"So he knows we're coming," Archie said with a grim, meaningful glance from Jake to Derek.

The Guardian nodded. "Jake was right. We'd better strike fast before he's back to his old self. We stopped the gargoyles, but lost the element of surprise."

Old Sack stood by fretting as Madam Sylvia returned with the sage.

With her colorful cloth bag full of magical equipment over her shoulder, she shooed them out, then flipped the sign in her shop window to *Closed*.

As soon as she locked the front door, they hurried to the carriage.

But when Derek opened the door for the lady and started to hand her up, Madam Sylvia suddenly screamed and recoiled in shock. "What is *that?*"

Jake rushed over to her side. "Oh, sorry! I forgot to tell you about my Gryphon. It's all right, he's friendly."

"A-a gryphon?" she cried.

"His name's Red. Really, he won't bite you."

"B-b-but..."

The Gryphon blinked innocently, as if to say, *What's wrong with her?*

Unfortunately, Jake had forgotten that he had left the beast hiding in the carriage while they had gone into the shop. "Trust me, he's a really good ally to have when you're going into battle."

Which it seemed they suddenly were.

The old woman looked at Jake in astonishment, but gave no further protest. When they had all climbed into the carriage, however, Madam Sylvia stared at Red in trepidation the whole way out to the school.

CHAPTER TWENTY-FOUR
Harsh Lessons

Under dismal gray skies, the Harris Mine School loomed ahead as they turned in at the drive, passing through the tall wrought-iron gates. The spiky trees were bare and the whole place seemed bleaker than ever as a biting wind rasped across the bald face of the hill.

When they pulled up in front of the school's entrance, Derek slowed the carriage to a halt. Everyone warily got out, except for Red; Jake ordered him to stay in the coach for now. The Gryphon growled unhappily at this command, but Jake would only call him in as a last resort.

Having the creature seen by countless schoolchildren and their teachers would only complicate *all* their lives.

Archie shrugged the Phantom Fetcher over his shoulder. Derek touched the scabbards of his knives on each hip in a habitual gesture, armed and ready. Madam Sylvia pulled her colorful cloth bag full of charms and crystals higher up onto her shoulder.

Jake tucked another yew wood wand from the Archive into his back pocket, along with a folded-up copy of the Lightriders' previous spell for vanquishing Garnock. Then he turned to his companions. "Everyone ready?"

They nodded, then they all walked up bravely onto the school's shadowy stone porch.

Derek banged on the door with his fist.

No one answered.

His chest tight, pulse pounding, Jake glanced nervously over his shoulder and saw Red peeking out the carriage window, watching the proceedings.

That was when he noticed an orb streaking toward them over the hill. In the next moment, Old Sack reappeared on the porch beside them.

"Hurry," he said anxiously, "you might as well go in. Nobody's going to answer the door. They can't. That's what I was trying to tell you."

"The headmaster's here. He says we should just go in." Jake brushed Derek aside and seized hold of the doorknob himself, then frowned. "Locked."

The warrior shrugged, stepped back, then lunged forward, kicking it open.

When it had blasted back with a bang, they walked into the gloomy foyer, everyone on guard, looking around in all directions. The four classroom doors that led off the foyer were closed. Since there were four rooms and four of them, they separated to look in through the classroom windows.

Before Jake had even reached his door, Derek let out a curse and rushed into the room he was checking. The others followed— and gasped. The children were littered around the classroom, some half-conscious at their desks. Others had collapsed on the floor.

"What's he done to them?" Archie cried.

"Blimey," Jake breathed.

"It's as I told you," Old Sack replied, nervously following. "Garnock's been draining the life out of them!"

"Dr. Sackville was right. It *was* a feeding frenzy," Madam Sylvia murmured. "This is almost as bad as the séance. Are they dead?"

At once, Derek and Archie hurried down the aisles between the desks, checking all the kids.

"Alive," Derek reported.

"This one, too," Archie said.

As warriors, all Guardians were trained in battlefield medicine to help the wounded, while Archie had sat in on some medical courses at Oxford. Madam Sylvia also knew about healing, though her specialty was in apothecary herbs.

With their various training, all three got to work helping the victims. While they raced from one listless, inert kid to the next, checking their pulses and trying to revive them, Jake restrained his rage over Garnock doing this to them and carefully scanned the classroom.

As the only one who could actually see spirits, he alone was able to confirm that Garnock wasn't still in the room.

He wasn't. Obviously, the warlock's work here was already done. Jake strode out to check the other classrooms and found the students in the same condition, but there was still no sign of Garnock.

As he hurried back to tell the others that the kids in the other rooms needed attention, too, another, even more ominous question suddenly occurred to him.

Where are all the teachers?

They would have tried to help their students, surely, and Garnock wouldn't have liked that.

Jake rushed over to one of the older boys—he looked familiar. Yes, one of the stronger lads who had been assigned to help them carry in the presents.

Jake figured that the older, larger boy would have weathered Garnock's attack better than the littler ones. He pulled the woozy kid upright at his desk, then started slapping him lightly on the cheek. "Hey, wake up. What happened here?"

"Huh? Please let me sleep. So tired..."

He shook him. "Where's your teacher?"

But he had no sooner spoken the question than a muffled *"Help!"* came from somewhere nearby.

Jake glanced around. His eyes widened.

He had been so appalled by the condition of the students that he only just now noticed signs of a struggle up at the front of the classroom.

All the bookcases had been knocked down.

A mountain of books had fallen off the shelves, and Jake had a feeling the teacher was buried under them. He released the groggy boy. His head thunked back down onto his desk as Jake ran to help.

Another low, muffled call came from underneath the pile of books and toppled bookcases.

"I'm coming! Hold on!"

Blimey, the poor scholar was buried under an entire encyclopedia.

Unfortunately, the bookcases were too long and awkward for him to manage alone. When he lifted one end, trying to pull it up, the other end sagged all the more heavily.

He was afraid of hurting the teacher underneath. He almost yelled for Derek to come and get the other end, but Derek was attending to the kids in the classroom across the hall.

Scowling at the risk of any of these half-conscious students seeing him use his freakish powers, Jake had no choice but to summon up his telekinesis. He had to free the teacher before he or she was well and truly crushed under all that weight.

Once Jake had discreetly floated the bookcases back to where they belonged, it only took a moment to dig the teacher out from under the avalanche of books. Unfortunately, the little man was so hysterical over the supernatural events he had already witnessed that all he did was babble incoherently.

"Hey!" Jake snapped his fingers in his face. "It's all right, you're safe now, calm down."

But as soon as the teacher did so, he leaped to his feet, ran out of the room, and fled the building, his black robes flapping out behind him. Jake saw him out the window, tearing off down the drive, and shrieking at the Gryphon in the carriage as he passed.

"You're welcome," Jake muttered with a scowl.

Then the other three came in.

"They seem to be all right," Jake told them, but Derek and Archie gave the students a cursory check anyway. "It's the teachers I'm worried about."

While he explained how he had found the teacher in this room buried under books, Madam Sylvia took some white candles out of her bag and hurried to set them in the four corners of the room, lighting them.

She then lit a little bouquet of dried sage tied with a string and began waving it slowly in the air, walking around the perimeter of the room and speaking some sort of chant, a white-magic incantation.

She continued this in the other classrooms, "clearing" the first floor of evil energy, so she claimed, while Archie and Derek made sure none of the kids were in too bad of shape, especially the little ones.

But in all the classrooms, they found the kids in a similar state: draped over their chairs, snoring on their desks, or sleeping on the floor in exhaustion, as if they had been subjected to the most boring lesson of their lives.

By feeding on their life-force, according to the Spell of a Hundred Souls, Garnock had clearly stolen all their energy.

Hopefully, a good nap, a meal, and some time would restore them to their normal selves.

For the teachers, it was a different story.

Some had been dealt with more severely than others, probably depending on how hard they had fought back, trying to defend their students. Prim little Miss Tutbury was locked in her classroom closet, which had been sealed up by some devilish spell.

"Try to be calm in there," Madam Sylvia told her through the door. "It may take some doing, but we will get you out!"

Miss Tutbury had fared better than the art teacher, who had been stuck to the ceiling by her own classroom glue.

Dr. Winston, the current headmaster, must have abandoned his flask of liquor long enough to try to find out what was going on. He had made it as far as the second classroom on the left, where he had been confined in a magic circle that Garnock had drawn on the classroom floor with the chalk from the blackboard.

Whenever Dr. Winston tried to reach his hand or step with one foot or move in any way over the chalk line, a burning sensation engulfed that part of his body, forcing him to pull back again in pain.

The bewildered man was stuck inside the circle. "That piece of chalk is possessed, I say! It just floated up from the blackboard and started writing b-by itself!" he whispered, wide-eyed. "Perhaps this is a dream? Am I actually passed out somewhere? At my desk?"

"That's it," Jake assured him. "Just a dream. Don't worry, it'll be fine. Just stay in that circle for now, eh?"

They promised to free him at the first opportunity. But for the time being, at least he was relatively safe there and would not get in the way. For now, their number one task was finding Garnock and dealing with him before the wizard could do something worse to anyone else.

Indeed, his various punishments on the teachers served as a warning to them all that the sorcerer's strength had indeed grown after his feeding frenzy. Even if the black fog did not yet have a body, it was plain that Garnock had now grown strong enough to manipulate solid objects—from something as small as a piece of chalk or a bottle of glue, all the way up to sealing a door shut and knocking over those big, heavy bookcases.

They'd have to be on their toes.

"Where is he?" Jake muttered nervously under his breath as they pressed on in their sweep of the school.

"Hiding?" Madam Sylvia suggested, still waving her smoking sage bouquet in all directions.

"By now he knows we're here," Derek said in a low tone.

Meanwhile, Archie's head swiveled constantly back and forth, practically like an owl's, as the boy genius kept watching for him.

"I think Madam Sylvia is right. He's hiding from us," Jake said when they had swept the second floor and still saw no sign of the evil wizard.

"That means he's scared. Right?" Archie asked hopefully.

Derek shrugged. "Or he's setting up an ambush."

"I found him, here!" Old Sack suddenly yelled out, appearing in the open doorway of a room behind them.

Only Jake and Madam Sylvia turned.

"You've got something?" Derek asked quickly.

"Follow me!" Jake ran towards Old Sack, but before he could reach him, Garnock flew out of the wall with a sinister roar.

Jake stopped in his tracks, shocked by the change in the sorcerer's appearance. Below the waist, Garnock was still a black fog, but now, instead of a skeleton head, his face was distinct.

Though still swathed in smoke, his upper half was that of a middle-aged man with strong, lordly features and short, spiky hair, pale as moonlight. He now had a regular sort of neck and shoulders, a chest, the top of a back, arms, and hands.

But the rest of him was still a trailing dark cloud as he raced through the air, going after Old Sack.

"Run!" Jake shouted, only to grab his cousin's shoulder when Archie started to dash away. "Not you, the ghost," he muttered.

The headmaster ghost let out a shriek and instantly turned himself into a fast-moving orb. Old Sack flew out over the staircase, but he wasn't fast enough.

Garnock caught him in midair.

"Let him go!" Jake shouted.

"Oh, dear," Madam Sylvia whispered, lifting her hand to her mouth.

Grasping the orb between his newly formed hands like it was a crystal ball, Garnock shoved the whole thing into his mouth. To Jake's horror, the evil spirit's lower jaw unhinged like that of a shark, enabling him to swallow the orb whole.

Jake stood aghast. He couldn't move, could not believe what he had just witnessed. He stared, riveted with morbid fascination.

He could not think of a single thing to say.

Garnock gave a great gulp, then his jaw and head went back to normal.

He turned in midair to leer at Jake in sinister satisfaction. Then he licked his lips like a frog that had just swallowed a fly. "A little dry for my taste, like all these academics. That makes number ninety-six."

"You killed him."

"Good afternoon to you, too, Lord Griffon! The Lightrider's son. Yes, I know now who you are." Garnock's eyes narrowed. "And I know what you did to my poor little Mischief and Mayhem. My gargoyles."

"You're a monster!" Jake choked out, taking a backward step in the hallway as Garnock floated closer.

Moving under the school's dingy main chandelier, the black-fog warlock tilted his head back and laughed. "Thank you very much, my lad! I shall take that as a compliment. Some of my best friends are monsters. Now then, who wants to be number ninety-seven? Here's a tasty little morsel."

"You stay away from my cousin!" Jake belted out, throwing up his arm in front of Archie, and that was all the boy genius needed to hear.

Shoving Jake's arm out of the way, he slid the opened Spirit Box across the floor, then brought up the Phantom Fetcher with a yell and started firing wildly in all directions, cranking the brass handle at top speed.

The Phantom Fetcher blasted out a lightning-like net of crackling, bluish energy.

Garnock threw himself out of the way in the nick of time, then turned, looking outraged at this unexpected device. As soon as the sorcerer righted himself, he fired back at the boy genius with a ball of dark magic that only Jake could see.

"Arch, look out!"

It flew out of Garnock's hand and barreled into Archie's chest, sending him flying against the wall behind him.

Jake stepped in front of him as Garnock swooped toward his cousin to feed. "Don't even think about it."

"Quick, the spell!" Archie said, pushing his spectacles back up after they had slipped down his nose.

"Everyone, all at once!" Madam Sylvia said.

They had all memorized the Lightriders' spell and together began reciting it. Jake brought up the wand and pointed it at Garnock, concentrating on the ancient magical words with all his might.

"Thrice cursed,
be thou bound
who evil chose
we now enclose
in dark and doom—
be thou entombed!
So we swear it by our blood
And victory of Holy Rood,
Banished be forevermore."

Garnock drew back with a look of fear when he heard the incantation. He must have remembered its previous effect on him all too well, for he lifted his hands as if to shield himself, and immediately began chanting a counter-spell.

Jake and the others spoke louder, reciting the Lightriders' spell over and over in unison while Archie climbed to his feet, but nothing seemed to be happening to Garnock.

If anything, every repetition only seemed to make him stronger. He was getting bigger and the human part of his body was growing more distinct; he now had a waist.

Apparently, he couldn't help laughing. "You fools! Did you think I sat in that tomb all those centuries twiddling my thumbs? What do you take me for? Leave it to a Lightrider to show a total lack of originality. Ho-hum!"

"Everyone, stop!" Jake ordered. "He's turning our magic against us."

"Very good, my clever little nugget! Maybe you're not as thick as you look. Love the white hair, by the way. It suits you."

"I take it the spell didn't work," Archie said in a tight voice. "So what do we do now?"

Jake glanced over his shoulder at his cousin, at a loss.

This wasn't in the plan.

Madam Sylvia took charge and stepped to the fore, holding up a handful of crystals on chains and waving them at Garnock, although she couldn't see him, which Jake thought extremely brave.

She proceeded to lay a curse on him in the potent bardic language of old Welsh, her tone dire.

Garnock flinched as though someone with good aim had just thrown a rock at him, but he shook it off and sneered.

"Take that, you hag!" He threw out his hand and cast another ball of dark energy, which jolted Madam Sylvia off her feet and carried her backward toward the staircase.

He meant to throw her down the steps.

But before Jake could even summon up his telekinesis to save her, Derek dove, wrapping his arms around the old woman's waist in order to take the brunt of the fall.

Jake and Archie winced and ran to the top step as the two went bumping down the staircase, tumbling as they rolled. Madam Sylvia fainted along the way. Then Derek landed under the medium with a grunt of pain.

Setting the dazed old woman safely aside, he came up angry. "Point to him, Jake."

Jake pointed at Garnock, and Derek instantly hurled his first Bowie knife. It flew right through the smoky black substance of Garnock's body and stuck in the wall behind him.

Garnock looked over his shoulder and arched a ghostly eyebrow in amusement at the knife hilt still shuddering in the wall. "That wasn't very nice."

"Did I hit him?"

"Yes, but it didn't matter."

"Oh, really?" Derek threw the second knife with a growl of frustration.

Garnock's eyes narrowed. "Ah, now it's my turn." The sorcerer hurled a jagged silver bolt of energy at the Guardian.

"Derek, look out!"

The warrior crouched down and started to spin out of the way to duck behind the wall, but the bolt of magic caught him in the knee; he gasped in astonishment just before he was suddenly frozen in place.

"What have you done to him?" Archie cried, then he raced to the nearest window and threw open the sash. "Red! Come! We need you!"

"You are an irritating little thing," Garnock declared.

"Don't you dare!" Jake yelled, but there was nothing he could do to stop him.

Garnock sent out an orangey-green bolt of magic from his fingertips with a snicker, and when it hit the boy genius, Archie started shrinking right before Jake's eyes.

His voice turned high-pitched, like the squeak of a mouse; down and down he went, until he was only pixie-sized, and when Red swooped in through the open window with an angry *"Caw!"* he got the same.

"No!" Jake yelled.

Garnock laughed hysterically as the Gryphon shrank down to the size of a dragonfly. Miniaturized Red landed on the ground beside tiny Archie, who was hollering squeaky protests at the top of his teensy lungs.

Burning with outrage, Jake zapped Garnock with a furious bolt of telekinesis, and though the wizard had no solid matter to affect, he *did* stop laughing.

Perhaps he recalled the effect that trying to feed on Jake had had on him before.

"I'll get you for this," Jake vowed. "Put them back the way they were!"

"Or what?" Garnock taunted.

Jake's answer was another bone-jarring jolt of telekinetic power. He sustained it for several seconds, ignoring the risks to himself of doing so.

It would weaken him, but he was too furious to care.

Besides, it also seemed to weaken Garnock, who dropped a few feet lower in the air when Jake cut off the beam.

Garnock panted after Jake released him. "I'll make you sorry for that. But first..."

He swooped over and fed off Archie with a mighty inhalation through his mouth: ninety-seven.

Aghast, Jake shot at him again with telekinesis, but had to be careful of hitting his itty-bitty cousin. He didn't want to accidentally throw tiny Archie across the room.

Garnock apparently didn't dare feed off Red, but flew away and drained off some of Derek's powerful life-force next in the same fashion: ninety-eight.

"Get away from them!" Jake bellowed, racing down the steps as Garnock went over and inhaled more energy off the unconscious Madam Sylvia.

"Ha, that's ninety-nine!" the sorcerer declared, wiping his mouth on his sleeve. He looked younger, stronger; his face almost had some color, and Jake could see that Garnock's spiky hair was turning blond. "I'd hide if I were you, Lord Griffon. You have very little time to run before I come back for you. Now if you'll excuse me, it's time to find a unicorn!"

With that, Garnock whooshed through the foyer and flew out of the school.

Jake knew he had to go after him, but he couldn't leave Archie and Derek and Red in this condition. He turned to Madam Sylvia, who had managed to rouse herself from her swoon.

"Go on, hurry." She waved him off. "I'll look after these two."

"Three. He got Red, too."

"Fine, just go! You mustn't let him finish the spell!"

Just then, an angry squeaking from the top of the stairs drew his attention. He turned and saw Archie standing on the top step, jumping up and down to get his attention and waving him on.

"What?" Jake tilted his head, listening harder.

"Hurry!" his cousin chirped. "The girls!"

He drew in his breath. "You're right!"

Instantly, he dashed off, though he had no idea what he could possibly do to Garnock by himself once he caught up to him. He'd just have to figure something out when he got there.

With a sick feeling in his stomach, he rushed across the foyer, burst through the front door and strode across the porch, into the overcast afternoon.

Ahead, Garnock was a small black cloud sweeping down the drive.

Jake narrowed his eyes. His pulse pounding, he leaped off the porch steps and went chasing after him.

Alone.

CHAPTER TWENTY-FIVE
Keeper of the Unicorns

G arnock could almost taste his victory. Now for the final step in the spell, and then it would be complete. He flew toward the unicorn sanctuary at Plas-y-Fforest, ignoring the twinge of pain when he crossed the threshold, passing over the old, faded-out protective spells.

They might have worked on him a few centuries ago, but not anymore. He felt little more than a sting.

Nothing would stop him now.

As he flew up higher to gain a better vantage point from which to search for the unicorn herd, he skimmed the forest just above the treetops, no more than a passing shadow, like the fleeting memory of a bad dream.

But soon he'd be so much more, he thought eagerly. He'd be real again. And, ah, *then* he would finally get the chance to settle some old scores...

There!

Movement among the trees below proved to be the elusive herd.

Garnock swirled lower, unseen, unsensed by the animals and the two young girls he found keeping watch over them.

The smaller child, a ginger-haired little wisp of a thing with freckles, was humming to herself and playing with some odd sparkling dust.

A few yards away, a lovely blonde stood on guard, a little older, though not yet of marriageable age.

Garnock narrowed his eyes.

The white staff she was holding marked her as the Keeper. Garnock smirked. The chit looked too delicate to harm a fly. No, he thought, these two were of no concern to him, but best to make sure there wasn't anyone else on hand that he should worry about.

From high above, he made a quick pass around the edges of the herd to assess the situation and was glad he did, for he also spotted a black-haired woman standing watch, her yellowish-green eyes glowing slightly in the forest twilight, like a cat's.

She had a fey quality and a tall, slender build like the elven folk—but no, she was human, more or less, he thought, still unsure what she was.

Witch? Shapeshifter, perhaps? He just hoped she wasn't a clairvoyant, or she might be able to see him.

Not taking any chances now that he had finally made it to the last step of the spell, he approached just close enough to use the same spell he had used on the Guardian and froze her where she stood.

The two girls never even noticed. Satisfied—indeed, gloating a little—Garnock floated closer to the unicorns, studying the animals and choosing his target from out of the herd, like any good predator—lion or wolf.

One colt in particular seemed a little weak.

He homed in on the animal, studying its movements, until the sudden shriek of a tree goblin who had spotted Garnock broke his concentration. He looked over with a low snarl; several small tree goblins scattered up higher into the branches and fled from him.

Unfortunately, when he turned back to look at the colt, he saw that the tree goblin's cry had drawn the attention of the girls.

He held perfectly still, melting into the shadow of the thick tree trunk beside him.

The girls exchanged a glance and moved a little closer. The magnificent unicorn stallion trotted past, tossing his horned head restlessly, almost sensing something.

Garnock held his breath.

But after a moment, when nothing more happened, the girls shrugged off the tree goblin's yelp and went back to what they were doing.

The little redhead went back to singing to herself, looking bored with her duties, while the blonde patrolled along the edges of the herd, staff in hand.

The unicorns grazed a trifle fretfully around the girls, their pastel-colored tails swinging rhythmically as they swatted away a few straggling summer flies.

Satisfied that the girls were not going to bother him, Garnock returned his attention to the colt. Grazing, it kicked its hind leg idly at an insect.

This is it, he thought, his excitement building. It was as good a chance as he could hope to get.

He gathered himself, recalling all those centuries in his tomb. In a few short moments, he would be truly free.

Now!

He launched out from behind the tree and attacked, zooming up to the colt and opening his mouth. Hovering just above the innocent mystical animal, he began drawing in a huge inhalation, pulling the creature's life-force into himself.

The colt could not see him, but it knew something was wrong. It let out a frantic whinny and moved to the right and the left, trying to escape, but Garnock followed it each way, siphoning out its life-force until the weakened creature stumbled.

The colt's anxious mood and clumsy movements startled the herd. As the other unicorns started speeding away, the red-haired girl stopped singing.

"Isabelle, where are you going?"

Having drunk his fill and already reeling with victory, Garnock released the colt from his dark magical hold. But now the young animal was too weakened to run.

Garnock pulled back and turned dazedly, only to find the Keeper running toward the colt, leaping over rocks and logs in her path. She had lost all semblance of a neat young miss and ran like a young barbarian warrior princess, an Amazon of old, wielding her white staff like a spear.

He saw fury in her bright blue eyes—and Garnock was afraid.

There were few magicks on earth like that of an innocent Keeper. Most never even knew how mighty they were until it was too late.

This one was magnificent...and as much as she terrified him, he was suddenly inspired. What a gift she'd make! An exquisite peace offering to placate a certain devil of his acquaintance who was still waiting to collect a soul from him.

Aye, the debt he owed would be written off as paid if he handed over this bright young beauty in his place.

"Isabelle, what is it? Where are you going?" the little ginger yelled.

"He's here!" she shouted back rather savagely.

"Where? I don't see anything!"

"Neither do I, but I feel him," she added coldly under her breath, scanning the grove.

Garnock was standing inches away from her, but he was still in spirit form.

She rushed right past him, breathing heavily from her sprint. She glided over to the colt, went down on one knee, and put her graceful arms around it.

He could hear her speaking softly to the creature, comforting it, asking what was wrong, but Garnock quit listening as he noticed the Spell of a Hundred Souls starting to take effect now that the final step was completed.

He could feel the most startling change coming over him. *It's happening! It worked!*

The world seemed to be spinning. He felt tingly all over. A wind rushed through the woods with a roaring sound and made the autumn leaves on the ground scatter and whirl.

The Keeper was still protecting the colt, and the little redhead was running toward the pair, asking Isabelle what was wrong.

Garnock felt giddy and lightheaded as he looked down and saw his body flicker into being, starting to materialize. A real, physical body—flesh and blood!

It did not remain constant yet, but phased in and out of materiality like a distant star.

It felt wonderful.

The first sound out of his newly formed mouth was a shocked, triumphant laugh. He began running his newly made hands all over himself, checking to feel if everything was there. Face, ears, head, arms, legs, feet. All the parts right where they should be.

"I'm alive." He lifted his arms and threw his head back, screaming at the sky in defiance, *"I'm alive!"*

Whack!

His shout of victory was short-lived, for in the midst of his rejoicing, he failed to take into account that he was now also visible to the two young ladies.

The Keeper wasted no time in expressing what she thought of him. Once again, the blonde lifted her staff and swung it at him with all her strength, welcoming him back into the world with a second blow that sent him reeling.

Garnock winced with tears of pain smarting in his eyes, but even though it hurt like the blazes, he couldn't stop laughing. "Do you know how many centuries it's been since I could feel physical pain?" he asked aloud—rhetorically—from where he lay laughing on the ground. "I almost welcome it! At least now I'm able to feel something."

"Good!" The little redhead loomed over him, hands propped on her waist. "Then maybe you'll like this, too." She kicked him in the ribs as he started to sit up and sent him sprawling onto his back once again.

Their beating on him ceased to be amusing. He stayed down for a while to make them stop, waiting for his strength to return.

Instead, he lay there balled up on the ground to protect his new innards, reveling in the weight of having a body again after so long, feeling the solid texture of the earth beneath. Having a nose again with which to smell the rich forest moss and autumn leaves!

When they stopped kicking him, he just lay there, savoring these simple luxuries and waiting for his full powers to come in. He had known it might take a short while. Most magic wasn't instantaneous, after all, and in those first few minutes of having his new body, he was as weak as a baby.

But not for long.

He whispered a summoning spell for his ring and it appeared on his finger. With every second, he could feel his strength growing. His heart raced.

From the corner of his eye, he saw the two girls glance at each other in confusion at the way he lay inert.

"Hullo?" The redhead waved her hand before his face. "Isabelle, did we kill him?"

Garnock played dead to avoid getting cracked in the head again, waiting...

"Why isn't he getting up?" she whispered.

"I don't think he can," the Keeper replied.

"But I didn't hit him that hard!"

They both leaned closer curiously. And that was their mistake.

He opened his eyes to slits. Two young heads were peering down at him with the sky and the trees behind them.

The girls looked at each other.

"Something terrible must have happened at the school," the redhead whispered. "Isabelle, Jake and your brother must've failed! Why else would Garnock be here? How did he make it past them? They could be dead for all we know!"

"You mustn't say that..."

As the Keeper argued with her companion in low tones, Garnock felt his full strength rushing back into him, flooding his new body, tingling down every nerve ending.

He had never felt more alive.

The two girls screamed when he shot his hand out and grasped the Keeper's wrist.

"Ouch! Let go of me! It burns!"

"Miss Helena, help!" the redhead shouted into the distance while his blond captive twisted and squirmed and tried to pull her arm free.

Garnock sat up but simply refused to let go.

"Take your hands off me!"

"Oh, but I have a use for you, my dear."

"You let her go!" The redhead charged as if she meant to tackle him, but with his free hand, Garnock tossed her into a pile of dead leaves with a casual bolt of magic from his fingertips.

Ah, yes, he was feeling *much* more himself now.

"Dani!" the blonde screamed.

"Stay out of my way, you little Irish barbarian."

"Leave her alone!" the Keeper protested.

"I'm not interested in her, actually. Isabelle, isn't it?"

She went still, eyeing him in cold distrust. "What do you want with me?"

"You must come with me, my dear. I have a friend you really have to meet."

"I'm not going anywhere with you. Let me go!"

"Garnock!" a voice suddenly thundered as she struggled.

Garnock looked over with a hiss as the Lightrider's son appeared at the far edge of the clearing. He was red-faced with running, his chest heaving. Persistent, that one.

"Take your hands off my cousin," the young Lord Griffon

commanded, angrily striding toward them.

But Garnock had no intention of complying.

With a sneer at the lad, he clutched the girl's wrist harder, then uttered a one-word teleportation spell and vanished, taking the Keeper with him.

CHAPTER TWENTY-SIX
A Cruel Trade

"*I* sabelle!"

Dani's piercing scream rang in Jake's ears, a sound of pure panic that echoed his own overwhelming horror.

Garnock had simply vanished with his cousin in a puff of black smoke.

"Where did they go? They couldn't just disappear!"

But they had.

Dani was becoming hysterical, running around the grove looking for her friend in wild disbelief, as if Garnock and Isabelle might be hiding with her somewhere here just under their noses.

Jake grabbed her arm to stop her and tried to calm her down. "Shh, it's all right."

"No, it isn't!" Her green eyes welled with terrified tears. "Jake, he took her!" she choked out.

"We're going to get her back."

"How?"

He swallowed hard. "I don't know yet. I'll figure it out. But you have to calm down. This isn't helping."

His firm tone helped her settle down slightly. "Where's Derek? Where are Red and Archie? Is everyone all right? How did Garnock get past you?"

"The Lightriders' spell didn't work. He had already figured out a defense."

"I knew it!" she yelled, her cheeks flushing with a burst of anger to match her bewilderment. "I knew your stupid plan would never work! Oh, why do you always do this?"

"What?" he cried, taken aback. "It isn't my fault!"

"Yes, it is! You always have to rush headlong into everything. Why couldn't you just wait until your aunt wrote back and told you what to do?"

Jake's first impulse was to defend himself, but he realized she was beside herself at the moment after seeing Isabelle abducted right before their eyes.

He strove to be patient. "I would've gladly waited if I had a choice. The headmaster ghost came and warned us that Garnock was going crazy feeding on the children." He paused with a pang at the awful memory of how Old Sack had been devoured.

But he dared not mention it to Dani—let alone how Archie and Red had been miniaturized, and Derek had been frozen. "You should have seen the way we found the students at the school. They were practically comatose."

"Well, what do we do now?"

He shook his head, at a loss, but before he could think of any possible answer, a welcome sound came from above, filling the skies.

"Caw!"

He looked up and saw Red soaring toward them at top speed. Even better, Archie was riding on the Gryphon's back. "They're all right," he breathed.

"What do you mean?" Dani asked.

"Never mind." Jake waved anxiously to Red. "We're down here! Hurry!"

"Red, help us!" Dani yelled.

A moment later, Red and Archie landed in the grove.

Jake and Dani ran to them. Archie slid off Red's back. "I'm so glad to see you two back to your normal selves!"

"What are you talking about?" Dani asked.

Jake ignored her as Archie glanced around. "No worries, coz. Where's my sister?"

Jake winced and dropped his gaze, and Dani started crying.

"Where is she?" Archie demanded in sudden dread.

Dani let out a sob. "Oh, Archie—Garnock took her!"

Red roared in fury at this news, rearing up on his hind legs and slashing at the air with his front claws.

The boy genius turned white. "What do you mean he took her?"

"I'm pretty sure he used a transport spell. Then they

just...vanished." Jake reached out and steadied his cousin as Archie began wobbling on his feet.

"We have to get her back!" her brother fairly screamed, which made Dani cry harder.

Jake gulped. "We will." Their reactions really weren't helping. "How's Derek?"

"Madam Sylvia's still working on him," Archie said.

"What happened to Derek?" Dani cried in renewed horror.

"He got frozen. Don't worry, Madam Sylvia seemed to think that she can fix him. It'll probably just take some time," Jake assured her with far more conviction than he felt. "Where's Miss Helena, by the way?"

Dani turned to him with a low gasp. "We haven't seen her."

They rushed off to look for her and soon found the frozen governess, immobilized by the same spell Garnock had used on Derek.

"Don't worry, we'll get Madam Sylvia up here to work on her next," Jake told the younger two.

"Mother Mary, we're all doomed," Dani said.

Hearing the despair in her voice, Red got hold of his own wrath and came over to the kids to help calm them down. He spread his wings around the boys' shoulders and gave Dani a comforting nuzzle with his feathered cheek.

It made them feel much better to be reminded that although their adult chaperones might be frozen, at least they still had Claw the Courageous on their side.

"All right, it's down to us now," Jake said after a moment. "We've got to work together if we're going to rescue Isabelle."

Dani took a shaky breath. She nodded. "Just tell us what to do."

"Did Garnock say anything about why he was kidnapping her or where he might have gone?" Jake asked Dani. "Did you hear him say anything useful?"

She furrowed her brow. "Well, after he threw me in the leaf-pile, I heard him say he had a friend he wanted her to meet."

Oh, no.

"Maybe he meant the Dark Druids," Archie whispered.

Jake shook his head. The sick feeling returned to his stomach. He hoped with all his heart he was wrong, but he had a feeling...

"I don't know," Jake lied, for he dared not tell them his suspicion, especially Archie, "but I'll bet I know where he's gone. I need to get back to the Tomb."

"What, down in the coalmine?" Dani asked in confusion.

"Hang it! I almost forgot about the rockfall."

"I can get you in there. I just need to mix up some explosives," Archie said at once.

"That sounds dangerous," said Dani.

The boy genius glanced at her. "I'd do anything to save my sister."

Jake clapped him on the shoulder. "That's the spirit, coz. I'm sure Emrys will have whatever you need—"

"I already have it in my chemistry set," Archie cut him off.

"You brought your chemistry set on holiday?" Dani muttered.

"Of course." Archie turned to Jake. "But why would Garnock take my sister to the tomb?"

"Is he going to kill her?" Dani whispered, wide-eyed.

"No." Jake strove to find the most tactful way to put it, but he couldn't bear to tell them his theory.

It was only logical.

Now that he was back among the living, the last thing Garnock would want was to have to keep looking over his shoulder and worrying about the devil on his tail.

What better way to make amends with the demon ally he had betrayed than to offer up another soul to take his place? There were probably few souls of higher value than the unusually pure type belonging to a Keeper of the Unicorns. If Garnock offered up Isabelle in his place, he'd be off the hook—free to enjoy his unnatural new life without worrying about the devil coming to collect on their bargain.

And if he succeeded, then poor Isabelle would be stuck in that horrible netherworld for all time, prisoner of the demons, unless Jake could save her.

"Are you sure about this?" Archie was asking. "Because we can't afford the time if you're wrong."

"Sure enough," he replied, dodging the need to explain. His suspicions about Garnock's reason for taking Isabelle would only terrify them more. "Come on, then. Enough gab. Are we going to go and rescue her or what? Let's go down to the cottage and get our supplies."

"What about Miss Helena?" Dani asked as all four of them started running down the trail. "What if the tree goblins start sniffing around her? Don't they bite?"

"We'll send Snowdrop up to stand guard over her until Madam Sylvia can come and unfreeze her."

It seemed to take forever to reach the cottage, but when they got there, they gave Snowdrop her instructions. She was appalled to hear how badly it all had gone, but sped out to the woods at once to watch over poor Miss Helena.

Archie immediately began collecting the needed items for the explosion. At least knowing he'd have the chance to blow something up seemed to make him feel better. It was one of his favorite things.

Dani turned to Jake. "What can I do?"

"You need to get down to the Harris Mine School and tell Derek what's happened as soon as he's unfrozen. Nimbus can drive you. Once Madam Sylvia's done with Derek, bring her back here to fix Miss Helena. Tell Derek to follow us down to Garnock's lair. We may need his help once he's back in action."

"But that mine is huge. How's he going to find it?"

"He'll have to sing. When Red and I went down there, I left a trail of Illuminium behind us like breadcrumbs so we could find our way back out. All he has to do is sing and he should be able to follow the Illuminium trail just fine."

"So you're out of Illuminium," Dani said, nodding. "Here, take mine. It may come in handy down there in the dark." She offered him her pouch of the powder. He accepted it with a grateful nod and tied it to his belt.

Then Jake hollered for Nimbus to get the carriage ready for Dani.

"All set," Archie said, marching back up the hallway with the Vampire Monocle pushed up onto his head and a satchel full of explosives over his shoulder. "We're in luck. I had a few sticks of dynamite left over from the Invention Convention. Some American railroad engineer gave them to me. If they can blast through the Rockies with this stuff, it should work for us."

Jake and Dani took a wary step back from him at this announcement.

"So he just carries these sorts of things around with him?" she murmured.

Jake nodded. "I know. He's a traveling laboratory."

But it seemed the moment had arrived. Red prowled over into their midst, ready to carry the boys to the coalmine.

"Well, this is it, then," Dani said. "Promise me you'll both be careful."

"We will," they said.

"Don't blow yourselves up. And Jake, bring Isabelle back to us. We need her." Dani's voice caught on the threat of another sob as she spoke these plaintive words.

Jake couldn't stand for her to start crying again, so he distracted her—shocked her was more like it—by giving her a quick hug. "Don't you start that again, carrot-head," he mumbled, and gave her a brotherly kiss on the head.

She pulled back and looked at him like he was a tree goblin.

Jake grinned. "Gotcha."

Fortunately, his unexpected show of affection had the effect he'd hoped. She forgot all about crying.

Instead, she backed away from him as if he had a disease, then turned and ran outside to the carriage.

Through the window, they saw her climb up onto the driver's box beside Nimbus Fingle. Then the brownie coachman slapped the reins over the horses' rumps and they went tearing off for the Harris Mine School.

Jake glanced at Archie, who backed away, putting his hands up. "Don't even think about hugging me."

Jake laughed and clapped him on the shoulder. "C'mon, coz. We've got a Keeper to rescue."

Archie nodded, his jaw clenched in resolve.

Then the boys climbed on the Gryphon's back. Jake leaned down to murmur in his mount's ear: "All right, Red. The Lightriders dealt with this devil once before, but it's our turn now. So let's go and finish it."

"Caw!"

Red took a few running steps then leaped into the air, his scarlet wings pumping powerfully as he rose into the air with his passengers.

The October sky was cold and windy as he bore them aloft, but nothing would deter them now.

Both boys held on tight as the Gryphon carried them over the mountains to the mine.

CHAPTER TWENTY-SEVEN
Light in a Dark Place

Jake had always suspected that Archie's love of blowing things up would come in handy someday.

Deep in the coalmine a short while later, having left Red out in the woods where he wouldn't be seen, the boys crouched at a safe distance down the tunnel from the rock pile blocking the collapsed tomb.

Jake held his ears while the boy genius lit the long fuse with a gleeful look of intensity. The spark burned its way along the ground to where he had packed the dynamite in among the rocks.

"Wait for it..." Archie murmured.

BOOOOOM!

The deafening sound of the explosion reverberated down the tunnel, followed a moment later by a rolling cloud of dust.

The boys coughed a bit, waving the dust away, then peeked around the bend in the tunnel, lifting their lanterns to see if the entrance to Garnock's tomb had been cleared.

Jake clapped Archie on the back as soon as he saw that the sticks of dynamite had done the job.

The huge mound of rocks from the collapse that had trapped him in the tomb had now been pulverized.

They raced down the tunnel, but when they arrived at the newly formed opening, Jake held Archie back. "Stay out here. I don't want to risk another collapse. The chamber will still be unstable without a few support beams. Learned that the hard way."

"I'm coming with you! She's *my* sister!"

Jake knew his cousin was terrified for Isabelle—they all were—but he shook his head in adamant refusal. "It's too dangerous. You already got shrunk! What if he does something worse to you next time? Please, just stay back. I'm the only one he seems the least bit afraid of, because of my Lightrider bloodlines. Please. I'll take care of Isabelle. Just stay back and send Derek in, if he reaches us in time. I'll holler if I need you, I promise."

Archie grumbled, peered longingly through the hole into Garnock's lair, but finally nodded in reluctance. "Be careful, Jake. Save her."

"I'll have her back to you in no time."

"I know. I believe in you, coz," he said.

Touched by his cousin's words of encouragement, Jake gave Archie a grateful nod, then turned to face the tomb.

Blimey, he did not like caves any more now than he did when he had first arrived in Wales. Nevertheless, he climbed over the rubble left by Archie's explosion and entered the tomb once again.

He shuddered upon arriving, lifting his lantern high. He did not say it aloud, but privately, he could not believe he had to come back in here.

At least this time there weren't any gargoyles trying to bite his face off. No, he thought dryly as he crossed the chamber warily, now he only had to contend with their master. An enemy far older and far more powerful than he. An enemy that, frankly, he had no idea how to defeat.

But there had to be a way. There just had to. Isabelle's life was at stake. No, actually, more than her life, he thought. Her soul. Her afterlife. Eternity. Because the underworld was where bad people were sent to endure eternal punishment. She, of all people, did not deserve what would happen to her if he failed.

Then Jake's blood ran cold, for as he went down the dark stone steps into the second room with the skull-shaped doorway, he suddenly heard her screaming.

He drew in his breath, momentarily paralyzed with fear. *Good Lord.* He had never heard anyone scream like that before. It was a sound of pure agony and raised the very hackles on his nape.

He's torturing her!

At that realization, Jake instantly forgot all about his own terror, racing across the room and through the skull doorway to save her.

He would never forget the sound of those screams for as long as he lived—and if he failed, he knew he would never again be able to face Archie or Dani or Aunt Ramona.

As he burst through the door into Hades, which Garnock had left propped open, the smoke briefly choked and blinded him. He brought up his hand to shield his face. It was all as unpleasant as he remembered. The fiery heat, the sulfur smell, the wailing and gnashing of teeth from millions of dead souls who had earned their torment. Thieves and murderers, cheats and swindlers, liars and maniacs of all kinds.

And the innocent Keeper of the Unicorns.

Jake stopped at the top of the stairs, taken aback when he spotted her below. The moment his vision cleared, he saw, thank Heaven, that Garnock wasn't torturing her.

He wasn't even touching her.

On the flat rocky plateau at the bottom of the stairs, she was tied up with her arms over her head to a wooden frame resembling a gallows.

The sorcerer himself was standing, arms raised, at the cliff's edge, shouting into the void to summon his former demon ally, Jake supposed—the one he had betrayed with his trickery.

No doubt he had some making up to do after cheating the devil of his promised soul.

Neither Garnock nor Isabelle had noticed Jake's arrival yet, but for his part, a chill ran down his spine despite the river of fire nearby as he suddenly realized *why* such bloodcurdling screams were coming out of his poor cousin.

Isabelle was an empath.

Her particular gift was feeling what other people felt. Only now did it dawn on Jake how this terrible place of suffering would affect someone with her abilities.

Of all the people to be dragged down here! he thought. She couldn't even stand to be in a crowd in all the hustle and bustle of London. Even that was too overwhelming for her exquisite sensitivity, so finely attuned was she to the emotions and attitudes of everyone around her.

It was what made her so compassionate toward others, but in this place, no wonder she was screaming like that.

Isabelle was in agony, drowning in a sea of other people's pain and horror and regret. Sharing the despair of the damned. He swallowed hard.

She'll go mad if she stays down here much longer.

Jake knew he had to get her out of here.

He also knew that Garnock was going to do everything in his considerable power to stop him.

Given that the sorcerer was still flickering between spirit and solid form, Jake wasn't sure what—if anything—he could actually do to him. Nevertheless, he started rushing down the stairs, despite his lack of any particular plan.

Well, he thought, using his telekinesis to push Garnock off the cliff sounded like a decent start.

He filtered out Isabelle's tormented screaming as best he could because it so unnerved him. Then he cleared his mind, focusing on the wizard's back.

Determined to shove her captor off the ledge into the canyon below, he summoned up every ounce of magical ability at his disposal.

Now!

From the very core of him, power rocketed out of his palms, amplified by the presence of the great quartz crystals just outside the skull door.

Garnock didn't have a chance. He went shooting over the cliff as though he had been blasted by the water from the strongest fireman's hose that ever was.

Jake sustained the beam and did not stop until the sorcerer had disappeared over the stone ledge with a shout, plummeting into the dark, fiery pit beyond.

Where he belonged.

Jake's chest was heaving when he finally dropped his hands to his sides. He was a little dazed by the outpouring of power and could already feel his temples starting to throb. But as draining as that had been, he was still in much better shape than Isabelle. He pulled out his runic dagger and ran to cut the ropes binding her wrists.

Having seen him, she had stopped screaming.

"Jake," she said weakly. Her blue eyes were glazed with pain. Her face was smudged with ashes.

"Don't worry, I'm going to get you out of here."

He lifted his knife to free her, but she glanced past his

shoulder and gasped. "Jake, look out!"

Knife still in hand, he whirled around and was astonished to find the sorcerer floating back up over the side of the cliff again, his black robes billowing in the breeze.

"Surprise," Garnock said sweetly, gliding up higher into the air. "Now it's my turn," he snarled. Suddenly brandishing a twisted black wand, he aimed it at Jake, and a snakelike wave of dreadful magic came crackling out of it, so powerful it emitted a deep, droning hum.

Shielding Isabelle with his body, Jake instinctively raised his hands to ward off the current of dark magic barreling toward them.

He was not entirely sure what he had expected to happen, but even he was shocked when, somehow, his telekinesis bent the beam of magic coming at him and deflected it toward the red underworld sky.

Garnock was visibly outraged by this trick, though Jake was as bewildered by it as the sorcerer was.

The wizard redoubled his efforts, and Jake continued to channel the furious current of power elsewhere. He and Izzy remained unscathed—for the moment.

Garnock finally gave up on that, slightly winded.

Heart pounding, Jake tried to hide the fact that he, too, was rather exhausted from the effort.

Garnock studied him through narrowed eyes. "Well, you're just full of surprises, aren't you, little Lord Griffon? I didn't hear you come in. But honestly! Shooting a fellow in the back? Hardly worthy of a young Lightrider."

"That's the least you deserve." Bristling, Jake stood his ground in front of Isabelle, with sweat from the fires of Hades dripping down his face. "You kidnapped my cousin. You killed Brother Colwyn. You shrank Red and Archie and froze Derek Stone. You nearly drained the life out of all those students, and terrorized their teachers."

Garnock smiled. "To be sure, I am such a naughty man."

"Man? You're not even human anymore, after you changed yourself into a black fog. You might have got your body back, but you're still not a real person. I'm beginning to doubt you ever were."

"Insulting me isn't going to save you, you insolent snail." Garnock floated down from the air and landed on solid ground, studying him intently. "Tell me how you did that. Bent the stream of magic away? I heard no chant. You don't even carry a wand. What's the trick?"

"How should I know? But you better not come near me or my cousin, or I'll give you something worse," Jake warned.

Garnock laughed. "Such threats! Boy, you may have a prodigious amount of natural talent, but it's obvious you have no idea what you're doing. All that power, wasted on a cheeky little numskull. But...you've got courage, coming in here. I'll give you that. I daresay with the proper training, you could actually be something someday, couldn't you?" the sorcerer mused aloud.

Indifferent to the volcanoes in the distance and the screams echoing from the city of the condemned, Garnock pocketed his wand and held up his hands to show he was unarmed. Then he started walking closer, step by cautious step. "Perhaps I was hasty in trying to destroy you. I could use a new apprentice."

"Forget it."

"Ah, ah, remember, I've looked into your mind, Jake. At the séance."

Jake growled under his breath at the memory of how Garnock had terrified him that night, projecting the awful vision into his head of himself as the future leader of the Dark Druids. Even now, his fears whispered: *Is this how it begins?*

"You have no right to do that to people! Why don't you mind your own business?"

"What fun would that be? Besides, I had to keep you still somehow, so I could feed on your life-force. Yes, as you guessed, that is how it works. It's quite a handy trick. I could teach it to you if you like."

"Not interested."

"Think it over," Garnock chided. "Think of all that you could do, the way you could control the idiots around you. You see, in my research, I've found that nothing can paralyze a person more swiftly than showing them the picture of their worst fears. I've seen yours, Jake, don't forget—along with your greatest desires, even the secret wounds you think you hide. Poor boy," Garnock continued with artificial sympathy. "I also glimpsed your memories of your rookery days inside that head of yours. So sad. You've had a hard life, Jake. Robbed of your parents. Unloved at the orphanage..."

"Don't listen to him, Jake," Isabelle whispered through her suffering. "He's only trying to manipulate you."

"Beaten by your apprentice masters. Then the scrabble to survive on the streets. Begging, stealing. Half starved to death, and nobody even caring whether you lived or died."

"Dani cared," Isabelle rasped, dangling by her wrists from the ropes that bound her. "She was always there for you. Still is. And you have us now."

"Don't listen to her!" Garnock snapped. "How can this sheltered little rich girl, this pathetic china doll, understand the cruel things you went through? She has no idea what it's like to face a winter's night without a roof over your head! But I know. I've seen it in your mind, in your heart."

"She's seen it, too. She *is* an empath," Jake said stiffly.

"Ah, yes." The wizard sneered at Isabelle. "An empath who can't handle anything difficult. Look at how weak she is, Jake. What good are you, girl? Quit your sniveling!"

"I am not weak," Isabelle ground out, sobbing, and Jake suddenly understood that this very accusation was *her* greatest fear.

That was exactly why Garnock was saying it. The enchanter was like a snake weaving back and forth before its prey to mesmerize it before striking. "Little porcelain doll. She'll crack under the slightest pressure. She can't do anything like ordinary girls. Helpless. Weak. She can't even go into London."

"Leave her alone! She's stronger than you know!" Jake said furiously.

"Well, whatever she is, she's too *innocent* and *pure* to understand what the struggle to survive can do to a person. Those of us who have tasted the bitter side of life like you and I, Jake, we know how such experiences harden a person. But that's not necessarily a bad thing," Garnock admitted. "Indeed, I find that nasty streak of survival in you rather a promising sign. You're not like the others. You could actually be something, with the right guidance." He stepped closer. "Maybe we should talk."

"Stay away from me."

"Come, Jake, you already know the truth, deep down. The Lightriders are weak, just like her. You don't want to be like them. Look at how your own parents failed you!"

"Stop talking," Jake ordered.

But Garnock shook his head, offering the drug of self-pity. "Poor, poor boy. No wonder you've always felt abandoned. I mean, really, I know you admire your precious Lightriders and want to be just like them. But if you think about it, they're the ones who ruined your life. How could those unconscionable fools lose track of such a special boy as you? With your gifts? Your abilities?"

First terror, then temptation. Now it was flattery. Jake shook his head. This bloke was good.

"You really think they're going to do any better by you in the future? They'll only fail you again. They don't deserve you, Jake. You deserve better."

"Look, I know what you're trying to do and it isn't going to work," Jake informed him, trying to shake off the depressing effect of the wizard's words.

It did rather make him recall that Aunt Ramona could not even be bothered to answer his message.

"I'm only giving you the truth, Jake. The Elders of the Order will never let you reach your true potential. They're already scared of you, I wager. They'll always hold you back. I'll tell you what," he ventured. "Why don't we make a bargain? I'll free the girl right now if you will agree to become my apprentice."

"Your apprentice?"

Isabelle struggled against her bonds. "Don't do it, Jake. That's how the Dark Druids started out."

"What say you, Jake?" Garnock asked in a coaxing voice. "I'll teach you how to use all that marvelous ability you were born with. Then you can become something greater than your parents ever were."

He shook his head, aghast at the offer. "Never."

"How selfish of you, boy! Tsk, tsk, selfish as usual. I'm giving you the chance to set your cousin free. Do you realize what will happen to her if you don't take the deal? We're talking about eternal torment here."

"It's a trick, Jake. He lies. Don't let him fool you," Isabelle whispered weakly from behind him.

"You're right, Izz. Even if I agreed to it, he'd never let you go. So let's quit wasting time." Jake moved boldly behind Isabelle to avoid turning his back on Garnock.

He lifted his runic dagger and started to cut the ropes around her wrists, but Isabelle suddenly screamed.

Garnock's wand was aiming at her.

Jake froze.

Garnock lowered the wand and Isabelle heaved for breath, mercifully granted relief. "Try that again and I'll hurt her even worse."

Jake stared at him in bewilderment. He hadn't expected that. "Why are you doing this?" he cried as he stepped back out from behind his cousin. "And to her, of all people? Isabelle would never hurt anyone!"

Garnock grimaced like he couldn't stand a goody two shoes. "It's nothing personal. I have an old debt to cover, and she's to be my payment."

"Oh, really?"

"I had an unfortunate falling out a long time ago with a very powerful friend down here. The sort of friend who holds a grudge and never forgets a debt. He should be here any moment to collect. Which means you have only a minute or two to take my offer, Jake. I'll free her right now, like I said, and find some other way to pay my debt another time. I suggest you take the deal. Otherwise, the china doll will serve as payment in my place—and you know how easily fine china shatters."

"So, the old story's true," Jake said, stalling for time until he could think of another solution for how to free Isabelle without risking Garnock torturing her again by magic. "You really did promise the devil your soul? Did you really think you could actually make him serve you?"

Garnock sighed. "It seemed like a reasonable idea at the time."

"What a fool! You're the one who's weak," Jake baited him. He figured that if all else failed, he could draw Garnock's fire to himself instead of Isabelle.

After all, if he had one natural, non-magic talent, it was his gift for annoying people. He had honed it well on Dani O'Dell.

"I mean, look at you!" he taunted, pressing harder, turning the wizard's own sly tactics against him. "Only a coward would feed on schoolchildren and helpless tree goblins—and the only way you even got this far was by being invisible. Now anyone can have a crack at you. How are you ever going to make it in the nineteenth century? You're a relic of a bygone age. You must be completely bewildered by all our new machines."

"That's why I need you," Garnock countered. "You help me, I share my knowledge with you. A fair exchange."

"I want nothing to do with you." Jake shook his head, scoffing at him. "I hope you get run over by a train. I'll bet you don't even know what that is. And I'll tell you something else, old man." Jake moved closer and stared into the sorcerer's fiery eyes. "You will never substitute my cousin in your place. You're the one who made the bargain. You're the one who'll pay the price."

Garnock forced an approving smile. "You catch on fast. Last chance, Jake. I think I'm being very fair. I'll set her free and even remove the unpleasant memory of all this from her pretty head to sweeten the deal. Can't you see how she's suffering? I wouldn't want to be an empath here myself," he said. "This way, I can pull out the memory like a thorn, and the poor, sensitive little thing won't even remember the horrors she's witnessed here. If you really cared about her, you'd do this for her. Let her go.

"All you have to do is agree to serve me as your apprentice master. Learn from me, Jake. I'll be like the father you never had. Or..." Garnock paused. "Both of you can stay here, trapped underground forever. Just like your ancestors tried to do to me," he added coldly.

Jake laughed in his face. "Aye, well, you deserved it," he replied, and that was not what the sorcerer wanted to hear.

Garnock let out a garbled shout of rage and charged straight at him.

He seemed to have decided that if he couldn't kill Jake by magic, he was perfectly happy to strangle him to death.

Jake was not prepared for the ferocity of the attack.

Garnock's hands wrapped around his throat and shook him violently as he sought to choke the life out of him.

As a grown man, Garnock had the advantage of height and strength over Jake. As a wizard, he had the advantage of dark magic, as well. And as someone who still technically owed the devil his soul, he also had the wild strength of utter desperation.

But Jake had Risker.

With his eyes bulging and his face turning from scarlet to an air-deprived shade of blue, he reached for the dagger at his side and pulled it out to slash at the man.

But Garnock uttered a spell and the knife glowed hot.

Jake dropped it in pain while Isabelle cried his name in the background.

The magic Viking dagger tried to fly back into his hand, wrought, as it was, by the same great smith of Asgard who had forged Thor's hammer. But when it tried to come back to him, Jake knocked it away, his fingers already burned.

Garnock leaned closer and gave him a sinister smile as Jake continued to struggle. "I don't care how bad you taste, with your Lightrider blood. Your powers will be worth it when I steal them along with your life-force. Let's try this again now, shall we?"

Then his mouth opened up, the jaw unhinging as it had before—only now, it was much more horrible, since the sorcerer had an actual human head. His whole face became distorted, demonic.

Jake panicked as Garnock took a deep breath and started to suck the life out of his very soul. He thrashed and pulled and tried to throw himself out of the way, but he couldn't breathe and the ruthless wizard wouldn't let him go.

His knife was still too hot to touch, and his powers were spent after defending himself from the wizard's evil magic and from hitting Garnock so hard before with his telekinesis.

I'm going to die down here, he thought in astonishment, watching the vapor of his spirit rushing into Garnock's gaping maw. *He's stealing my soul!*

Scrabbling for any sort of weapon, while lack of oxygen sent worrisome black dots drifting before his eyes, all his searching hand found was Dani's pouch of Illuminium.

But Garnock was still inhaling, ignoring the sickening effect of a Lightrider-related soul.

Weaker by the second, Jake yanked open the pouch and reached into it, grabbing a big handful of Illuminium dust.

It was better than nothing.

He flung it like sand in Garnock's face, and given the nature of his attack, the sorcerer breathed in a cloud of it.

Garnock at once started coughing.

More annoyed than ever, he released Jake, throwing him to the ground.

Garnock gagged a bit on the Illuminium powder that had rushed into his lungs, then he kicked Jake once where he lay. "That should shut you up for a while."

Coughing again while Isabelle wept nearby, Garnock pounded his chest and roughly tried to clear his throat. "Still alive, eh? Well, you're more stubborn than I thought. But no matter. Here comes my friend. You might've refused my offer for now, but after you've spent a month down here under his care, I daresay you'll be ready to reconsider. Indeed, let's give Beelzebub a few weeks to work on you. When I come back, I'm sure you'll agree to anything."

Garnock kicked him again in the stomach one last time. Jake curled up on his side, gasping for air, his head pounding where he had banged it on the ground.

Through eyes only open to slits, he watched Garnock walk back toward the cliff's edge to await the huge approaching demon.

Jake closed his eyes in defeat. But then a thought occurred to him.

Illuminium...

The question in his mind was enough to make Jake drag himself upright.

The sorcerer was standing on the cliff's edge, arms raised, while in the distance, a massive horned demon left the city of the damned and started wading through the river of fire, heading their way.

Jake's throat seemed broken from Garnock's stranglehold, but somehow, having barely caught his breath, he forced out, in a rasping voice, a few bars of the first song that came to mind.

The 'Souling Song' of the beggar children.

Garnock didn't even hear him at first, too busy shouting praises to his demon friend.

"Hey, ho, nobody home.
No food, no drink, no money have I none..."

He could hardly force the words out. But Isabelle heard him and realized his intent, and instantly she joined in, singing through her tears.

"Yet will I be merry..."

Odd words from a girl, captured and tormented, and a boy who had nearly been murdered a moment ago. Nevertheless, they sang louder.

"Hey, ho, nobody home."

Repeating the simple refrain, they saw Garnock turn, rubbing his chest with an odd, puzzled wince.

They sang it again, louder. Garnock coughed. They did not know what exactly he was experiencing, but a look of panic flashed across his face; he clutched his chest with a wince, then started trying to spit out the residue of the Illuminium powder as though it was burning his mouth.

"Hey, ho, nobody home. No food, no drink, no money have I none..." Jake started climbing to his feet, with all the memories of those hard days as an orphan on the streets stirred up by Garnock's efforts to manipulate him. Oh, yes, he had sung this song before. *But it doesn't matter what you or fate or anyone does to me. What I do or don't have. You will never break me.*

That was what the song meant. That was why the beggar children sang it. It was the only act of defiance they could afford with empty pockets and no shoes on their feet, and not a soul in the world who cared.

"*Yet will I be merry!*"

At that instant, a tiny ray of sunlight or something very like it burst out of Garnock's chest.

Illuminium.

Its shining brilliance was unmistakable as it pierced the sorcerer's black robes. Garnock looked down at himself in horrified confusion. Another hole appeared, another bright pinpoint of light, more, shredding him from the inside.

He screamed in sudden terror and pain, trying to plug the holes of his emptiness with his hands.

Jake almost felt sorry for him.

Isabelle didn't. She sang louder still, though her voice sounded nearly as broken as Jake's was, after all her screaming.

They both forced themselves, directing the frequencies of the music straight at him like the dwarves had shown them to do to drive off the darkness, while in the distance, the demon came ever closer, walking now through the waist-high canyon, its every footfall like an approaching earthquake.

"What have you done to me?" Garnock screamed a second before a beam of light poked out of his throat.

In the next heartbeat, he exploded into a puff of black ashes and shimmering Illuminium, and all that was left of him was his magic ring. It thunked onto the ground with a metallic clang and rolled.

Their song stopped.

Jake instantly picked up his now-cooled knife and ran to Isabelle, cutting the ropes that bound her wrists. He steadied her as she stumbled against him.

"Can you walk? Uh, better make that *run!*" Still holding his ribs, Jake thrust her ahead of him toward the stairs.

The most terrifying voice Jake had ever heard—deep, hideous, and gurgling—engulfed them as they ran up the stairs toward the skull doorway.

"Fair game," the demon rumbled. *"You are in my territory now."*

"Go!" Isabelle stumbled, glancing over her shoulder. Jake quickly helped her up.

"All my devils! Imps! Hellhounds! Out, out into the world of men! The Portal is open!"

"Run!" Jake yelled.

Reaching the ledge where Garnock had stood moments ago, the demon swiped at them as they fled, its huge hand blood-red with great black-clawed fingernails.

It barely missed them.

Meanwhile, the hellhounds and an army of gargoyles were racing over the desolation of that terrible realm, intent on catching the intruders and tearing them apart.

Jake and Isabelle made it up the stairs, and just as they rushed out of the skull door, Derek was running in.

"Jake! Izzy! What is that noise?"

The demon dogs were barking riotously and howling while the devil roared: *"After them!"*

Jake didn't bother answering, turning the warrior around. "Tell you later. We've got to go—now!"

Even Derek gasped, and they all jolted back in shock when the devil thrust his giant hand through the skull doorway and reached into the cave, trying to grab them.

"You're mine," it taunted in its warped voice as deep and dark as the Harris Mine itself.

Its hand was blocking their way out.

"What do we do?" Jake cried.

The hand pulled back. The devil tilted its giant horned head to peer at them through the doorway. Its burning eyes gleamed with malice.

"It's trying to get out!" Isabelle said.

They both clung to Derek.

"Get out of here," he ordered, pulling out his Bowie knives. "I'll hold him off."

"Are you insane?" Jake yelled while the hellhounds' barking grew louder. "It's a suicide mission!"

"Just go!" Derek marched toward the skull doorway.

Before he reached it, however, there was a blinding flash of white light in their midst.

A second flash appeared, piercing through a mountain's worth of stone like a column of white light. A third and fourth joined it, seemingly out of nowhere.

Powerful winged figures appeared in the beams.

Jake and Isabelle clung to each other and stared.

"Dr. Celestus?" he breathed.

In full battle regalia, the angel from the stained-glass window and three of his fellow warriors rose from their crouched positions, where they had slammed to earth.

"Go, Guardian Stone," Celestus commanded. "This is a battle beyond your power." They drew out their shining swords and marched toward the skull doorway with gliding grace.

When Derek and Jake and Isabelle all failed to move, paralyzed with shock, the pale-haired angel who had once saved Dani's life turned and said harshly to them: *"Go!"*

Then they ran. Derek steadied them as the stone chamber started shaking behind them.

Chunks of rock began falling from the ceiling as they ran out through the tomb.

The whole place was coming down—for good this time.

Archie grabbed hold of his sister the moment they cleared the hole he had blown in the wall. "Isabelle!"

"Hurry!" Derek yelled, pushing them all before him.

Archie had the only lantern and he held it up for them as they all went racing up the tunnel, trying to escape the coming collapse.

It was already starting. The whole mine shook around them. Jake was not surprised, considering the battle royal going on back there.

"We're not going to make it!" Archie yelled, when all of a sudden, a little door cut right into the tunnel wall popped open and Ufudd peeked out, beckoning to them.

"Friends! Over here!"

Dani was with him, gesturing wildly. "Hurry! Everybody, this way! Oh, Isabelle!" She gave the older girl a quick hug as Ufudd rushed them all through the dwarves' secret door where, apparently, the two mines abutted.

As Jake stepped through the doorway, he was startled to find Emrys sitting at the front of a line of mining carts waiting for them on the tracks. "All aboard, and make it quick! It's an earthquake!"

"Er, not exactly," Jake muttered, but there was no time to explain.

They jumped into the mining carts and Emrys threw the switch. The shaking continued, but they all held on for dear life as the carts whizzed up and down over the crazy tracks, zooming them back up to the surface.

Minutes later, they whooshed out into blinding sunlight at the top of the White Lace Falls, safe within the bounds of Plas-y-Fforest.

Red was already there, roaring for them.

Dani quickly explained that after leading Madam Sylvia to the frozen governess in the woods, she had run over to the secret goldmine entrance to tell the dwarves what was happening, since Master Emrys always seemed to know what to do.

As they all leaped out of the mining carts, Jake seized the chance to mumble an apology to Emrys for going off alone with Red during the gargoyle hunt.

The head dwarf waved him off. "Never mind that. I'm just glad you're safe, lad."

Then they all ran toward the vantage point atop the waterfall, where they could see a section of the Harris Mine collapsing in the distance.

The ground still shook as from an earthquake while the angels battled the demon and his minions back into their fiery prison.

The enemy must have been putting up quite a fight.

Jake and the others stood together with the river coursing past them until, a few minutes later, the shaking stopped.

Everyone held their breath, unsure what to expect.

They yelled out in surprise when a section of the mine suddenly cratered with a deep groan, burying the tomb and the skull-shaped portal under so much earth this time that no one was ever getting out.

What about the angels? Jake wondered.

Just then, Miss Helena came running out of the woods (in her human form) to hug a very relieved Derek Stone.

Madam Sylvia followed a few steps behind, and everybody welcomed her into their midst.

"Look!" Isabelle cried all of a sudden, pointing at the sky.

The angels must have done their job. Four streaks of brilliant light shot up out of the hillside and went zooming up into the blue, vanishing behind the clouds.

They all stared for a long moment in speechless wonder, waiting for any further glimpse of them, but there was none.

At length, Jake shook his head and whispered, "Amazing."

EPILOGUE
First Snow

S nowdrop Fingle outdid herself with the food for the celebration they had later that evening at the cottage.

To be sure, they had many reasons to rejoice.

Isabelle was back safe and feeling much better with the help of a gryphon feather's magical healing properties. Jake was alive. Red and Archie were once again their proper sizes. Derek and Helena were free to move about at will, and Madam Sylvia was also unscathed after having freed the teachers at the Harris School from Garnock's various torments.

Likewise, to help speed the students' recovery after the evil sorcerer had preyed on their souls and drained half the life out of them, Jake had ordered party foods sent to the school. Cakes and candy worked wonders for a kid's general happiness, in his experience. Snowdrop, of course, had been overjoyed to have dozens more people to cook and bake for.

The real fun started, however, when the dwarves arrived. Earlier, Miss Helena, looking very happy to return to her normal governess duties, had instructed Jake that it was proper to return the hospitality the dwarves had extended to them a few days ago. So they were all together again: Emrys and his family, Ufudd, and a few of the other leading citizens of Waterfall Village in attendance.

The little mayor presented Jake with a fresh pouch of Illuminium to take with him after hearing about his victory.

But the surprise guest of the night was none other than everyone's favorite fairy courier, Gladwin Lightwing.

"Her Ladyship was worried when she got your telegram, so she sent me personally to check on you all and see if everything was all right."

"Pfft," said Jake.

Gladwin looked at him in confusion at this answer.

"What took her so long to reply?" he retorted. "Didn't she get my Inkbug messages?"

Gladwin frowned. "Oh, er, we had a bit of a tragedy with the poor Inkbug while you were away, I'm afraid. It seems he got out of his box and one of the maids—well, I'm sorry to say, somebody stepped on him. Most unfortunate."

They groaned.

"So she never even got my first two messages?"

"No, the first one she received was the regular telegram. I know you said you needed her advice about some spells, but I hope it wasn't too terribly inconvenient. I'll be happy to take back any answer you like—"

"No, please, don't fly off so soon, Gladwin! Stay with us awhile," Dani begged her, which pleased the little fairy greatly—although Gladwin did seem puzzled about why the boys were laughing.

"Oh, no, it wasn't too *terribly* inconvenient," Jake said wryly.

"Pardon?" the fairy asked.

"Never mind."

"It is too bad about the Inkbug," Archie remarked.

Jake nodded at him. "I don't imagine they're easy to come by."

"Well, the important thing is, Her Ladyship did as you asked. Here are the refresher spells you are to use, along with some instructions."

Jake took the fairy's tiny, scrolled message in relief, then nodded. "I'll go see to this."

"You can't leave your own party," Dani protested when he stood up to go.

He rumpled her red hair. "It's important. Besides, I'll be back." The truth was, he rather needed some time alone. He had a lot to think about, still digesting all that had happened between him and Garnock and Isabelle and the demon. It was not every day that a lad saw such things.

Jake retreated quietly from the gathering, reviewed Aunt Ramona's instructions, then put on his coat, got a wand from the Archive room, and stepped outside.

The autumn night was crisp and black, and the moon rode

high over the mountains. He took a deep breath, glad to be alone, then he set out to walk the boundary of his property, renewing the old magical protection spells, per his great-great aunt's instructions.

Every twenty steps, he had to flick the wand and say a couple of lines in Latin, some sort of white-magic blessing. He hesitated the first few times, unsure if he was doing it right.

A cheerful sparkle-trail in the darkness proved to be Gladwin, following him out. "Mind if I join you?"

Jake shrugged. "Sure, but I'm not much in a talking mood."

"Is that why you left the party?"

He nodded. "I guess so."

Fluttering near his face, the tiny fairy studied him in worry, but did not intrude on his thoughts, flying along beside him in silence.

The only sound was the crunching of the leaves beneath his feet and his awkward repetitions of the Latin words. She corrected his pronunciation, then chuckled in her high-pitched, tinkling voice. "Not to nag, but who knows what'll happen if you say it wrong."

Jake smiled at her. "Good point."

They moved on.

"This could take a while, you know," he warned. "I've got a lot of ground to cover."

"I don't mind." She gasped, hovering in midair when they approached the field near the chapel ruins. She pointed. "Unicorns!"

"Better keep my distance in case the stallion tries to impale me," Jake muttered. "Thankless brute."

The fairy's laughter in response sounded like little silver wind chimes.

"Did you know we have pixies here, too?"

"Ugh, pixies." She wrinkled her nose in slightly haughty distaste, then it was Jake's turn to laugh at her.

"They said you fairies think you're too good for everyone."

"Well, we are," she answered with a grin, and tugged on the white lock of his hair. "What is this new look you're trying? It's silly."

"It wasn't on purpose! Stop that!" He waved her away like he would an insect, chuckling. "I wonder if this spell will get rid of the tree goblins. Though, to be honest, I'm with Emrys—I don't mind them. I kind of feel sorry for them."

"Tree goblins?" She was still scanning the branches overhead with a wary look as Jake stepped out of the woods into the field, keeping well clear of the unicorn herd.

"Keep up, eh?" he called as he marched toward the ruins.

"Where are you going? Isn't the property line over there?"

"I have to check on someone first."

Gladwin followed.

He didn't know if Brother Colwyn would still be haunting the ruins now that he had his head back. He just wanted to let the friar ghost know that Garnock wouldn't be murdering anybody anymore.

Upon arriving at the edge of the lonely ruins, however, he found that the place seemed deserted.

When Gladwin caught up, he nodded to her. "Come in here a second. You've got to see this."

She flew after him as he led her through what was left of the hollowed nave and into the side chapel, where he showed her Sir Reginald's tomb.

He gestured at it. "The original Lord Griffon."

She ooh'ed and ahh'ed, while Jake reflected on how he had changed after all he'd been through in Wales. Right now, he felt confident that if he were to find a gryphon egg, he, too, would have given it back to the mother without hesitation.

Turning around, still lost in his thoughts, Jake was nearly startled out of his skin to find Brother Colwyn standing—well, floating politely—in the archway behind them.

"Blimey, guv, you gave me a fright." He clutched his chest. It wasn't like him to be so jumpy, but he'd had enough surprises for one day.

"Sorry, I didn't want to interrupt," the ghost said.

"It's all right." Jake quickly did the introductions.

"Nice to meet you," said Gladwin with a midair curtsy.

"Likewise, miss."

"I wasn't sure if you'd still be here. How's the head? It looks good on you," Jake jested as the monk ghost beamed.

"It fits perfectly," Brother Colwyn replied with a grin. "Actually, I am glad you're here. You're just in time."

"For what?"

"Tonight," he answered, eagerly floating closer. "It's time. I finally get to go. You know, up there. Meet the Boss in person." He pointed discreetly toward the sky.

"Really?"

"That must be particularly exciting for a man of the cloth," Gladwin said with an earnest nod.

"Oh, yes! Celestus is in town picking up the others even now. He'll be taking us all up shortly."

"How exciting."

"Others?" Jake asked.

Before Brother Colwyn could answer, the angel himself appeared with the noisy crowd of ghosts he would be escorting to Heaven. Jake was astonished, recognizing many faces from the séance. The miners, the soldier ghost—even the phantom dog was there—but there was one among them that made Jake's jaw drop.

Old Sack!

"You're alive!" he exclaimed.

"In a sense," the headmaster ghost answered with a chuckle.

"But I saw Garnock *eat* you! How? All of you..." He looked around in confusion. "I thought he destroyed you."

Dr. Celestus strode over to him with a laugh. "Don't hurt your brain trying to make logic from it, Jake. Souls are eternal, and that's that. Surely you, of all people, must have realized that by now after all you've seen. And by the way, congratulations on a battle won."

"To you, as well," Jake responded. "I don't know what would have happened if you hadn't come."

The angel waved off his concerns. "Ah, he tries to get out every now and then. We just keep putting him back. Dreadful-looking these days, though. Shocking to see how much he's let himself go since we used to work together. To think he was once considered the handsomest of us!"

Jake pondered this. It was hard to imagine that that horrible demon used to be an angel.

"How's your cousin?" Celestus asked.

"She's doing much better, thanks. I think it'll be a while before she's entirely herself again, though. You know how sensitive she is."

"Perhaps I should pay her a visit later. I could help."

"I'm sure she would appreciate that if you're free."

"Well!" He clapped his hands together and rubbed them back and forth, turning to his band of heaven-bound souls with an otherworldly smile. "Everyone ready?"

"Wait. Have you really been hanging around my family since the time when this chapel was built?" Jake asked, pointing at the stained-glass window depicting the very angel who now stood before him.

"You look shocked," Celestus replied, then he shrugged, stretching out his big white wings. "We all have our assignments. Greetings, Lord Crafanc!" he added as Red came flying down from the dark skies and landed with a pounce in their midst.

The ghosts murmured in shock at the arrival of the Gryphon. Red bowed to Celestus—a rare honor. Then the angel smiled at him.

"See you around, Jake." He glanced at his following. "All right, everyone. Take hold of my sleeves here, or catch hold of the edge of my sash. The rest of you join hands. I'll have you all home in a twinkling of..."

They disappeared before he had even finished the sentence.

Jake, Gladwin, and Red stared at the empty space where the group had stood.

"Well!" the fairy said at last. "I suppose that's that—like he said."

Red nudged Jake affectionately with his head like a giant housecat and let out a brief purr. "Aw, what's the matter, boy?"

"I think he came to bring you back to the party," Gladwin observed, folding her tiny arms across her chest as she balanced on the back of an ancient pew.

Jake put his hands in his pockets. "I guess I could always finish up the spells tomorrow."

"Becaw!"

"All right, boy. I wouldn't want to be rude."

"That's a first," Gladwin teased.

Jake snorted and gave her a droll look, then swung onto Red's back. As the Gryphon lifted off, Gladwin kept pace, flying through the dark sky beside them.

The cottage was in sight below, its windows warmly glowing,

when all of a sudden, a cold puff of wind blew past, carrying with it the first snowflakes of the season.

"Oh, how beautiful!" Gladwin exclaimed.

"I guess winter comes early up here in the mountains," Jake agreed.

Lacy snowflakes went spinning past them on all sides, each one unique.

"It'll be Christmas before you know it," Gladwin said. Then she turned to him in surprise. "Your first Christmas with a family!"

"Aha," Jake murmured, "and presents! Red, I'm going to need some gold for shopping—"

The Gryphon banked hard to the left at that comment, nearly spilling his rider off his back.

Jake hung on with a laugh. "I was only joking! All right, all right, we can talk about my allowance later. Let's go tell the others to come outside and see the snow!"

Red snorted and swooped back the other way, throwing Jake into an upright sitting position on his back again.

With a grin from ear to ear, Jake leaned lower over the Gryphon's neck like a jockey, while snowflakes starred his lashes and clung to his rosy cheeks.

"Brrr, it's cold!" Gladwin said, shivering in her tiny fur-trimmed coat. It had holes cut in the back for her delicate wings to poke through. "Race you!" she challenged all of a sudden.

"You're on. Hey, no fair!" Jake cried as she tore off in the blink of an eye, disappearing in a streak of golden sparkles.

Red let out an indignant roar and pumped his scarlet wings harder, but there was no catching up to a fairy courier moving at top speed.

"Showoff!" Jake yelled merrily after her. But in truth, he was just happy to be returning to the party and his friends and the warmth that was home.

And, of course, the food.

Definitely the food.

The End

Now Available!

It's Jake's first Christmas with a family, but nothing's ever quite what you'd expect. Celebrate a Victorian Christmas with a Gryphon Chronicles holiday novella.

JAKE & THE GINGERBREAD WARS

Peace on Earth, Goodwill to Men...And Gingerbread Men?!

Look for the next full-length Gryphon Chronicles Novel coming in Spring/Summer 2014!

The United States of *Ahhhh!*-merica

50 States of Fear

By E.G. Foley

Come along on a journey – if you dare – from sea to shining sea!

Welcome to the spine-tingling new series of strange and spooky tales, with hair-raising happenings in all 50 States! Get ready for frightful chills and thrills as we visit every star on the flag. From Civil War ghosts in Alabama to weird Wyoming cowboy legends, there's always something to scream about in *Ahhhh!*-merica.

ALABAMA – Now Available!
By day, sunshine and Southern hospitality. But by night, the ghosts of the Old South come alive…
I knew my Alabama Grandma couldn't wait for me and my sister to come down from New York to see her new apartment in a grand old Southern plantation house. Of course, I had no idea the place was crawling with ghosts—or that a simple trip to Grandma's would doom me to four nights in a haunted mansion.

More States Coming Soon!

ALASKA - *Land of the Midnight Sun…and the Black Helicopters?*

I'm not some kind of weird conspiracy nut. Really. At least, I wasn't until my famous dad invited me to tag along on his summer trip to Alaska to film a wildlife documentary. But what we found hidden in that vast wilderness was something even scarier than grizzly bears. A secret research facility, where the government is building a weapon of indescribable power. Now the Men in Black are after me…

ARIZONA - *Starry nights. Painted deserts… Giant Tarantulas??*

I was staying at my uncle's ranch when my dog ran out into the desert, barking at something mysterious in the night. I knew I had to get out there fast and bring him home safe. Like my uncle always says, the desert is full of dangerous things. Rattlesnakes, mountain lions, coyotes. Too bad he never mentioned the giant mutant spiders.

Hooray for the Red, White, & BOO!

ABOUT THE AUTHORS

 E.G. Foley is the pen name for a husband-and-wife writing team who live in Pennsylvania. They have been finishing each other's sentences since they were teens, so it was only a matter of time before they were writing together, too.

They are the authors of "The Gryphon Chronicles" historical fantasy adventure series (*The Lost Heir, Jake and the Giant, The Dark Portal*), as well as a contemporary series of shorter books called, "The United States of *Ahhhh!*-merica: 50 States of Fear" – spooky stories for kids set in all fifty states.

"E" is a 7-8th grade teacher of students who regularly use more than 10% of their brains, world traveler, ice cream connoisseur, and martial arts enthusiast. "G" loves big books and small fluffy creatures, and if she hadn't become a writer, would have pursued a career as either a princess or spy—or possibly both. With millions of copies of her nineteen adult novels from Random House and HarperCollins sold in sixteen languages worldwide, she has been hitting bestseller lists regularly for the past decade.

Visit them on the web at EGFoley.com for fun story "Extras" (you can listen to the real, historical *Souling Song*, for example!), as well as videos, creative games, and tips for aspiring writers of all ages. While you're there, please sign up for the E.G. Foley Newsletter, so you can be notified as soon as their next book is available.

Thanks for Reading!

About The Illustrator

Josh D. Addessi has been drawing ever since he could hold a pencil. He has since honed his skills and passions at Huntington University, where he is currently a Professor, teaching Digital Illustration and Hand Drawn Animation to aspiring artists.

After being mentored by renowned illustrator, Bryan Ballinger, Josh has thoroughly explored the fantasy art genre, painting all manner of fantastical worlds and the characters who live in them—from dragons and monsters, to heroic knights and beautiful princesses, faeries and more.

Most of all, Josh enjoys bringing smiles with his art. That's all he wants. Just a smile. To see more of his work, visit him on the web at joshaddessi.blogspot.com.